CHRIS GRABENSTEIN

PRESENTS

SUPER PUZZLETASTIC MYSTERIES

Short Stories for Young Sleuths from Mystery Writers of America

Mystery Writers of America Presents

HARPER
An Imprint of HarperCollinsPublishers

Library of Congress Cataloging-in-Publication Data

Names: Grabenstein, Chris, author.
Title: Super puzzletastic mysteries : short stories for young sleuths from Mystery Writers of
    America.
Description: First edition. | New York : HarperCollins, 2020. | At head of title: Chris Grabenstein
    presents. | Audience: Ages 8-12. | Audience: Grades 4-6. | Summary: "New York Times
    bestselling author Chris Grabenstein and his all-star cast of contributing authors team up for
    Super Puzzletastic Mysteries, a group of interactive short stories that invite the reader to solve
    the mystery themselves"-- Provided by publisher.
Identifiers: LCCN 2019035482 | ISBN 978-0-06-288421-3 (pbk.) Subjects: LCSH: Detective and
    mystery stories, American. | Children's stories, American. | CYAC: Mystery and detective
    stories. | Short stories. | Literary recreations.
Classification: LCC PZ5 .S9618 2020 | DDC [Fic]--dc23
LC record available at https://lccn.loc.gov/2019035482

Typography by Torborg Davern
23 24 25 PC/BRR 10 9 8 7 6 5 4 3
❖
First paperback edition, 2021

Contents

INTRODUCTION

For me, a lot of the fun of reading mysteries comes from trying to solve the story's puzzle before the characters in it do.

I think this fun started one Christmas when Santa brought me a book: Donald Sobol's *Two-Minute Mysteries* (Sobol was also the creator of Encyclopedia Brown).

There would be some sort of crime, the clues would be presented, and the story would end without a solution. I had to rack my ten-year-old brain and try to figure out whodunit or what happened.

I confess, I seldom got the answer right, but I had fun trying. When I ultimately flipped to the back of the book to read the author's solution, I usually slapped my forehead with the palm of my hand and said, "Doh! Of course. I knew that. I just forgot to think it."

Such was the inspiration for this collection of *Super Puzzletastic Mysteries*, created by some of the best criminal masterminds from the Mystery Writers of America organization and the world of kidlit.

Here you will find twenty stories—some by authors you're familiar with, some by authors you'll want to read more of—all of them filled with clues, red herrings, and clever sleuths. The stories will take you right up to the brink of a solution . . . and then you'll have a chance to match wits with the characters and attempt to solve the mystery on your own. (Or with your classmates. These stories were all written to be the perfect length for a classroom read-aloud.)

And yes, you'll find the solutions in the back of the book to make sure your deductions are correct!

I was so lucky that so many terrific writers accepted an invitation to contribute to this collection—a number of whom, like Donald Sobol, have been singled out by Mystery Writers of America committees judging the prestigious Edgar awards:

Edgar nominee Stuart Gibbs will take you to the world of his Fun-Jungle series, where some "Monkey Business" has led to chaos and confusion in the cages. It's a case that must (with your help) be solved.

The always hysterical (and Edgar-nominated) Steve Hockensmith will introduce you to the funniest superhero you've ever met: Possum-Man. With the help of his niece, Janet—and, of course, you—will Possum-Man be able to avert disaster?

Edgar winner Kate Milford will take you camping in "The Dapperlings." But, at this camp, solving puzzles (not making lanyards) is the number one activity.

Edgar nominee Lamar Giles will introduce you to a brainy young man who is only called a nerd because he is so much better at unraveling puzzles than all his classmates. Will he be smarter than you?

Edgar winner James Ponti will treat you to "TRICKED!" a new tale in his amazing Framed! series. There's a reason twelve-year-old Florian Bates is a consultant with the FBI. He's very good at making observations and solving mysteries—something you'll be great at after you work your way through these twenty mysterious puzzlers.

And my own story? Well, let's just say it's based on something I actually saw out the library window when I did a school visit the day after a snow day.

I hope you enjoy *Super Puzzletastic Mysteries*. I know I did when I first read the stories as they came in.

Could I solve 'em all?

Of course not. But that's half the fun!

—Chris Grabenstein

SNOW DEVILS
A Riley Mack Story
By Chris Grabenstein

The FART was huge.

The biggest one Riley Mack had ever seen.

"Looks like somebody enjoyed their snow day yesterday," Riley said to himself with a grin.

The towering word had been cleverly shuffled into the deep snow on a hill facing the school library windows. Each letter was at least twenty feet tall and surrounded by the daintier boot prints of the mystery writer moving from one leg-plowed letter to the next. The F-A-R-T spanned at least forty feet across the backyard of a house on the other side of the school's perimeter fence.

"Mr. Ball's not going to like that," said Riley's friend Ben Markowitz, who was sitting with him at a table in the library that more or less served as Riley's office.

Mr. Ball was Fairview Middle School's vice principal. Its disciplinarian. The guy who liked nothing better than running detention hall. He'd strut up and down the rows of chairs, tapping a ruler behind his back, his eyes darting from one inmate to the next, just itching to whip out his pink pad and give one of the troublemakers *another* hour in the after-school punishment zone.

Troublemakers.

That's what some grown-ups called Riley and his friends Ben, Briana, Jamal, and Mongo (whose real name was Hubert Montgomery but, because he was so huge, everybody called him "Humongo," which quickly morphed into "Mongo").

In truth, Riley's crew didn't make trouble. They were fixers. The school's go-to team of Robin Hoods. They only tried to right wrongs, protect innocent kids from bullies, look out for abused animals, and, basically, use their talents to do all the good they could.

Riley had a strict ethical code for his team's operations, too. They would never execute a caper that was just plain wrong. For instance, on Monday, an eighth grader named Steve Duffy had come to Riley's office in the media center, begging for help.

"What do you need?" Riley asked.

"The answers to my history makeup quiz."

"Excuse me?"

"I missed the quiz last week. So Mrs. Henkin is going to give me a makeup exam Thursday morning with all new questions! And I'll be on my own. Jenny Myers won't be sitting next to me."

Riley arched an inquisitive eyebrow.

"She's smart," Duffy explained. "Always knows what answer to circle. I sometimes copy her moves."

"I see," said Riley.

"But I don't need Jenny Myers. I saw where Mrs. Henkin stashed the answer key."

"Oh, you did, did you?"

"Top right-hand drawer of her desk. The one that locks. I figure your guy Jamal could sneak in after school, pop it open, copy the answers, and BOOM! I'm golden. But we have to hurry. Like I said, my makeup test is first thing Thursday!"

"Nope," Riley told the eighth grader. "Not gonna do it."

"Why? What's your problem? I can pay you ten dollars. Twenty! Okay, thirty."

"That's not how we roll, Steve."

"Why not?"

"Because I might need brain surgery someday."

"What?!!"

"You think I want to be operated on by some Dr. Dingus D. Doofus who cheated his way through middle school, then high school, and all the way through medical school?"

"Oh," fumed Steve. "Funny. Guess Brandon Kilmeade was right. He said you and your crew were yesterday's news. He'll do the same job for twenty bucks. But I came to you first, Riley Mack. Out of respect."

"Steve?"

"Yeah?"

"Why don't you just study for the test? You say it's not till Thursday. Today's Monday. You have three whole days."

"Um, no, I don't. Every single one of my after-school hours this week is spoken for. I made it to the next level of Alien Annihilator. I can't miss a single online Thrash or my avatar will lose his force field *and* his bludgeon balloon."

Riley shook his head in disbelief, remembering that Monday morning conversation.

"So, Ben?" he asked his friend. "Who do you think's the prime suspect for the FART art?"

"I'd go with Sam Morkal-Williams," said Ben, tapping the glass of his smartphone, pulling up a database. "Kid's a real cutup and class clown. This looks like his kind of prank."

"You have to admire his craftsmanship," said Riley. "It's not easy bulldozing letters into snow while making the minimum number of moves necessary to hop over to the next letter."

Ben nodded. "The leap from the right leg of the *A* to the left leg of the *R* is amazing. Winter Olympics–caliber stuff. Kudos to Sam."

Ben was the brainiac in Riley's crew. He used words like *kudos* a lot.

"OMG, you guys?!!" Briana Bloomfield made a dramatic entrance into the library. She was their actress. She could imitate voices, create disguises, and become whoever Riley and his team needed her to be. Her locker was full of costumes, hats, wigs, makeup kits, and all sorts of disguises. She was so theatrical, almost *every* entrance she made was dramatic. "Did you guys see the FART?"

"We're kind of looking at it right now," said Riley.

Briana gasped. "That thing is huge. No. It's ginormous! Who do you think did it?"

"Sam Morkal-Williams," said Ben.

"That's what I thought," said Briana. "Although it could've been Elyssa Shapiro. That girl is hard-core."

"Interesting choices," said Riley. "Any idea whose yard that is?"

"Old Man Jenkins," said Briana. "I mean, Old Man probably isn't his real first name, but that's what everybody calls him."

"Is he old?" asked Ben, innocently.

Briana rolled her eyes. "Uh, yeah. He's also a widower. Doesn't really like kids. You do *not* want your ball to end up in his backyard. If it does, you will never see it again. They say the inside of his garage looks like a sporting goods store."

Jamal Wilson came strutting into the library. He was the youngest and newest member of Riley's "gnat pack." That's what Fairview's sheriff, Big John Brown, called Riley Mack and the "other known troublemakers" he associated with. The sheriff thought they were a bunch of annoying little pests. Probably because the bully they busted most often was his son, Gavin Brown.

Riley didn't mind the gnat pack label. In fact, he kind of liked it. Gnats were small, almost microscopic creatures. But they could drive full-grown adults crazy.

"Dag," said Jamal. "That FART out there is elephantine. You know what that word means, Riley Mack?"

"Yeah. Big."

Jamal was good with his hands and could crack open just about any lock you tossed his way. He also liked memorizing big words out of the dictionary.

"It is positively behemothic," Jamal continued. "Man, I wish I'd thought to write something in the snow yesterday. I know so many better words than *fart*. For instance, *flatulence*. You know what that word means?"

"Yeah," said Riley. "Fart."

"Correct. But I spent the whole day yesterday sledding with Mongo over on the golf course. Let me tell you—that dude is strong! He gave me such a mighty shove downhill, I was flying!"

"Hey, speaking of Mongo, has anybody seen him this morning?" asked Riley.

Everybody shook their heads. Mongo was the group's muscle. Sure, he was a seventh grader, but he was growing so fast that he was already bigger than most high school kids.

"Maybe he's in the cafeteria," suggested Ben. "He sometimes needs a second breakfast."

"And a third," said Briana.

Riley and his crew usually met up in the library every morning before the first bell. After school, they'd meet up again at the Pizza Palace on Main Street. They were a little like firefighters or the Avengers. They were always ready to spring into action at a moment's notice.

"Excuse me, guys," said the librarian. "The first bell is about to ring. I'm going to need these tables. Mrs. Henkin is still snowed in so she asked me to give a makeup quiz for her."

Riley nodded. He figured Steve Duffy's private history quiz had slid back a day on account of yesterday's snow.

"No problem," he said to the librarian. "Come on, guys."

Riley and his crew stood up from the table.

"Enjoy the view," cracked Jamal, nodding his head toward the big FART outside the window.

"Oh, my," gasped the librarian. "Who did that?"

"That," said Ben, "is today's sixty-four-thousand-dollar question."

Riley led his crew out of the library.

"Dag," said Jamal when they were in the hall. "There's a reward? Sixty-four thousand dollars? For finding the FART felon?"

"It's just an expression, Jamal," said Briana. "It was the title of an old TV game show back in the 1950s."

"Now," explained Ben, "whenever a question is extremely important or difficult to answer, we call it a sixty-four-thousand-dollar question."

"Really?" said Jamal. "I mean y'all might do that, but not me. I'd call that question onerous. Or troublesome. Maybe even enigmatic. You know what all those words mean?"

"Yeah," said Riley. "It won't be easy for Mr. Ball to figure out who wrote FART in the snow."

"Mr. Ball thinks I did it," said Mongo.

On his way to his first period class, Riley had seen his friend Mongo, the gentle giant, sitting in his stocking feet on the bench outside the school's main office.

"He told me to wait right here while he investigated. So that's what I'm doing. Waiting. Right here."

"Why aren't you wearing any shoes?" asked Riley, sitting down on the bench alongside his friend.

Mongo wiggled his toes. His brown socks were decorated with cute little teddy bears. Not that anyone at Fairview Middle School would dare make fun of him for it.

"Mr. Ball took my boots," he explained.

"Why?"

"He wants to go see if they match the boot prints near that big FART in Old Man Jenkins's backyard."

"He thinks you did that?"

"Yeah."

"But you were at the golf course yesterday. Sledding with Jamal."

"I know. I told Mr. Ball. He didn't care. He said I was a miscreant and ne'er-do-well." The big guy furrowed his brow and scrunched up his eyes. Riley could tell he was thinking. Hard. "Hey, Riley?"

"Yeah, Mongo?"

"What's a miscreant and a ne'er-do-well?"

Riley winked. "They're both very important members of any top-notch gnat pack."

"Oh. Cool."

Mr. Ball came through the front doors wrapped in a dull gray parka that made him look like a quilted pork sausage. He stomped snow off his rubber boots; shook it off his pant cuffs. Then he wiggle-waggled the large pair of tan hiking boots he held in his hand.

"If the boot fits, Mr. Montgomery," he said with a sneer as he marched over to the bench, "wear it."

"Okay," said Mongo. "Thanks. My toes were getting kind of cold . . ."

"What are you doing here, Mr. Mack?"

"Sitting."

"Shouldn't you be on your way to class?"

"No, sir. Not when one of my best friends is shoeless and the Real-Feel temperature outside is fifteen."

"Your 'friend,' as you put it, Mr. Mack, is not wearing shoes because he was wearing boots. These boots. The ones I hereby hold in my hands. But now they are more than boots, Mr. Montgomery. They are evidence!"

Mongo nodded. "Okay. But can I still wear them?"

"No! Not until you confess!"

"To what?"

"Writing that foul word in the snow."

"Oh. I didn't do that."

"Oh, yes you did. You're the only student at Fairview Middle School who wears a size fifteen shoe or boot."

"How can you know that?" asked Riley.

"Because I keep statistics, Mr. Mack. Why? For situations just like this one! Plus, Mr. Montgomery, these are Timberland brand boots. They leave an extremely distinctive, easy-to-identify footprint pattern in the snow. The same pattern I found at the scene of the crime."

"Wait a second," said Riley. "Timberland boots are very popular. And who said a student from Fairview wrote that word in the snow? Some adult with size fifteen feet could've—"

"*Ha!* Don't make me laugh, Mr. Mack. *Ha, ha, ha.* Look at me. I'm laughing. I warned you not to make me do that."

Briana came up the hall, hugging her books to her chest, trying to blend into the background of lockers. Riley touched his ear. She nodded and moved to the nearby water fountain where she could eavesdrop.

Riley stood up. "I can prove Mongo, I mean Hubert, didn't do it."

Mr. Ball gave Riley some snide stink eye. "Oh, really? How?"

"I'm not exactly sure," said Riley. "But you definitely don't want to accuse the wrong student. Remember what the new school superintendent said about false accusations and lawsuits."

"Mrs. Worthington said something about lawsuits?" Suddenly, Mr. Ball's left eye was twitching. "She's a very important person," he sputtered. "We haven't met, not yet, but, well, I, of course, respect her opinions . . ."

Briana touched the tip of her nose and slipped around the corner where, right on cue, she speed-dialed Mr. Ball.

The phone inside the chest pocket of his sausage parka started chirping. (Ben had loaded all the personal cell phone numbers of the teachers and administrators in Briana's and Riley's phones for just such an emergency. He'd also blocked the caller ID function.)

"Hello?" Mr. Ball snapped into his phone. "This is Albert Ball. To whom do I have the pleasure of speaking?"

His eyes went wide.

"Superintendent Worthington? Why, I was just talking about you. I loved your most recent memo . . ."

Riley grinned. Briana was on the case.

"I see," said Mr. Ball. "You're writing a new memo? About avoiding lawsuits? Fascinating. Oh, I agree, Mrs. Worthington. False accusations are the worst. However, I think if you have solid evidence and a prime suspect— Right. Lawsuits. Need to be one hundred percent certain. What? Yes, as a matter of fact I do have a student eager to lead an investigation but— Oh. You think that's a good idea? You know, now that you mention it, so do I. Thank you, Mrs. Worthington. And, if you have a minute, might we discuss the current pay scale for vice principals in the district? As you may not know— I see. You have to run. No, later would be fine. We'll chat later. Thank you for the call."

Mr. Ball tapped the off button on his phone just as the second class-change bell rang.

"You have until the end of the day, Mr. Mack. Otherwise, I am turning Mr. Montgomery over to the authorities."

"Thank you, sir," said Riley.

"May I have my boots back, Mr. Ball?" asked Mongo.

"No, you may not. I'm confiscating them."

"Huh?"

"I'm keeping them! They're evidence."

"They're also warm, sir. Warmer than just socks."

"For goodness' sake, Hubert. Go to the gym. Put on your sneakers."

"Good idea, sir," said Riley, grabbing Mongo by the elbow. "Let's hit the gym."

As they walked, Riley thumbed a text string.

Bathroom Emergency.

NOW!

Meet us outside the boys' locker room.

Riley and Mongo hit the gym. Mongo went to his locker and quickly slid on his size fifteen sneakers.

"These won't be good for walking home in the snow."

"Don't worry, Mongo," Riley assured him. "You'll have your Timberlands back before school's out for the day."

When they stepped into the hall outside the locker room, Ben, Briana, and Jamal were there, waiting for them.

"Why, hello, Mr. Mack," said Briana in a snooty, lockjaw voice, like she went to college in Connecticut. "I'm ever so delighted to see you again."

"Is that the voice you used on Mr. Ball?" asked Mongo.

"Yuh-huh. I went full-blown Ivy League. It can be very intimidating."

"Good job," said Riley.

"Thank you," said Briana in her normal voice. "An actor makes choices. The secret is believing in those choices. Keeping them real."

"Yo," said Jamal. "That was supposed to sound real? Because, if I may, I have a few notes on your performance that I'd be happy to—"

"Not now, guys," said Riley. "The clock's ticking."

Ben nodded and waved a green card. "I could only score a five-minute bathroom pass."

"Me, too," said Jamal.

"Okay," said Riley. "We have to clear Mongo."

"I didn't do it," said Mongo.

"Cool," said Jamal. "So, uh, what exactly are people saying you did?"

"Mr. Ball thinks I'm the one who wrote FART in the snow."

"Nah, man. That's not your style. You're more physical than verbal. Me? I'm something of a wordsmith. Love to play with words, experiment with them."

"Jamal?" said Riley. "We only have until the end of school today. So far, the evidence against Mongo is pretty solid. The snow writing was done by someone wearing size fifteen Timberland boots."

"Like Mongo wears," said Ben.

"Exactly. We don't have the time to pull together a full-blown operation. We need to peanut butter out the tasks and see what we can learn about those other suspects."

"Um, what other suspects?" asked Ben.

"You mentioned Sam Morkal-Williams. Class clown. Known prankster. You and Jamal get close to him at lunch. If Sam did it, he's going to be eager for someone to find out. The guy lives for the spotlight. Briana?"

"Yeah?"

"This Elyssa Shapiro you mentioned."

"Nuh-uh. No way. I told you, she's hard-core. I think she has tattoos. I know she dyes her hair. That's why it's so black it looks bluish. The girl is extremely Goth. She'll be giving me noogies on the cafeteria floor if I even come close to her table. Goth chicks don't like drama geeks."

"Then put on a disguise. Become somebody new. Maybe a new kid. Pretend this is your first day at Fairview. You're looking for girls even Gothier than you are . . ."

Briana nodded. Slowly. "Okay. Yes. I can do this. I am an *ac-tor.* Sure, it'll be a challenge, but all good roles are."

"What do we do, Riley?" asked Mongo. "You and me?"

"You stick to your class schedule and be on your best behavior. Me? I'm going to visit Old Man Jenkins after lunch. I have a free period."

"No, Riley!" said Ben.

"That old man is old *and* cranky," said Jamal. "They could call him Old Cranky Man Jenkins. He might come after you with his Weed-wacker."

Briana arched an eyebrow. "In the middle of winter?"

"Hey, some old dudes keep their Weedwackers handy all year long, just to chase kids off their lawns. And who knows what else he might have hidden in that garage. Sledgehammers. Hedge trimmers. WD-40 he could spray in your eyeballs."

Riley just grinned. "He might also have a pair of Timberland boots. Size fifteen."

Riley and his crew all had lunch at the same time.

Usually, they sat together and fielded requests from kids who needed help righting wrongs. Today, they split up. Ben and Jamal sat with Sam Morkal-Williams and his friends, who called themselves the Goofballs. They were Fairview Middle School's premier practical jokers and class clowns. The best of the best.

Briana would hit the locker room, change into her New Goth Girl disguise/costume, and then try to find a seat at Elyssa Shapiro's table. It shouldn't be hard. Nobody much wanted to sit with Elyssa except her nose- and eyebrow-studded friend with the purple hair, Charlotte Edelman.

Mongo and Riley ate their lunches at their regular table.

"See?" said the weasely looking kid, Brandon Kilmeade. He and Steve Duffy shuffled past Mongo and Riley's table, carrying trays loaded down with double desserts and double chocolate milks. "Riley Mack is old news. He can't even protect his pal Mongo. Check out the shoes."

"*Ha!*" laughed Steve. "He's wearing canvas high tops the day after a snowstorm? His socks are gonna stink when he gets home."

Brandon nodded. "His feet are gonna itch, too."

Mongo slammed down both fists on the table and jangled all the silverware.

"My boots have been confiscated for evidence!" he declared.

"We heard," said Brandon. "If you need help getting out of that jam, let me know. I charge by the job, not the hour."

"Hey, Riley?" taunted Steve. "Guess who aced his history quiz this morning? Me. Answered all four questions correctly. Scored a big fat one hundred."

Meanwhile, over at the Goofballs' table, Jamal and Ben were listening to Sam Morkal-Williams regaling his fellow jokers with his funny tale of woe.

"Oh, man, I so wish I had thought of that," he said. "Writing something funny in the snow? That's like the ultimate stunt. Although I might've gone with the word *poop*. *Poop* is always funnier than *fart*. *Underpants* would've been funny, too."

"Y'all talk about this kind of stuff every day?" asked Jamal.

"Nah," said Sam. "Usually we just tell jokes and try to make everybody else laugh so hard, milk comes shooting out their noses."

"Cool," said Jamal. "Nice grabbing lunch with you dudes. We gotta run."

"Yeah," said Ben. "This was fun. And, you know, funny. Sorry I didn't laugh much."

"It's nothing personal," said Jamal. "Ben never laughs. Except when he's watching that British guy Mr. Bean. Go figure, huh?"

As Ben and Jamal took their trays to the drop-off window, they passed Briana in a jet-black wig. She was dressed in black from head to toe. Even her lipstick was black. She had raccoon circles around her eyes, wore a jagged necklace, and had plastered all sorts of temporary tattoos up and down her sleeveless arms.

She sat down at the table where Elyssa and Charlotte were sitting, each girl twirling the dyed tips of her hair. All Briana had on her tray was a small plate cradling a wobbly hard-boiled egg. The other girls were eating bowls of gloomy-looking gruel. Or grits. It could've been grits.

"Hey," said Briana, sounding totally bored.

"Hey," said Elyssa.

Charlotte just grunted.

"I'm new," said Briana, with a yawn. "First day."

"Cool," said Elyssa.

Charlotte grunted again.

"So," said Brianna, "which one of you total bad apples wrote *the word* in, like, the snow?"

Elyssa and Charlotte put down their spoons and glared at her.

"You think I wrote FART?" said Elyssa. "In the snow?" She sounded like she might rip out somebody's hair sometime soon.

"Totally," said Briana.

"You don't wear coffin creeper boots like these in the snow, idiot!" snarled Elyssa.

"They cost like a hundred and thirty dollars," added Charlotte.

"Snow could ruin the leather," said Elyssa. "And do you know how much we paid for these pants?"

"Oh-kay," said Briana. "Good fashion tips. Thanks."

She picked up her tray, turned around, looked over to where Riley was sitting, shook her head, and mouthed two words:

"No. Way."

That meant it was up to Riley.

He had to sneak over to Old Man Jenkins's house and see what he could see.

He had a free period right after lunch that he usually spent in the media center working on "independent studies."

"Excuse me?" he said to the librarian. "I need to go outside and gather some samples for science class."

"Samples?" the librarian answered skeptically.

"Yeah," said Riley. "I'm going to catalog snowflakes. See if they're all really different. I mean, come on, one or two have to be the same, am I right?"

The librarian stared at him. For a full second. "Be sure to wear your coat."

"Yes, ma'am."

Riley put on his snow boots and coat and trudged across the ballfields to the scene of the "crime." The edges of the FART letters were crusting over with ice. Riley wondered why Mr. Ball hadn't sent out the custodians to plow away or cover up the word. Probably because it was on Old Man Jenkins's property, not the school's.

Riley scooched through a hole he knew about in the fence and carefully headed toward Mr. Jenkins's elevated back porch. It was made of concrete and free of snow, shielded by an angled aluminum awning overhead. As he moved closer, Riley could see the tops of a pair of tan boots peeking out of a wooden crate pushed into a corner where the porch's railings met the house's brick wall.

Riley tiptoed up the stoop's three steps and took a look inside the boots. He checked out their size. It was printed on the label sewn to the tongue.

Fifteen.

Mr. Jenkins had the same size feet as Mongo.

But were his boots Timberlands?

Riley gingerly extracted one boot out of the box and read the logo stamped into the side of the heel.

Eddie Bauer.

He eased the boot back into the box and sighed.

It was nearly one o'clock. School would be over in two hours.

And he didn't have a single piece of evidence.

Or did he?

He quickly texted Mongo.

WHERE DO YOU STORE YOUR BOOTS AT NIGHT?

Mongo texted right back.

IN MY ROOM.

Not the answer Riley was looking for.

But then he saw the bubble and dots letting him know that Mongo wasn't done texting. His second message finally *blooped* onto his screen:

UNLESS THEY ARE WET.
THEN MOM MAKES US PUT THEM ON THE PORCH.

Yes! Riley thought. He hurried away from Mr. Jenkins's house, slipped through the fence, and went back into school.

He needed to talk to Steve Duffy.

The class-change bell rang. Riley strolled over to where he knew Duffy had his locker.

"What are you doing here, loser?" Duffy asked when he swaggered up the hallway to grab what he needed for his next class.

"I think you're lying," Riley told him. "No way you scored a one hundred on your makeup history quiz."

"Ha!" said Duffy, digging a sheet of paper out of his notebook. "Read it and weep. The librarian graded it for Mrs. Henkin. See? One hundred percent! Nailed all four multiple choice questions."

Riley glanced at the exam sheet. Up in the right-hand corner, he saw the *100* circled in red. The librarian had also added a smiley face.

Riley checked out the first question:

1. Who was president at the start of World War II?

A. *Harry Truman*   C. *Franklin D. Roosevelt*

B. *Dwight D. Eisenhower*   D. *None of the above*

Duffy, of course, had circled the correct answer. C. He'd answered the other three questions correctly, too.

Riley handed the quiz back to Duffy and didn't say another word.

He and Mongo needed to go see Mr. Ball.

Because Riley Mack knew who had written FART in the snow and why.

For the solution to this story, please turn to page 317.

POSSUM-MAN AND JANET

By Steve Hockensmith

It was nine o'clock at night, and Janet was walking her dog, Albus, before getting ready for bed.

Something moved in the darkness between two houses.

Albus turned toward it and growled.

Janet stopped on the sidewalk and peered into the shadows.

"Hello?" she said. "Is someone there?"

A shape emerged—tall and broad, with gray fur and round black eyes and a long, hairless tail. It spoke to Janet in a deep, raspy voice.

"I am the night," it said.

"Oh," said Janet. "Hi, Uncle Jim."

Albus wagged his tail.

The man cleared his throat. He didn't like being called "Uncle Jim" when he was in costume.

"Janet Goffman," he said, his voice still low and gruff, "Cleveland needs you."

Janet sighed.

"It's late," she said.

"It's never too late," said Uncle Jim, "for justice."

"I'm tired," said Janet.

"I am, too," said Uncle Jim. "Tired of the criminals who prey on our city."

"I have a math test tomorrow," said Janet.

"We're all being tested. All the time," said Uncle Jim. "And you don't want to flunk doing the right thing."

"'Doing the right thing' would be walking Albus and brushing my teeth and going to sleep," said Janet.

"Crime never sleeps," said Uncle Jim. "Or brushes its teeth."

"I'm in the fifth grade," said Janet. "I shouldn't be running around with a superhero."

"Please?" said Uncle Jim, his voice going up an octave. "Please, please, please?"

"Oh, alright," said Janet. "But I can't stay out long, and I want to bring Albus."

"Albus?" said Uncle Jim.

Albus wagged his tail again. He'd always liked Uncle Jim.

"He'll get hair in the Night Glider," Uncle Jim said.

"OK, fine," said Janet. "You wait here while I finish walking him and put him inside and tell Mom you dropped by and need my help. I should be back in twenty minutes or so. Maybe."

Uncle Jim held up a black-gloved hand.

"There's no time for that," he said, his voice dropping low again. "Bring him."

He turned and stalked away.

Janet followed him through her neighbors' yards.

"Let's go, Albus," she said. "You're coming with me and Uncle Jim."

Uncle Jim looked over his shoulder, and even in the darkness Janet could tell he was scowling.

"I mean 'me and Possum-Man.'" Janet sighed.

Albus trotted along beside her still wagging his tail.

The Night Glider—the large black hoverdisc Uncle Jim flew in around Cleveland—was parked on a baseball field nearby. A gray-haired man was standing near the bleachers staring at it, a leashed Chihuahua at his side.

"Hi, Mr. Getzler," said Janet. "Hi, Amy."

Amy the Chihuahua whipped around and started barking at Albus. Albus—five times her size—ignored her.

Mr. Getzler turned and stared in wonder at Janet and Uncle Jim.

"Geez Louise," he said. "I heard it, but I didn't believe it. You actually know Opossum-Man?"

Janet put a finger to her lips.

"It's supposed to be a secret," she said.

"There's no O, citizen," growled Uncle Jim. "It's just Possum-Man."

"Yeah, well, I appreciate everything you've done for us, *Possum-Man*," Mr. Getzler said.

Uncle Jim kept heading toward the Night Glider.

"No need to thank me, friend," he said.

"I know you've saved the city a dozen times," Mr. Getzler went on.

"Two dozen," Uncle Jim said, still not slowing down. "All in a day's work for Cuyahoga County's cowled crusader."

Janet knew Mr. Getzler well enough to know what was coming next.

"Beautiful afternoon," he'd usually say when he spotted her walking Albus. "But do you have to let that big elephant of yours do his business so close to my daffodils?"

Or "Lovely evening," he'd say. "But could you keep it lovely and not talk on your cell phone so loud? Some of us appreciate peace and quiet."

Mr. Getzler scowled at Uncle Jim and jerked his thumb at the baseball diamond.

"Well, hurrah for you," he said. "But FYI, that isn't an airport. Didn't you notice that your No-O-Possum-Plane or whatever is squashing the pitcher's mound?"

Uncle Jim slowed to glower at Mr. Getzler. It was a good glower, too. Janet had seen it strike fear into the hearts of hardened criminals. But Mr. Getzler didn't even blink.

"That field's township property," he said. "My tax dollars pay for that."

Uncle Jim broke off his glare.

"I'll send a check," he grumbled.

He pushed a button on his Possum Belt, and a ramp lowered from the Night Glider. He led Janet and Albus up it as Amy the Chihuahua continued to yap at them.

"Bye, Mr. Getzler!" Janet said.

"Tell your buddy to use Uber next time!" Mr. Getzler called back.

Uncle Jim, Janet, and Albus stepped onto the flight deck of the Night Glider, and the ramp started to pull itself up.

"Prepare for takeoff," Uncle Jim said.

He sat in the pilot's seat, buckled himself in, and started pushing buttons and flipping switches.

Janet walked to the copilot's seat and found a neatly folded unitard and goggles sitting on the cushion. It was an outfit just like Uncle Jim's, except that the tail was fluffy with black rings and there were two red initials on the gray fabric: RG.

"What's this?" Janet asked.

"Your new costume," said Uncle Jim, "Raccoon Girl."

Janet heaved a sigh. At least it was an improvement over the last name Uncle Jim had come up with. For months, he'd tried to convince her to be "Trash Panda"—even after she'd refused to wear anything with "TP" written on it.

Janet picked up the new costume, put it on the floor, and sat down.

"So . . . where to this time?" she said as she strapped herself in.

Uncle Jim looked down at the Raccoon Girl outfit. Albus pawed at it, then curled up on it as if it were a dog bed.

"The Museum of Art," Uncle Jim said. "There's been a robbery."

"Wow," said Janet. "Shocker."

She was being sarcastic. When Uncle Jim came to her dressed as Possum-Man, it wasn't to go get pizza.

The Night Glider rose over the suburbs where she lived and streaked toward Cleveland.

Ten minutes later, the Night Glider landed on the museum roof. It was hard to get Albus to stay—he kept running down the ramp beside Janet—but finally Uncle Jim remembered that he had some Possum Bars, and he broke two into pieces and scattered them across the flight deck floor. (The "Possum Bars" were just Pop-Tarts, Janet knew, but she didn't contradict him.)

Uncle Jim and Janet hurried out and retracted the ramp while Albus happily snorked up Possum Bar bits.

"Now," said Uncle Jim, "to the scene of the crime."

He was still using his Possum-Man voice, which sounded like someone with laryngitis impersonating Darth Vader.

He led Janet to a hole in the roof. It was about eight feet across, and far below it, on the museum floor, was a pile of rubble.

"Subtle," Janet said.

"It worked," said Uncle Jim. "They were able to get in and disable the alarms. Only one thing gave them away."

"The big hole in the roof?" Janet said. "Which you happened to see when you flew by on patrol?"

Uncle Jim gave her his Possum-Man nod: a single, brusque, downward jerk of the head. "Exactly. You have a sharp mind, Raccoon Girl. That's why I—"

"Janet," Janet corrected. "Just Janet." She pointed down into the museum. "Could we move this along, please? Test in the morning, remember?"

There was a loud, deep *woof* behind them, and they turned to see Albus watching them from the pilot's seat of the Night Glider.

"You don't want to leave him alone in there long," Janet said. "We'd just started our walk when you showed up, know what I mean?"

Albus barked again and wagged his tail.

"Right," said Uncle Jim.

He drew his Possum Gun from his Possum Belt, shot a Possum Hook into the roof, and tossed the attached Possum Cable into the hole.

He held an arm out to Janet. She gritted her teeth but stepped forward and let him wrap his arm around her and take her down the cable to the museum floor.

Uncle Jim wasn't the world's greatest superhero, but he was really good at dropping dramatically through rooftop holes.

He swung them out past the debris as they descended, and they landed on the marble floor of a long, dimly lit hall. Uncle Jim let Janet go, and she turned to find a gleaming silver figure looming over her.

She froze.

Killer robots? she thought. *Again?*

She quickly realized her mistake: It was just a suit of armor. There were more scattered throughout the hall, along with sculptures and vases and pictures.

"Over here," said Uncle Jim.

He led Janet around the rubble to a display case against one wall. The top of the case had been shattered, and all that was in it now were bits of broken glass. Hanging on the wall to the left of it was a painting of a man with horns and hairy legs and hooves lounging on grass beside a flute. To the right of it was an old tapestry showing a bunch of dudes in tights trying to capture a horse with a long horn growing from its forehead. Under the tapestry, beside the display case, was a sign. Written on it was this:

HOLY CROWN OF HUNGARY
A.D. 1000
ON LOAN FROM THE HUNGARIAN PARLIAMENT BUILDING

Janet only glanced at the sign. She was more interested in the note affixed to the wall beneath it.

It's stolen, and I'm to be blamed
I'm guilty, and yet I've been framed
To find where I've gone
Just look to the faun
And find who you seek clearly named.

"So . . . he's back," Janet said.

Uncle Jim gave her another Possum-Man nod. "That's right. The diabolical Haiku Master has returned."

"Haiku Master?" said Janet.

Uncle Jim threw her a nervous look out of the corners of his eyes.

"Uhh . . . Sonnet Lady?" he said.

Janet shook her head.

This was why Uncle Jim needed her. He was great at the physical superhero stuff. Appearing out of nowhere. Crouching dramatically on gargoyles. Beating people up. Even foiling nefarious schemes, so long as they were really, really obvious. But actually following clues and solving mysteries? Not so much.

"*Da-da da-da-da da-da-da-bay*," Janet said. "*Da-da da-da-da da-da-kay. Da-da da-da-bee. Da-da da-da-tee. Da-da da-da-da da-da-fay.*"

"Raccoon Girl!" Uncle Jim cried. "Are you having a seizure?"

Janet groaned and dropped her face into her hands.

"Don't try to talk anymore—you might swallow your tongue!" Uncle Jim said, fumbling with his Possum Belt. "Hold on while I get you a Possum Tranquilizer!"

Janet lifted her head and shook it. "I'm not having a seizure. I'm trying to remind you how a limerick works."

"A limerick?" said Uncle Jim.

Janet pointed at the note. "That's from Limerick King."

Uncle Jim's eyes narrowed behind his Possum Goggles.

"Of course," he said. "It's been a while since we last heard from that madman. Now he's back to steal himself a crown—but like always he felt compelled to leave us clues in verse."

Janet nodded, appreciating another of her uncle's superhero skills: exposition.

"This one's really obvious, too," she said.

"It is," said Uncle Jim.

Janet waited for him to say more.

After a long moment of silence, he said it.

"Um . . . it is?"

"'It's stolen, and I'm to be blamed / I'm guilty, and yet I've been framed,'" Janet said. "Get it?"

There was another moment of silence.

Janet waved at the wall before them—and the artworks hanging there.

"Like a picture frame?" she said.

"Oh! Right!"

Uncle Jim stepped forward and reached for the tapestry.

"What are you doing?" Janet said.

"'To find where I've gone / Just look to the faun,'" her uncle said. "Like you said: It's obvious. There's another clue behind this thing."

Janet pointed at the tapestry. "That's not a faun."

"I know. But it's the closest thing in here to a baby deer," said Uncle Jim. "And anyway, what rhymes with *unicorn*? Limerick King must have been stumped."

Janet fought the urge to bury her face in her hands again.

"It's not fawn, F-A-W-N. It's faun, F-A-U-N." She nodded at the painting on the other side of the smashed display case: the one of a half-man, half-goat lying in the grass. "As in the mythological creature?"

"Ohhhhhhhhh," said Uncle Jim. He squinted at the painting. "I thought that was what's-his-name. The god of sheep or flutes or whatever. Flan?"

"Pan," Janet corrected. "And that might be him, I don't know. But he looks the same as a faun. So—"

"Right!" said Uncle Jim.

He moved over to the painting, lifted one side and peeked behind it.

"A-ha!" he said.

He slid his other hand behind the picture and pulled out a sheet of paper. He handed it to Janet, who read what was on it out loud.

Good work! You've found my next note
But you've no time to stand there and gloat
To send me to the jailer
Don't look to a tailor
Though I've gone where there's millions of coats.

Your pal,
Limerick King

"Millions of coats, eh?" Uncle Jim mused, rubbing his square jaw. "JCPenney?"

"Uh . . . no," said Janet.

"Goodwill?" said Uncle Jim.

"You're being too literal," said Janet. "It's probably a pun."

"No," said Uncle Jim. "That's the Punster. He's still in prison. The fiend."

"Trust me. Limerick King uses puns, too," Janet said. "His hideouts are usually in old factories and warehouses, right? Is there anything like that around here?"

Uncle Jim went back to rubbing his jaw. "Well, there's the Bakedwell cookie factory. No coats there. The Grass Devil lawn mower factory. No coats there. The Spreadz-Easy paint factory. No coats there. The Ties-Rite shoelace factory. No coats—"

"Hold on," said Janet. "There's a paint factory?"

"Yeah. Over in the Flats. But you don't paint coats."

"No," Janet said. She spun her hands slowly in the air. "But you do use . . ."

She kept spinning her hands as she waited for her uncle to finish her sentence.

He just stared at her.

". . . coats of . . . ," she prompted.

She kept spinning her hands.

"Wool?" said Uncle Jim.

Janet dropped her hands.

"Paint," she said. "Coats of paint. It is a pun. He's at the Spreadz-Easy factory."

"Good work, Raccoo . . . uh, Janet! To the Night Glider!"

Uncle Jim sprinted to the Possum Cable and hooked it to the Possum Spool on his Possum Belt.

Janet reluctantly shuffled over to join him. Coming down on the Possum Cable could be daunting, but going up was worse.

Uncle Jim wrapped an arm around her and hit a button on the

Possum Belt. The Possum Spool activated, whipping them off the floor. Janet squeezed her eyes shut as they shot upward. Just when she would have expected them to flatten their heads on the ceiling, she felt Uncle Jim swing to the side so they'd pop through the hole in the roof. A second later they landed on their feet with a thud, and her uncle let her go.

"Now how did that happen?" she heard him say.

There was a rhythmic squeaking sound she didn't recognize. When she opened her eyes, she found herself momentarily blinded by a bright light.

It was the Night Glider. The spotlights running along the front had been turned on. The windshield wipers were going, too—that's what was squeaking.

As Janet's eyes adjusted to the light, she could make out a large white-and-black shape leaping and wriggling inside the Night Glider. It started barking.

"Albus!" Janet called out. "Calm down!"

It had the same effect telling Albus to calm down always did: He started barking louder and jumping higher. His paws smacked onto the control panel in front of him.

The windshield wipers turned off, but something else turned on—a black panel that slid aside beneath the cockpit to reveal four red-tipped tubes.

"He's armed the Possum Rockets!" Uncle Jim gasped, sprinting toward the Night Glider.

"Possum Rockets?"

Janet never knew her uncle was flying around with *rockets*.

She really, really, *really* wished she were home in bed.

Uncle Jim hit the button on his belt that dropped down the ramp into the Night Glider. Albus bounded out, his leash dragging beside him, and bolted toward a silver ventilation duct sticking out of the roof.

"What is it, boy?" Uncle Jim asked as the dog streaked past. "Someone hiding there? You see a clue?"

Albus stopped by the metal duct, sniffed it, and lifted one of his hind legs.

"Oh," said Uncle Jim.

"I told you we weren't done with our walk," Janet said.

Uncle Jim coughed.

"OK, well, get him back on the Night Glider," he said. "We don't have a moment to lose."

He whirled around and jogged up the ramp.

Janet hurried to Albus and picked up his leash.

"Sorry, Al," she said as she tugged him away. "Maybe when we get to the paint factory . . ."

The second the Night Glider was parked on the pavement beside the Spreadz-Easy plant, Uncle Jim broke up another "Possum Bar," threw it on the floor, and ran down the ramp.

"Time to knock Limerick King off his throne!" he said.

Janet sighed and started after him.

"Sorry," she said to Albus as he sucked up Pop-Tart crumbles. "We're almost done . . . I hope."

When she was outside in the chilly night air, Uncle Jim hit the button on his belt that retracted the ramp. He'd already reached a side door into the factory, and he knelt in front of it and pulled out a slender silver tool. After some fiddling, he pushed the door open and rushed into the dark hallway beyond.

Janet didn't follow.

"That was easy," she said.

"The Possum Pick opens anything," said Uncle Jim, already so deep in the darkness Janet couldn't see him.

"Those limerick riddles were easy, too, now that I think about it," she said.

"Limerick King isn't as clever as he thinks," said Uncle Jim.

"Or he's more clever than *we* think. What if this is a trap?"

Janet heard her uncle scoff.

"There isn't a trap on earth," he said, "that can catch Possum . . ."

There was a swirl of movement in the blackness in the factory, followed by a *bonk* and an *oof*. Then everything went still and silent beyond the door.

"Uncle Jim? You alright?"

A new voice came from the shadows—one Janet hadn't heard in a long time.

"I'm afraid it's just as you thought," it said. "You've stumbled right into my plot."

The sound of slow, steady footsteps echoed out of the hallway, and Janet could make out a gray silhouette moving toward her.

"Your uncle's knocked cold," the voice said, "so it's time you were told."

A man stepped into the moonlight. He was wearing a crown and a long red robe trimmed with white fur.

Limerick King.

Someone flicked on a light behind him, and Janet saw a pair of burly women dressed in fancy coats and tight trousers and powdered wigs like eighteenth-century dandies. She remembered them well. They were Punk and Skunk, two members of Limerick King's "royal court."

Uncle Jim was crumpled on the floor by their buckled black shoes.

Janet turned to run and found three more henchwomen—Thug, Mug, and Lug—lined up behind her.

"This *was* a trap, kid," Limerick King said. "And you're caught."

Punk and Skunk picked up Uncle Jim. Thug and Mug grabbed Janet. Lug turned to look at Albus, who was barking wildly in the Night Glider.

"Uhh . . . want me to get the dog, boss?" Lug asked.

"No," Limerick King said. "What I'm going to do to these two I wouldn't do to a dog."

He cackled and swept back into the factory. His flunkies followed with Janet and Uncle Jim in tow. Limerick King led the procession down the hallway, through another door and onto the factory floor.

A huge silver tank loomed before them, fifty feet across and thirty high. A hatch-like door in the side was open, and Limerick King and Lug stayed back while the rest of the gang went through it.

Thug and Mug shoved Janet toward the far side of the tank. Punk and Skunk dumped Uncle Jim on the floor. Then the four lackeys marched off. When they were out of the tank, they took up position just beyond the door.

Uncle Jim stirred.

"Why yes, I'd love to see the Batcave," he muttered. "Can I call you Bruce?"

He reached back groggily, pulled the tail of his Possum Suit over himself like a blanket, and curled into a ball.

Janet knelt and gave him a shake. "Uncle Jim. Wake up."

"Huh? Wha'?"

Uncle Jim sat up and looked around.

"Darn," he mumbled when he registered where he was. "So . . . a trap, huh?"

Janet nodded. "A trap."

Uncle Jim slowly pushed himself to his feet. Janet helped him. When he was standing straight, he took a wobbly step toward the doorway.

"Oh," he said to Thug, Mug, Punk, and Skunk. "Hello, ladies."

Thug, Mug, and Punk just glowered back at him. Skunk cracked her knuckles.

Uncle Jim turned to take in the rest of the tank. The interior wasn't shiny silver, like the outside. It was coated in dried paint all the way to its domed top. Five holes, each half a foot across, ran along the bottom of the tank opposite the door. Above the holes was a white sign with blocky red letters. Uncle Jim stepped closer to peer at it though the message was clear—just one word over a skull and crossbones.

"It says Danger," someone said.

Janet and Uncle Jim turned to find Limerick King standing in the doorway, Thug, Mug, Punk, and Skunk packed in behind him. He held a gleaming gold bulb the size of a bowling ball in one hand: the Holy Crown of Hungary.

"I wasn't sure he could read," he said to Janet.

She was staring at the crown.

"Like it?" Limerick King said, giving it a jiggle. "I've already sent a ransom note to the Hungarian government. We'll see how much they're willing to pay to get it back. I put it on eBay, too." He shrugged. "I'll go with the highest bidder."

"Whatever you have planned for me, I'll face," Uncle Jim said. "But let the girl go."

Limerick King scoffed. "Oh, *now* you're worried about her safety. *After* dragging her around chasing criminals you're too thick to catch yourself." He shook his head. "Sad."

"I'll show you 'sad,' villain," Uncle Jim growled. "Roses are red. Violets are blue. In two and a half seconds, I'll be handcuffing you!"

He slapped a hand to his side—then looked down with a frown.

His Possum Belt was gone, along with all its gizmos.

"Does he think that was a limerick?" Limerick King asked Janet.

She just sighed.

Limerick King looked at Uncle Jim again. "I had Punk and Skunk take your little toys. I'll put those on eBay, too. They'll be collector's items . . . for fans of the late, great Possum-Man."

"You ready, boss?" Lug yelled from somewhere in the distance.

"Indeed, I am!" Limerick King called back. "It's time to paint the town red!"

There was a squeaking sound, like a rusty tap being turned, followed by the clattering of unseen machinery.

A loud *glug-glug-glug* turned Janet and Uncle Jim around to look behind them.

A viscous blue liquid was flowing from one of the holes under the Danger sign.

"Hey! I thought the paint was gonna be red!" Limerick King said.

"There wasn't enough to fill the tank, so I switched to blue!" Lug called back.

"You should've told me! It ruined my zinger!"

Uncle Jim and Janet backed up as the paint slowly spread across the bottom of the tank.

Limerick King rubbed his chin, then grinned. "Looks like you're going to die a true-blue hero, Possum-Man!"

"Nice improv, boss!" Lug cheered.

Janet waggled her hand—the international sign for "meh."

"Leave the one-liners to the Punster," she said as the blue goo started to swallow the toes of her shoes. "It's not really your thing."

Limerick King shot her a glare, then shifted his gaze to Uncle Jim.

"And now, we've had our last brawl," he said. "I get to see my arch-enemy fall. Is there a way to get free?" He looked around the tank, then smirked and shook his head. "None I can see. For you, the writing's on the wall. Ta-ta!"

He slammed the door shut, the deafening *clank* echoing through the tank like thunder.

Uncle Jim threw himself at the door, but it was already sealed tight.

There was a squeal of rusty metal, and the *glugging* from the holes at the far end of the tank grew louder.

The paint wasn't just oozing in now. It was pouring in. Almost immediately it was over Janet's and Uncle Jim's ankles.

Uncle Jim pounded on the door with his gloved fists.

"I'm Possum-Man and I'm here to say!" he bellowed. "With this you're not going to get away!"

"Still not a limerick," said Janet.

Uncle Jim turned toward her, broad shoulders sagging. "I'm sorry I got you into this, Janet."

"Don't be," she replied. She looked down at the rising pool of paint around her. It was already up to her knees. "Not yet, anyway. Limerick King told us how to get out of here."

Uncle Jim sloshed over to her through the thick blue liquid.

"It must be fumes from the paint," he said, flapping a hand in front of her face.

"What?" said Janet.

"You're hallucinating. Limerick King didn't tell us how to get out of here. It's just a dream, Janet. A beautiful, beautiful dream."

Janet grabbed her uncle's hand and pushed it away. "Listen! The last thing Limerick King said to us! It was a limerick!"

Uncle Jim cocked his head. "'Ta-ta' is a limerick?"

Janet gritted her teeth.

"Not 'ta-ta,'" she said. "Something, something, something brawl; something, something, something fall. 'Is there a way to get free? None I can see. For you, the writing's on the wall.'"

"Oh. That." Uncle Jim shook his head sadly. "Janet, that's called a taunt."

"No! That nut can't help himself! It's a clue!"

"Janet, 'the writing's on the wall' is an expression. It means something's been set in motion that can't be stopped. Which is exactly what's happening." Uncle Jim turned away and brought his hand to his eyebrow as if saluting some unseen flag. "Farewell, Cleveland. I wish I could've fought for you longer."

Janet let out an exasperated groan, then started spinning slowly, scanning the stained walls of the tank.

It was up to her—and the paint was up to her waist.

"We need to take it literally," she said, speaking to herself more than her uncle. "'The writing's on the wall.' But there's old paint all the way to the top. If there's any writing, it would be buried under layers of . . ."

She stopped turning.

She was facing the Danger sign.

The *white* Danger sign. Without a single drop of paint on it.

Janet waded toward it.

"This sign is new," she said. "Otherwise it would be stained, like everything else in here."

Uncle Jim stopped saluting nothing. "Interesting. But I don't see how *Danger* and a skull and crossbones help us."

"They don't," said Janet.

The paint had reached the bottom edge of the sign—which, Janet noticed before it disappeared into the blueness, wasn't perfectly smooth. In fact, there were wrinkles here and there all over the sign, she could see now.

It was just a sheet of paper glued to the wall. Perhaps *over* something else.

Janet moved closer and picked at the sign's top left corner. The paper came unstuck slowly at first, then tore into a long strip. As it peeled away from the wall, chips of old paint came away with it, revealing writing beneath the paper—as well as a large, round button.

Uncle Jim leaned to look past Janet at the *real* writing on the wall. Half of it was still covered in plastered-on paper, but this much was visible:

NUAL

RRIDE

SH IN

SE OF

ERGENCY

"It's gibberish," Uncle Jim said.

"No, it's not!" Janet shot back. "Don't you see? This is how we get out!"

Uncle Jim squinted at the letters like they were an eye test chart.

"Uhh . . . we're supposed to 'nual rride sh in se of ergency'?" he said.

"No," Janet said. "We're supposed to do *this*."

And she brought up her right hand and did it.

For the solution to this story, please turn to page 320.

MONKEY BUSINESS
A FunJungle Mystery
By Stuart Gibbs

I was getting a corn dog at FunJungle Wild Animal Park when some idiot tried to steal a squirrel monkey.

Apparently, they thought you could steal a monkey the same way a burglar might swipe some jewelry: break into where it was kept, snatch it, and run off before anyone noticed. Maybe that would have worked with a more sedentary animal, like a small tortoise, or a banana slug, or even a sloth. But no monkey was going to let you grab it and run, especially a bundle of energy like a squirrel monkey. Imagine a kindergartener hopped up on three pounds of candy and a couple highly caffeinated sodas. That's what a squirrel monkey is like.

The thief had used a crowbar to pry open an access gate on the squirrel monkey cage at Monkey Mountain. After that, everything went wrong. The only squirrel monkey out that day was a two-year-old female named Zipper, who quickly slipped the thief's grasp and bolted for freedom.

It was a busy day at FunJungle and the walkways around Monkey Mountain were crowded with tourists. Anyone Zipper encountered reacted to the monkey's sudden arrival in two distinct ways: they either recognized she was an escapee and tried to corner her—or they thought she was potentially dangerous and ran in terror. Both reactions freaked Zipper out.

The closest security staff member to Monkey Mountain at the time was Marge O'Malley, who was often a bit overzealous in her attempts to do the right thing. Upon spotting Zipper, Marge immediately began pursuit.

That's when I got involved. I was at the Gorilla Grill, which was the closest place to eat by Monkey Mountain.

My name is Teddy Fitzroy. I'm only thirteen, but everyone at Fun-Jungle knows me because both my parents work here. We live in the employee housing behind the park, and I have my own official Fun-Jungle ID so I can enter whenever I want. My school bus stop is by the entry gates, so I always pass through the park on the way home, usually stopping to get a snack and visit a few exhibits on the way.

I was just about to order my corn dog when I heard a chorus of screams outside. Through the window, I saw Zipper bound across a series of tables. Startled tourists yelped as a medium-sized primate sent their french fries flying and knocked over their $11.99 souvenir mugs full of soda. Zipper still did less damage than Marge, however, who came barreling through, knocking tourists aside left and right in pursuit of the monkey. She made a desperate lunge for Zipper, but missed her and landed on a few ketchup squeeze bottles, which discharged all at once, splattering a poor Japanese family with red goop.

I abandoned my place in line and joined the chase, partly to help catch Zipper—and partly to try to make sure Marge didn't cause any more trouble. Sadly, I didn't move fast enough.

Just beyond the Grill was an open plaza where several of FunJungle's mascot characters had gathered for photo ops with the guests. The characters were merely adults dressed as animals. It always struck me as odd that tourists would wait up to half an hour in the hot sun to take pictures with pretend animals when there were *real* animals all around them. But the guests loved it and were dutifully waiting in line when Zipper and Marge came charging through.

Zipper made a beeline for Uncle O-Rang, perhaps mistaking the fake orangutan for a real one and thinking that a fellow primate would protect her from the crazed security guard bearing down on her. What Zipper didn't know was that the person playing Uncle O-Rang had an irrational fear of squirrels, having been attacked by a rabid one as a child. Now, a squirrel monkey doesn't really look like a squirrel at all. Squirrels are short and squat while squirrel monkeys are lean and spindly with long, prehensile tails. But it was notoriously hard to see out of the giant heads of the costumes. To the poor actor playing Uncle O-Rang, Zipper was just a blur of fur that *could* have been a rabid squirrel. He saw her racing toward him, then felt the thud as she leaped onto his enormous orangutan head. Zipper was only looking for comfort, but the actor mistakenly believed she was attacking him. He promptly screamed in terror and began to flail his arms wildly. He didn't come anywhere close to dislodging the monkey on his head—although he did ape-smack an unfortunate grandmother from Toledo.

At this point, Marge arrived on the scene and, rather than attempting to calm the frantic fake orangutan, she decided this would be the perfect time to ambush Zipper. The squirrel monkey was certainly distracted, desperately clinging to Uncle O-Rang's mega-cranium like a tiny bull rider as he thrashed about beneath her. Unfortunately, stealth was not exactly Marge's forte. She came barreling in like an angry rhino and lunged at Zipper. The monkey easily saw her coming and leaped to the safety of a jacaranda tree while Marge plowed headlong into Uncle O-Rang. The two of them smashed into Zelda Zebra, and all three tumbled into the landscaping. The head of Zelda's costume popped off, mortifying a group of kindergarteners who thought that Zelda was real—and that they had just witnessed her decapitation.

Zipper fled onward into FunJungle.

I helped the mascots get back to their feet, then headed back toward Monkey Mountain. I figured I'd need the help of some of the primate specialists to recover the escaped monkey.

It turned out that, while Marge had been causing chaos in her pursuit of Zipper, a significantly more competent group of security guards were back at the scene of the crime, doing their best to apprehend the criminal. A keeper who had been on duty nearby had identified three tourists who had all been close to the squirrel monkey exhibit at the time of the attempted primate heist. While there were thousands of security cameras all throughout the park, none looked directly at the squirrel monkey exhibit, but a few covered the nearby walkways, and security was able to quickly confirm the proximity of each suspect.

When I came along, the three suspects had been rounded up and were seated in the shade of a large oak tree near Monkey Mountain, under the watchful eye of FunJungle Security. Chief Hoenekker, the head of the security division, greeted me gruffly as I wandered up. "Hello, Teddy. I figured I might be seeing you. You're never far away when there's trouble."

"I didn't have anything to do with this, I swear," I said.

"I know," Hoenekker replied, then looked to the primate keeper, who was a middle-aged woman with the name Padgett on her official uniform. Padgett was petite, with a short haircut and a dark tan from long days working outside. "Did you see any of these people approach the exhibit?" Hoenekker asked her.

"No," Padgett replied. "I was busy with the colobus monkeys. But I know they were all close by when the attack occurred."

"I didn't go anywhere near that exhibit!" the first suspect exclaimed. He was a short, pudgy guy in a baseball cap and a FunJungle T-shirt. He looked to be in his twenties and was kind of twitchy and nervous. "I would never try to steal a monkey! I'm an active conservationist!" He quickly reached into his pocket.

All the FunJungle guards went on alert, going for their Tasers, as if fearing the guy was reaching for a gun.

The suspect raised his hands in fear, now with his wallet clutched in them. "Don't tase me!" he cried. "I was just getting out my membership card from the World Wildlife Fund!"

The security guards all relaxed a bit. Hoenekker snatched the wallet away and looked through it. Sure enough, there was a WWF membership card in it, along with a FunJungle annual pass and a FunJungle credit card.

"I'm innocent, too," the second suspect said quietly. She was a meek teenager in dark clothing with a long overcoat. The clothing looked like it was some sort of personal statement to me, because it certainly wasn't practical for a summer day at FunJungle, where it could often be over ninety degrees. "I didn't even know I was anywhere near the squirrel monkeys. I was trying to find the Polar Pavilion. I'm supposed to be meeting my friends there." Her phone started buzzing. "That's probably them now. Can I answer it?"

"No," Hoenekker told her. "None of you talks to anyone until I'm done with my questioning." He shifted his attention to the third subject, an older man in a spiffy suit that seemed very out of place compared to the shorts and T-shirts most tourists wore. "How about you? What's your story?"

The third suspect started speaking rapidly—in Italian. The words poured out of him in a torrent. I couldn't understand a thing, but I got the sense he was confused about what was even happening.

"Whoa!" Hoenekker shouted, signaling him to calm down. Then he spoke loudly and slowly, as if that would possibly make the man understand him. "Do . . . you . . . speak . . . English?"

"*Inglese?*" the man asked. "*No Inglese. Italiano!*"

Hoenekker sighed, exasperated, then looked to his team. "Does anyone here speak Italian?"

"I visited Italy last year!" one guard volunteered. "I learned a little bit."

"Do you have any idea what that man is saying?" Hoenekker asked.

"*Er* . . . Not really," the guard admitted. "Most of the words I learned had to do with pizza."

Marge O'Malley suddenly came along, triumphantly bearing Zipper. She had managed to catch the monkey in a large butterfly net and had then twisted the netting around, the same way one might close a bag of bread, to keep the monkey from escaping. Zipper didn't seem to appreciate this at all and was chattering angrily. "Our crisis is over!" Marge announced proudly. "I have recovered the monkey!"

"In a net?" Keeper Padgett gasped. "Oh, the poor thing!"

"She's not hurt, I assure you," Marge said. "I caught her way over by the giraffe exhibit."

"Must have reminded her of home," Padgett said, taking the net from Marge. Then she looked at Zipper, who was tangled in the netting, and said, "Don't worry, sweetie. I'll get you out of there as fast as I can." She turned to Hoenekker. "Do you mind if I take her? She's had a traumatic day."

"Of course not," Hoenekker said. "Take good care of her."

Padgett hurried off, Zipper still bound in the net. As she passed the suspects, the young monkey suddenly began squawking wildly. The suspects recoiled in surprise. A tiny tuft of dark fabric slipped from Zipper's hand and wafted to the ground.

Hoenekker snatched it up and examined it closely. It was only half an inch long and extremely fuzzy, like a woolly bear caterpillar.

"What's that?" Marge asked. "A clue?"

"Whatever it is, it's not mine," the first suspect said.

"Mine either," said the second suspect.

The third suspect said something in Italian.

"It's not his either," said the security officer who had been to Italy. "I think. He either said that or asked where the bathroom is."

Hoenekker sighed again. "I think we should all go someplace air-conditioned," he told his people. "We're in for a long round of questioning."

"No, we're not," I said. "I know who tried to steal the monkey."

For the solution to this story, please turn to page 322.

THE FIFTY-SEVENTH CAT

By Sheela Chari

The manager said there were fifty-six cats. And Div wanted to meet every single one.

Div loved cats. She loved their cat eyes and cat fur and that cat expression they had when they checked you out and decided you were okay.

It was humid in Key West and Div's hair was frizzing like crazy, even though they had flown in just a few hours ago. There was a line when they got to the museum, but it moved quickly. Everyone was dressed in shorts and tees and summer dresses—tourist clothes in December. One couple was not. The man wore a red suit and the woman, a white beaded dress fringed with feathers. Feathers? Red suit? Who were these people?

"One adult," Mom said to the ticket seller. "One eleven-year-old," she continued, eying Div, then Anya. "And she's nine."

"That's two children and an adult," the ticket seller said pleasantly. She took Mom's credit card. "Where y'all from?"

"New York," Anya said. "It was snowing when we left this morning."

"Well, aren't you glad you're in Florida?" the woman asked. "Enjoy your visit! And the cats."

"Cats?" Div repeated.

"Oh, yes. Do you like them?"

"My sister is bananas about them," Anya said. "But our mom won't get one. She says we're enough work for her."

Div poked her sister. Sometimes Anya said too much.

The woman pointed to the man in the front taking tickets. "He's the manager. He'll tell you about the cats," she said.

And that's when they found out about the fifty-six cats in Hemingway House.

"Goodness!" Mom said. "Why so many?"

"Because Hemingway loved cats," the manager said, beaming. "And this is where he lived. Some of the cats are *polydactyl*. Do you know what that means?"

Anya and Mom did not. But Div had read about it in a book from the library.

"It means they're six-toed," she said immediately.

The man was impressed. "Well, I'll be a crab shell. What's your name?"

"Div," she said, flushing. "Short for Divya. But everyone calls me Div."

"Listen, Div, because you're so smart, I'll give you a puzzle to solve." His voice dropped down a pitch. "Everyone will tell you there are fifty-six cats here. Except there are actually fifty-seven. Let's see if you can find the fifty-seventh cat."

Div suddenly grinned. She loved challenges, and she loved cats.

"What will you give us if we do?" Anya asked.

"Anya!" Div tugged on her sister's arm. "It's just for fun."

The manager nodded. "That's right. Just for fun. But if you find it, come tell me and you'll get a special prize! Good luck, girls!" Then he was off talking to the other tourists.

"Come on," Mom said. "There's a lot to see." She went ahead, entering the house.

"Who in the world has fifty-six cats?" Anya wanted to know. "I don't see a single one."

"Me either," Div said. "No, wait, Anya, look!"

There on the lawn strolled a gray tabby cat. Cat number one. And stretched out near a tree was an orange one. Cat number two. And two long-haired cats snoozed nearby. Three and four. Div ran to the tabby. It sniffed her fingers and allowed Div to stroke its head. She examined the cat's feet and counted the toes. Six.

By now her sister had caught up to her. "It's a polydactyl, Anya!"

"That's four cats. How will we keep track?"

Div kept stroking between the tabby cat's ears. "We'll write it down. You have that notepad you brought on the plane, right?"

"Yeah," Anya said. She pulled it out of her backpack. "We'll keep track by color. One: gray. Two: orange. Three: white and shoot—where did four go?" While they were talking, the other long-haired cat had wandered off. "This is harder than I thought!"

"No, Anya," Div said. "This will be fun! So many cats!"

They circled the grounds, walking past pink and white camellias in bloom and the base of palm trees dotting the corners of the yard. And everywhere there were cats: little, big, striped, plain, large-eared, long-haired, friendly, snarly, snoozing, sharp-clawed, timid, and bold. Div loved all of them. Tourists snapped pictures, their voices murmuring like bees in the sun.

"Fifteen," Anya declared, by the time they made it to the back, past the cat houses and onto the pebbled walkway leading to the gift store.

"Let's go inside," Div said.

The store was filled with books, postcards, and posters of Hemingway. Mom said he was a very famous writer. She had studied Hemingway in high school, and she figured Div and Anya would someday, too. Div walked around and at one of the tables, she picked up a cat calendar painted in bright, tropical colors.

"Cute, right?" asked a saleswoman with a pretty, suntanned face. Her name tag said Judy. "You gotta love the cats."

Anya shoved her way forward. "Actually, we're looking for the fifty-seventh cat. Do you know where it is?"

"Hmm," Judy said. "You should ask Shel. He's our cat keeper."

Anya's eyes grew round. "You have a *cat keeper*?"

Judy smiled. "Shel is the best. And Shel is . . . well, do you want to meet him?"

"Um, sure," Div said, surprised.

Judy showed them out the back door, her heels clicking against the pavement. Outside, they found a young guy in a green polo shirt and jean shorts near the cat homes, which resembled bird houses stacked one on top of another.

"Excuse me, you're in Marilyn Monroe's way," he said to Div.

Div looked bewildered until Judy gently pulled her back and a slender white cat flashed past them and jumped into Shel's lap.

"All the cats are named after famous people," Judy explained.

"That's Marilyn Monroe, Shel's favorite, right, Shel?" she asked him shyly.

Shel didn't seem to hear. "Does the lady Marilyn want her snack?" he said to the cat tenderly.

"You must love cats," Anya observed.

"I love *Hemingway cats*," Shel corrected her. "Isn't that so, Shirley Temple?" he crooned to an orange tabby. In his hand he held cat treats shaped like small, delicate fish. Marilyn Monroe and Shirley Temple were chomping them up.

"Do you know about the fifty-seventh cat?" Div asked.

Shel's face instantly clouded over. "You're not one of *those* people," he said.

Before she could ask what he meant, a voice called out. "Shel, Fred Astaire has gotten into the magnolia bush again. We need you to fish him out."

Shel nodded curtly at the girls. "Excuse me. Duty calls." He grabbed an extra handful of treats and was off.

"What was that about? He seemed mad," Anya said.

Judy looked unhappily in the direction Shel went. "He's very sensitive about the cats. But every time a cat does something wrong, Shel's the one who gets blamed."

Anya watched her. "You really like him," she said in a singsongy way.

Div poked Anya. There she was, saying too much again.

Judy blushed, but she didn't say no to Anya either. "Somebody has to look out for the guy," she said. Abruptly she excused herself to go back to the store.

After Judy left, Div said, "Anya, you can't just say whatever you're thinking!"

"What? She *does* really like him. I can tell."

Div reached down to pet Marilyn Monroe. "Well, even if she does! How many cats now?"

Anya consulted her pad. "Seventeen. I don't think we're going to get to fifty-six."

"Maybe we don't have to," Div said thoughtfully. "Maybe we just have to find the fifty-seventh one."

"Isn't that the same thing?"

Div shook her head. "There's something we're not seeing yet. A trick. Come on, let's go inside the house."

They entered from the front and stepped into the drawing room, which had shelves full of Hemingway's things: typewriters, books, papers, photographs, a pair of reading glasses, an old pair of binoculars. Just then, Div felt someone jostle past her. It was the man in the red suit, and he was talking to the woman in the beaded dress and feathers. He seemed upset. "I can't rest until I have it," he said.

"It's just a cat," the woman muttered. She gave a look of disdain. "Speaking of which, I'm not a big fan with the whole bunch of them crawling around here."

The man was aghast. "What are you saying? Are you forgetting what we do?"

The woman sighed. "Of course not. Just not my taste."

Div listened in fascination. The man didn't mean he wanted one of the cats, did he? He did give off a weird vibe. But did that make him a cat burglar? Div decided to follow them.

"Wait," Anya called out. Div signaled to her to be quiet, then went upstairs where the couple was headed. She couldn't hear what they were saying anymore because a tour group crowded in between them. But she stayed close behind until everyone was inside Hemingway's bedroom.

"Here we have Hemingway's room," announced the tour guide.

"Another cat!" Anya pointed to a bed that was roped off from everyone. Everyone laughed. Square in the middle of the roped-off bed was a dozing black-and-white cat.

"Good thing he's sleeping, right?" The tour guide winked at Anya. "No telling what he'll do when he's awake!"

As Anya wrote in her pad, Div saw the couple next to a display in the back, peering at it intently. Div wondered what could be so important. Another typewriter?

"There you are!"

Div jumped at the sound of her mom's voice.

"I've been looking around for you two," Mom said.

"Mom, we found eighteen cats and I don't think we can find any more," Anya pouted, holding up her pad.

Mom smiled. "I'm sure they're hiding from all these people."

Div craned her neck to hear what the couple was saying but they were already walking to the next room. She shuffled around the tour group until she got to the display. When she bent down to get a better look, what she saw made her pause for a whole moment and then she grinned wide.

Div and Anya argued on the way downstairs.

"I'm sure the manager man meant an alive cat," Anya said.

"But even you said there's no way we can find fifty-six cats. The fifty-seventh has to be something else. It has to be that statue!"

SHEELA CHARI

"Who is Picasso anyway?" Anya asked Mom as they reached the bottom of the stairs. "I thought the Hemingway cats were famous. Now there's a Picasso cat, too?"

"Picasso was a famous artist," Mom said. "The cat statue on that shelf was a gift he gave to Hemingway. That's what the sheet next to it said."

"Is Picasso as famous as Hemingway?" Anya asked.

"They're both famous," Div said. "For different reasons."

Last spring she'd gone to a Picasso exhibit with her dad. She remembered the paintings she saw of women with faces and eyes in the wrong place. Dad said it was called cubism, whatever that was. Even the Picasso cat didn't look completely like a cat either. Dad said that was what made art interesting—things not being where you expected them.

She couldn't wait to talk to him on the phone. He was still in New York finishing up with a client. She'd tell him how she'd solved a mystery in Key West—her first one!

At the bottom of the stairs, they ran into the woman from the store.

"Hey, girls," Judy said. "Have you seen Shel?"

"Wasn't he at the magnolia bush?" Anya asked.

Mom was surprised. "How do you know that? Who's Shel?"

Judy gave them a distracted glance. "Sorry to bother you. One of the cats is missing. He's a frisky one, and might be in the house. I can't seem to find Shel either. I guess I have to look for Elvis Presley myself." With that she went upstairs.

"Wait," Mom said. "Did she just say she was looking for Elvis Presley?"

Div shrugged. "Cat stuff."

On the front lawn, they saw the manager talking to Shel, who had a long-haired cat in his arms. Div knew Anya would interrupt them, so she

58

grabbed her sister. "Don't say anything," she whispered. "They're talking."

"The magnolia bush has to go, Mr. Frost," Shel said to the manager. "Fred won't stop eating the flowers and it's making him sick."

"Shel, we can't relandscape because of the cats," Mr. Frost said. "Let's be reasonable."

"Mister, we found the fifty-seventh cat!" Anya exclaimed, butting in like she always did.

Div frowned. Was there no way to stop her interrupting sister?

Still, Div couldn't help adding, "It's the Picasso cat." After all, *she* was the one who solved the puzzle.

Mr. Frost beamed. "You figured it out! Such smart girls!"

"I know!" Anya burst out, smiling.

Mr. Frost was looking ahead at the water fountain, where Div noticed that same couple from before. The man in the red suit still seemed agitated, and the woman still bored. The man waved a red business card in the air.

Mr. Frost sighed. "Here's that prize we talked about. Some complimentary postcards of the Picasso cat! Good work. Now please excuse me." He headed off to talk to the man in the red suit.

"Postcards?" mumbled Anya. "I thought we would get candy."

As Mr. Frost and the odd man talked, Shel stroked Fred Astaire nervously. "I have a bad feeling," he said.

"About what?" Div asked.

"They think that money talks. But there are some things money can't buy." Shel walked off with Fred Astaire.

"Wait, Judy was looking for you," Anya called out.

"He didn't hear you," Div said. "He was too busy being mad about something."

Meanwhile Mr. Frost finished talking to the man in the red suit.

"You have my business card," said the man. "The offer stands until New Year's Day."

Mr. Frost sighed again. "I'll let you know, but realize you can't just walk in and change a tradition."

"We'll be around," the man in the red suit said over his shoulder.

The woman in the beaded dress tugged on his arm. "I want a selfie," she said.

"You know I hate those," he whined.

"Just one by the pool," she said. "But no cats!"

They laughed, sauntering away.

"Now where's Shel?" Mr. Frost murmured.

"He went that way," Anya said, pointing.

By now, Mom was ready to leave. "Next stop," she said, "swimming with the dolphins!"

"But I want a picture with a cat," Anya said.

So did Div. They took several photos around the gardens and pool and verandah.

"Hey, there's Judy again," Anya said. "I wonder if she found Shel."

Near the back door, Judy stood, her eyes darting back and forth. She opened her hand and Div saw what Judy was holding. They were the treats Shel was giving to the cats. Then Judy did something really strange. She stuffed them in her mouth!

"What on earth!" Div exclaimed. "Did you see, Anya? She ate the cat biscuits!"

"*Haha*, maybe she's the fifty-eighth cat."

Div giggled.

"Let's go," Mom said. "We have enough pictures."

They got to the entrance when they saw a crowd at the gate. Not only that, the gate was locked with two police officers standing in front! Mr. Frost waved to everyone to be quiet. "Ladies and gentlemen, we require your assistance. Please form an orderly line. We need to ask each of you a few questions before you leave. Single file please." Everyone looked baffled.

"What's going on?" asked Mom. "We have reservations at Dolphin Paradise in one hour."

Murmurs went through the crowd.

The man in the red suit was angry. "You can't hold us against our will!"

"Yeah, due process, people," said the woman in the beaded dress.

"They're holding us because of what happened," said a woman in baggy pants, standing behind Div.

"What happened?" asked Mom.

"The statue—it was stolen," said the woman in the baggy pants. "Didn't you hear? A few minutes ago. In broad daylight!"

"The Picasso statue?" Anya asked, surprised.

"Yeah, that's the one," the woman said.

"They can't hold us," the man in the red suit repeated. "It's against the law."

More murmurs went through the crowd. Meanwhile, Div looked up and down the line. Did the police and Mr. Frost think one of the visitors had taken the statue?

"I don't get it," said Anya. "Didn't we just see the statue?"

"No, remember we stopped to take pictures," said Mom. "I knew we should have left already. We'd be on our way to Dolphin Paradise by now. Let's see if I can move the reservation." She got out her phone.

On the ground, Div spotted something—a red business card. When she picked it up, she remembered the man in the red suit holding it out to Mr. Frost. On the front it said "Wally Stevens & Lizzie B., Art Buyers, specializing in rare art. 'We get what we want and so will you!'"

Art dealer! Cats! The pieces suddenly clicked together.

"That couple wanted the Picasso cat!" Div whispered to Anya. "Only Mr. Frost didn't want to sell it. And neither did Shel!"

"How do you know?" Anya whispered back.

"I just do. Any time someone says they're thinking about something, it means no," Div whispered again. "And Shel . . ." There was something odd about the cat keeper but Div couldn't put her finger on it. "Mom, Anya and I are going for a walk," Div suddenly announced.

Mom was still on the phone with Dolphin Paradise. "Don't go too far off," she told them. "The line is starting to move."

Div looked ahead where one by one, each visitor went off to one side to talk to the police and then a few minutes later was released through a separate exit. So far, no one had any clues about where the statue had gone. And no one had the statue hidden in their shoulder bag.

"Where are we going?" Anya asked.

"To investigate," Div said. "We were the last ones to see that statue." She studied the postcard, and the brilliant blue, yellow, and red hues of the Picasso cat. "Keep your eyes and ears open, Anya."

When they went upstairs though, they discovered that one whole wing had been cordoned off with yellow tape.

"Sorry, kids," a man said, who stood in front of the bedroom. "This is a crime scene."

But Div wasn't ready to give up yet. She remembered the balcony wrapped around the entire second floor. "Come on, Anya," she whispered. They went to the other side of the floor, through the doors that led to the balcony. From there, they would be able to look inside the windows of Hemingway's bedroom. But when they rounded the corner, Div and Anya found the balcony packed with tourists, all with the same idea of trying to sneak a peek.

"This is crazy," one man said. "Count me out." He backed away. The rest of the tourists continued pushing to get a view.

"What's there to see?" Anya asked. "Isn't the statue missing?"

"No one knows for sure," someone told her. "But it's very exciting!"

Div tried to get closer to the window but there were too many people. "I guess we should go back down, Anya," she said, disappointed. "Mom is probably wondering where we are." Besides, what had she hoped to find? She wasn't a trained investigator. And she didn't know anything about Hemingway. The only thing she knew about were cats.

They got to the back stairs when Anya said, "Hey, it's the cat from Hemingway's bed."

"A tuxedo," Div said. "That's the kind of cat it is."

The black-and-white cat stood, watching them.

"*Meow*," the tuxedo cat said.

"Hi, kitty," Div replied. She patted its head gently. "What a sweet kitty."

"*Meow, meow*," answered the tuxedo cat.

"Let's see if you're a polydactyl. Kitty, show me your paws." Div checked and saw the distinctive six toes. "Anya, it's another one."

"*Meow, meow, meow*," said the tuxedo cat, this time a little more insistently.

"What's wrong, kitty? Are you trying to tell us something?" And then Div saw it, lodged between the tuxedo cat's fifth and sixth toe, a colorful shard of clay. Div pulled it out and held it up. "Kitty!" she exclaimed.

The cat stared at her as if to say, *I told you so.*

Div looked from the tuxedo to the shard, which had yellow, red, and blue colors. "That must hurt, Kitty. So many colors and . . ." Suddenly she could barely speak. "Anya, it's from the Picasso cat. I just know it."

"You mean . . ." Anya's voice trailed off.

The tuxedo cat regarded Div for a moment, then started down the stairs.

"Let's follow it," Div said excitedly.

They ran after the tuxedo as it wove around visitors, climbing steadily down the stairs. Soon they were all at the bottom, then on the pebbled walk that went to the cat houses and eventually the gift store. The cat picked up speed and so did Div and Anya. The cat sensed it was being followed, which seemed to fill it with even more urgency. It bounded into the encircled area of the cat homes.

Shel was standing in the middle and saw the tuxedo. "Elvis Presley!" he exclaimed.

The tuxedo dived into a cat house.

"Shel, I'm sorry but we have to search that cat house," Div said.

"Wait, what?" Shel said. "Of course you can't. That's Elvis Presley's house and—"

Div debated half a second then leaped forward, jamming her hand in.

"Div!" Anya yelled.

Shel lunged but it was too late. Div pulled out a brightly colored object. She held it up, a clay statue that was heavier than she imagined, brilliant in shades of yellow, red, and blue, a cat statue only because of its tail and paws, because it was now missing a head.

Shel gasped. "What? Oh no! Elvis! What have you done?"

Before anyone could say anything, up the path came Mr. Frost and the two police officers, one of them holding a ziplock bag.

"Shel!" exclaimed Mr. Frost. "What's going on? We found cat cookie crumbs on the display shelf. And now the statue is here—and what happened to its head?"

"It was hidden in Elvis Presley's cat house," Anya said.

"Anya!" Div cried. Could nothing stop her sister from blurting?

"Shel, this is a grave situation," Mr. Frost said. "I don't even know where to begin."

"First we'll take fingerprints," one of the police officers said.

"Wait, I didn't take the statue!" Shel sputtered. "Why would I?"

"Well, you sure didn't want me to sell it to Wally," Mr. Frost said slowly. "Even if the money would mean we could keep the house operating for many more years."

"But . . . but . . ." Shel was choking on his words.

Div's mind rapidly calculated everything she had seen so far: Shel's devotion to the cats, the art couple insisting on buying the statue for their collection, and finally the crumbs in the ziplock bag that the police officer held. And then she remembered something else: how art might be the right thing in the wrong place. That's what made it interesting. Where else had she seen that—the right thing in the wrong place?

Div spotted someone on the pebbled path and she stood up suddenly.

"Shel didn't take the statue," she said. "But I know who did!"

For the solution to this story, please turn to page 323.

THE PERFECT ALIBI
By Fleur Bradley

Time just wasn't on my side that day.

I was running late, *really* late, so I yanked my bike off the main road and took the shortcut home from George's house. He's my best friend and we were so into the Lego robot we were constructing, I left later than I should to beat my mom's deadline. George lives across town. It takes about half an hour on my bike to get to his apartment.

I didn't have a half an hour.

So, like I said, I took the shortcut—the one that goes through the forest (super creepy, especially once it gets dark), and passes the big stone church and the Cumberland Mansion.

More on that place later.

I raced on my bike, past the church where the clock in the stone steeple told me I was in trouble.

It was seven fifteen.

I was supposed to be home by seven. And the church clock was meticulously set to the correct time by the maintenance man every Monday. Boring but true. We once did a school field trip to the church, where we met the man and saw his clunky set of clock-setting tools.

Anyway, like I said, all my hurrying wasn't enough to get me home on time. And my mom wasn't listening when I tried to explain why I was late and how close George and I were to a mega breakthrough in the robot department.

"Francesca," she said when I dashed through the back door and tried to act nonchalant, "you have to start following the rules around here." She was at the kitchen table grading papers for the high school English class she teaches. "This is the fifth time you're late this month."

Sometimes it stinks to have a mom who keeps track of stuff so accurately.

"You know you need to be home before dark," she continued. "Even on a Friday."

Then she sighed. It's always worse when she sighs.

"I need some time to figure out your punishment. I'll tell you what it is later."

I went to bed dreading what she might dream up.

I found out soon enough. The next morning at breakfast, Mom looked way too pleased with herself. My punishment was going to be brutal. I could tell.

I ate my cereal and waited. It seemed as if the cinnamon in my Cinnamon Toast Crunch had a little extra bite to it. Maybe it was helping Mom punish me.

Mom smiled as she wiped down the kitchen counters.

It was time for me to take my punishment.

"Francesca," she said, "I was putting away the garbage can last night when all of a sudden, I had a brilliant idea. You know Mr. Griffin, from across the street?"

"Uh-huh."

Our neighbor Mr. Griffin is a grumpy old guy who complains about everything: my older brother's skateboarding on the sidewalk, my water balloon fight's leftover balloon bits ("They mess up my lawn!"), dogs even thinking about sniffing one of his trees to do their business. Mr. Griffin is always watching you from his window, even when you think he isn't.

"He was complaining the other day about how his garage was so full of stuff he couldn't even park his car in there." Mom gave me an even bigger smile. "You're going to help him."

"Do what?"

"Clean out his garage."

I was about to say "B-B-But" when Mom said, "No ifs, ands, or buts about it."

From the look on Mom's face, I knew there would be no appealing my sentence. So, after I finished breakfast and my morning chores, I mustered up all my courage and walked across the street. I climbed Old Man Griffin's porch steps, and with my eyes closed, I rang his doorbell.

I opened my eyes when I heard the garage door rolling up.

Mr. Griffin was standing in front of the garage, a dark, cluttered cavern full of who knows what. He had a sour look on his face and his arms crossed over his chest. He looked even less thrilled than me about the prospect of our spending the day together.

"What's your name?" he asked when I (very slowly) walked to the garage. The place smelled like motor oil mixed with old garbage and wet newspapers.

"Um, Francesca?" Yes, I said it like it was a question. What can I say? I was scared.

He arched a bushy eyebrow. "Francesca?"

"Everyone calls me Frankie. My mom told me I should come over and—"

He waved his hand dismissively. "I know what she told you. She told me, too. Called me up on the phone. Thought it was another one of those salespeople calling about credit cards. I hate those calls." This time he waved his hands to dismiss the world. "Your mother says you've come over here to help me clean up. What'd you do?"

I was about to tell him when he waved his hand to dismiss me for the third time.

"Never mind. I don't much care. Besides, you and me have work to do."

I followed him into the garage. There were boxes stacked on top of boxes. A bunch of broken lawn furniture stacked in a tangled heap. Old lawn mowers leaking ancient oil. Tangled strands of Christmas lights. String-tied bundles of magazines and newspapers. A workbench buried under grimy tools. A wheelbarrow filled with dirt and a dead plant. There was even a wrinkled plastic swimming pool piled in a clump.

I checked my phone.

It was 10:05.

This was going to be a very long day.

"We'll deal with the lawn furniture and busted swimming pool tomorrow," Mr. Griffin said.

Tomorrow?

Mom hadn't said anything about me doing two days of community service.

I was about to say something when Mr. Griffin wheezed up a laugh. "Ha! Gotcha. Don't worry, Frankie. Your prison sentence ends today."

I smiled. "Thank you."

"Don't thank me. Your mother is the judge, jury, and appeals court on this one."

He pulled a box out of one of the tallest stacks and dropped it on the concrete floor with a thump.

"These are my old files. I'll go through them, you shred what I give you." He nodded toward the industrial-sized paper shredder jammed into the corner near the workbench. The one I had thought was another hunk of junk to be dragged to the curb.

I counted the number of file cartons climbing up to the garage ceiling. It was a teetering cardboard skyscraper. And the stack behind it? Those boxes were labeled "files," too.

I groaned—inwardly. I'm polite that way.

For thirty minutes or more, Mr. Griffin glanced at sheets of paper, grunted, and handed those papers to me, five at a time. Any more and the machine would clog up. I took those five pieces of paper over to the shredder and fed them into the thing's hungry mouth.

When I went back for more, Mr. Griffin was staring at a stack of pages. He seemed caught up in whatever he was reading.

"What's that?" I asked.

"An old case," Mr. Griffin mumbled.

"What kind of case?"

"Burglary."

"Were you a lawyer?"

Mr. Griffin shook his head. "Police detective."

I guess that sort of explained why he was always policing our street from his living room window.

"What's the case?" I asked.

I love a good mystery. I read mystery books all the time, but this was a real-life one. That was pretty exciting.

Mr. Griffin didn't answer me for a good minute. I stood there waiting for him to hand me the papers so I could go shred them.

Mr. Griffin tapped the pages and frowned. "You know, this one always stumped me. And it irked the heck out of me."

"What was stolen?"

"A million dollars' worth of jewelry, the entire Cumberland family's collection. Several pieces of art. Plus, twenty thousand dollars in cash."

"Whoa," I mumbled. I mean who has a million dollars' worth of jewelry? I have a necklace and this sparkle ring I bought at the mall that turned my finger green.

"I was never able to figure out what happened to a good portion of the loot, or who all was involved. It's a cold case." He hesitated, then handed the file to me. "Go ahead and shred it. I'll never solve that one."

I took the file. "Can I look at it?"

Mr. Griffin shrugged. "Knock yourself out, kid."

I opened the file just as George walked up the driveway pushing his bike. "Hey, Frankie. Your mom says you're doing community service."

"More kids?" Mr. Griffin huffed. "I'm not running a local youth group here, you know."

"Hey, George," I said. "You can help if you want." I smiled eagerly. I'd do anything to get a friendly face in the garage with me.

"Cool," said George.

"Who the heck are you?" growled Mr. Griffin, putting on his extra-grumpy face. I think he saves that one for kids.

But George didn't mind. He doesn't pick up on social cues too much and is friendly to even the nastiest bullies in school.

"I'm George, sir." He extended his hand to shake but turned it into a friendly wave when Mr. Griffin just gave him another grunt and a frown. "Nice to meet you. Frankie and I build robots. Do you have any robots in your garage?"

"Listen, *George*," said Mr. Griffin, "unless you're here to help, you probably want to scram." He turned back to his box of files.

"I'd be happy to help, sir." George parked his bike and came into the garage. "Frankie and I were going to work on our robot, but this looks more exciting. What's in that file? Is it something secret?"

"It's a cold case," I said. "Mr. Griffin used to be a detective. With the police. We were shredding papers and he found an unsolved mystery."

"We should solve it!" George said eagerly. "You and me, Frankie!"

He plopped down next to me on the concrete floor.

Mr. Griffin laughed. "I was a detective for twenty-three years, and I couldn't crack this case. Now you two kids are going to do it?"

George ignored him. "Let me see what you've got so far, Frankie."

I took the pages out of the file. There were forms and more forms, plus a stack of hand-scribbled notes. Then there was a photograph—what they call a mug shot on TV—the kind they snap when someone gets arrested.

His name was Petey Miller. He looked grumpy. Then again, I probably wouldn't be smiling for the camera if I just got arrested.

"That guy, we caught," Mr. Griffin said.

George examined the photo. "What happened, exactly?"

Mr. Griffin hesitated, but began to tell us the story. "Do you kids know the Cumberland Mansion?"

We both nodded. I said, "I bike by that place every day, when I go over to George's to work on our robots."

"Well, you kids might be too young to remember, but the Cumberland Mansion was burgled five years ago. The thieves got away with a lot of valuables—mostly jewelry and art." He pointed to the mug shot. "That's Petey Miller. We busted him trying to sell what he stole. But we never caught any of the other burglars."

"I'll bet Frankie can figure this out," said George, pulling a lawn chair out of the heap so he had a place to sit. "She's a wiz at puzzles."

Mr. Griffin gave me an incredulous stare.

I get that a lot—people think because I'm a kid, I couldn't possibly be good at solving a mystery.

"You might've missed something, Mr. Griffin," I said very politely. "Our science teacher, Ms. Willow, tells us that sometimes it takes a fresh eye to see something that was there all along."

"And there's no *I* in team," George added. "Right?"

I wasn't sure if that was really the point we were trying to make, but I nodded anyway.

Mr. Griffin huffed but didn't argue.

George pulled a sheet off another old chair. Dust flew everywhere. "Sit down, Frankie. We can be armchair detectives! Here's a chair for you, too, Mr. Griffin."

He yanked back another sheet. George looked pretty funny, trying to swat away that cloud of dust. It made me laugh. You can't really be grumpy around George. Unless you were Mr. Griffin. He still looked like the oldest member of the Sour Patch Kids.

I found an old pin board filled with old-fashioned metal thumbtacks and used one to pin up the mug shot.

"So what other evidence do we have?" I asked.

Mr. Griffin flipped through the file. "Well, the burglary took place on a Sunday morning, March tenth. Mrs. Cumberland was hosting a brunch at her mansion—her annual Spring Fling. Once a year, she'd 'fling' open her doors and let folks tour her mansion. It was an annual charity event. People were coming and going all morning."

"So anyone could have stolen the stuff," said George.

"Not anyone," said Mr. Griffin. He pulled out a paper with names written on it. "It was a 'by invitation only' event. Here's her guest list and the names of the catering staff." He gestured toward the mug shot. "The brunch and open house were scheduled for ten a.m. to noon. Petey Miller was a waiter at the mansion that day."

There were about thirty names on the guest list. Half a dozen with the catering company.

"That's a lot of suspects." I used another thumbtack to pin the lists next to Miller's mug shot.

"Mrs. Cumberland went up to her bedroom a little before noon," said Mr. Griffin. "She took off her diamond necklace and went to the bathroom to freshen up. When she came back to her bedroom, the necklace was gone."

"So the burglar struck at noon!" I said.

Mr. Griffin nodded. "At least that's when he or she stole the diamond necklace."

There were some other pictures in the file folder: the mansion, its luxurious rooms, the empty jewelry cases, the blank spots on the wall.

"Mrs. Cumberland is elderly," said Mr. Griffin. "She was only able to give us a partial inventory of what was missing."

There was another photo in the file, but it didn't look like it was taken at the mansion. It showed some rich-looking guy in a tux holding a fancy-looking pocket watch, standing in what appeared to be a hotel ballroom.

"Who's he?" I asked Mr. Griffin.

"Meet Mr. Charles Cumberland, Mrs. Cumberland's only grandson. This photo was taken a month after the burglary, at another charity gala—downtown at the Reed House Hotel. Charles, of course, wasn't talking to his grandmother at the time. In fact, he hadn't talked to her since New Year's Day when she informed her one and only grandson that she'd rewritten her will. Suffice it to say, Charles wasn't thrilled with what she had decided would be his inheritance."

"Maybe he's the thief," George said, saying what I was thinking.

"Totally," I said. "I mean, he definitely had a motive. If his grandmother wasn't going to leave him stuff in her will, maybe Charles just decided to grab as much as he could at the Spring Fling."

"Not possible," Mr. Griffin said. "Charles was out of town on the day of the burglary."

"Where?" George and I asked at the same time.

"France."

"Oh." George sat back in his chair. "Bummer."

"Indeed," Mr. Griffin said. He still pinned the photo to what was becoming our evidence wall. "Anyway, a couple weeks after the burglary, we caught Petey Miller with about a third of the stolen jewelry. He was trying to sell it to a local pawnshop."

"Busted," said George. "Hey—how do you know some outsider who wasn't on the guest or catering list didn't just break in when nobody was looking to steal stuff?"

"The mansion had a security team monitoring every entry and exit that Sunday," said Mr. Griffin. "And there are video cameras outside the mansion, recording everybody in and everybody out."

"What about *inside* the mansion?" I asked.

Mr. Griffin shook his head. "No cameras. At the time, Mrs. Cumberland thought that would just be extravagant."

"I bet she wishes she had them now!" blurted George.

Mr. Griffin actually smiled. George will do that to you.

"So it had to be someone at the party," I said. I looked at some more pages in the file. There were notes on interviews and grainy security camera stills of guests entering and exiting the mansion.

Mr. Griffin pulled a photo from the file and pinned it to the workbench wall.

"This is a shot of the catering van being loaded after the party," he said. "I'm pretty sure that's how they escaped with the loot. There's Petey Miller. Who knows what he has hidden inside that butler's trolley? And this shadowy figure here, we thought that might be Petey's girlfriend— Shana Cooper. The photo is too fuzzy to make a positive ID."

"Doesn't that solve your case then?" asked George. "She probably has the rest of the loot in that covered rubber tub she's carrying."

Mr. Griffin shook his head. "Shana had an airtight alibi. See the time stamp in the corner? That photo of the catering van was taken at twelve p.m. And Shana was seen going to church that Sunday—precisely at noon."

"Says who?" I asked. "Maybe the person who gave her the alibi was lying."

"It wasn't one person. More than a dozen people saw her walk up the church steps at noon. Ms. Cooper was wearing a bright red dress— she was hard to miss."

"Bummer," I mumbled.

"Yeah, there were a lot of bummers in this case," said Mr. Griffin, getting up from his chair. "We searched Shana Cooper's apartment and just about anywhere she could have hidden her share of the treasure. We even looked inside the church." He shook his head. "I told you kids: it's a cold case for a reason."

George and I were both silent. This *really* was a cold case. Maybe even frozen. Despite our enthusiasm, I wasn't sure we could help Mr. Griffin solve it.

We all stared at the evidence wall for about a minute.

Then, frustrated, we went back to shredding papers.

Maybe an hour later, George glanced at his watch.

"I have to get home—Dad was making cookies for us when I left, Frankie. Can you come?"

I looked to Mr. Griffin.

He waved his hand in dismissal.

"Go, go. Maybe you can help me finish this up another day."

"I'd like to." I looked at the cold case evidence wall one more time. I was actually sorry to go. This was just the kind of puzzle I liked: one that seemed to stump everyone, but you knew there was an answer to it. You just had to know where to look.

"Let it go, Frankie," said Mr. Griffin. "I worked on this thing for months. It can drive you crazy. And make you cranky."

No lie. Mr. Griffin was about the grumpiest guy I'd ever met.

George and I took off on our bikes and retraced my usual route to his place. We went down the hunter's path and past the Cumberland Mansion, which looked extra mysterious now that we knew about the cold case hanging over it.

George followed my gaze as we pedaled down the path. "Makes you look at that place in a whole different light, huh?"

I nodded. My eyes went from the mansion's grand entry down to the road. "What if Shana Cooper took our dirt path instead of the road to get to church?" I said. "That would be fast, right?"

"You're forgetting that she has an alibi for exactly noon. Remember?" said George as we pedaled past the church. The clock stood high in its tower and was, of course, set to the correct time.

"There has to be a clue we're missing here," I said. I stopped, and straddled my bike.

The answer was right there in front of me. But I just couldn't see what we were missing.

"Um, there are chocolate chip cookies waiting for us," said George. "Triple chocolate chip. Your favorite?"

"What was the date of the burglary again?" I asked George.

George thought for a second. "Mr. Griffin said Sunday, March tenth. Why?"

It was like a coin dropped, an alarm bell dinged, and a lightbulb went off over my head at the exact same time. "Let's go back to Mr. Griffin's. I think I know how to solve the mystery!"

"I knew it!" George said. "I knew you'd crack the case! *Woo-hoo!* This is better than cookies!"

A few hours later, Mr. Griffin's former colleagues on the police force arrested the grandson, Mr. Charles Cumberland. "I was in France at the time of the burglary," he argued.

"But you're the mastermind," said Mr. Griffin. "We have proof."

Thirty minutes later, the same police officers arrested Shana Cooper. They even gave retired Detective Griffin the honor of cuffing her.

"But I have an alibi!" Shana exclaimed. "I couldn't have been at the mansion—I was at church."

Mr. Griffin grinned. "Actually, Ms. Cooper, it's your perfect alibi that did you in." He nodded to George and me. "And you can thank these kids for cracking the case."

For the solution to this story, please turn to page 326.

THREE BROTHERS, TWO SISTERS, AND ONE CUP OF POISON

By Lauren Magaziner

There was poison inside the vial. It was tasteless, odorless, and disastrously deadly if ingested.

The vial rested on the countertop for a solid hour. Waiting to be found, waiting to be used. Then, quietly, someone tipped it into a goblet.

Six hours earlier:

Hannah Friedman looked in the mirror. "I'm a cupcake," she groaned, looking at her very frilly dress. It was pink with ruffles up the front, bows down the back. It cinched at the waist, which was a fancy way of saying that it pulled her lungs so tight she could barely breathe. She looked at her grandmother, and said, "Bubbie, I'm literally a *cupcake*."

"I think you look very nice," her bubbie replied.

From the doorway, Hannah's brother, Isaac, tugged at his collar. "At least you don't have this *thing* choking you!" He tried to loosen his tie, but he pulled it just a bit tighter. "Dressy clothes! Are torture machines! For children!"

"Your great-aunt Bea will love it."

"If she's our aunt," Isaac said, "then why haven't we met her before?"

"My sister and I have not spoken for over twenty years. We are estranged."

"You're not *that* strange, Bubbie," Isaac said.

"*Estranged*, not strange." Hannah groaned. "It means they've been fighting. There's been a rift between them."

"That's putting it mildly," said Bubbie.

"What caused the fight?" asked Isaac.

Bubbie didn't respond.

"Well . . . why are we going to see her now?"

At that, Bubbie smiled, showing off every one of the big teeth in her dentures. "I have to deliver a message."

"What message?" Isaac said.

But Bubbie shook her head. Her meaning was clear: the only person who would hear the message was Great-Aunt Bea herself.

They piled into the car. When they left, the day was clear, and the sky was bright. But the more they coiled around mountains and through valleys, the more the air around them became thin and foggy. Before too long, it was getting dark.

Isaac fell asleep right away, as he often did in cars. But Hannah was too uncomfortable to nod off.

Something was troubling her. Bubbie had a telephone. She had a computer. She had all the conveniences of modern technology, which included a hundred different ways to call, email, video chat, text, and more to reach her sister. What sort of message needed to be delivered in person? Why was Bubbie making them drive three hours to say something? What couldn't be written down?

It was all very suspicious.

When, at last, Hannah thought she was about to *burst*, the car approached an iron gate. A camera zoomed in as Isaac popped up from his armrest pillow. "Where are we?"

"Here," Hannah said as the gate swung wide to let them in.

"And where is here?" Isaac asked, surveying the stark mountains, the low-hanging moon, the dusky evening sky.

It was like driving into a movie, really. The dirt driveway—which curled through evergreen trees—was ridiculously long. There was no end in sight; for all they knew, this was the road to infinity.

Then, at last, there was a light ahead. A cottage, hidden in the shadow of the mountains, beside a very still lake. Great-Aunt Bea's cottage was the only house on the lake.

"Aunt Bea likes her privacy," Bubbie said as she parked.

The cottage was small, but fancy. Through the windows, Hannah caught a glimpse of a house that was dressed to impress: a dining room table with very ornate chinaware, napkins folded into the shape of swans, and golden goblets—except for one special silver one sitting at the head of the table.

The door knockers were lion-shaped and made of iron. "Can I?" Isaac asked, and without even waiting for an answer he slammed the knockers over and over again. Hannah rolled her eyes. She knew this was inevitable. Isaac had a bad habit of wanting to touch everything.

The door swung open.

"Come in," said a man.

In the light of the lobby, they could see he had a head of curly brown hair and dark eyes that danced behind round glasses. His smile wide, his face round, and his chin clean-shaven.

And there were three of him.

"Twins!" Isaac gasped. "Three identical twins!"

"Or . . . ?" Hannah said. "Triplets?"

"Oh. Right."

The men all frowned in the same exact way, at the same exact time. They were all dressed in the same dark blue suit, with the same light blue tie, with the same black loafers, the same horn-rimmed glasses. Not a single curl on their head was unalike. Hannah could already tell it was going to be a nightmare, trying to tell them apart.

"Hello," they said together. "Our names are—"

"Huey, Dewey, and Louie!" Isaac shouted.

"Wow! How did you know?" said the triplet on the left, with an enormous grin. A dimple dotted his left cheek.

"Wait . . . really?"

"No. Not really," said the triplet in the middle. He was neither smiling nor frowning. He was perfectly even-keeled.

Meanwhile, the triplet on the right stared at Isaac with deep disdain.

"I am Blake," said the triplet on the left.

"I am Jake," said the triplet in the middle.

"And I am—"

"Let me guess! Cake?" said Isaac.

"Fake?" ventured Hannah.

"Drake," the angry triplet said sourly.

"Welcome to our lake," said Jake.

Hannah shook her head. This was getting ridiculous.

Blake smiled and gestured to the kitchen. "I hope you like steak."

"For goodness' sake." Bubbie groaned.

"This is giving me a headache," Isaac said, grinning.

"You're all Aunt Bea's children, yes?" Bubbie said, before anyone else could rhyme again. "Which one of you lives here and takes care of your mother?"

"We do," said Blake and Jake.

"And which one of you wrote me about my sister's failing health?"

"I did," said Jake, the bland triplet. He was as exciting as a cream-colored wall.

Bubbie frowned. "Hmmm."

Hannah looked between the triplets and her bubbie. *Something* was going on here. Was anyone going to clue her in?

"What do you do?" Hannah asked Drake. "If you don't take care of Aunt Bea here?"

Drake's frown got even deeper. "I moved to Los Angeles."

"To become an actor?"

"To become a life coach, happiness guru, and motivational speaker."

Hannah and Isaac exchanged a glance.

"You? An expert on happiness?" Hannah said, trying very hard to keep the skepticism out of her voice.

"I am a very happy person," Drake said with a glower.

"Oh . . . yes. Totally. I see it now," Isaac lied.

Jake, the middle-of-the-road triplet, held out his arms. "Can I take your coats?"

Bubbie placed her coat in his hands, and Hannah and Isaac followed her lead. Then Bubbie glided between Blake and Drake, waltzing into the dining room like she'd been here a million times before—and maybe she had, for all Hannah knew.

At the head of the table was Great-Aunt Bea herself. She looked ill. Her skin was sallow, and her eyes were sunken. Her mouth pressed into a tight line, like she was in great pain. Hannah thought she looked like she would much rather be lying in bed than sitting rigid in her dining room chair, in fancy earrings, with her hair piled atop her head.

Bubbie hugged her sister, but Aunt Bea did not hug back. Instead, she feebly patted Bubbie's back.

"How are you feeling?" Bubbie asked.

"Perpetually ill," Aunt Bea said with a weak smile. "Thank goodness I have Blake and Jake with me. Although . . . not all the time. They rotate."

"Why, where are they when they're not with you?"

"Blake works part time at an auto repair shop, and Jake works part time at a soup restaurant." Aunt Bea looked down at her feet. "I didn't expect to see you again . . . not after our last argu—"

"Let me introduce you to my grandchildren," Bubbie interrupted. "Hannah, she's twelve, and Isaac is ten."

"Hi," Hannah said shyly.

Isaac burst forward. "Nice to meet you, GAB. Can I call you GAB?"

"Gab?"

"Great-Aunt Bea!"

"Bea or Aunt Bea, will do just fine." She turned to Bubbie with a glare. "I expect you want a slice of my inheritance now that you've shown me these *adorable* children?" *Adorable* was dripping in sarcasm.

"Hey!" Hannah said. "We're pretty cute!"

"Really cute!" Isaac said, and he let out a toot accidentally. "Oops."

Bubbie leaned forward, nose to nose with her sister. "It's not *your* inheritance, Bea. It was supposed to be *our* inheritance. And besides, that's not why I'm here."

Aunt Bea raised her eyebrows. "It's not?"

"No. I have a message. I needed to deliver it in person. I couldn't risk it getting intercepted."

"And what is this critical message?"

"Despite our feud, despite everything that's happened," Bubbie said, "I came to tell you, you're in terrible da—" She stopped and looked up at the doorway. There stood Blake, Jake, or Drake, a curious expression on his face.

"Oh my," said the mystery triplet. "I'm interrupting something important, aren't I?" He sat down at the table with a smile.

No, a smirk.

"Drake," Aunt Bea said. "Why don't you go help your brothers in the kitchen?"

"Oh, you've made it very clear that I am no help at all, Mother." Drake folded his arms and plopped into a chair. "No, I think I'll stay right here."

Aunt Bea looked at Bubbie, and Bubbie looked back at her, and they seemed to say something with their eyes. Something that was clear to the two of them . . . and absolute gibberish to Hannah.

The spell was broken when Happy Blake and Plain Jake brought in the trays of food and drinks. Dreadful Drake sat across from Hannah, scowling at his brothers.

What a weird family, Hannah thought. When at last the serving plates were laid out, Aunt Bea raised her cup, a unique silver goblet with a grapevine pattern.

Bubbie squinted. "Is that our pop-pop's kiddush cup? The necklace wasn't enough for you? You took the cup, too?"

Aunt Bea sniffed. "To . . . reunions," she said, staring at her sister.

To Hannah, a toast was an invitation to start eating. She reached for food.

"No, mamaleh," Bubbie whispered, putting her arm across Hannah. "Wait a second."

Isaac's stomach growled. "But we're hungry."

Jake, meanwhile, was piling his plate high and digging in with neither a smile nor a frown on his nonexpressive face. He was a quick and messy eater. Chewing with his mouth open, licking his fingers, he dived in for seconds before anyone else had firsts.

Drake was watching Bubbie very carefully as she pulled a pen out of her purse and began to scribble on a paper napkin. When Bubbie was done, she folded the napkin and held it in her palm.

"Eat, Drake!" Aunt Bea demanded. "Eat, Blake!"

"I'm not very hungry," Blake said with a smile. "And I want to make sure our guests have enough food. It's discourteous to eat and drink before they do."

Aunt Bea gestured at the well-prepared food. A platter of juicy steaks glistened at Hannah, and the smell of mashed potatoes was making her mouth water. Isaac put his chin down on the table and started having a staring contest with a piece of homemade challah. Hannah knew that face; they only had about ten seconds before Isaac attacked the food in sheer hunger.

Aunt Bea stood up, red in the face. "You're all being very impolite!

All except my Jake!"

Bubbie stood up, too. Eye to eye with her sister, she slipped Aunt Bea the napkin note. "Snake," she spat.

Aunt Bea's face scrunched into an angry ball. But her expression changed completely as she stared at the napkin. Her eyes bulged, and her mouth parted in surprise. The napkin began to tremble in her hands.

"B-But how do you know?" Aunt Bea said, her voice quivery.

"I got a letter from one of your sons with your symptoms," Bubbie said. "I knew right away, from my work. But I'm not sure if your boys knew I was a forensic scientist."

Aunt Bea's complexion turned almost greenish. She put down her fork. "Excuse me," she said, standing shakily to her feet. "I must go make a phone call."

All eyes followed her as she exited the room—except for Hannah, who was watching her brother steal the napkin from Aunt Bea's place setting.

"I have to go to the bathroom," Isaac said.

"I'll go, too!" Hannah said quickly. "To make sure he doesn't get lost."

The two of them scurried out of the room and shut themselves inside the kitchen pantry. Isaac unfolded the letter.

P

TRUST NO ONE

A   IS

"P trust no one a is?" Isaac said. "What in the world does that mean?"

Hannah squinted at the letter. Bubbie had said *snake* as she handed Aunt Bea the letter. At first, it seemed like Bubbie was calling Aunt Bea a snake. But now Hannah was not so sure. It was either a word that meant something to them or instructions on how to read the letter.

"There must be a message hidden inside the message!" Hannah said thoughtfully. She traced her fingers in a snakelike shape through the letters. Then she started laughing.

"Well? What is it?" Isaac demanded.

"Start with the letter R in the word *trust*," Hannah said. "And if you read in a snake shape, instead of left to right, you'll see it, too."

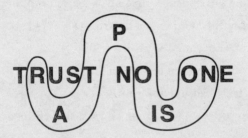

"Rat poison! But what does that mean?" He scrunched his eyebrows together.

"This is what Bubbie came here to say . . ." Things were beginning to click for Hannah. "Bubbie got a letter from Jake saying Aunt Bea was sick. He listed her symptoms. And because Bubbie is a forensic scientist, she knew *right away* that Aunt Bea was being slowly poisoned by one of the two sons that was caring for her."

"Blake or Jake?" Isaac said. "Blake is so happy. It must be Jake."

"But Jake wrote Bubbie the letter. Why write her if he were the one doing the poisoning?"

"Maybe Jake made a mistake."

"Give me a break."

Isaac shook his head. "Not this again! Too much rhyming!"

Hannah sighed. "Look—Bubbie had to come here, to Aunt Bea's house, to deliver the message in person. If she wrote a letter about the rat poison, it's possible the wrong brother would have intercepted her warning and thrown it out."

The doorknob to the pantry turned, and Isaac quickly grabbed Bubbie's note, stuffed it in his mouth, and swallowed it.

"Isaac! That's disgusting!"

"I'm hiding the evidence," he said. "Plus, I'm *starving*."

The door opened and one of the triplets towered above them.

"Which one are you?" Hannah asked.

"Which one do you *think*?" he said nastily.

It had to be Dreadful Drake.

"What do you want?" Hannah said, as Isaac cleaned bits of napkin out of his teeth.

"My mother is finished with her phone call, and she requests everyone's presence in the dining room . . . *now*."

They followed Drake back into the dining room. And if Hannah had any doubts that it was actually Drake, she knew for sure when Aunt Bea said, "Thank you for fetching them, Drake."

He nodded at his mother, then sat down in his chair across from Hannah.

"Boys," Aunt Bea said, raising her silver goblet. "Let's make a toast."

"What are we toasting?" Blake said, raising his glass.

"My new will."

Blake's smile slid off his face. Jake dropped his fork. Drake looked at their mother curiously.

Aunt Bea continued, "As of right now, my will states that after my death, Blake will receive my mother's green emerald pendant, our family's most precious heirloom, worth three million dollars. And Jake would be getting the house, worth one million dollars. And Drake, who abandoned me in my old age and did not care for his poor, ailing mother, would get *nothing*."

Drake frowned.

"But I have just called my lawyer. At midnight, he is coming over to change the will."

The room was still and oh-so-hushed. It was so quiet you could hear a pin drop. So quiet you could hear a spider scuttle. So quiet you could hear the silent-but-deadly release of three nervous farts from all three identical brothers.

"Drake," Aunt Bea says, "will now receive *everything*. Every last item, every last penny I own."

Drake looked both dumbfounded and gleeful. He grinned widely, looking happier than Hannah ever thought the grumpy triplet could look.

"WHAT?" Jake and Blake fumed, and they both slammed their palms on the table.

"Why?" Jake demanded.

"Because I can't trust either of you! Someone has been making me sick . . . on purpose," Aunt Bea said.

Rat poison, Hannah thought, but she didn't dare say it aloud.

"Not me! I've done nothing but care for you!" Blake said. "If anyone's untrustworthy, it's Jake!"

Jake pursed his lips. "Blake is lying! Let me prove that *I'm* the trustworthy one."

"That's an excellent idea," Blake agreed. "If I can definitively prove that I'm telling the truth, can you keep me in your will?"

Aunt Bea considered. "Okay," she finally answered. "If you can prove yourself innocent by midnight, I'll give the inheritance to the one who has been taking care of me . . . and *not* making me ill. And we will save this toast until then." She placed the cup back on the table.

Jake and Blake got up from their chairs and ran from the room; Hannah could hear them arguing, even from across the house.

Drake looked nervous. "Mother, if you'll excuse me." And he left as well.

Aunt Bea looked sharply at Bubbie. "You don't have to be here anymore. You delivered your message. Consider me thoroughly warned."

Bubbie frowned. "We'll stay until midnight. I have to make sure you're safe."

"More like you want me to give the inheritance to *you*!" Aunt Bea snarled, and then she, too, excused herself.

Bubbie sighed and turned to Hannah and Isaac. "That's what our fight was about. All those years ago. Bea got my mother's precious necklace. She was always the favorite, and she lorded it over me. I was hoping that if she saw you two, she would consider gifting me my mother's necklace—letting it pass to our side of the family."

Hannah frowned. Given what little she knew about Aunt Bea, that seemed *highly* unlikely.

Bubbie sighed. "I'm sorry for dragging you kids out here. I should have delivered the warning by myself. We'll leave at midnight, don't

worry. But until then . . ." Bubbie dug into her purse. "Here's a few granola bars. I know you kids are hungry."

"No kidding," Isaac said, "I ate your napkin. Informative but *not*
filling!"

As they waited,

    and waited,

    and waited,

    and waited,

night ensnared the lakeside cottage. It was dark, and it was quiet. Yes,
the cottage itself made noise—there was the ticking of a grandfather
clock, the creaking of the house's old bones, and the hiss of the radiator
in the corner. But the triplets and Aunt Bea were nowhere to be heard.
The still inside the house wasn't peaceful—it was tense.

Hannah couldn't stop thinking about Blake and Jake. One of them
was poisoning their own mother, and both of them were accusing the
other brother. So one was telling the truth, and one was lying—but how
was Aunt Bea supposed to know which one was which? And would
they be able to prove their innocence—or the other one's guilt—before
midnight? Or would Drake swoop in and take the inheritance?

It sure seemed like Drake had a lot to gain.

And Blake and Jake had a lot to lose.

Eventually, Bubbie fell asleep on the couch, and Isaac dug in her
bag for more food to eat. It was an unsuccessful mission, turning up
only three lemon drops, a stick of gum, and denture toothpaste, which
he actually tried (and spit out into one of Aunt Bea's decorative bowls).

Clang! Bang!

The noise was coming from the kitchen—pots and pans being

moved around. At first Hannah thought that her ears were playing tricks on her, but Isaac looked at her eagerly. "We should check it out," he said.

Hannah glanced at Bubbie, who was snoring slightly. Bubbie could sleep through an earthquake. In fact, she *had* slept through earthquakes in her lifetime.

Clink! Clang!

"Let's go," Hannah said. She and her brother tiptoed to the door, opened it a crack, and peered into the kitchen.

There was a bottle with a rat on its label sitting on the counter, next to Aunt Bea's silver goblet. And beside the goblet was a triplet—

But *which one*?

Curse these identical triplets!

Hannah frowned. Their uncle—whichever uncle it was—was grinning. Not smirking, but actually smiling. He seemed to be *very* happy. Glowing, even. The dimple in his left cheek danced. He held the poison in his hand . . . and then he burped quite loudly and patted his stomach. "Ugh, I am so full," he groaned.

Then the triplet turned the vial of poison over and tipped it into the cup.

"He's poisoning her cup—*right now!*" Hannah whispered.

Isaac took a deep breath and shouted, "HELP! HE'S THE CULPRIT!"

The triplet bolted out the other kitchen exit—so fast that Hannah and Isaac couldn't catch up. They chased after him, but he disappeared around the corner. He had the advantage of knowing the cottage well. Unlike Hannah and Isaac, who had no idea where they were going.

"POISON!" Isaac shouted again.

Moments later, all three triplets dashed into the kitchen. Aunt Bea also came running. And Bubbie got up from the couch.

"What is it? What do you want?" Aunt Bea demanded, looking at Hannah and Isaac like she'd regretted letting *children* into her home. "I was having a lie-down!"

"This cup is poisoned," Hannah said. "And we saw one of them pour it in!" She pointed at Blake, Jake, and Drake.

"I'm innocent! I've been alone in my room this whole time," said Blake.

"It wasn't me! I've been alone in my room this whole time," said Jake.

"How dare you! I've been alone in my room this whole time," said Drake.

"Well, which one did the poisoning?" Aunt Bea asked.

Hannah looked between her identical uncles. Which one *did* do the poisoning? Cheerful Blake? Emotionless Jake? Miserable Drake?

"I . . . I don't know," Hannah admitted. "Maybe you shouldn't trust any of them."

This, of course, caused the triplets to erupt into angry shouts. Bubbie, quiet from the corner, walked over to the countertop. Toward the poisoned goblet and the bottle of rat poison.

Bubbie began to chuckle. And that chuckle grew into a laugh. And that laugh grew into an all-out guffaw.

"*Why* are you laughing?!" Aunt Bea shouted, stamping her foot.

"Because you don't have rat poison in your system! You actually had ethylene glycol poisoning."

"Ethel—what?"

"It's a type of antifreeze—it lowers the freezing point of water-based liquid in cold environments. It's *very* lethal in large doses. But in small doses, it's nearly impossible to detect in the body, since the symptoms can be confused for lots of other diseases and illnesses. In tiny doses, it can take months to poison someone to death."

"So why did you tell me it was rat poison?"

"Somehow," Bubbie said, "I didn't think you'd know ethylene glycol. So I just wrote down rat poison. It is very curious that suddenly the poison would switch from ethylene glycol to rat poison when I show up. Which of your sons did you tell?"

"None. I swear! I didn't know who to trust."

All three brothers crossed their arms at the same time.

"What is going on? Who is responsible for making me ill?"

Blake pointed to Drake. Drake pointed to Jake. Jake pointed to Blake.

Hannah suddenly stood up. "Aunt Bea," she said breathlessly, "I know."

For the solution to this story, please turn to page 326.

THE HAUNTED TYPEWRITER

By Gigi Pandian

The day after eleven-year-old Tara Chandran founded her first detective agency, a magician moved in down the hall.

Tara didn't consider herself superstitious—she loved Friday the thirteenth, she walked under ladders, and Halloween was her favorite holiday—but she took this as a good omen. A magician was sure to bring mystery to the building. There wasn't nearly enough mystery in her life that gloomy San Francisco summer, even after the burglary in their apartment building four days ago, which had prompted Tara and her best friend Kevin to form the Moon Raven Detective Agency.

"Auspicious," Kevin had said when he heard about the magician. Whatever. He was always using bigger words than he needed to. He could have simply said it was lucky.

Of course, the magician wasn't actually a wizard who could do magic. He was a grown-up who got paid to do tricks on a stage. He didn't have any kind of mystical powers that could help them figure out who'd stolen Kevin's mother's diamond earrings.

So even with a magician in the building, the week after sixth grade ended wasn't as magical as it could have been. People in the building were unhappy about the theft, of course, and Tara had heard a few of them yelling at Ms. Weber, the building manager. Security in the building was supposed to be good. It was an expensive building with a dozen apartments in San Francisco's SoMa neighborhood, which stood for South of Market, the area south of the diagonal Market Street that stretched across the foggy city where she'd grown up.

Tara gazed out the kitchen window as she stirred her soggy cereal, the milk turning brown. It was chocolate granola her mom had bought at the farmers' market as a treat. She had summer camp and a visit with her grandparents coming up later that summer, but nothing besides the detective agency with Kevin planned for another two weeks. But they had no leads in the case of the purloined earrings! And no other cases, either. Their parents wouldn't let them build a website, so nobody besides a few friends and people in the building knew Tara and Kevin were official detectives.

Suddenly, there was a banging at the front door. It was so loud, Tara dropped her spoon.

"Tara?" Kevin shouted on the other side of the door as he beat his fist against it again.

"Manners, young man!" Tara's father commented as he walked to the door, shaking his head.

"Sorry, Mr. Chandran," Kevin said as the door swung open. "Uh, it's an emergency. Can Tara come over?"

"An emergency?" said Tara's dad.

"Yeah," said Kevin, trying to catch his breath. "We have our first lead in the case."

Tara's dad chuckled and looked from Kevin's uncombed hair to the Star Wars slippers on his feet. He turned back to his daughter. "Finish your breakfast. Then you can go."

"Mmm, hmmm," Tara said through a mouthful of soggy granola. "All done."

Her dad laughed again. Tara knew her dad thought Kevin's mom had simply forgotten where she put her diamond earrings—because both she and Kevin's dad worked long hours at a start-up company called Technology for Change, and were tired at the end of the day—so he saw no harm in Tara and Kevin helping her find the earrings. But Tara? She knew in her heart there was more to it.

"What's going on?" she asked Kevin as they ran down the hallway leading to his apartment.

"I knew we were right about Mom's earrings. They were stolen. And now we know who did it."

"You do? Who was it?"

"A ghost."

"A ghost?" Tara repeated, staring at Kevin.

"A ghost?" said another voice. This one was older. "Ah, at last. Now this place is finally getting interesting."

Tara and Kevin turned and saw the magician peering out of his doorway. His front door was across from Kevin's, one of the four apartments on the top floor.

Tara didn't have strong feelings about magic, but Kevin's older brother, Braden, was in a junior magicians' club. Braden was the one who'd recognized the new tenant on the floor as the Hindi Houdini. He didn't go around calling himself that, of course. His real name was Sanjay Rai. The Hindi Houdini was his stage name.

Sanjay Rai looked like he was from India, just like Tara's dad, but he had the same California accent as hers. He was nice, too. When they'd first met, he'd asked Tara and Kevin to call him Sanjay. He also told them they and their parents could have free tickets to attend one of his magic shows. Now he held a steaming mug in one hand, his feet were bare, and his thick black hair stood up at funny angles, just like Kevin's.

"The ghost left a message for us on my dad's typewriter," Kevin told them both.

"Your dad has a typewriter instead of a computer?" Sanjay asked.

Tara laughed. "The Byrnes love collecting old stuff. Kevin's dad, especially. He has a room of antiques he calls his office, with stuff like a letterpress—those old machines made of iron and wood that books used to be printed on—and a really old telephone that looks like one of the ones its inventor Alexander Graham Bell made."

"And the typewriter that my dad's parents had when he was a little kid," Kevin said, "before they had a computer. But the typewriter's letter keys haven't worked as long as we've lived here. There's no way a message could have been typed on the typewriter."

Sanjay frowned. "Oh. I'm sorry, but it sounds as if your father simply fixed his typewriter. No ghost."

Kevin shook his head. "The message was signed *The Ghost of SoMa*."

"As in the South of Market area," Sanjay murmured. "Then, perhaps, he is our friendly San Francisco neighborhood ghost."

Kevin's front door flew open, and his parents bustled out. Kevin's older brother, Braden, trailed behind.

"I can't believe you're going to work after what we found," Braden whined to his parents.

"Kevin?" said his dad. "Your mom and I have to get to work. You know the rules. Until you start summer classes next week, no leaving the building unless you're with Braden, or with Tara and her parents."

Braden scowled at his father. "You don't, like, even care about a threatening note? You're totally leaving me and Kevin alone with a ghost, and you haven't even figured out what it wants, why it's haunting us!"

"The note is nonsense," Kevin's mom said to Braden. "Our building manager simply has a mean sense of humor. That's all this is. Ms. Weber has a key to every apartment. She started this nonsense to get back at me for raising my voice when I spoke to her about the building's security."

Kevin shook his head. "The message is written in code, Mom. That's why I went to get Tara."

His mom smiled and kissed the top of his head.

"I know you see codes everywhere," she told Kevin. "Have fun working on codes with Tara today." She turned to Sanjay. "Good morning, Sanjay. Sorry for the disturbance."

"No trouble," Sanjay said. "I love a good ghost story to start my day."

Mrs. Byrne smiled, but it looked to Tara like it was a fake sort of smile. "Our children both have well-developed and sometimes overactive imaginations."

"What about the sound of the typewriter keys tapping?" Braden asked. He was still scowling.

At least Tara thought that's what he was doing. Since he turned thirteen, he'd been letting his hair grow out and it usually covered his eyes.

"We must've heard something else," said Mr. Byrne. "We just thought it was the typewriter. We have to run. Keep your brother out of trouble. See you guys tonight."

Kevin's parents hurried down the hall to the elevator and disappeared into it.

"So," said Sanjay when they were gone, "you said you *heard* the keys typing the note?"

"We sure did," said Braden, flicking his bangs out of his eyes.

"Fascinating. Why, that's even more mysterious than a note found on a broken typewriter."

"You want to see?" Braden asked.

"Of course. This is a mystery I can't turn down. Just let me go inside and put on some shoes first. Back in a few seconds."

"He's not kidding," Braden said, smiling for the first time Tara had seen in weeks. "It'll take him like a nanosecond. One of the things he does in his act is a quick-change routine. He can change complete costumes in a flash."

As predicted, Sanjay was back a few seconds later, his hair combed and perfectly laced sneakers on his feet. Tara and Sanjay followed the two brothers into their apartment.

"We were all eating breakfast together," Kevin said, "when we heard the sound of tapping coming from this empty room."

Breakfast was the one meal of the day the Byrnes ate together. Though it was brief, it was meant to be quality family time, so no electronic devices were allowed at the table.

"We thought at first Dad left one of his laptops in here and some video started playing from the internet," Braden said. "But there were no working electronic devices in the whole room. Only this note in the typewriter. The typewriter that's still broken."

He held up the note for all of them to see.

```
\ / \ /
/ \ / \

S...W...I...T...O...R...W...W...D...P...R.
.T.P.O.K.N.A.T.C.R.O.E.E.E.S.I.L.I.A.P.A.
..O...R...G...F...M...J...L...L...S...E...

SINCERELY,
THE GHOST OF SOMA
```

Tara shivered. She didn't believe in ghosts. Not really. But how could anyone have typed the note on a broken typewriter—and then disappeared?

"Wow," Sanjay said, "that's a really polite ghost. See how they sign off with *sincerely*? Very polite. But the first part of its message is scrambled."

He was right. The three lines read:

```
SWITORWWDPR
TPOKNATCROEEESILIAPA
ORGFMJLLSE
```

"It's a cipher," Tara said, studying the letters and dots as Sanjay looked at the typewriter itself.

"I knew you'd see it, too," Kevin said.

"Almost," Tara whispered. "I *almost* see it. It's a coded message, and I know we can crack the code. What I'm more worried about is *how* the note appeared."

"A ghost did it," blurted Braden.

"I'm curious as to how the perpetrator disappeared," said Kevin, using another one of his favorite big words.

"It's a ghost," said Braden. "It can walk through walls."

"The note has to be related to the theft," said Kevin. "Right, Tara?"

Tara nodded. Two strange occurrences in Kevin's apartment within one week. It would be too much of a coincidence if they weren't related.

The burglary was why Tara had suggested to Kevin that they form the detective agency. The two of them had always loved mysteries, ever since they first met the summer before second grade. And some of the biggest mysteries were codes. Tara and Kevin had invented several to communicate over the years. Tara's favorite was still the first one they'd invented. The one that changed her name to *Star Moon* and Kevin Byrne's to *Kind Raven*. Even though they'd outgrown communicating like that, they still liked their idea of changing words to reveal the secret meaning of each word. That's why they'd become Moon Raven Detective Agency.

They got their code names from their real names. The Sanskrit meaning of Tara Chandran's name was *Star* for Tara and *Shiny* and *Moon* for Chandran. The meaning of Kevin Byrne's Irish name was *Kind* and *Handsome* for Kevin and *Raven* for Byrne. *Shiny* sounded weird, so they went with *Moon*. And *Handsome*? Eww. So their second grade code names became *Star Moon* and *Kind Raven*. Kevin's brother Braden's name meant a wise fish from Irish mythology. They had looked up the meanings behind other words they wanted to use in front of their parents without the adults knowing what they were saying.

"You two are investigating the theft?" Sanjay asked.

"Indubitably," Kevin said.

"He means *yes*," Tara said, scowling at Kevin.

"I don't know why he doesn't just say 'yes,'" muttered Braden.

Kevin darted out of the room.

"Oops," said Braden. "Did we upset him?"

"I hope not." Tara sighed.

When Kevin came back a few minutes later, he handed Sanjay a flyer he'd printed with the logo Tara had designed. Along with the text, "Moon Raven Detective Agency," was an illustration of a bird silhouette on a full moon.

"I'll keep you two in mind if I ever have a need for sleuthing," Sanjay said, "and file this away for the future." He held up the flyer in his hand—and it disappeared.

Tara clapped.

"Braden performs the same illusion nearly as well," Sanjay said.

Braden shrugged. When they'd all met Sanjay earlier that week, Tara had heard the magician talking to Braden about misdirection, which was how magicians fooled their audience. But Tara was sure she'd been looking directly at the flyer when Sanjay made it invisible.

"Can we focus on the ghost's message?" asked Kevin.

"Well," said Tara, "because it took you so long to find our flyer, I've already solved the cipher."

"You have?" Kevin and Braden said at the same time.

"Look at the diagonal lines' crisscross pattern at the top of the paper. I thought at first it was just a mistake, like someone testing the keys. But that's the clue to what kind of cipher it is."

"A rail fence cipher!" Kevin said.

```
\ / \ /
/ \ / \

S...W...I..T...O...R...W...W...D...P...R.
.T.P.O.K.N.A.T.C.R.O.E.E.E.S.I.L.I.A.P.A.
..O...R...G...F...M...J...L..L...S...E...

SINCERELY,
THE GHOST OF SOMA
```

Tara nodded. "So we don't read the letters on each line from left to right. We follow the letters at a diagonal angle, starting on the left and moving to the right at an angle."

Kevin began writing on a fresh sheet of paper. He read aloud as he wrote each letter. "S-T-O-P."

Sanjay shook his head. "This isn't right."

"It's right," Tara said. "The first letters even spell out a word. 'Stop.'"

"I'm not talking about the note," Sanjay said, pointing at the typewriter. "This machine is broken. There's no way it was used to type the note. You're sure you heard the sound of keys tapping?"

"Definitely," said Braden.

"I'm done decoding the message," Kevin said. "Here's what it says: STOPWORKINGATTFCORMOREJEWELSWILLDISAPPEAR."

"We need to add spaces to separate the words," Tara said. "STOP WORKING AT TFC OR MORE JEWELS WILL DISAPPEAR."

"TFC?" asked Sanjay.

"TFC," said Kevin. "That's Technology for Change. Seems like the ghost wants our parents to quit their jobs."

Braden called their parents on the cell phone he'd gotten for his thirteenth birthday, but they wouldn't come home. They again insisted it was the building manager, Muriel Weber, who had written the note and left it in the typewriter.

But that night they came home before dinnertime, which was such a rare occurrence that Kevin invited Tara to join them for dinner. Tara, Braden, and Kevin watched as Mr. and Mrs. Byrne searched the room with the typewriter thoroughly before locking the door.

"I'm the only person who has the key to my office," Kevin's dad said. "The mystery ends here."

But Mr. Byrne was wrong.

While the five of them shared a dinner of takeout Chinese food—the spring rolls dipped in sweet and sour sauce were Tara's favorite—she heard a noise that made the hairs on her arms stand up.

"That sound . . ." she whispered.

"Keys tapping," Kevin said. "The typewriter!"

Everyone dropped their chopsticks and ran toward the study. Mr. Byrne got to the door first. He jiggled the handle.

"It's still locked!"

"That typewriter doesn't even work," said Mrs. Byrne as she glanced around nervously.

"The sound of keys tapping stopped," Braden said. "Dad, can you open the door?"

Mr. Byrne nodded and unlocked the door.

"Look!" Braden shouted as the door swung open. "Another note!"

He rushed forward and pulled a white sheet of paper from the type-writer. He held it up in his hands. "Another code."

"Cipher," Kevin corrected him, taking the paper from his brother's hands. "Codes are word substitutions. Ciphers are letter substitutions."

Braden rolled his eyes at his brother.

"This cipher looks different," Tara said.

```
/ \ / \
\ / \ /

N . . . . . H . . . . . E . . . . U . . . . L . . . . N . . . . . D
. E . . . I . C . . Y . R . . I . O . . . I E . . . O . G . . . O .
. . R . L . . . R . O . . . O . G . . . Y . K . . . M . R . . . I . N . .
. . . D . . . . . U . . . . . N . . . . E . . . . E . . . . T . . .

SINCERELY,
THE GHOST OF SOMA
```

"There's a different marking on top," said Kevin. "And an additional line."

"But if we follow the diagonal pattern we did last time," Tara said, "it doesn't make real words. N-E-R-D-L-I-H-C-R-U."

Even though it wasn't as easy as the first cipher, Tara was confident they could figure out the message. But the locked room? *How* did someone get into a locked room, write a note on a broken antique type-writer, and get out again? That's what worried her most.

"How did the note get here?" Kevin's mom asked. "David, didn't you lock the door properly before dinner?"

"Yes," said Mr. Byrne. "And I'm locking it again right now. Then we're calling the police."

"I don't think you want to do that," said Kevin. He was hastily scribbling letters on a piece of paper. It looked like he'd solved the new cipher.

Meanwhile, Tara had solved a different mystery. She had an idea about the locked room. An idea that formed because the magician had made her detective agency flyer disappear from right in front of her eyes.

Tara glanced at Kevin's decoded message. Her heart began to pound as she realized what the message meant.

"Oh no," she said, looking up at Kevin. "I think I know who did it. You do, too, right? That's why you don't want your mom to call the police."

Kevin nodded. "*Salmon*," he said, using their old code name for the person they both thought it was. "The person who left the notes and who stole Mom's earrings. It's the same person."

"Salmon?" said Braden. "There's nobody in the building named Salmon. Do you mean Sanjay? The magician?"

"No," said Mrs. Byrne. "He didn't move in until after my diamonds were stolen. I still say it was the building manager. She's the only one who could have both bypassed security to steal my earrings and gotten into our apartment."

"But she doesn't have a key to this inside door," said Mr. Byrne.

"Neither of you are correct," Kevin said.

"But, in a sense," Tara said, "Mr. Byrne *is* correct that Sanjay Rai is involved. He's the one who gave the ghost the idea to haunt the typewriter. Probably without realizing he'd done it."

Kevin elbowed her. "You'd better explain what we mean. I think they're going to burst if we don't tell them."

For the solution to this story, please turn to page 331.

SURPRISE. PARTY.

By Lamar Giles

rica, in her lacy pink dress, with matching bows tying her swinging pigtails, had been a good birthday girl for the whole party.

She smiled at all of her guests, even the ones Daddy made her invite. She'd suffered through dumb party games like Pin the Tail on the Robot (because in her family they don't harm animals). She'd forced applause when kiddie magician the Sorcerer Farnsworth pulled a quarter out of her ear. But Erica was most concerned with opening her gifts, especially the biggest, brightest (and what had to be the best-est) gift on the present pile. A huge box, wrapped in metallic red paper, with a golden bow. From Mommy.

"Your mother really outdid herself this time," Daddy said of the wrapping when he hefted the box onto the folding gift table he'd set up before the party's start.

As more guests had arrived, more boxes piled up around that centerpiece gift, making Erica anxious with anticipation. What could it be? Maybe a new dollhouse. Perhaps a Sea Breeze Blue fashion mirror for when she and her best friend, Paisley, played dress up. Or, even better, a surprise gift that would blow her expectations out of the water to make up for this being a "Daddy Weekend" and Mommy having to work all the way on the other side of the country, meaning she couldn't be there.

Once the games were done, and after the rabbit in the magician's hat bit him, Daddy finally announced it was time to cut the cake (no candles to blow out, though, because in her family they don't intentionally spread germs). Everyone knew what came after that.

"Okay, sweetie," Daddy said, "which one do you want to open fir—"

Erica swept aside all the presents blocking her path, nearly throwing herself across the gift table to reach the red box. When she snatched it, she almost tossed it to the ceiling because it was so light, something that panicked her because no dollhouse should be nearly weightless!

She dropped the too-light box at her feet, ripped away the bow and tossed it over her shoulder.

She shredded the wrapping paper and pried the box top open. She peered inside with bulging eyes, and felt her face redden with fury. Registering the box's contents, she shrieked.

Because there was nothing inside.

Surprise.

A full five minutes of fear and chaos passed while Erica threw a tantrum of legend. Outside, by the pool, Sherman Tisdale—her fifth grade classmate and an amateur sleuth—absentmindedly noted the screams of terror and the hurried motion of his classmates fleeing the no-longer-festive festivities. Some rushed from the house so fast, they toppled into the pool. Sherman observed the huge waves his falling, splashing peers created, forcing water to lap the pool's edge, wetting his plaid socks. Pity. Sherman despised wet cotton.

One boy, James, who'd somehow cut his foot and had a bandage covering the sole, hobbled past moments before Erica loudly stomped out onto the patio. She was also shoeless, and growled at anyone in her path. Sherman decided it best to take two steps away from the pool.

A moment after he moved, another classmate backpedaled into the space he'd just vacated, toppling in with the others. Sherman wondered if there were any napkins available to soak up the moisture on his toes.

While he searched the nearby patio tables for the most absorbent material available, Erica approached him, her fists clenched, and her teeth exposed by her scowl. "Hey!"

Sherman remained focused on his napkin quest.

"Hey, freak!" She tapped him on his shoulder.

Fortunately, his blazer, the V-neck sweater beneath it, the pressed oxford shirt beneath that, and the collarless white T-shirt beneath *that* provided sufficient layers to keep her unusually sharp nails from breaking skin.

"Yes, Erica?"

"You're smart. You can do stuff, right?"

"By stuff, you mean . . . ?"

"Figure things out! I've heard about you finding the person who was stealing the standardized tests from the main office. And that thing with the school's track and the missing hurdles."

Sherman nodded. Yes, he'd deduced the culprit in both instances, gaining copious gratitude from Principal Smithers on both occasions.

"Then," Erica shouted an inch from his nose, "FIND! MY! GIFT!"

"Sweetie," her father called, feigning civility with an exaggerated frown clearly in place for Sherman's benefit. "That's no way to talk to your guest."

"*Your* guest, Daddy! You're the one who invited this dweeb!" She stomped one foot. "I want my present!"

"Sugarplum, I don't know what could've possibly happened to your mother's gift. Maybe she forgot to put it in the box when she sent it, honest mistake. But you shouldn't be rude and ignore all the other lovely gifts everyone gave you. In our family we treat our guests pleasantly."

More stomping. More quivering from the spectators. "I want my big gift."

"I don't know what else to tell you, Lollipop. I—"

Sherman cleared his throat, corralling everyone's attention. "Mister Erica's Dad, for your gratitude and willingness to order a sausage and mushroom pizza just for me—"

"Ewwww," someone said as they clawed their way out of the pool.

Sherman continued, "—I am willing to expose the criminal, or criminals, in our midst."

Mister Erica's Dad squinted at him, like he was a curious bug or a dancing squirrel. "You're willing to . . . what?"

Clasping his hands behind his back, Sherman sidestepped Erica and her father to get a better look at the scene. "Time is of the essence, of course. My mother will be picking me up in an hour to assist with her Saturday evening grocery shopping. Let us not waste a moment."

As he entered the house, he caught Erica's dad whispering to her, "You win, sweetie. Next time you have complete control over the guest list."

The party crowd kept their distance from Sherman, each person processing their own strange and different impression of the boy who'd been at their school less than a year, but who'd gained quite the reputation as a "scary-smart freakazoid."

Aware of his audience, but mostly engrossed by the day's mystery, Sherman shimmied out of his blazer, folded it neatly over the arm of the sofa, then knelt over the pile of torn wrapping that had covered the empty box. You could see scratches in the paper's metallic finish where the girl had dug her nails in. Erica hadn't completely shredded the wrapping, though. She'd torn through the top, and the box had slipped free, leaving an intact bottom. Sherman could make out the edges where the paper had been neatly cut, folded, and taped. Interesting.

"The magician did it," someone squeaked just over Sherman's shoulder.

"Hey!" said the Sorcerer Farnsworth. Erica's dad gave him a swift head shake, as if this was all too silly to debate.

Sherman stood, faced the frail boy who'd made the statement. "Your name is Otis."

"Yep." His dark hair and equally dark freckles were in stark contrast to his otherwise pale complexion.

"You're a talented artist who draws murals on huge swaths of construction paper at our school."

"Yep."

Sherman stroked his chin. "A shame you don't create your art from sturdier material. I might implore my mother to acquire some for her collection. You should consider a different medium. Also, different subject matter. Poofy clouds and smiling yellow suns are beneath you. It could be quite lucrative."

Otis's eyes bounced from Sherman to the skeptical crowd. Clearly confused. "Errrr . . ."

Sherman said, "Explain your accusation."

Otis shifted from foot to foot. "He pulled a bouquet of flowers out of Tonia's armpit, so he's gotta be able to pull a gift out of a box right. I mean, who else could?"

Erica stomped to the middle of the room, waggled her finger at the magician. "Arrest him, Daddy!"

"Gumdrop, I don't know what your mother allows when you're at her house, but here you shouldn't point fingers at people without proof."

"He's innocent," Sherman said, definitively. "Though, Otis, I do understand your line of thinking and applaud your initiative."

Otis blushed. "How do you know it's not him?"

"Simple." Sherman abandoned the paper and the box, approached the dapper magician, who sweated guiltily despite clearly having an advocate in Sherman. "He's not dressed properly."

The Sorcerer Farnsworth said, "Excuse me! I'll have you know this is a tailor-made tuxedo."

"Yes, and it's fine work. But it's too heavy for the weather."

"You just took off a blazer."

"Correct. But the layers I'm wearing aren't causing me to sweat like you. Part of it may be your high salt diet—"

"How—? Have you been talking to my wife?"

"—But I'm willing to bet the forty-or-so pounds of magician's equipment hidden in your suit has become a strain."

"You're not supposed to tell our secrets!"

Sherman spun toward the slack-jawed crowd. "Don't worry, I won't go into details. But the Sorcerer Farnsworth's entire act is predicated on the devices hidden on his person. For him to have rigged a way to slip the gift from the box in such spectacular fashion, he would've needed more preparation, and a tightly controlled environment. The decals and phone number stenciled on his 'Magicmobile' suggest he's come from two towns over. Also, I can't imagine being a party magician is a stable career—"

"Hey again!" said the magician.

"—so taking such a risk would ruin his business. This is a crime that required both motive and opportunity. Who here would have both?"

"Paisley!" Erica shrieked.

The red-haired girl whom Sherman often saw loping after Erica in the school corridor perked, quaking. "What's wrong? What'd I do?"

Erica aimed that deadly finger her way. "You slept over last night. That's the opportunity, right?"

She'd craned her neck toward Sherman for confirmation. "Yes," he said, "that could be an opportunity. What about motive, though?"

"She's jealous of me," Erica said. "Always has been."

"What?" Tears brimmed in Paisley's eyes.

Sherman said, "I was under the impression you two were best friends."

Not exactly the truth. There was a clear alpha and beta relationship here.

Erica continued berating her "friend." "You knew my mommy was sending me the best gift ever, and you wanted to ruin my party."

Paisley's cheeks and forehead flared, nearly matching her hair. "That's not true!"

Erica's father gripped her shoulder. "That's enough! You should not talk to your friend like that."

"She's not my friend if she stole from me."

"It wasn't her," Sherman said.

The look Paisley shot him was overly grateful. Then she sprinted and threw her arms around his shoulders. He stood stiffly in the embrace, unsure how to respond, worrying her tears might stain his sweater.

"Thank you for believing me."

Gently—trying not to seem too freaked out—Sherman pried himself free, brushed imaginary wrinkles from his slacks. "It's not a matter of *believing* you. It's a matter of objective fact. Allow me to explain."

Sherman shuffled to the remaining gifts on the gift table, and the crowd shuffled after him. He perused the boxes of various sizes until he spotted the one he'd guessed to be Paisley's. The wrapping paper featured a pattern of two angelic little girls skipping and holding hands. "This is yours, yes?"

Paisley nodded.

The box was a cube, only protruding slightly beyond the width of Sherman's hand. "Notice the wrapping. The corners are poofy and imprecise. There's excessive tape. There's even a gap at the bottom seam because it wasn't measured properly, so there isn't enough paper. If someone removed the gift from this box, they would need to have reapplied the wrapping paper neatly. I don't think Paisley is concerned with such cosmetic details."

Sherman tore the paper away, revealing a box with a clear plastic face, and a demure teddy bear inside. The bear held a heart with a phrase stitched into it: "For My BEARY Best Friend."

"I believe her concern was your friendship," said Sherman.

Erica reached for the box, but Paisley beat her to it, snatching the bear away and running from the room.

Erica didn't chase her, turning her full wrath on Sherman. "Who stole it then, super-smart detective? Huh? You don't know, do you?

You're a joke!"

The crowd was silent, undoubtedly considering Erica's claims.

Sherman said, "This is a gift from your mother?"

"Yeah, I told you that."

"Shipped from across the country just in time for the party?"

"Yes!"

"Shipped in what?"

"Huh?"

Sherman spoke slowly. "Where is the box this box was shipped in?"

Erica looked to her daddy, and he said, "It came just like that. I took off the mail label."

Sherman said, "Hmm."

"Hmm," said Erica, "what does *hmm* mean?"

"It means I know what happened, and why. Gather around, everyone, and I'll show you."

For the solution to this story, please turn to page 335.

THE DAPPERLINGS

By Kate Milford

You had *one job*."

Milo Pine stood in his pajamas in the bleak light of just-before-sunup, drowning in his cabinmate Kip's disapproval and hating life. He had not wanted to come to camp in the first place. He was deeply uncomfortable with surprises, social interactions, and almost any changes to his routine—and the camp experience was basically a bubbling mess of those things, plus mosquitos. But his father had gone to Camp Bewilder as a kid and had waxed poetic about how it was all adventures and puzzles that had been tailor-made for role-playing game enthusiasts like himself and Milo. Mr. Pine had laid the salesmanship on thick until Milo had grudgingly agreed to be delivered to this campground deep in the Nagspeake woods.

Upon arrival, Milo had been duly sorted into a cabin called Cat Dapperling, which turned out to be the name of a fungus. The campground was on the former estate of an eccentric mycologist, so all the cabins were named after fungi, and in moments when Milo started feeling like this venture had been a terrible idea, he reminded himself that at least he was not among the six poor saps who had to troop home each night to Weeping Toothcrust.

The Dapperlings—Milo, Kip, Phero, Josh, Toby, and Rayhan—got along pretty well, all things considered, with the occasional exception of Kip, who ditched them periodically to hang out with his best friend from a different cabin. (Only ten kids out of sixty this year were returning campers, and despite various requests to bunk together, they'd been divvied up so that each cabin got a veteran, which was how Kip had wound up in Cat Dapperling while the powers that be had stuck Kent in Chicken of the Woods.) Still, the other guys were pretty cool, and they'd won a nontrivial number of the games and puzzle challenges. If asked, Milo would have grudgingly admitted that he'd had a pretty good time so far, right up until the morning they got up and Milo discovered he'd lost the cabin's team flag, which wasn't a flag at all but a small cylindrical specimen container from the nature resource lab containing the preserved remains of an actual Cat Dapperling mushroom.

"One job, Pine," Kip repeated, staring down his short nose at Milo. "And you blew it. You only had to keep the thing safe for one night. One more night, and we were in the clear."

"That guy's kind of a twit," said the seventh person in the boys' cabin, a girl with short red hair who sat perched on the footboard of the nearest bed. Milo forced himself not to reply, or even to let his eyes flick in the speaker's direction. Meddy had been dead for more than thirty years, and Milo was the only living person who could see or hear her.

Red-faced, he folded his arms, refusing to wilt under the glare of the Senior Dapperling. "The jar was accounted for at lights-out. The door and the windows were locked. We all checked. What could I have done to keep it safer than it was in our own cabin, with everything locked and all of us here? Swallow the thing?"

"Could've given it to me," said Meddy. Milo, who knew perfectly well that none of the other guys could hear her, cringed anyway. It took getting used to, being buddies with a ghost. "But no, *you* said that wasn't in the spirit of the game."

Milo clamped his mouth shut. She was right, but giving his team's creepy dead mushroom specimen to his equally dead best friend to keep another team from stealing it just hadn't seemed sporting.

Camp Bewilder's version of Capture the Flag had been running for two days. It had a constantly evolving set of excessively complicated rules crafted, as far as Milo could tell, specifically to be able to extend the game almost without end. The basic premise was simple enough, though: each cabin got a hundred-year-old mushroom in a jar from the massive collection of spores, molds, and fungi that the former owner of the property had bequeathed to the camp. The original idea was that campers had to keep their jar from getting stolen (or broken) for the whole week, and whichever team managed to capture the most specimens from other cabins would be the winner.

Of course, it wasn't that simple in practice. For one thing, nobody was actually sure who was in the lead at the moment, because over the last couple days several cabins had claimed their jars had disappeared—not that they had been captured through legitimate play under the rules of the game, but that they'd vanished outright. It was almost certainly just a bit of tactical deception, a way for those cabins to try to hold on to their jars by trickery rather than strategy, and the result was that the already confusing game had rapidly devolved into chaos. Or maybe it would've done that anyway. The counselors had tried to combat the confusion by adding more rules and more jars, leading to more frustration and more missing specimens. It was not the camp's most successful game, and the adults had announced at dinner that they'd be putting the kids out of their misery the following day at breakfast.

The Dapperlings had only managed to capture one other cabin's jar (a thumb-sized test tube nicked from the gentlemen in Scurfy Twiglet), so they weren't really in the running to win. Still, you couldn't officially *lose* if you hung on to your own 'shroom without breaking its container, so all Milo and his bunkmates had to do at this point was keep control of their jar until the end of breakfast on Wednesday. And now, here they were, a half an hour before the beginning of that very meal, their weird little specimen was inexplicably gone, and the other five boys were looking at Milo like it was his fault.

Or four of them were, anyway. "The Twiglets' tube is gone, too," reported Phero, hauling his duffel out from under his bunk in a panic and dumping the contents on his bed. When every scrap and stitch of sock and spare underwear had been tossed out and the duffel was empty, he looked up in horror. "The tube was *here*," Phero insisted, jabbing a finger into the duffel. "Right here in the side pocket. It's *gone!*"

One missing mushroom could be chalked up to Milo's being a blockhead. *Two* missing mushrooms: that was troubling. Kip abandoned the stare down, folded his arms, and addressed the group. "All right, Dapperlings. Let's focus. This is just one more puzzle we need to solve. We have"—he shook his pajama sleeve back and checked his watch—"twenty-five minutes before we need to be at the mess hall with these stupid mushrooms. The mushrooms can't have gone far."

Milo felt himself start to relax just a bit. Camp pushed a bunch of his most uncomfortable buttons, but this was the kind of thing that made him want to power through all that: the group coming together as a team and working through a challenge.

Meddy hopped down to stand at his side as Kip gave his little pep talk. Milo glanced expectantly at her out of the corner of his eye. "I know, right?" Meddy said. "Every time Kip calls you all Dapperlings it's all I can do not to giggle." Milo risked an impatient glare. "Sorry," she said apologetically. "And before you ask, I didn't see a thing. I spent last night haunting the woods instead."

"Great," Milo whispered sourly. "Super helpful, thank you."

Meanwhile, the rest of the Dapperlings had moved on to searching the cabin. Josh was gingerly emptying the trash can by the door of candy wrappers, old batteries, and tinfoil from a batch of cookies Toby's mother had sent. "Nothing here," Josh reported, dumping it all back in.

"Maybe they rolled into a corner," Rayhan suggested, eyeing the uneven floor. He and Phero circled the perimeter of the room from opposite directions. It didn't take long; Cat Dapperling cabin was comprised of a single room, and the only furniture was their six bunks, the six chairs that served as bedside tables, and the writing table in front of the cabin's crumbling stone fireplace. For good measure, Toby even rolled up the rug: nothing.

Milo watched the search, shaking his head. "But the Twiglets' tube was in an inside pocket, zipped into Phero's duffel. It couldn't have rolled out. And ours was inside my shoe, under the bed. It couldn't have rolled out, either. I don't think the jars are *lost*."

The unspoken, terrible thought hung heavy over their heads. "Do we think we've been robbed?" Phero asked at last, instinctively dropping his voice to a whisper. "Is it possible somebody snuck in overnight?"

"Oh my God, the other cabins' jars, the ones that went missing—"

Kip gasped. "I *told* you guys it wasn't just a clever ruse. We've been hit by the Jar Thief."

Milo glanced at Meddy again. "Didn't see anything," she repeated. "I mean, there's some *very* weird stuff out in the woods, but I didn't see anything weird going on *here*."

"Is that even allowed, to take stuff from our cabins?" Rayhan asked. "I thought our cabins were, like, *base*. Safe."

"Who can keep all the rules straight?" Phero grumbled. "They add a new one like every day."

The boys checked every possible entrance to the cabin. Again, it didn't take long: there were windows to either side of the single door and another two windows on the opposite wall. "All secure," Rayhan reported.

"All except for that one," Josh said, pointing to the narrow rectangular window over the door. "We didn't leave that open, did we?"

"I don't think it's been open all week," Milo muttered as they all looked at the aperture in question. It was the width of the door and only about a foot high, but it really was more vent than window, and Milo wasn't sure any of them could've squeezed through it—assuming any of them could even *get* to it. "And none of us opened it?" The other campers shook their heads.

But at his side, Meddy held up a finger. "It was open last night."

"You sure?" Milo asked, after making sure the question could reasonably be a response to his cabinmates' head shakes as well as to Meddy's statement.

"Positive," confirmed five humans and one ghost.

Another moment to be sure his next question worked for both the living and the dead in the room, then: "And we don't know when it got opened?"

The boys glanced around at each other, then shook their heads. Meddy made an apologetic face. No luck there.

"Well, if everything else is locked, that must be how someone got in," Kip said decisively. "No one could've snuck in the front door anyway. It sticks and it creaks. No way to be sneaky about it."

Milo shook his head. "But *nobody* would fit through there. And even if they could, how would they have gotten up and down from it?"

"Maybe if they stood on the shelf?" Phero pointed to the little ledge to the right of the door, where a spare flashlight, a lantern, and the cabin's first aid kit stood ready in case of emergencies.

Meddy and Milo made doubtful noises at the same time. "That thing's not strong enough to hold a person," Milo said. "And even if it was, nobody could've climbed on it without knocking that stuff down or moving it all first, in which case they also had to put it back when they left."

"I'd love to hear whatever alternative idea you've got," Kip snapped. "But if you *haven't* got one, quit wasting time. If we can figure out how whoever got in here *did* get in here, maybe we can find a clue that will lead us back to them, and we might just have time to get the jars back before breakfast. Everything else is locked and none of us opened that window, so that's got to be the answer, even if it seems like a long shot."

"I really want to kick him," Meddy said thoughtfully. "Or, like, keep untying his shoes over and over for like an hour, except maybe once every fifteen minutes or so, tie them together instead."

"Milo's not wrong, though," Rayhan put in. "The shelf doesn't look sturdy enough and the window doesn't look big enough. Let's test it. I'm the smallest. I'll give it a try, and if I can't do it, I don't think it can be done."

He passed Milo the big spare flashlight and handed the first aid kit in its plastic box to Kip. Then, as he lifted the lantern, he gave a yelp of surprise. "Look!"

The Dapperlings gathered around and stared, disbelieving, at a vague and smudgy, dusty gray crescent that was unmistakably the toe end of a footprint made by some kind of sneaker.

"Now," Meddy said appreciatively, "that's interesting." She tilted her head. "And weird." She rose effortlessly off the ground and proceeded to lever herself up and down from the shelf to the window and back. She took care to make sure one foot or the other always touched down, however briefly, on the crescent toe print. She managed it, but it seemed awkward from every angle, and it really didn't look like she'd have been able to use the window if she'd actually had to maneuver the mass of a living kid.

Milo shook his head. "That print's more than weird, it's not *possible*. And it makes no sense for it to have been *under* the lantern. It must be from some other time."

"Some *other* time when someone had a reason to climb up on that shelf?" Kip asked, rolling his eyes. "No."

"I don't think it was under the lantern," Rayhan said. "I think I just couldn't see it until I *moved* the lantern. I *think*," he repeated dubiously.

"I'm convinced," Kip announced with obnoxious finality. "Impossible as it sounds, somebody must've climbed through that window last night and taken the sample tubes. What we need to do now is find the person whose shoe matches this print."

"Ugh, Kip," Meddy complained, sitting on the shelf and letting her feet dangle. "What's he think, that all the other kids are just going to line up and show you the toes of their shoes?"

Milo folded his arms and glowered at Kip. "It's barely a print at all. There's no tread visible. Without the tread pattern, how could we possibly match this to anyone's shoe?" He glanced at the clock on the wall between his bed and Rayhan's. "We have fifteen minutes, plus what, a half-hour for breakfast? There are fifty-four other kids here. Even if we could line them all up and make them show us their shoes one by one, which obviously we can't—"

Kip took a deep, frustrated breath and let it out, exhaling the words "WHAT IS YOUR SUGGESTION THEN, MILO, IF YOU KNOW SO MUCH ABOUT EVERYTHING" at the same time.

Meddy reached down to whack Kip on the back of the head, a gesture he couldn't possibly have seen or felt but that still somehow managed to make him flinch. But it was too late—suddenly the whole cabin was looking at Milo. His face began to burn.

"Hey." Meddy spotted the flare-up. She leaped down from the shelf and stood at his side. "You're up against a blackjack, Milo. A trickster, just like in our role-playing games back home. Just like *you*, when you play. We know how to deal with blackjacks. Shake it off and focus."

"Whoa," Phero said quickly at about the same time. "Let's not fight with each other. There's got to be a way—hey!" He snapped his fingers. "What about—what's it called, trace evidence? In movies the forensic people are always using trace evidence to link the crime scene to the criminal. What about the dirt? Maybe we can match it to the area around someone's cabin."

"Not unless they teleported from their cabin to ours, we can't," Milo said glumly.

"Yeah," Meddy agreed, looking over his shoulder at the crescent toe print again. "If they crossed the campground, their shoes'll have dirt from all over."

The two of them looked down at the crescent toe print together. Then Milo frowned. Dirt from all over the campsite . . . yes, that's what *should* be there: some unremarkable mix of dirt and grass and whatever else accumulated on the bottom of a shoe in the course of a day spent outdoors. But the print they were all looking at didn't look like it was made of transferred dirt at all. The gray of the print had no brown or green to it. The particles . . .

Milo took a breath and puffed out a quick breath of air, and tiny motes swirled up away from the print. "It's not dirt," Meddy said softly. "It's dust. Or maybe not even dust."

"Yeah." He glanced sharply over his shoulder at the fireplace, then looked at his cabinmates. "I think it's *ash*."

"Let me see." Kip elbowed his way past Milo for a look. "I don't see how you get ash from that," he argued. "Probably he—whoever he was—just stepped in the dust already on the shelf."

But the rest of the Dapperlings loved the fireplace idea. "The one way in we didn't think of!" Toby crowed, darting over to the stone hearth with Rayhan, Phero, and Josh in tow.

"You really think someone climbed down the chimney?" Kip protested, following reluctantly. "That's even more ridiculous than the window idea!"

It was as if Kip hadn't spoken at all. "Somebody see if the ash here matches the stuff on the shelf," Phero suggested. "Who's got a shoe handy?" He glanced over to Kip's stuff, which was closest. "Kip, pass me one of yours."

Kip snorted. "Get your own shoes filthy. Are there even any footprints in there?"

The Senior Dapperling was not enjoying getting dragged along with a theory he didn't like. It was almost enough to lift Milo's mood, especially now that Milo himself wasn't the focus of everyone's attention. "Here, use mine," he said, tucking the flashlight he was still holding under one arm, grabbing one of his own shoes, and tossing it into Phero's waiting hands.

Phero rubbed the shoe into a blackish smudge in the corner of the fireplace, then carried it over to the shelf, stamped it next to the toe print, and examined the results. "Looks like the same stuff to me."

"The way this thing is falling apart, I bet there are toeholds all the way up," Josh said, kneeling on the stones and peering up into the murk of the chimney. "It's definitely wide enough for a kid. Somebody pass me a flashlight."

"I can look," Meddy volunteered. She crossed to the fireplace, edged past Josh, and vanished up the chimney.

Meanwhile, "Take my light," Kip said quickly, heading for his bag.

"Never mind. I've got the big one." Milo still had the emergency flashlight from the shelf under his arm. Josh held out his hands, and Kip cringed as Milo tossed it just as he'd tossed his shoe a moment before.

But Josh, thankfully, caught the flashlight flawlessly. He leaned back into the fireplace, aimed it up into the chimney, and flicked the switch. Nothing happened. "Huh." He shook the flashlight, rattling the batteries inside, and tried again. Still nothing.

Meddy popped back down the chimney and returned to Milo's side. "He doesn't have to worry about it. There's nothing to see up there."

Kip made an impatient noise. "The batteries are probably dead. Here," he said, offering his own pocket-sized flashlight. "Just use mine, do whatever, and let's get out of here. If you think we need to be looking for soot on somebody, fine, but I'm telling you, if we're going to find whoever did this, we need to get moving."

The boys swapped flashlights and Josh peered up. The others waited for his pronouncement. A little fall of ash and tiny bits of mortar fell as he reached up into the chimney stack to test some potential foothold.

Milo watched it all with an irritated sort of itch beginning to scratch at the back of his mind. A thought was coming together, and he badly wanted to talk it out with Meddy, but there was nowhere in the single-room cabin where the two of them could converse unobserved.

"So?" Kip said peevishly.

Josh emerged from the chimney, his face and hair now lightly dusted with gray. "I don't know," he admitted. "The stone's plenty uneven, but it would be a pretty tough climb. And," he said, looking down at the debris at his feet, "I feel like there would've been evidence."

"If whoever it was got in and out through the chimney," Milo said slowly, "there'd be no reason for a footprint on the shelf." The idea was solidifying. He didn't much like it—in fact, the possibility made him furious—but it made a certain kind of sense. "And if whoever managed to get in and out through that window, what on earth reason would there be for them to go anywhere near the fireplace?"

"I really do think it matches the ash, though," Phero protested, looking down at the two prints: the one they'd found and the one he'd made. "Come see for yourself."

Milo shook his head. "I don't need to see it. I believe you. But I don't think it means what you think it means."

"What are you thinking?" Meddy asked.

Now he had everyone's attention, which was the opposite of how Milo preferred it. On the other hand, he suspected he had the answer and nobody else had worked it out yet.

"This is a locked-door mystery," Milo said thoughtfully, "and we're up against a blackjack."

"A locked—" Meddy's mouth opened in an O, and Milo permitted himself a short nod. She was no slouch. It was coming together in her mind now, too.

"Excuse me?" Phero said. "A *blackjack*?"

"Yeah, I think so." Milo looked around, past his cabinmates and his ghostly best friend to take in the single-room cabin that was Cat Dapperling. *This* is *a locked-door problem. I'm sure of it.* "I think there are only a handful of solutions to a locked-door mystery," he said aloud. "But I'm pretty sure they're all variations on the idea that if it doesn't look like someone could get into or out of a room without a secret passage, then—unless there *is* a secret passage, and I don't think these cabins are that fancy—nobody *did* get in or out."

Josh sat on the hearth and scratched his head, sending up a puff of soot. "Meaning?"

"Meaning the reason we can't figure out how a person could've snuck in and out again undetected last night is that nobody *did*. But someone did a lot of work to make us think an outsider broke into the cabin and stole our jars." Milo nodded at the shelf with the prints.

"That's why that nonsense footprint is there. Somebody had to make it look like an outsider had used that shelf to get up and down from the window, but he couldn't actually go outside to get dirt for a fake footprint, because Kip's right and the door creaks like crazy; one of us would've woken up. So he used the fireplace ash instead." Milo looked around at the staring faces. "Nobody snuck in last night. Somebody definitely took the jars, though—but for the moment, they're still here. And so is the thief."

"And it's one of them," Meddy pronounced, just as Rayhan said quietly, "So the thief is one of us."

Milo nodded. "That's exactly what I mean."

"Not possible," Toby protested. "If we lose our jar, we lose the game. None of us would sabotage the cabin. Anyway, what would be the point?"

"Well, we're not going to lose the game, because I know where the jars are," Milo said. "As to why—I'm not totally positive, but I have an idea." He smiled sourly at Kip. "Do you want to explain it, or shall I?"

The other four of the Dapperlings gasped. "Me?" Kip retorted. "Explain what? Don't be ridiculous. I didn't take the jars. Search my stuff if you want. All it's going to do is make us late for breakfast."

"I don't have to search your stuff," Milo snapped. "You could've swiped any of our shoes to make the fake print on the shelf, but you probably didn't think you needed to be that sneaky since the idea was to make it look like someone outside the cabin did the thieving. You wouldn't let Phero use your shoe to make a print with the ash because you knew even though you'd cleaned it off, the shape of the toe would match the print and give you away." He nodded to Kip's shoes, which were lined up under his bed. "Go ahead. Prove me wrong."

Five angry pairs of eyes turned on him. Kip said nothing for a long minute. Then, "I can't," he said quietly.

"Why on earth would you do that?" Phero exploded. "We were already not going to win. Why'd you want us to actually *lose*?"

Still Kip didn't answer. Milo sighed. "Well, if you're not going to say anything, I'll make my guess. He didn't *want* us to lose," he told the others. "But he was playing a parallel game with a different team, and he wanted *that* team to win. Right, Kip?"

"What on earth game were you playing?" Josh demanded, grabbing at his own hair in frustration, which had the unfortunate effect of sending a bunch of ash sifting down right into his face.

"Either him and Kent, or all ten of the returning campers," Milo explained. "I suspect it was all of them. They were sort of playing the same Capture-the-Jar game we were, they just decided to form their own separate team and not tell anybody. That's where the disappearing jars have been going—the ones that disappeared, but that no cabin took credit for taking."

"It was all ten of us," Kip said dully, sitting at the edge of his bed. He looked up at the others mutinously. "I feel like I ought to say something here about how we would've gotten away with it all, if not for . . ." He sighed. "I'm sorry. It was a crummy thing to do."

"You were bored, so you made up your own rules," Milo said. "I can sort of relate, right up to the point where you would have torpedoed your own cabin." He glared at Kip. "And now you're stuck between two teams and I bet that feels utterly crappy."

"Yeah," Kip grumbled. "That is accurate."

Toby snorted. "Forgive me for not feeling sorry for you."

Josh shook his head. "Me either."

"If we didn't have to bunk together for three more days," Rayhan said coldly, "I would be planning some very humiliating revenge for you right now."

"I'm still planning humiliating revenge," Phero muttered.

The four aggrieved campers began to speak all at once, berating the traitor and promising a minimum punishment of a jug of orange juice down his pants as soon as they got to the mess hall. But Milo hesitated. All right, yes, they'd had a sleeper agent in their midst the whole week, but apart from that, the Dapperlings had made a pretty good team, and they'd had a pretty good time. Torn between the wish for retribution and the wish to have his cabin team back while they still had half a week of camp left, Milo thought fast.

"New rule," he announced, shouting over the raised voices. "New rule!"

"Good grief, what now?" Kip demanded. "This game had too many rules from the beginning, and I'd just as soon get on with whatever suffering I've got coming my way."

"Just listen." Milo cleared his throat. "I hereby declare that, if a spy is discovered on any given team, he may be turned into a double agent by capturing his contraband back." He pointed at Kip. "You haven't told us where the jars are: *don't*. If we can figure it out and steal them from you, we win you back over to our team, and you help us steal back the jars the secret team took." He looked at the others. "Agreed?"

"What if we don't want him back?" Josh mumbled.

"One moment." Rayhan motioned to him, Toby, and Phero, and the four of them ducked into a huddle by the fireplace. There a moment's hushed discussion followed this. Then, "Fine," Rayhan announced. "We accept. Kip?"

"I also accept," said the disgraced Senior Dapperling.

"Do I get a vote?" Meddy asked. "Because I vote yes, as long as I can still untie his shoes for an hour."

Everyone looked to Milo. "This is acceptable," he said. He took a deep breath. "The specimen jars are in—"

For the solution to this story, please turn to page 338.

CODENAME: MOM

By Laura Brennan

ost people think spies are cool. And they are. James Bond (a fictional spy), Mata Hari (who may have been a double agent), and James Armistead Lafayette (one of the first Revolutionary War spies).

But it's a little less cool when your mom is a spy.

I mean, it's so weird. There she is, packing lunches and changing your sister's diaper, and in between she's catching bad guys and saving the free world. Or at least, that's what I imagine she's doing. In front of me, she only ever graded papers and put together symposiums. She tells people that she's the Chair of the Math Department at the private university where we live. And she is. But I know that's just her cover job.

"It's brilliant," I told her one night. She was helping me with my homework while Dad put my sister, Rosa, to bed.

"Math?" Mom smiled at me. "Well, I've always loved it . . ."

I rolled my eyes. "Not math! Your cover story. Not only does being a professor explain your trips all over the world—"

"Mathematics is a universal language," she said for the hundredth time.

"—it also bores people to death! I mean, you just have to mention that you do math for a living and everyone changes the subject. It's a perfect way to keep them from snooping. You're a genius."

"Thanks. I think. Next question: what is five to the third power?"

"How did you become a spy?" I asked. Mom sighed and gave me her I'm-almost-losing-my-patience face.

"One hundred twenty-five," I said, answering the math question. "It's five times five, which is twenty-five, times five. Now will you tell me?"

"Honey," she said. "I'm not a spy."

"Let's look at the facts." I ticked the reasons off on my fingers. "One, you're always flying off to 'conferences.'" I went big with the air quotes to show how little I believed that. "Two, people call you in the middle of the night from places like Beijing and Paris. And three, you always keep your papers locked in your briefcase. What else could you be except a spy?"

For a second, I thought she'd crack. But spies are made of tougher stuff. Instead, Mom picked up a pencil and made a mark in the margin of my homework. "What is that?" she asked.

This was not rocket science. "It's a line," I answered.

She put the number three after it. "Now what is it?" she asked.

I had no idea where this was going, but I answered anyway. "It's a minus sign. Minus three."

She nodded and erased the three. Instead of the number, this time she wrote the letter *a* next to the minus sign. "What about now?" she asked.

I shrugged. "Still minus, I guess."

Mom shook her head. "Not quite. With the variable a instead of a number, that short pencil line would be read as 'the opposite of a,' not 'minus a.' It's the same line each time, I haven't changed it, but it's a different thing depending on the context."

I grumped and sank back into my chair.

"Blake," she continued, "I travel because I'm on too many committees, the phone rings at night because some of my colleagues have trouble remembering time zones, and I keep my papers locked up because once Rosa started walking, nothing in this house was safe anymore." She erased the line. "But thanks for giving my overscheduled life a glamorous context for a change."

And that was it. I finished my homework, Dad came in and broke out the ice cream, and there was no more mention of spies.

Not then, anyway.

But I kept my eyes open. I took note of anything unusual that happened and copied it down in my notebook. I practiced shadowing people around campus and discovered how much more often college kids head to the coffee shop vs. the library.

"Spycraft is science in action," Dad told me. He had taken time off from teaching when Rosa was born. I think he was more excited than I was at the excuse to break out his old chemistry set. Dad helped me make invisible ink with lemon juice and listen through walls with drinking glasses. Even Mom eventually got into the spirit of things. She started writing me lunch notes in a substitution code, which meant she'd swap one letter for another. They weren't too hard to break, but it was fun, even though they never said anything more interesting than "Don't forget to eat your apple slices."

It was a month later, and Mom was dropping me off at school. I usually walked, but all that week, Mom had come up with reasons to drive me in and pick me up. I sat in the back, listening to the car radio and thinking about hanging out with my friends after class. All of a sudden, Mom turned the volume down and gestured toward the rear-view mirror.

"Without turning around," she said, "can you see the car behind us?"

I craned my neck to see in the rearview mirror. It was just a black Toyota behind us, nothing special. "I scc it," I said.

"Did you look at the license plate?"

I jockeyed around a bit until I could see the plate. It was reflected in the mirror, but not hard to figure out. "11SUS17," I read.

"That mean anything to you?" she asked.

I thought for a minute. If it meant something to Mom, then it probably had to do with math. The numbers were 11 and 17, or three ones and a seven. I thought about what they had in common. Then I smiled.

"They're all prime numbers," I said.

"Good job," Mom answered. "So with that license plate, I'd say that guy is a 'prime suspect.'"

I looked again. Prime plus SUS. That was pretty funny.

"I hope he's not a bank robber," I said. "That would be tough luck, having that license plate."

"Tough on him," she said as she pulled up to the drop-off spot. "Lucky for the police."

I scrambled out of the car and reached into the front seat for my backpack.

"Don't forget your lunchbox," Mom said.

She handed it to me and waved. I waved back. I noticed the Prime

Suspect car was still behind her as she turned the corner. Then I got swept up by the rest of the kids going through the school gates and forgot all about the car. Until lunchtime.

I was sitting with my friends Luisa and Dwayne when I unzipped my lunch bag. There, tucked next to the leftover chicken potpie, was my mom's cell phone.

"That's weird," I said. "How'd my mom's phone get in my lunch?"

"Are you sure it's hers?" asked Luisa.

"It's got her phone case," I said, looking at the bright yellow case covered in math equations. I hit the On button and the screen lit up. There was the picture of me, Mom, and Dad at the school fair last year. We had all entered the pie-eating contest and our faces were covered with blueberry gunk and pie crust crumbs. We looked super-dorky, but we all had these massive grins. I guess that's why Mom liked the picture enough to use it as her phone screen.

I hit the button again and the prompt came up to unlock the phone. Six numbers or letters. I didn't know her password.

"Maybe it fell out of your mom's pocket," Dwayne said.

"And into my closed lunchbox? Which then zipped itself up again after the phone fell in?" I asked. "Mom must've put it there on purpose."

"Why would she do that?"

I didn't answer. I couldn't. I didn't have enough data. As lunch ended, I slipped Mom's phone into my pocket and tried to concentrate on class. But all I could think of were possible passwords.

I expected to see Mom's car waiting out front when school let out, but it wasn't there. Either she didn't need her phone that bad or for some reason she couldn't come get it. I decided to skip hanging out with my friends after all. As I walked home, I thought about her password and things that came in sixes. Birthdays were six numbers if you only used the last two numbers for the year, but Mom was nothing if not fair. I didn't think she'd use my birthday but not Rosa's, or use Dad's instead of either of ours. She wouldn't want anyone to feel left out. Of course, it might be her own birthday . . .

I had just decided to try 01/18/82 when I turned the last corner and saw the car pull up to our house. A black Toyota, 11SUS17. I ducked behind a tree. A man got out and went up to our door. In that moment, I realized Mom had pointed that car out to me for a reason. She must've known the man was following her. She had slipped her phone into my lunchbox to make sure he didn't get it. All of a sudden, the fun of playing at being a spy was replaced with the responsibility of actually needing to think like one. Mom had trusted me with her phone; I had to keep it safe.

As the man rang our doorbell, I pulled out my own phone and took off the case. I put Mom's math equations case on my phone and slipped it into my backpack. My jacket had an inside, zippered pocket, so I put Mom's phone there for safekeeping. Then I took a deep breath, grabbed my backpack, and headed down the sidewalk.

Dad stood in the doorway holding Rosa. He looked completely relaxed as the Prime Suspect man stood there smiling and talking, but I could tell he was blocking the door on purpose to keep the man from going inside.

"Hi, Dad!" I said, moving up the steps to the house.

"Hey, Blake," Dad answered. "This gentleman says Mom sent him to get her phone from you. She thinks it fell into your backpack by mistake. Do you know anything about that?"

I tried to look surprised. "Huh, let me look." I unzipped my backpack and pretended to rummage. "Oh, yeah, here it is."

I pulled out my phone, wrapped in Mom's bright yellow case. I could feel Prime Suspect tense at the sight of it. "Here you go," I said. The man reached for it.

"Hold up," Dad said. "What's the magic word?"

The guy smiled. If he was a spy, he was pretty lousy at it; he oozed fake charm. "Please?" he asked. Dad narrowed his eyes and pulled out his own phone.

Just then, Mrs. Gupta rounded the corner, walking her German shepherd. "Hi, Mrs. Gupta!" I called.

She looked up and waved as she always does. I waved back and managed to "accidentally" drop the phone in the grass. Prime Suspect was on it in a flash.

"Thanks!" he said.

"Wait!" Dad tried to make a grab for him, but he was still holding Rosa. The guy ran to his car and took off. Dad managed to snap a few photos before the guy roared down the street and vanished.

"It's okay, Dad," I said. "I have his license plate number."

"But he has your mom's phone." Dad looked really upset.

"No, he doesn't," I told him. "I switched phone covers. He has my phone."

The one thing about Dad is, he never asks dopey questions. He didn't want to know why I did it, or when, or how. The only question he had was the important one.

"How long until he figures it out?" Dad asked.

"Twenty minutes," I answered. "Maybe twenty-five."

"Get in the car," Dad said.

I did. Dad buckled Rosa into her car seat. Within ninety seconds, we were pulling out of the driveway.

I thought we'd be heading for the police station or at least Campus Security to report Mom missing, but instead we went to our favorite diner. Dad parked around back so the car couldn't be seen from the street.

"Take Rosa inside and get us a booth. I have to make a quick call."

"The CIA?" I asked. Dad smiled.

"No, kiddo," he answered. "Just a friend who can help us. What was that license plate?"

I told him, and then I took Rosa inside and picked a booth in the back corner. The waitress came with waters and menus. Rosa loved pie, so I ordered a slice of apple for her and blueberry for me. After a couple of minutes, Dad joined us.

"Okay," he said. "My friend is on it. She thinks your mom may have some information on her phone that can help us. Can I see it?"

I handed him the phone. He turned it on. There was the goofy picture of the three of us at the pie-eating contest. I expected him to smile when he saw it, but he didn't. I realized he must be really worried. The prompt for the password came up.

"Do you know how to unlock the phone?" I asked.

He shook his head. "Your mom's pretty private about her stuff," he said.

"Try her birthday," I suggested. "That's what I was going to do when I got home."

He did. 0-1-1-8-8-2. Nothing.

"Good idea," he said. "But I bet Mom picked something a little harder to guess."

Suddenly, I remembered what Dad said when the man had reached for the phone. "You asked that man for the magic word," I reminded him. "It wasn't 'please.' So what is the magic word?"

"Euclid," he answered.

Of course Mom would use the name of the father of geometry to signal that all was well. But Euclid also had six letters. "Try it," I suggested.

Dad put it in. No luck.

"What about our birthdays?" I asked.

Dad tried them all. He put in mine and Rosa's and his own, and even Grandma's and Poppy's. He tried Mom's middle name, which had six letters, and the name of her first pet, which I'd never even heard of, but he knew because it was one of the security answers on their bank account. Nothing. Meanwhile, time was ticking away. I didn't know what Prime Suspect would do when he realized he'd been tricked. I didn't want to think about it.

The waitress arrived with our pie. Rosa reached into hers with both hands. Dad was so busy with the phone, he didn't try to stop her.

"I don't think your mom put this in your backpack just to keep it from that man," Dad said. "I think she gave it to you because she thought you'd know how to open it."

"I don't know if it helps," I said, "but she didn't put it in my backpack, she put it in my lunchbox."

"*Lunchbox* is too many letters," Dad said. "And *lunch* is too few."

"Maybe she wanted to let us know she was using a substitution code," I said. "Like the notes in my lunchbox."

"If so," said Dad, "we'll never figure it out. We don't know what word she's substituting or the code. It would just be six random letters."

As he thought of another combination to try, I watched Rosa eat her apple pie. Somehow, she had already managed to get crumbs in her hair and on her chin, even in her eyebrows. I thought of the picture on Mom's phone. I remembered how happy we had all been, covered in blueberry pie. For the first time, I was afraid that we would never be that happy again.

And then all of a sudden, I knew what the password was.

"Dad!" I almost knocked over my plate as I jumped out of the booth. "I've got it! Here are the numbers to type in!"

For the solution to this story, please turn to page 340.

THE RED ENVELOPE

By Lara Cassidy

Catherine McCleary nudges a bulging backpack toward Mr. Michael's classroom with her knee.

Her bright blue eyes dart between the math book nestled in the crook of her left arm and the history timeline clenched in her right fist. She conjugates verbs in Latin as she inches down the hall.

Mr. Michael's placement exams are deceptively simple: one question, any subject. Answer correctly to join Mr. Michael's middle school honors class. Answer first to win the Golden Answer Award.

"Hey, McClever, it's too late for studying now." Kevin Lane stands directly in front of Mr. Michael's classroom door. He is a tall boy with short brown hair, the captain of the middle school basketball team. "Just because you get the best grades in class doesn't mean you'll win."

Catherine drags her eyes away from her math book. "Challenge accepted," she whispers to herself.

Nine students soon gather outside Mr. Michael's classroom. A buzz of questions and answers, whispers, and nervous giggles fills the air.

Catherine stuffs her math book into her backpack, retightens her low blonde ponytail, and sizes up the competition.

Two boys join Kevin near the door. Peter Montgomery has curly red hair that stands out in every direction. Tony Boyle is a head shorter than the other boys, with jet-black hair and large brown eyes.

Janie Garcia, a petite girl with auburn hair that swings around her face, weaves through the crowd to Catherine. "You can do this," she says. "Golden Answer all the way."

"Not so fast, Garcia." Kevin overhears her. "I'm kickin' it into high gear. Pullin' away from McClever for the victory lap. Especially if the question involves sports. Carrots here"—he arcs his thumb toward the redhead, Peter—"knows grammar backward and forward. If the question is about science, it'll be Tony Boy for the win."

"I'm hoping for a history question," Margo Holla chimes in. "That's my best subject."

"Geometry," says Linda Ochoa.

"Geography," adds Bill Trident.

"Art," says Andrea Cicero.

Suddenly, the doorknob to Mr. Michael's classroom turns from the inside, and the door squeaks open.

"Welcome. Come in." Mr. Michael beckons the students to enter his classroom as if they were invited to a party rather than an exam. He is a slender man with smiling eyes and a bushy mustache that holds more gray hair than the rest of his nearly bald head. His checked blazer has brown leather patches on the elbows. A stack of note cards juts out of his lapel pocket.

Catherine enters and looks around the large classroom. Four neat rows of student desks face a teacher's desk with a black rotary-dial phone on one corner. A long high-top lab table spans one side of the room. Cabinets labeled "Science Equipment," a deep sink, and a mirror cover the wall beyond. On the opposite side of the room, a reading lamp and globe sit atop a rolling cart. The far wall is lined with floor-to-ceiling shelves jam-packed with books.

Catherine claims a student desk in the front row, comforted by Mr. Michael's cheerfulness. The exam question can't be too hard if he smiles like that. Janie sits next to her. Kevin heads to the back row with Peter and Tony. The other students find seats in the middle.

Mr. Michael walks to the front of the room. "You have each taken a significant step toward joining my honors program by coming out for this exam.

"The Golden Answer Award will be given for the first correct answer to the question in this envelope." Mr. Michael sets a red greeting-card envelope onto his desk, next to a stack of smaller white envelopes. "But first, the rules." He takes the note cards out of his jacket pocket.

"Number One: You may use any resources in this room to answer the question, including each other. No electronic devices are allowed. I will not be in the room, so you may not ask any questions of me.

"Number Two: Enclose your answer in a white envelope, write your name on the outside, and deliver it to me in the teachers' lounge down the hall. Once you submit, you may not return to the classroom for the remainder of the exam.

"Number Three: Think critically before submitting. The question may have more than one possible answer, but I am looking for only one *right* answer.

"Number Four: You have one hour to complete the exam. Once time expires, I will not accept any further envelopes. Do you understand?"

Nine heads nod.

Mr. Michael beams. "Your time will begin as soon as Miss McCleary reads the question out loud to the group."

Catherine's head jerks up in panic. Reading the question aloud puts her at a disadvantage for jotting down an immediate answer and winning the Golden Answer Award. But she stands, walks the few steps to the front of the room, and picks up the red envelope.

Mr. Michael crosses to the door. "Remember, one hour."

Catherine opens the envelope and removes the question with trembling hands. She takes a deep breath and reads: "This man's name is synonymous with the order of things."

"Dewey!" shouts Margo, even before Catherine finishes. She jumps out of her chair, races to Mr. Michael's desk, and grabs a white answer envelope. "The Dewey decimal system is named after Melvil Dewey, who invented it in 1876. His name is synonymous with the order of books in the library. Dewey is the answer and I'm first!" The door slams behind her as she rushes out.

Catherine stares after Margo slack-mouthed. All her hard work down the drain. Margo has claimed the Golden Answer Award.

The rest of the class looks equally dejected. Kevin stubs his toe into the floor in the back row.

"Wait." Janie's voice is calm. "Mr. Michael told us to think critically. That means not jumping to conclusions." She takes the slip of paper out of Catherine's hand and examines it closely. A smile comes to her lips.

Catherine looks over and sees what Janie sees. "Tiny writing." She squints but can't make out the words.

Tony rummages through the marked science cabinets. "Microscopes, prisms, flashlights . . . *aha*!—magnifying glasses." He strides to the front of the room, pumping his fist.

Tony deciphers the tiny words haltingly. "Do we know . . . the answer? Not . . . yet."

"It's not Dewey." Catherine laughs with relief. "Get it? 'Do we know' means 'Dewey, no.'"

"Great, McClever," Kevin calls from the back row. "We know who it's not. Any idea who it is?"

"Not a clue," Catherine says. "Tony, please study the page again, and the red envelope."

Tony doesn't find any more words.

Catherine gazes at the long wall of books. "The Dewey decimal system puts books in order. Margo was right about that. We need to find the book in those shelves that is not in order."

"That's like finding a needle in a haystack," Linda groans.

"If the books are organized the way they should be," Catherine responds, "it's more like finding a science book in the literature section."

Tony looks at his watch. "Fifty-four minutes left. Let's get started. The clock is ticking."

"I'll take this section." Catherine points to the first set of bookshelves. "Spread out along the wall, everyone."

Tony and Janie hop to the next two areas, but the rest of the students remain in their seats.

"I know we each want to win the Golden Answer Award," Catherine says, "but to have any chance of finding the book in time, we have to work together."

Reluctantly, the students fan out across the library wall.

"What are we supposed to do?" Linda huffs. She tosses light brown hair with blue streaks over her shoulder.

Catherine considers for a minute. "Start with the call numbers along the bottom of each book spine. Books on the same subject are grouped together in number order. Fiction books are organized alphabetically by author's last name."

Precious minutes pass.

"I found it!" Bill waves a book over his head. "*Erik the Red Discovers Greenland* was not with the right call numbers."

"Me, too," says Janie. "*Green Threads*, a book about sewing, was sandwiched between books about flags."

"Maybe Betsy Ross stuck it there," jokes Kevin.

"Maybe she also put the poetry book *Cowboys, Tenderfoots, and Greenhorns* with books about philosophy." Peter holds up another out-of-order book.

Catherine raises a heavy textbook with both hands. "*Chlorophyll in the Boreal Forest* should have been with other plant books. It was shelved in computer science."

"*A Beginner's Guide to Eco-Travel* does not belong with the dictionaries." Andrea reports her discovery.

"One more," Tony says. "A novel called *The Leprechaun's Treasure Map*. The author's last name is Green, but the book was shelved with the *r*'s."

They line up the six books on the long science table.

"Green!" Andrea shouts. "Greenland; green thread; greenhorns; a leprechaun book by someone named Green; chlorophyll; the boreal forest; and an eco-travel guide, which is about ecology, a different kind of 'green.'"

"Are you sure the boreal forest is green?" Linda sounds unconvinced.

"Definitely green," Bill responds, and Catherine recalls that geography is his favorite subject. He retrieves the globe from the rolling cart. "The boreal forest is the forest ring that circles the top of the globe. It covers parts of Canada, Norway, Sweden, Finland, Russia, and even Alaska." He hesitates. "Greenland isn't part of the boreal forest, though. It has too much ice."

Catherine's eyes light up with an idea. "Greenland may not have the boreal forest, but it's famous for something else that uses the word *boreal*: the aurora borealis."

"The northern lights?" Janie asks. "I've heard of them, but I'm not sure what they are."

Science fan Tony jumps in: "The northern lights are colorful bands that light up the far-northern sky when particles from the sun collide. The lights can show up in almost all the colors of the rainbow. Pale green and pink are most common, but they also can be red, yellow, blue, or violet."

"I don't think we need to worry about the northern lights," interrupts Kevin. He holds up a yellow sheet of paper with a series of marks on it.

"I found this page in the Greenland book," Kevin continues. "It looks like a message of dashes, dots, and slashes."

$$- \bullet\bullet\bullet\ /\ \bullet\ /\ \bullet - \ /\ - \bullet\ /\ \bullet\bullet\bullet\ /\ \bullet - - \ /\ \bullet\ /\ \bullet - \bullet\ /\ \bullet\ /\ - \bullet\bullet$$

"I've seen that before," says Peter. "It's Morse code, like they used to send telegraphs in the old days."

"Samuel Morse invented it," Andrea adds excitedly. "Morse was a well-known painter. He got interested in electricity and developed the code with some scientist friends."

"Did he paint anything green?" Kevin cracks another joke.

Catherine rolls her eyes. "Anyone know Morse code?"

"Dot-dot-dot, dash-dash-dash, dot-dot-dot means SOS." Tony taps the table as he speaks. "It's the international distress signal. You send it when you're in trouble." His voice falters. "That's all I know."

"We should send an SOS signal now," Linda complains. "We need our phones or a computer to translate the code."

"We have everything we need." Catherine points to the library wall. "Books."

"I saw dictionaries earlier." Andrea returns to the shelf she reviewed. "Maybe one of them has a Morse code chart . . . Yes!" She carries the open dictionary to the table.

"Dash-dot-dot-dot . . . then a slash. I bet the slash divides the letters." Andrea studies the dictionary. "The first letter is . . . *B*. Next is a single dot, which is the code for *E* . . . B-E . . . Be." She writes the letters down on the yellow page. "Then *A* . . . Be a." Her eyes go back and forth between the message and the dictionary. "*N* . . . B-E-A-N . . . Bean? . . . Be an?" She continues translating. "*S* . . . Beans."

Just then, Janie finds another sheet of yellow paper taped in the middle of the sewing book. "Another code—numbers this time. It looks like an enormous locker combination."

2-5-19-15-18-20-5-4

Catherine and the boys crowd around Janie for a look at the new message.

Suddenly, Andrea jumps out of her chair, races to the front desk for a white envelope, and flies out of the room.

Catherine retrieves the now-decoded Morse code message that Andrea left behind: "BE ANSWERED." Catherine shakes her head in dismay. "Andrea just submitted Samuel Morse."

"Morse's name is synonymous with the order of dashes and dots in his code," Tony agrees. "But I don't think Morse is the *right* answer to Mr. Michael's question." Six faces look at him.

"Remember Rule Number Three? The question can have more than one possible answer, but only one right answer." Tony holds up a third yellow sheet with a grin.

"This message is written in braille, the raised dot alphabet for the blind," Tony continues. "That means its inventor Louis Braille is a *possible* answer, just like Samuel Morse."

"We need to translate the braille message." Catherine points to the dictionary. "But we share the answer with the whole group. No more rushing off like Andrea did."

"Who put you in charge, McClever?"

Tony whirls to face Kevin. "Her name is McCleary. Catherine McCleary. She's the reason we looked for the books and found the messages. Listening to her and sticking together is our only chance of answering the question. The least you can do is get her name right."

"Cool it, Tony Boy. I'm the captain of the basketball team."

"Too bad you aren't a team player."

Kevin lets out a deep breath. "I'll figure out the braille message," he mumbles, "and I'll share what I find."

"The message 'BE ANSWERED' came out of the Greenland book," says Bill. "I'll study that book more closely."

"Janie and I will work on the number message," says Catherine, picking up the yellow paper.

"Peter and I will search for messages in the other books," Tony says. "Forty-two minutes to go."

"The braille message says 'BE CAUGHT.'" Kevin closes the dictionary. "It came out of the leprechaun book, right? What does a little Irish dude have to do with being caught?"

Peter looks up. "If you catch him, you get the pot of gold at the end of the rainbow."

"Speaking of gold, or yellow at least, here's another message." Tony tugs a yellow page from the index of the chlorophyll book and hands it to Kevin.

"It's music." Kevin looks at the page. "Garcia, I mean, Janie, you play violin." It's a statement, not a question. "Take a look at this. Please."

Janie takes the page and hums the tune softly. "I don't think it's a song. It just repeats the same notes over and over again."

"Musical notes can be written as letters, right?" Bill looks up from the Greenland book. "E-G-B-D-F, E-G-B-D-F, these are the lines of the treble clef." He smiles sheepishly. "Third grade music class."

"I learned it as Every Good Boy Does Fine," Janie remembers. "Both ways are useful mnemonics, or memory aids, for the notes on the staff."

"My Very Extravagant Mother is the beginning of a popular memory aid to learn the planets in order," Tony says.

Janie looks at the musical message again. "B-E-F-A-C-E-D. The notes spell 'BE FACED.'"

"Eureka!" yells Catherine.

"You know what 'BE FACED' means?" Janie looks at Catherine incredulously.

"No, I solved the number message." Catherine slides her yellow page to the middle of the table. "The other messages started B-E. I guessed this one did, too. I replaced the number two with a *B*, and the number five with an *E*. Then I saw the pattern. Here's the chart." Catherine flips the yellow paper over. She has listed the numbers one through twenty-six in one column, and the letters of the alphabet next to them. "Once I had this, the message was easy to read."

"What does it say?" Janie asks.

"BE SORTED."

"BE SORTED. BE FACED. BE CAUGHT. BE ANSWERED." Kevin ticks off the messages the group has solved so far. "What do they mean?"

Catherine motions toward the remaining books. "We need more yellow clues."

"These sheets are well hidden." Tony pulls a clue from the poetry book. "I missed this one the first time around."

bɘwƨɔɒͶɘdbɘwƨɔɒͶɘdbɘwƨɔɒͶɘd

Peter barely glances at the yellow paper. "It says BE WASHED." The other students stare at him. "It's mirror writing, like Leonardo da Vinci used. Check the mirror if you don't believe me."

Catherine smiles. "You really do know grammar backward and forward. Tony, which book is left?"

"The travel guide." Tony flips through the book page by page. He unfolds the pull-out map stapled in the back. "Here it is." He blinks. "It's blank."

"Blank?" repeats Kevin.

"Nothing on it," Tony confirms.

"Invisible ink!" Catherine rushes to the sink and dampens a paper towel. "I'll wet a corner and see if anything shows up."

Kevin frowns. "Water might ruin it. We should hold it over the reading lamp. Heat could make the ink appear."

"Hold on." Tony heads to the science cabinet and pulls out a small flashlight. "Bill, please turn off the room lights." Tony flips on his flashlight, which casts an eerie blue glow. "Black light," he says, shining it at the page. Words appear: "BE GLOBAL."

"The globe again." Bill flips the lights back on and walks over to the globe still sitting on the science table. "Greenland, the boreal forest, Ireland and leprechauns, seven continents, five oceans, north pole, south pole, equator." He drums his fingers on the base of the globe, picks it up, turns it over, and hears a rattle. "Something's in here!"

Bill pries the bottom off the base. He sticks two fingers inside and retrieves a blue plastic bag filled with small items. "Puzzle pieces," he announces.

Catherine turns to Tony. "How much time is left?"

"Twenty-nine minutes."

"Bill and Linda, you start putting the puzzle together. Fast. Everyone else, search the room for more puzzle pieces."

"I think 'BE FACED' means the mirror," Peter says. "That's why we had the mirror-writing message." He runs his fingers across the top of the frame and finds another blue bag.

"'BE WASHED' . . . the sink!" Catherine finds a blue bag taped to the bottom of the outflow pipe.

"BE ANSWERED. BE CAUGHT. BE SORTED." Janie chants the remaining clues. "What gets sorted? Papers? Maybe there's a filing cabinet."

"How about recycling?" Linda looks up from the puzzle. "Sorting trash for recycling fits the 'green' theme."

Janie thrusts her arm deep into a green wastebasket with the recycling symbol on its side. "Got it!"

Bill stands up. "I'm terrible at jigsaw puzzles. I'll help search for the bags."

Catherine scans the science table. "Fortunately, Linda is awesome!" The straight-edged puzzle border is mostly in place. Inside the frame, Linda joins matching green stems and dark blue blossoms into a flower bouquet. The flowers aren't violets or bluebonnets; the color falls somewhere in between.

"Puzzles I can do." Linda sounds happy at last. "It's geometry. The angles make sense."

"*Woo hoo!*" Tony rushes over another bag. "'BE CAUGHT' led me to the butterfly net in the science cabinet."

Linda continues fitting pieces into the puzzle. "The picture has a bowl of fruit, a note, and flowers. We need more pieces to read the writing on the note."

The boys mill around the classroom turning over random objects. "BE ANSWERED . . . BE ANSWERED . . . BE ANSWERED."

"*Ha!*" Kevin laughs. "We can't use our phones, but the room still has one." He picks up the old-fashioned black phone sitting on Mr. Michael's desk and finds the sought-after blue bag taped to the bottom of the housing. "Last bag."

"Nope." Linda bursts his bubble. "We're still missing puzzle pieces."

Catherine matches up the green books on the table, the yellow clues, and the blue puzzle bags. "This is a complete set. Six of everything."

"We need a seventh green book." Kevin looks over at the book wall. "Did we miss a shelf before?"

The students retrace their earlier steps.

"Oh!" Janie cries. "I found the sewing book here." She points at the shelf in front of her face. "I didn't look any higher. Can someone tall help me out?"

Kevin searches the top two shelves in Janie's area. He pulls down a kelly-green paperback titled *The Mathematical Papers of Sir Isaac Newton*. "This probably shouldn't be with books about painting."

"That's it!" Catherine cheers.

"Quick, find the message," Tony says. "We only have fourteen minutes left."

Kevin pulls out the now-familiar yellow sheet. "It's a crossword puzzle."

ACROSS

1   First-timers in sports and leisure activities
2   In all places
5   Be commanded to do something
6   Go completely around something

DOWN

3   Have in the mind
4   Devices originated after experimentation
7   Lengthy
8   Units of revolution around the sun

"No time to waste." Peter studies the page. "One across is 'First-timers in sports and leisure activities.'"

"*Beginners,*" says Bill.

Peter fills out the squares. "Two across is 'In all places'—ten letters."

"*Everywhere*," Janie answers.

"Next is five across: 'Be commanded to do something'—four letters."

"*Tell? Told?*" Janie throws out possible answers.

"*Told* sounds better." Peter writes it down. "Six across: 'Go completely around something.'"

"*Detour*," says Tony.

"*Encircle*," Bill suggests, still thinking of the globe.

"Forgot to say nine letters."

"How about *encompass*?" Catherine offers a longer alternative.

"*Encompass* fits. Now the clues going down. Number three is 'Have in the mind.'"

"*Know*," says Bill.

Peter shakes his head. "Five letters, second one is an *h*."

"*Think*," says Tony.

"I am thinking," cries Janie. Everyone laughs.

"Four down has ten letters: 'Devices originated after experimentation.'"

"That could be anything. Skip to the next clue," Bill urges.

"Okay, but four down is plural—'devices'—so the answer needs to end in an *s*. That means *told* is wrong for five across."

"Five across is *must*," says Tony firmly. "If someone is commanded to do something, they must do it."

Peter changes the letters. "Seven down is 'Lengthy.'"

"The clue or the word?" asks Janie.

"The clue." Peter consults the puzzle. "The word has four letters."

"*Long*," Janie responds.

"Eight down—five letters: 'Units of revolution around the sun.'"

"*Years.*" Everyone answers at once.

"Back to four down. Ten-letter word for 'Devices originated after experimentation.' So far, we have 'blank-blank-V-blank-N-blank-blank-O-blank-S.'"

"*Inventions,*" Janie answers.

Peter holds up the completed puzzle. "Anyone see the clue in here?"

"Try reading the answers in number order," Catherine suggests. "I saw that in a book once."

Peter reads out loud: "'Beginners everywhere think inventions must encompass long years.'"

"Nonsense." Kevin waves his hand.

"It sounds like a memory-aid thing," says Tony. He takes the crossword from Peter. "B-E-T-I-M-E-L-Y. The first letters of the words spell 'BE TIMELY.' The clock!"

The students turn to the front of the room, where a large clock on the wall shows that they have less than five minutes left to answer the question.

"Peter, hold this chair steady." Kevin climbs up and reaches his long arm toward the clock. "I can see the blue bag, but I can't reach it." He looks around. "Stand back, it's dunk time."

Kevin squats down, then jumps up in the air, as if jamming a basketball into a hoop. He swipes the blue bag from the top of the clock mid-jump, and lands in a graceful crouch on the floor.

He gives the blue puzzle bag to Linda. "I didn't come here to put puzzles together. Basketball is the only game I want to play. Later." He grabs an answer envelope, scribbles something down on it, and walks out the door without a backward glance.

Linda fits the final pieces into the puzzle and the picture becomes complete: a still life with a bowl of oranges, a vase of blue-purple flowers, and a handwritten note poking out of a purple envelope. The note says, "For a round seven."

"Two minutes, Catherine." Tony consults his watch. "Ready to submit?"

"Yes." Catherine shows the other students her answer. "I put all of our names on the envelope."

Tony smiles. "Maybe we should call you McClever after all."

Mr. Michael reassembles the nine test takers in his classroom. "The Golden Answer Award for this year's exam goes to Catherine McCleary."

Catherine looks pleased, but surprised. "I put all of our names on the envelope. How did I win?"

Mr. Michael smiles broadly. "Why don't you tell everyone the answer to the question, and we can find out together."

For the solution to this story, please turn to page 342.

WHIZ TANNER AND THE PILFERED CASHBOX

A Tanner-Dent Mystery

By Fred Rexroad

hiz! Joey! You're gonna wanna hear this!"

Bonnie Bachmann raced into Whiz's driveway and skidded her bicycle to a halt—just inches from where Whiz and I were leaning on ours.

"Bonnie . . ." Whiz remained unfazed even though she almost ran over us. "To what do we owe this excited entrance?"

"A crime . . . a big one . . . just committed . . . at the school fundraiser." She huffed and puffed as she tried to catch her breath.

"What happened?" I asked.

"Thorny stole the cashbox! Maybe Chuck, too. Just now! I heard it had over five hundred dollars in it."

"Thorny!" I let that out under my breath, and then a bit louder I added, "I knew he was no good. He probably needs the money for that drone with a panoramic camera he's been talking about for weeks."

"Let us not jump to conclusions, Agent K." Whiz, also known as Agent M, was the Chief Investigator for the Tanner-Dent Detective Agency, and one of his strong points was stepping back to analyze all the clues before jumping to a conclusion. But I guess it's not jumping if you've analyzed the clues first—is it?

"Well, it certainly looks like Thorny did it." Bonnie was still breathing hard. "He was the only one near the cashbox when it disappeared."

"Tell us the facts, Bonnie," said Whiz. "We need the what, when, and where of the situation."

"If she tells us the how and who, we'll have the five Ws that news reporters are always talking about." I gave a little chuckle, but nobody laughed. Well, I wasn't expecting a laugh from Whiz—he doesn't get most jokes anyway. But he did respond.

"You misunderstand the five Ws, Joey. However, if she knew the how and who we would not have a mystery to solve. Determining the method used and the perpetrator involved is our job. Please continue, Bonnie."

"Certainly, Agent M," she responded with a big smile. Whiz winced a little bit. He's very uncomfortable with our secret code names being known by civilians—and Bonnie was definitely a civilian. She did know our secret identities but, basically, she's cool about it. I don't think she's ever told anybody.

"Fill us in on the details as we ride," said Whiz. "We should visit the scene of the crime before too many clues become compromised."

With that, we rode off, Bonnie in the lead.

We rode fast. Bonnie and Whiz were ahead of me, so I didn't hear everything she told him.

What I did get was that there's a fund-raising event going on at the community center today. The Jasper Springs Combined School Parent-Teacher Organization was raising money to repave the track around the high school football field. Even though it's the high school's field, it actually sits smack in between the high school on one side and the elementary and middle schools on the other. We sixth graders use it as much as the high schoolers.

A couple of classmates of ours, Thorny—his real name was Arnold Rose—and Chuck Boyles—his real name may be Charles, but nobody's ever said so—were cashiers and sat at a table in the back corner with a couple of cardboard boxes full of coffee mugs and T-shirts in various sizes and colors. They also had a cashbox. Chuck left for a few minutes to take a bathroom break. When he returned, Thorny was digging through one of the boxes on the floor and there was no cashbox on the table. Everybody looked but they couldn't find it anywhere. Naturally, since Thorny was the only one near it, he got the blame.

I knew he would turn crooked someday. He and a few other kids have tried to join our detective agency since we started. Whiz and I actually let Thorny help on some of our minor cases—nothing important, of course, just legwork when we were too busy to do it ourselves. But I never really trusted him, and now I'd been proven right.

The three of us skidded to a halt in front of the bike rack at the community center. We locked our bikes to the rack and followed Bonnie toward the door where a Jasper Springs policeman, Officer Van Dyke, was entering. There was a small traffic jam at the door—nobody wanted to get in the cop's way. After the scene cleared, several kids came out, including Jennifer Patterson—a high schooler—who was carrying, of all things, a fishing pole, and Megan Fields, who had a big wad of paper towels wrapped around her hand.

"Gangway," yelled Tyrone, one of the high schoolers who referees our middle school soccer games. "We've got an injured woman here. Let 'er through." He acted like he was in charge, the way he did on the soccer pitch—he could be tough.

"Oh, stop that, Tyrone. It's just a little jab." Megan held up her wrapped hand as if that was supposed to prove something to Tyrone.

"Being hooked like a fish can be very dangerous," replied Tyrone. "You could get gangrene and lose your whole hand . . . maybe the arm. Or you could get tetanus. You know they call that lockjaw? If your jaw locks, you might not be able to talk again . . . or eat."

"It was just an accident." Jennifer grabbed Megan's arm and led her away. "Come on, Megan, my house is close by. We have plenty of bandages there."

The two girls rushed off with Tyrone right behind. He kept talking about how dangerous it could be as they got out of earshot. "Maybe you could get mercury poisoning . . . ya know fish have mercury in them and the last fish Jennifer caught may've had a lot."

When the crowd cleared, the three of us entered. Being a gentleman, I held the door for Bonnie—Whiz went in right behind her. I was still holding the door as two adults went in. Then I hurried in before anybody else got the idea I was their doorman.

The building was basically one big room like the cafeteria at school, but bigger and taller. At one end were food-serving counters with the kitchen behind them. To the side were the restrooms and a coat-check place. The ceiling was very tall so there was enough room to play basketball, volleyball, or other sports without the ceiling being in the way. They also had little cage-like catwalks and braces hanging from the roof so they could hang lights and string microphones when they used the place to put on plays. If you really tried, you could get a basketball stuck up on one of the catwalks. Then someone would have to go to the back of the kitchen and climb the ladder up to the catwalks to get it down. A very multipurpose building, and now a crime scene.

Whiz stopped dead as he entered the room. The two adults nearly knocked him over as they swerved around him. I've banged into him enough to learn to expect him to do the unexpected. Whiz looked everywhere. He analyzed and cataloged every inch of the big room. The guy has a photographic brain.

I looked over the big room, too. It was set up with a bunch of chairs facing the stage at the opposite end from the kitchen. There were supposed to be different acts going on all day: local bands, singers, actors putting on plays, a magician, poets and authors reading from their works, and almost anything else that a stage could be used for. They even had a raffle drawing about the time of the theft.

Thorny sat at the cashier's table and Officer Van Dyke was talking to him. Chuck stood next to Thorny. Nobody looked happy, especially Thorny. The rest of the people hung around in groups as they talked among themselves—I'm sure the topic in all the groups was who stole the money. Whatever was supposed to be happening at this event had stopped.

When he snapped out of his trance, Whiz walked directly toward the cashier's table where Thorny and Chuck were focused in on the cop.

"Hello, Officer Van Dyke," Whiz announced, as we got close.

The officer turned around, looking at Whiz and me—and Bonnie.

"Well, I should've known the Tanner-Dent Detective Agency wouldn't be far away."

"Crime news travels fast in Jasper Springs," Whiz replied.

"It just disappeared," said Thorny. "We've searched everywhere. Lots of people have searched. Some adults are watching the doors to see if anybody leaves with it. It just disappeared."

Whiz was looking around the whole time Thorny talked. At one point, he almost touched the table with his nose as he eyed the area around where the cashbox should have been. He even wiped his fingers along the tabletop—back and forth across some red spots that appeared to be drops of paint. He then looked closely at a small chunk of dirt he brushed up. He sniffed it and then brought it close to his lips and breathed in through his mouth. I thought he might stick his tongue out and lick it—but luckily, he didn't.

"Very interesting," he said. He sniffed the dirt again.

"Do ya think you can get some fingerprints off that piece of dirt, Whiz?" I let out a laugh, but nobody else did. I guess Thorny and Chuck weren't in a laughing mood. Bonnie smiled, but it was one of those girl-smiles that said "boys are so dumb." Tough crowd—I guess I needed to put a hold on making jokes today.

"Never laugh at a clue, Joey. Plenty of truth can be discovered in the smallest one."

This is where he would've called me Agent K if there wasn't a crowd of civilians around.

"How can a piece of dirt be a clue to a robbery?" I wondered.

"Perhaps it is not evidence of the robbery. But, until we know how this insignificant piece of dried river mud got on top of this particular table, we cannot rule it out as a valuable clue."

"It's just a piece of dirt. It's no more a clue than those drops of dried red paint."

"It is a grave mistake to assume what things are until you have had ample time to investigate . . . Agent K." He dropped his voice very low as he said my code name. He wanted to emphasize the importance of maintaining professionalism while investigating a crime. "For instance, did you notice that Officer Van Dyke is not wearing his own pants?"

At this, Officer Van Dyke turned away from his interrogation of Thorny and Chuck.

"Of course they're his pants," I said. "It's part of his police uniform."

"No, they most certainly are not his."

"How did you know that?" Officer Van Dyke asked.

"You mean they're not yours?" Bonnie asked. She looked at Whiz with her mouth wide open.

"I spilled coffee on myself this morning," the cop explained. "I didn't have a spare uniform at the station, so Patrolman Edwards loaned me a pair of pants. How did you know they weren't mine?"

"Simplicity, sir. Your uniform is always very neat and clean. You take pride in it."

"Yes, we all do."

"That said, the bottoms of these pants end well above your polished shoes and your belt cinches the waistline, leaving some folded pieces of excess material. Those pants obviously belong to a shorter man with a larger waist. Patrolman Edwards was my deduction. But enough of these games, we have a case to solve."

He immediately looked around again. His eyes went from Thorny to Chuck and then toward the kitchen. He continued analyzing and cataloging the whole room. After gazing at the ovens and dishwasher— I think he was looking for places the cashbox could be hidden—he moved his eyes toward the rest of the room. He seemed to stop at each door and window—probably examining potential escape routes, and he even looked up at the ceiling for a long time. I watched his head move as he looked along the air-conditioning ductwork, the catwalks, the lights, and each of the big fans. He turned away from the table and looked at the front of the room where the main activity had been taking place.

While he was doing this, a few kids and parents from around the room gathered around us. They knew that once Tanner-Dent was on the job the crime would be solved very quickly, and they wanted to see it. From the murmuring it was clear they thought it was Thorny—and it sure looked that way to me, too.

"Whiz." Bonnie nudged him to bring him out of Whiz World—he zones out a lot as he thinks. "Officer Van Dyke asked us a question."

"Oh, sorry, sir. We do."

"What?" His mind must have been very far away. "We do what?" I asked.

"Officer Van Dyke asked if the Tanner-Dent Detective Agency had a theory yet on the robbery. My reply is yes, we do."

"You actually heard him? I thought you didn't hear us when you were off in Whiz World."

"I hear everything, Joey."

"That's amazing," said Bonnie.

Officer Van Dyke jumped back in. "So what's your theory, Whiz?"

"First of all, it is our opinion . . ." He actually said *our*. He's like that. The whole agency—which so far is only Whiz Tanner and yours truly, Joey Dent—got credit for everything we do. ". . . that Thorny was not involved. At least not wittingly."

"See, it's just like I said," Thorny responded. "I was digging through the box of T-shirts and it disappeared. Hey, what do you mean by wittingly? I was not involved at all—wittingly or not wittingly, whatever that means."

"Well, don't look at me," said Chuck. "I didn't take it either. I went to the boys' room and it was gone when I got back. Ask Megan, here she comes—she was here when I got back and the box was already gone."

Megan and Jennifer came back inside followed closely by Tyrone—he'd stopped talking about Megan's arm falling off or strange diseases attacking her. Megan had a more normal-looking bandage on her hand this time. Chuck waved at them to come over.

"Megan, tell them that I was in the restroom when the money box disappeared."

Megan snorted a laugh. "I can't tell them that. The money box wasn't even on the table when I got here."

"Yes, it was!" Thorny almost shouted. "I just closed it when you asked about a purple T-shirt."

"Well, I don't remember. But I wasn't looking for a money box. I just wanted a purple shirt."

"You were the only one here when the box disappeared." Thorny's voice trembled as he spoke. I think he felt the evidence piling up against him, even though Whiz had already said he didn't do it.

"Nobody else was at the table," huffed the high schooler. "And I didn't see any money box."

"But you were here when it vanished!" Thorny yelled.

"No, I wasn't! You and Chuck were here when I came up to the table and you guys were here when I left."

"That's right," added Megan's friend Jennifer. "Did you see her carrying away a big ol' box full of money? Did she stick it in her pocket . . . or up her sleeve? I don't think so. Thorny might have put it in one of the

T-shirt boxes so he could get it later. In fact . . . come to think of it . . ." She stopped talking and looked at Chuck. "Chuck carried a box into the kitchen before he went to the restroom. I saw him."

"Is that so?" asked Officer Van Dyke. He looked at Chuck.

Bonnie and I looked to Whiz. We expected him to jump in and save our fellow middle schoolers, Thorny and Chuck. But he just stood there, silently soaking it all in.

"Did you carry a box into the kitchen, Chuck?" Officer Van Dyke moved closer to Chuck.

"Yes, sir . . . several boxes . . . the empty ones," Chuck answered very slowly. "I wasn't trying to hide anything. You can check the boxes."

"That will not be necessary," stated Whiz, finally getting back into the game. "But, to be thorough in our investigation, we must inquire about Tyrone's whereabouts."

The high schooler—who's twice as big as me and Whiz, maybe combined—bristled. "Oh, really, Whiz kid? You need to 'inquire' about my 'whereabouts.'" He was speaking in air quotes—something my sister started doing when she was in the tenth grade, also.

"Indeed, I do, Tyrone," said Whiz, not the least bit intimidated by a guy whose growth spurts must've had growth spurts.

"Okay, fine," said Tyrone. "After I bought my raffle ticket, I wasn't near the table . . . or even this side of the room. I was working on stage sets . . . moving things around for the shows. Everybody saw me helping with the raffle when all the commotion started back here."

"*Ha!*" laughed Chuck. "A very convenient alibi. My big sister told me that you're trying to get enough money to go on that theater-class field trip to New York. The cashbox had over five hundred dollars in it."

"That's why I'm here. The PTO is paying me and if I won the raffle, that's fifty more dollars," Tyrone replied. "That would go a long way toward the field trip."

"Maybe Tyrone did steal it," said Megan, suddenly turning on her friend who'd been so worried about her injury.

"Yeah," exclaimed Jennifer. "Five hundred dollars would pay for the whole New York trip—with some left over."

"Artists don't steal," Tyrone replied. Somehow, he didn't look so big and intimidating as he said this.

"This is so confusing," said Bonnie. "Are all your cases this complicated, Whiz?"

Agent M didn't respond. His big brain was off doing its big brain thing again.

"Let's summarize this," said Officer Van Dyke. He cleared his throat. "We have Thorny closest to the cashbox all morning; Chuck with him, but leaving the scene around the time it disappeared. Megan was at the table either just before, during, or just after—but nobody saw her carrying the box away. Jennifer was in and out of the kitchen and saw Chuck stash empty boxes. And last, but not least, Tyrone was in the vicinity, with motive, but has a pretty good alibi, if enough people vouch for his working on stage."

"You have summarized the pertinent facts quite accurately, sir," offered Whiz. "The people facts, anyway."

"Thank you, Whiz. It's always nice to get the blessing of the Tanner-Dent Detective Agency."

Officer Van Dyke was kidding, but he does listen to us when the other police officers won't.

"Ah, here comes my backup." Officer Van Dyke looked up toward one of the doorways as Patrolman Bailey entered the center. "I want you all to grab some chairs and make yourselves comfortable as Patrolman Bailey and I interview each of you—separately."

A small crowd had gathered. I guess they figured our interviews were more of the day's entertainment. Sort of like one of those CSI shows on TV.

"Interviews will not be necessary, sir," said Whiz. "I know where the cashbox is . . . and who took it."

We all looked at Whiz.

"Okay, Whiz," Officer Van Dyke asked. "Who did it?"

"Thorny did it," yelled someone from the back of the crowd.

"I did not!" Thorny yelled back.

"Thorny is innocent and I can prove it!" Whiz exclaimed.

"How?" Bonnie asked, just as I was about to ask the same thing.

Officer Van Dyke, who usually takes charge but had been pretty quiet during most of this little show, looked at Whiz. "Are you sure?"

"Absolutely," replied Whiz.

"Well, Van Dyke," laughed Patrolman Bailey. "It looks like I wasted my time responding to this call. Whiz and his trusty sidekick have it all wrapped up."

I've been called Whiz's sidekick more than once around Jasper Springs.

"He's often right, Bailey, so let's listen to him." Officer Van Dyke then got a very serious look on his face. "Be careful accusing someone of a crime, Whiz, but who do you think did this?"

"Watch who squirms, sir," he replied quietly.

For the solution to this story, please turn to page 344.

THE MAGIC DAY MYSTERY
By Bryan Patrick Avery

Stop him!" someone shouted. "Don't let him get away."

A pack of shrieking first graders rumbled out of the gym and into the hallway. They nearly trampled me as they hurried down the hall. Just ahead of them, a small white rabbit bounded down the corridor.

"Our exhibit is getting away!" screamed a terrified six-year-old.

The speedy white rabbit hopped around the corner to escape the mob, which now included several older students. A moment later, I heard a scream, followed by a loud crash. I ran down the hall to see what had happened.

Grace Owens, seventh grade class president, lay sprawled on the floor. Around her, several toppled first graders struggled to get to their feet. The rabbit was nowhere to be seen.

Grace stood up and brushed off her leggings and oversized T-shirt.

She shook her head as she walked toward me, wading through the sea of fallen first graders.

"First graders," she sighed. "I really do think Magic Day is just too much for them."

I nodded. Magic Day had been a school tradition at George Roberts Elementary ever since Arthur Waldini joined the faculty decades ago. Each year, Waldini put on a magic show for the students. Soon, students began bringing their own magic tricks to perform or to display in what was called the Magic Fair. This was all, of course, before Mr. Waldini, physics teacher, became the world-famous Great Waldini.

After Waldini left, gaining fame at the Magic Castle in Hollywood, the school kept up the tradition. Now every year, the second Tuesday in May is Magic Day.

"I'm looking forward to your show later," Grace told me. "Everybody is."

Without Mr. Waldini on staff anymore, the school hired a professional magician each year to perform. This year, because of my newfound celebrity, Principal Greeley asked me, Marlon "the Magician" Jackson, to perform.

That's right. I'm twelve and I'm a professional magician.

I should probably explain. When the drama club teacher saw how serious I was about magic, she email-introduced me to Waldini. We corresponded almost every day for months. He became my mentor and even got me an opportunity to perform at the Magic Castle.

The crowd at the Castle, of course, was stunned to see a black seventh grader, dressed in magician's robes and sporting an afro, performing magic on that classic stage. The place is like the Carnegie Hall for magicians. It's hard to get a gig there. Anyway, the club taped my segment, and when it was replayed on several daytime talk shows and YouTube, I'd become a minor celebrity, at least in the magic community.

I checked my watch. I had come to school extra early to get prepared. I only had an hour before the first bell rang.

"Marlon!" A voice echoed down the hall. "There you are, man. I've been looking everywhere for you. Come on! I want to show you something!"

Jose Hernandez ran up to us.

"Hey, Grace," he said, a little too loud.

Grace grimaced. "Morning," she replied.

"What's up?" I asked.

"You have to see this!" he said.

"See what?" Grace asked.

Jose looked at Grace, then at me. He grabbed my arm.

"Excuse us," he said.

Jose dragged me down the hall toward the gym.

"Jose?" I protested. "I've got to get ready for my show—"

"Just wait till you see this," he said. "You're gonna love it."

The gym was nearly deserted. Folding tables lined the walls, leaving a large open space in the center of the floor. When it was time for the shows the students would sit in the center. The tables along the walls would be used to display items kids had brought (like, oh, a white bunny rabbit in a cage with the door wide open) for the Magic Fair, which is sort of like a science fair but for magic. A few students had already set up their exhibits.

Jose raced to a table at the far end of the line. He pointed to a small black case on the table.

"Well," I asked. "What is it?"

"Just open it, Marlon," he insisted.

"This better be good."

I unzipped the case, lifted the lid, and looked inside.

"Well?" he asked.

"Well, what?" I asked. "It's empty. I mean the velvet lining is pretty but . . ." I turned the case toward him.

Jose's mouth flew open. His eyes bugged and his bottom lip quivered. I thought he might be having a heart attack or something.

"No, no, no, no, no," he finally sputtered. "This can't be happening." He dug around in the box. He shook it. He held it upside down and shook it some more.

"Um, Jose?" I said, putting a hand on his shoulder. "There's nothing in it."

He put down the case. He looked like he might hurl.

"My dad is gonna kill me," he said.

"Why?" I asked. "What was in the case?"

"My grandfather's antique cups and balls set. The one he took to Buckingham Palace!"

"Oh."

This was bad. Jose's grandfather was Felipe Hernandez, the famous Mexican magician who had performed for heads of state and royalty all around the world. When he died, he left his entire magic collection to Jose's father. The most prized item in the collection was a cups and balls set Señor Hernandez had used to perform for Queen Elizabeth II. The handmade copper cups were painted blue and inscribed with various Mayan symbols. As a magic lover (some would say freak) I knew they were one of a kind and totally priceless. Now they were missing.

"*The* cups and balls?" I asked. I was sort of flabbergasted. "The royal cups and balls?!! How did you convince your dad to let you bring them?"

"I didn't."

"What?"

"He doesn't know I took them. We've got to get them back, man!"

I looked around the room. More students had begun to come in and claim places at the tables.

"Don't worry," I said. "We'll find them."

I tried to sound confident, even though, inside, I was freaking out almost as much as Jose was on the outside.

Jose followed me backstage. I stuffed my magic case and my costume into a closet just behind the curtain.

"Okay," he said. "Where do we start?"

"Maybe we should tell Principal Greeley," I suggested.

"No! We can't do that! The first thing she'll do is tell my parents. We have to find them ourselves."

"Okay, okay. Let's start at the beginning. Tell me everything you did today, up to the second we discovered the cups and balls were missing."

"Okay," he said, squinting hard. "I got up. Had breakfast. Froot Loops. I, uh, caught the bus. Got off the bus. Came in here, set up my table. Went out into the hall. Saw you with Grace. Grabbed you, and we came straight here."

"You didn't stop anywhere?"

"No. I wanted to get a good table. The royal cups and balls set is a primo exhibit."

I looked around the gym. I wasn't exactly sure what made the table he picked a good table but I kept that thought to myself.

"And then?" I asked.

"Uh . . ." He thought for a moment. "That's it."

"So how did you end up in the hall instead of in here guarding your family heirloom?"

"Oh, that was because of the rabbit. It got away from the first graders. Thing jumped out of its hat, cleared the cage, and took off running into the hall."

"Yeah. I saw."

"It was chaos, man. Everybody went running out after it."

"Including you."

Jose nodded.

"I just left my stuff on the table and went out into the hall. That's when I saw you and Grace."

I picked up the case.

"You're sure the cups were in here when you left?" I asked.

"Positive. They're heavy. And the case weighs almost nothing."

He was right. The empty case was very light.

"Okay, who knew you were bringing the cups to school?"

"Nobody," Jose said. "I haven't shown them to anybody. Besides you, I don't think anybody at school even knows Felipe Hernandez is my grandfather."

I looked around the room again. I was out of questions. I had only one idea, and I didn't think it was a very good one.

"Well, let's go find the first graders," I said.

"You think they stole the cups?"

"I doubt it," I answered. "But what if that rabbit getting loose wasn't an accident?"

We found the first graders still wandering the hall searching for their rabbit. A boy named Colin was crouched down looking underneath the lockers. I knew his name was Colin because someone had stitched his name on the inside of his shirt and his shirt was inside out.

"Colin, can I ask you something?" I said.

He looked up at us.

"Not now. I'm looking for our rabbit."

"I know," I said. "That's what I want to ask you about."

"He got away."

Jose sighed loudly.

"Yes," I said. "But how?"

Colin lowered his head and studied the tops of his shoes.

"Colin?" I prodded.

"I didn't do it," he said. "I swear."

I squatted down so I wouldn't be towering over him.

"I believe you. Can you tell me who did do it? Who let the rabbit out?"

"It was Benny!" Colin blurted and then he ran off down the hall.

I had a few more questions, like, you know, "Who is Benny?" but I wasn't in the mood to chase after a six-year-old kid. Jose and I watched Colin race down the hall. When he turned a corner and disappeared, Jose sighed again.

"Great. Now all we have to do is find a first grader named Benny."

"That shouldn't be too hard," I said.

I walked down the hall a short way.

"Hey, Benny!" I shouted. "Is this yours?"

A smaller-than-average first grader ran over to us. His light brown afro bounced as he moved.

"What is it?" he asked.

"Are you Benny?"

He nodded. I reached over and plucked a small red sponge ball from behind his ear. His mouth dropped open. I handed him the ball.

"Wow," he said. He studied the ball, grinning from ear to ear.

"Now," I said. "Can you answer a question for me?"

He nodded but didn't look up from the ball.

"Why did you let the rabbit out of its cage?"

"I didn't." He studied the ball more closely.

"Benny?" I said. "Are you telling me the truth?"

Benny slowly looked up at me. He nodded. Then, out of nowhere, he started crying.

"Hey, that's okay," I said, trying to soothe him.

He cried louder. Jose inched away from us.

"*Unh-unh*," I told Jose. "You're staying right here."

He gave me another one of his sighs.

Benny tried to explain, but through the crying and blubbering, I couldn't understand a word he said.

"Look," I explained. "You're not in trouble. My friend lost something very valuable in all the excitement when the rabbit got out. We're just trying to figure out if there's a connection."

Benny took a long sniff and wiped his nose with the back of his hand. I pulled a multicolored (and very long) handkerchief from my sleeve and handed it to him. He wiped his nose with it, blew his nose, and wiped again. Then, he held it out for me to take back.

"That's okay," I said. "You can keep it. Souvenir of Magic Day. Now, about the rabbit?"

"It wasn't my idea. It was the big kid."

Jose and I waited for him to continue. And, of course, he didn't.

"Big kid?" Jose asked.

Benny shrugged.

"You don't know his name?" I asked.

Benny shook his head.

"What grade is he in?" Jose asked.

Another shrug.

"Can you describe him?" I asked.

Benny shrugged again.

"Do you remember anything about him?" Jose asked.

Benny smiled.

"He gave me this," he said. He pulled a dollar bill out of his pocket. It was folded in the shape of a rabbit.

I looked at the dollar and then at Jose. We both said "Chase Matthews" at the same time.

We found Chase Matthews in his usual spot in the school library. He sat at a small table with a stack of purple and green papers scattered in front of him. Next to the stack was a menagerie of small origami animals. Among the group were several rabbits just like the one in my hand. I dropped the rabbit on the table in front of him. He stopped folding and looked up.

"What's that for?" he asked.

"You tell me," I replied. "We got it from a kid named Benny this morning. Is it one of yours?"

He finished folding a giraffe and set it aside. He picked up the rabbit.

"And if it is?" he asked.

I pulled out a chair and sat down across from him. Jose stood behind me.

"If it is," I said. "Then I want you to tell me why you paid him to let the rabbit out."

Chase's face turned bright red. Jose stepped in closer. "Benny told us everything," he said. "Where's my stuff?"

Chase looked surprised.

"Who's Benny?" he asked. "And what stuff are you talking about?"

I plucked the rabbit out of his hands and held it up.

"Benny," I said, "is the kid you gave this to earlier."

"Oh." He chuckled. "I had no idea that was his name. But look, I didn't take your stuff."

Jose snorted. "Yeah, right."

"Then why did you want him to let the rabbit out?" I asked.

Chase looked from me to Jose and shook his head. He reached into his backpack and pulled out a large sheet of rolled-up paper. He handed it to me.

"It was just supposed to be a joke," he said.

I unrolled the paper. It was nearly ten feet long. Chase had painted a message on it. I had to read it a letter at a time as I unscrolled his banner. When I put the letters together, I got the message: "Magicians are Morons."

I shook my head. "Seriously? You would do this? On Magic Day?"

Chase lowered his eyes.

"Sorry," he mumbled. "It was just a dumb joke."

"This is why you wanted the rabbit let out?" I asked.

He nodded. "I figured everyone would be distracted by the bunny so I could sneak backstage and hang it. Like, what do you call it? Misdirection."

"That's not really misdirection, but okay."

"Wait a minute," Jose interrupted. "If that was your plan, why do you still have the poster?"

"Because it didn't work," he said. "That tall girl, I can't remember her name, didn't leave. She just sat there with her basketball. So I gave up. Like I said, it was just a stupid prank."

Jose looked at me as if to ask, "Do we believe this guy?"

I half-nodded, half-shrugged. I wasn't certain, but I was pretty sure he was telling the truth. Plus, he'd just given us a great lead. The tall girl with the basketball could only be one person: Madison Reilly.

We found Madison in the gym. She was wearing her usual basketball shorts and sweatshirt. Her blonde braids were pulled back into a ponytail. Her basketball sat in her lap.

"Hey," I said.

"Hey," she answered. She looked at Jose. "Who's this?"

Despite being the tallest kid in school by far, Madison was only in the sixth grade. She didn't know many kids outside of her class unless, of course, they played sports.

"This is Jose," I said. "He has a problem we hope you can help us with."

"What kind of problem?"

"I lost something," Jose explained. "It's really valuable, and my dad will kill me if I don't get it back."

Madison wrinkled up her nose. "And I can help you because?"

"Were you here in the gym this morning?" I asked. "When the rabbit got out?"

She nodded.

"Well," I continued. "We think that's when the theft happened."

Madison stood up, cradling the basketball under one arm. We both had to look up at her.

"Theft?" she asked. "I thought you said you lost something."

Jose winced.

"Somebody stole it, actually," I explained. "It happened after everyone chased the rabbit out into the hall."

"I still don't see how I can help you. Unless you think I'm the thief."

Jose started to speak. I held up my hand to stop him.

"We don't have any reason to think that," I said. "But we heard you were here. Did you see anything suspicious?"

She thought for a moment.

"There was a guy here, too," she said. "He was holding this big roll of paper. He looked like he was waiting for someone or something. Then he left."

"Chase Matthews," I said.

"Chase what?"

"It was Chase Matthews. He's an eighth grader."

"Oh," she said. "I don't know him. Do you think he did it?"

"Not really," I said. "Do you mind if I ask you a personal question?"

She shrugged. "I guess not."

"Why were you here this morning? It doesn't really seem like Magic Day would be your kind of thing."

"It's not," she said. "I forgot it was happening. I came in to practice free throws and found all these tables set up. So I'm doing visualization exercises instead."

I was out of questions. Jose, Madison, and I stood for a moment, staring at each other. Jose cleared his throat.

"I think, maybe, we should get going," he said.

"Right," I agreed. "Thanks, Madison."

We were almost out of the gym when we heard her shout.

"I almost forgot," she said. She trotted over to us. "There was someone else here, too."

"Who?" Jose asked.

"That kid who does the food videos," she said.

"Malik Smith?" I asked.

"I guess."

"We know him," Jose said. "What was he doing?"

Madison shrugged. "Just hanging around. Kind of like me. Look, I gotta go. I hope you find your magic cups." She dribbled her ball out of the gym and into the hall.

"Well, let's go find Malik," I said.

Benny, the first grader we'd met earlier, was waiting for us in the hall. He had a friend with him. His friend had bright red hair and matching freckles and, from his watery eyes and runny nose, I could tell that he had been crying.

"This is my friend," Benny said. His friend snorted and then pulled a handkerchief—my long multicolored handkerchief—out of his pocket.

"That's really his," Benny told his friend, pointing to the handkerchief. The kid blew his nose. It made a sound like a really long note on a really wet tuba. Then he held the handkerchief out to me.

"Here you go," he said.

"That's okay," I said. "Keep it. What's up, Benny? We're pretty busy."

"Did you find your stuff yet?" he asked.

"Not yet," I said. "Why?"

"This is my friend," Benny said again.

"Does your friend have a name?"

"It's Kyle," Benny said.

"Okay. What can I do for you, Kyle?"

"I lost something, too," Kyle said.

"That rabbit?" I asked. He shook his head.

"Not the rabbit," he said. "A magic wand. I went to help catch Xavier and when I came back it was gone."

"Who is Xavier?" Jose asked.

The two first graders looked at each other, then at us. Benny shook his head in disappointment.

"Xavier is our rabbit," he said.

"Oh," I said. "You left the wand in the gym and now it's gone?"

Kyle nodded. He looked ready to burst into tears again.

"That's not all," Benny said. "I heard a fourth grader lost her top hat and someone else lost a magic book."

Jose and I exchanged glances.

"Sounds like we've got a thief on the loose," I said.

"Let's go find Malik," Jose suggested. I shook my head.

"We're running out of time," I said. "I'll find Malik. You see if you can find out what else is missing."

Jose and Kyle both gave me the same sad puppy face.

"Don't worry, guys," I told them. "We'll find your stuff." I hoped I sounded more confident than I felt.

I found Malik Smith in the cafeteria kitchen. He had agreed to make the snacks for Magic Day. In exchange, Principal Greeley agreed to let him film everything for his YouTube channel.

He was hard at work, chopping onions for salsa when I got there. Pans of chicken nuggets and sweet potato fries filled the counter behind him. He wore his usual black-and-white-checkered pants and a chef's jacket. He stopped chopping when he saw me.

"Marlon the Magician," he said. "The man of the hour. What brings you here?"

I had a hard time seeing Malik as a thief, but I was running short of options. Still, I knew I needed to be careful. Malik was very protective of his "brand," as he called it. He would not be happy if I accused him of stealing.

"I need your help," I said. "Can I ask you a question?"

He went back to chopping the onions.

"Sure. What's up?"

"Were you in the gym earlier?" I asked.

"Yeah," he said, then shook his head. "Man, that rabbit. I've cooked rabbit before, but I never had to catch one. I had no idea they were so quick."

We both laughed, then Malik got serious again.

"What's this about?" he asked.

"During the commotion with the rabbit, some things went missing."

Malik glared at me.

"Dude," he said. "I hope you're not here accusing me of something."

I glanced down at the very sharp knife in his hand and shook my head.

"No, of course not. But I heard you were there. I thought maybe you saw something."

Malik stared at me for a moment, then looked down at the knife. He set it aside and his face softened.

"Sorry," he said. "You know how I am about my brand."

He thought for a moment.

"After everybody went running after the rabbit, I wasn't the only one who stayed behind."

I tried to pretend that this was news to me.

"The basketball girl was there," he said. "Madison something."

"Reilly," I said.

"Yeah. Her. And the guy who does all the origami. He had a huge piece of paper with him. Like he was going to fold something really big."

"Did you see anybody else around?" I asked.

He shrugged.

"I didn't see anybody else," he said. "There might have been someone backstage but, if so, I wouldn't have known. Anyway, the origami guy creeps me out, so I left."

He picked up the knife again and went back to work on the onions. A thought started to form in the back of my mind. Something wasn't quite right, but I couldn't put my finger on it. The first bell rang.

"You need to head to class," Malik said. "I need to make salsa."

"Yeah," I said. "Thanks for your time."

I turned to leave, then stopped.

"Malik," I said. "You didn't ask what went missing."

He didn't look up.

"Don't really care," he replied. "Besides, on a day like today, I'm guessing it was magic stuff."

I made it back to the gym just as the second bell rang. Jose sat alone, holding his empty case. Principal Greeley gave us permission to skip homeroom so that we could prepare for the show. Other than the two of us, the gym was completely empty.

"Did you find out anything?" Jose asked hopefully.

"Sorry. Nothing useful. You?"

He fished a piece of paper out of his pocket and gave it to me.

Cups and Balls

Magic Wand

2 decks of cards*

Magic Book*

Bag of sponge balls

Top Hat*

"This all went missing this morning?" I asked. "Somebody was busy."

He nodded.

"Everything was taken from inside the gym. But get this. The ones listed with stars were missing *before* the rabbit got loose."

That thought was still forming in my mind, but it wasn't quite clear.

"What now?" Jose asked.

"I'm not sure. It might be time to talk to Principal Greeley."

Jose started to protest, then stopped. He nodded.

"Let's get you ready for the show," he said. "We can talk to her after it's over."

I was in no mood to perform, but there was no way I could back out. Jose and I got my props organized and I practiced a few tricks to warm up. The whole time, I had a feeling I had seen or heard something that would crack the case, but I had no idea what it was.

The bell rang, signaling the end of homeroom, and kids started filing into the gym. The younger grades sat up front, with the older grades in the back. Soon, the gym was buzzing with excitement. I hoped I could deliver on their expectations.

Jose went to sit with our class, but not before saying "break a wand." He'd come up with his clever phrase several years earlier as an alternative to "break a leg" and I didn't have the heart to tell him that, in the magic world, a broken wand signifies a dead magician.

I'd put on my outfit for the show. It was my usual black pants, black shoes, and black T-shirt. Over that, I wore one of my magician's robes. This one was red with silver stars and moons to match our school colors. Like all my robes, I'd made it myself.

I stood behind the curtain as Principal Greeley climbed the steps to the stage. She reminded everyone about staying in their seats, keeping quiet, and respecting the performer. Then she cleared her throat.

"Now," she said. "We're all in for a treat. This year's magician is one of your fellow students. He's been mentored by none other than the Great Waldini, who, years ago, started our wonderful Magic Day tradition. Our magician has appeared on television and was even invited to perform for the governor. Please give a warm George Roberts Elementary Redtail welcome to Marlon the Magician!"

The curtain opened, and the audience cheered.

I started with the trick I use to open all my shows. I called Mr. Davis, the gym teacher, up on stage and handed him three ropes. They were all different lengths. After he declared there was nothing unusual about the ropes, I took them back. Holding the ropes between my hands, I slowly pulled until all three ropes were the same size. Everyone cheered. Mr. Davis's eyes bulged.

"Don't worry," I told him and gathered the ropes together in my left hand. With my right hand, I very slowly pulled the ropes apart. They were once again three different lengths. Mr. Davis snatched the ropes away from me, stunned. I let him take them back to his seat. He fiddled with the ropes for the rest of the show.

The show continued. I did my cups and balls routine, which reminded me there was a thief on the loose. It's an audience participation trick with giant sponge balls. I also made an impossible number of coins appear from nowhere and drop into a large metal can.

The kids and teachers seemed to love it. Still, I was distracted by the mystery I hadn't been able to solve.

For my finale, I had planned a mind-reading effect where four audience members write down the name of a famous person and I guess the names. It's one of my favorite tricks because it stuns people. With my mind still focused on the missing items, I called up my four suspects, Benny, Chase, Madison, and Malik. I gave them each a pad and a pen.

"I want you each to think of someone famous," I said. "Once you have someone in mind, write his or her name on the pad and make sure I can't see it."

I walked to the front of the stage, so my back was to my volunteers. When they finished, I raised my hand to my head and thought.

"Benny," I said. "You wrote SpongeBob SquarePants. Is that correct?"

"Yes!" he shouted. He turned his pad around to show the audience. He had mangled the spelling, but it was clearly SpongeBob. Plus, he'd drawn a very helpful picture.

Next, I called on Malik.

"You wrote Prince Harry," I announced.

"No way!" he exclaimed and turned his pad around.

"Madison," I said. "You were thinking of Wilma Rudolph, correct?"

"Correct!" She flipped her pad over to show that I was right.

That just left Chase.

"Interesting choice," I said. "You wrote Abraham Lincoln."

Chase was speechless. He slowly turned his pad around.

"Abraham Lincoln," he said. "How did you do that without seeing our pads?"

I started to give him my usual answer, then stopped. The thought that was building in the back of my mind became crystal clear, and I knew who the thief was.

"With your permission," I said to the audience. "I'd like to do one more thing. This morning, several items went missing from right here in the gym. I spent time investigating, but was unable to figure out who the thief was. Until now. I sense that one of you feels very guilty."

A murmur moved through the gym. The four students on stage with me looked at one another. Next to the stage, Principal Greeley stood with her arms folded across her chest. Her usual frown had been replaced by an even more severe frown.

I turned to the kids on the stage and pointed at one of them. "It's you. You're the thief!"

In the end, the solution was pretty easy. Nothing magic about it at all.

It was the thief's own words that helped me solve this mystery.

For the solution to this story, please turn to page 349.

PUZZLING IT OUT
By Eileen Rendahl

he numbers danced in front of Jeremy's eyes. He threw his pencil down. "I can't do this." He shoved his chair back, making a screeching noise. Everyone else in the room stared at him.

Ms. Sullivan looked up from her desk. "What's the problem, Jeremy?" Her warm brown eyes focused in on him as if he was the only person in the room. It was part of why he liked Puzzle Club. He felt appreciated here, valued. There weren't many places a seventh grader could feel like that.

"I can't do this."

Puzzle Club had been Ms. Sullivan's brainchild. She was new to Darbyville Junior High, like Jeremy was. Like everything seemed to be nowadays—new and unfamiliar and frustrating.

"How far did you get?" Ms. Sullivan walked over to Jeremy and looked over his shoulder at his paper.

Jeremy looked down at the scribbled and crossed-out numbers. "Not far."

Chloe Romero walked over, too, copper curls bouncing like springs.

"You're making it more complicated than it has to be. Break it into parts and it gets simple again."

"I don't understand." He crossed his arms over his chest, unwilling to look at the stupid squares again. "All I see is a bunch of numbers that could add up to anything."

"You have to train your brain to see patterns in numbers. Did you find the magic constant?" Ms. Sullivan asked.

"Yes." The magic constant was the number everything was supposed to add up to. That he'd figured out, but only because Chloe had told him how. "I added all the numbers up, then divided that number by the number of rows." One plus two plus three plus four plus five plus six plus seven plus eight plus nine equaled forty-five. Divide that by three and you got fifteen. He hadn't known what to do next, though. There were lots of combinations that could add up to fifteen, but which one was he supposed to put where and why?

"Let me show you a trick to use with magic squares that have an odd number of boxes." Ms. Sullivan took his pencil and wrote the numbers one through nine in a row. "Which one is the middle number?"

"Five." Did she think he was stupid? Anyone could see that.

"Put the five in the middle box." She handed the pencil back to him.

He did. "What do I do now?" He sounded a little angrier than he'd meant to. He was frustrated, though, and he hated to be frustrated. Like really, really hated it.

"What do you have to add to five to make fifteen?" she asked.

"Ten." Duh.

"Find different combinations that add up to ten and arrange them around the five." She stepped back. "Remember, you can only use each number once."

Jeremy made a list. One plus nine. Two plus eight. Three plus seven. Four plus six. The pattern began to emerge. He plugged numbers into different squares. After a few false starts, he ended up with:

8	1	6
3	5	7
4	9	2

Feeling pleased with himself, he looked over at Chloe's paper and saw her square. It had thirty-six slots! "How did you solve that?"

She shrugged. "I treated each set of nine like it was its own puzzle."

He shook his head. "I'm not good at this kind of thing."

"Doesn't mean it's not fun to try," Ms. Sullivan said.

"I think it's the definition of not being fun," he grumbled.

"Maybe you and Chloe could work together on a few. That might help." Ms. Sullivan went back to her desk and straightened the already neatly stacked papers.

Jeremy's face got warm. He didn't like having to ask for help. He didn't want to work with someone else. He wanted to be able to do it himself.

But it was time to go anyways. There was no point in arguing and no time to work another puzzle. After gathering up their stuff, Jeremy and Chloe walked to the bike racks, Chloe's flowered skirt fluttering in the afternoon breeze. Their bikes were the only ones left. They'd stayed longer at Puzzle Club than Jeremy realized.

He had one foot up on the pedal ready to roll when a noise caught his attention. He looked around. "Did you hear something?"

"I think so. Where did it come from?"

"Over there maybe? Around the corner in the faculty parking lot?" Jeremy got off his bike and wheeled it toward the lot. They got to the corner and peered around it.

Ms. Sullivan stood by her car, talking to a tall guy with blond hair cut short. Jeremy had never seen him before. Had Ms. Sullivan been the one who yelled? She was speaking in an animated way, her hands flying as she spoke. The man grabbed one of her wrists.

Jeremy stepped out from where they peered around the building. "Hey!" he shouted. "What are you doing?"

Ms. Sullivan and the man froze for a second, then turned toward Jeremy. "What are you still doing here? You should be on your way home," Ms. Sullivan said. She sounded angry. She pulled her wrist away from the man and ran her hand over her head as if to smooth her close-cut afro.

"We're just getting our bikes. Are you okay?" He took another step forward, not sure what it was he was going to do, or even why he felt like he needed to. He just knew that he did and that it was making his heart beat way too fast.

"Well, go on home," Ms. Sullivan said. "I'm fine." She made a shooing gesture with her hand. "I'm just taking care of some business. Get the picture?"

"You're sure?" he called. He wasn't sure what she meant by him getting the picture. It sounded weird, not like something she would usually say.

"Absolutely." Ms. Sullivan made the shooing gesture again.

Chloe made a gesture for him to follow her. They left, but Jeremy felt uneasy about it.

"Did the way Ms. Sullivan told us to leave sound weird to you? That bit about getting the picture?" Jeremy asked Chloe as they rode.

Chloe thought for a second. "Sort of. Does it matter?"

"I suppose not." It was one more thing he didn't quite understand. He added it to the list of his frustrations and dropped it.

The next day, Jeremy and Chloe had science with Ms. Sullivan third period. He didn't register something wasn't right until he was through the door of the classroom. The room was silent. Usually there was a happy buzz.

"Take your seats, please," a woman with long dark hair pulled back into a ponytail tight enough to stretch her cheeks a bit barked at Jeremy and Chloe as they walked in. "We have a lot to cover."

Jeremy looked at Chloe whose eyes were opened wide in surprise.

"Come on," the woman said. "We don't have all day."

Someone else was sitting in the desk he usually sat in.

"Find your name tag and sit in that seat, please. I've assigned you places to make it easier to take roll," the woman said.

Jeremy turned in a circle, finally spotting his name on a desk in the dreaded front row. He threw himself into the chair and looked around again. Chloe was behind him three rows and to his left.

The woman clapped her hands. "I'm Ms. Hobson." She wrote her name on the whiteboard and underlined it three times. "I'll be taking over this course for the foreseeable future."

Jeremy raised his hand. "Where's Ms. Sullivan?"

Ms. Hobson turned slowly. "Please do not speak until I call on you to speak."

Jeremy put his hand up in the air and waited. After what seemed like hours but probably had been thirty seconds, Ms. Hobson squinted at his name tag. "Yes, Jeremy?"

"Where's Ms. Sullivan?" he repeated.

"She's taken a leave of absence."

"Why?" he asked.

She cocked her head to one side, like a bird looking at a worm it was about to eat. "I don't think that's really any of your business, Jeremy."

He was about to ask another question, but she spoke over him. "Take out your textbooks, please, and turn to page sixty-four. Lindsey, would you please read the first paragraph."

Class with Ms. Hobson had been excruciating. They'd read the text-book out loud. Each one taking a turn. No questions until they'd read the whole chapter. Jeremy's eyes had started to cross he was so bored by the time they finished.

"No way Ms. Sullivan would take a leave of absence and not tell us she was going," Jeremy said to Chloe as they left the classroom.

Chloe shrugged. "Grown-ups are weird. You never know what they're going to do."

It still didn't sound right to Jeremy. The weird grown-up thing was right, but not Ms. Sullivan. She was . . . different. Special. She cared about them. She wouldn't take off without telling them or leaving some kind of message. "Maybe something happened to her and they don't want to tell us. Maybe something with that guy from the parking lot."

Chloe dialed the combination on her locker and it sprang open like it had been booby-trapped. The duffel bag she'd shoved in earlier dropped out and her volleyball bounced across the courtyard. Chloe chased the ball while Jeremy picked up the duffel. As he bent over, he noticed something else next to Chloe's locker. A puzzle piece.

He held it up. "Is this yours?"

Chloe shook her head. "Never saw it before."

Jeremy shoved it in his pocket and they walked to his locker to leave his science notebook and retrieve his copy of *Wonder*. There were two puzzle pieces of about the same size as the ones at Chloe's locker under the book.

By lunchtime, they had found twenty-five puzzle pieces tucked everywhere from Jeremy's clarinet case to Chloe's gym locker.

"What do you think it means?" Chloe asked, moving the pieces around on the metal table where they ate lunch.

"I think it means we're supposed to put the puzzle together," Jeremy said.

"Great," Chloe said. "Let's do it."

"It's only twenty-five pieces. I can do it faster by myself." He looked for the colors and lines and shapes that went together. They leaped out at him the way numbers apparently leaped out at Chloe.

"Is that a picture of the rock wall in Gulch Park?" Chloe asked.

It sure looked like it.

"What should we do?" She leaned over the picture. Her curls tickled at Jeremy's nose.

"Ms. Sullivan asked if we got *the picture* and now there's a picture right in front of us. I think we should go there after school to find out."

Gulch Park was a few blocks out of their way on their regular route home. The rock wall from the puzzle stood at the edge of the park close to a set of picnic tables under some shade trees.

"Now what?" Chloe asked.

"I'm not sure." Jeremy got off his bike and slipped off his helmet. He pulled out his phone and found the photo he'd taken of the assembled puzzle. Chloe looked over his shoulder.

"I'm not seeing anything special. It's just a photo of the wall."

She was right, mainly. It was a photo of the wall, but it was taken at a different angle from where they were standing. "Maybe if we stand wherever the picture was taken from, we'll see something." He walked to his left. He was close, but it wasn't quite right. He backed up a few steps and clunked into a tree trunk. "Ouch!" He rubbed his head.

Chloe walked over to look again, too. "They were higher up when they took it."

Jeremy turned around and looked at the tree. "Do you think it was taken from up there?" He pointed at a branch almost within his reach.

"Maybe," Chloe said, standing on her tiptoes as if that would help.

"Only one way to find out, I guess." He put his phone away, rubbed his hands together, crouched down, and then jumped, managing to catch onto the branch. He planted his feet against the trunk and pulled himself up, wriggling onto the branch so he was straddling it.

"I could have given you a boost," Chloe said, arms akimbo as she looked up at him.

"I didn't need one." He took out his phone to look at the picture again and then looked at the rock wall. "This is it," he called to Chloe.

"Do you see anything?"

He looked around. Why would someone lead them here? He was about to climb back down when he saw a piece of ribbon tied around a twig a little farther out on the branch. He inched forward, stretching out. Good thing he'd had that growth spurt. He snagged the ribbon and tugged. It came free, bringing an envelope with it. He tucked it into his pocket and swung down from the branch to drop to the ground next to Chloe.

"What did you find?"

"I'm not sure." He pulled the envelope out and opened it. There were two folded pieces of paper inside. The top one was slick, like a page from a magazine. It was from a publication for employees of Dynamic Recreational Inc. with an article about their employee of the month, Lorinda Clarkson, a research chemist in the quality assurance department. Jeremy hadn't heard that name before, but he knew the face. "That's Ms. Sullivan!"

"I've heard of that place. What does Dynamic Recreational do?" Chloe asked. "And why would Ms. Sullivan pretend to be a research chemist for them?"

Jeremy tucked the article back into his pocket. He'd heard the name of the company, too. They'd been in the news. He'd look up the details when he got home. He unfolded the second piece of paper. It had a series of letters and pictures on it.

W + 🐬 - F + 💍 - R + W + 🔔 - 🐝

"What's that?" Chloe scowled at the piece of paper.

"It's a rebus." They'd done those before in Puzzle Club. A rebus combined pictures and letters to create words in unexpected ways.

Jeremy spread the paper out on a nearby picnic table and pulled a pen out of his backpack.

He wrote down "Wfish," then crossed out the *F* to get *Wish*. Then added ring to get *Wishring*. Take the *r* away and you had *Wishing*. He was pretty sure what the next word would be, but he worked the puzzle anyway. *Wbell* minus a *b* equaled *Well*.

He turned to Chloe. "The next clue is at the wishing well."

She peered over his shoulder. "The one at the grocery store?"

Jeremy gave her a look. "You know another one?"

She shook her head. "Nope."

Jeremy folded up the papers, stuffed them back in his backpack, picked up his bike and pointed it in the direction of the grocery store. "Let's go."

"Now?" Chloe got back on her bike, too, but didn't turn it to face toward the grocery store.

"Why not?"

"Because my mom will kill me if I'm not home in the next fifteen minutes."

Jeremy pulled out his phone and looked at the time. More time had gone by than he'd realized. His parents would be none too pleased if he was much later either. "Meet me there before school?"

Chloe sighed. "That's so early! Can't we go after?

"Don't you have volleyball practice?" Sometimes Jeremy thought he knew Chloe's schedule better than she did.

"Oh, yeah. See you there."

✦ ✦ ✦

Jeremy got home just in time to wash his hands and set the table for dinner. That, plus the actual dinner, plus helping his little sister clear felt like it took a bazillion years, even though it was only six thirty when he finally got to the computer and looked at the clock.

He plugged Dynamic Recreational into the search bar and hit return. The company website was big and colorful with tabs for brands and news and contact forms. The brand that took up the biggest part of the page was Origanisms, little stuffed animals that burst out of cubes if you entered the right codes. They'd been insanely popular last year. There'd been so much trading back and forth their sixth grade teacher banned kids from bringing them to school. He went back to the search results.

Over the next five entries he learned Dynamic Recreational was being accused of releasing toys that contained an unsafe chemical called chthalones. Someone from inside the company—a whistleblower—had tipped the government off there was something wrong with the Origanisms. The court case was scheduled to start tomorrow right here in Darbyville.

Jeremy typed Lorinda Clarkson into the search bar. The first item was a link to a professional networking site. He clicked on it. It was definitely Ms. Sullivan. Why would she be pretending to be Lorinda Clarkson? Finally, it dawned on him. Maybe it was the other way around. Maybe Lorinda Clarkson was pretending to be Ms. Sullivan.

The next morning, Jeremy pulled up to the wishing well in front of the grocery store. Chloe arrived five minutes later. "Now what?"

"I'm not sure. Do you see anything out of place?" he asked.

Chloe gazed around. "Do you think we have to climb a tree again?"

"There really aren't any." Jeremy wheeled his bike closer to the fountain, then walked around it. If he hadn't really been looking, peering down into the well, he would have missed it. Another ribbon like the one that had been attached to the tree tucked up under the concrete rim. He pulled it.

Another envelope. They sat down on one of the nearby benches and opened the envelope. They found a letter addressed to Chloe and him.

I'm sorry to make this difficult, but this information mustn't fall into the wrong hands. You've figured out who I am by now. I was put in a witness protection program until it was time for me to testify in the case against Dynamic Recreational.

Someone has betrayed me, someone from the inside. I've been suspicious for a while. I'd planted most of these clues as a fail-safe, knowing that I could quickly hide the puzzle pieces for you to find to start you on this journey. I couldn't leave plain directions in case someone else found them before you did, so I made them into puzzles and then made sure you would know how to solve them. I hid the data, too. I didn't want it to be on my person.

I'm not sure who to trust, except you two. I don't know who or where along the line the traitor is. I do know this, though. I need someone to bring me copies of the data that proves Dynamic Recreational knew Origanisms were dangerous and released them anyway, someone they would never suspect, someone they won't be watching.

There's one more puzzle for you to solve to get the data. It's in the BEST MEAN place.

Once you have it, bring it to me at 9 a.m. on Wednesday at the Darbyville Courthouse.

Ms. Sullivan/Clarkson

It was Wednesday and 9 a.m. was less than an hour away.

Chloe and Jeremy stared at each other. Did he look as shocked with his mouth hanging open like hers was?

Chloe pulled her feet up onto the bench and looped her arms around them. "We've got to tell our parents. We've got to find a grown-up to help."

Jeremy chewed his lip. "What would your parents do if you told them?"

Chloe stood up and began to pace. "Probably call the police."

"Mine, too." He rubbed his eyes with the heels of his hands. "Don't you think Ms. Sullivan—or Ms. Clarkson or whoever she really is— would have gone to the police if she thought she could trust them? Besides, there's no time."

Chloe kicked at the ground as she walked. "Who else could we go to? Principal Brethington?"

Jeremy shook his head. "He could be in on it, too. Dynamic Recreational has a ton of money. They could buy a lot of people's cooperation."

"But not Ms. Sullivan's."

"Not Ms. Sullivan's. Because she's one of the good guys. She's one of the people trying to keep kids safe and she needs our help to do it."

"Where do you think she means when she says the BEST MEAN place?" Chloe took the paper from him.

"It's got to be something with those letters," Jeremy said, casting through his mind for different kinds of puzzles they'd worked.

Chloe twirled one curl around a finger and tapped her feet, clear signs she was thinking hard. "Could it be an anagram?"

Jeremy took the paper back from her. "Yes. I bet that's exactly what it is."

He grabbed a notebook and a pen from his backpack and wrote down the letters:

BESTMEAN

He separated out the vowels from the consonants:

AEE

BSTMN

"Not many vowels there," Chloe observed.

"That means we need some of those consonants to pair up."

"There's S-T." She pointed.

"Would she have them together in the clue if they were together in the solution?" Jeremy asked.

"Probably not. It would make it too easy."

"What else could go together?"

"N-T?" Chloe suggested.

Jeremy wrote those two letters together and put an *E* in front of them to make E-N-T. "It's a place. Remember to think about places."

"Bent, sent, ment," she muttered.

"Ment!" Jeremy said. "What's left if we take out *MENT*?" He crossed letters out and came up with A-E-B-S.

In unison, they said, "Basement!"

"Which basement, though?" Chloe said.

Jeremy said. "It's got to be some place *we* can get to."

Once again, they spoke in unison. "School!"

Jeremy stood up. "Let's go."

It had been easy to get to the school basement. They'd just ridden to school, locked up their bikes, and walked in like it was any other day. It was 8:20 and lots of kids were arriving, streaming in and out of the school and going to their lockers. Chloe and Jeremy waited by the door for a moment when no one was near and scampered down the steps.

"What do you think we're looking for?" Chloe asked.

Jeremy looked around at the stacks of boxes, garbage barrels, mops and brooms and buckets, and bins of flat basketballs and soccer balls. He turned in a circle. There were so many places someone could hide something in here and they didn't have much time. So far, everything Ms. Sullivan had left for them as a clue was something other people might not notice if they weren't really looking. She wouldn't have made it obvious, but she wouldn't have made it impossible either. He chewed his lip. "Something that sticks out, but not too much. Something that's just a little out of place."

They walked the perimeter of the basement. It was lined with lockers similar to theirs, except these all had the kinds of padlocks that used keys instead of combinations. Except one. One locker had a combination lock. "Here," Jeremy cried. "This one. No one would notice the different lock unless they were really looking."

Chloe pulled on the combination lock. It didn't give. "How are we supposed to open this? How are we supposed to know the combination?"

Jeremy looked around. A little corner of white paper peeked out of one of the slots in the locker. Jeremy crouched down, grabbed the envelope corner and wiggled it out. He opened it up.

There was a square. A three-by-three grid with the number nineteen written in the center square. The squares of the middle row were outlined in red. Three numbers. Most combination locks had three numbers.

To find the combination to the lock, they had to solve the magic square.

For the solution to this story, please turn to page 351.

THE MECHANICAL BANK JOB

By Mo Walsh

I **wedged a penny in** the little dog's mouth and pressed a lever. The black terrier sprang through a silver hoop held by a clown in an old-fashioned yellow costume. With a metallic clink, the dog dropped my penny into a slot in the top of a red barrel.

It wasn't a video game, but it was still pretty cool.

"Good choice, Jill," said Mrs. Herzog, our fifth grade teacher. "The antique Trick Dog bank has always been one of the most popular." She handed a penny to the next student in line, who just happened to be my best friend, Kasey Aziz. She slid her penny into an elephant's trunk and pressed on its tail. The trunk curled up over the elephant's head and the penny plopped through a slot in the brightly colored seating platform strapped on its back.

Benny Tosca was up next. There were six mechanical banks spread out on the project table in our fifth grade classroom. Benny went with the firefighter. The squat figure with a wide red mouth sort of looked like he was ready to barf into his hand. It rolled its eyes, lifted its palm, and tossed a penny into its opened mouth.

No wonder the firefighter looked queasy. He had a stomach full of loose change.

"Imagine how children in the late eighteen hundreds and early nineteen hundreds would have been mesmerized and fascinated by these banks," said Mrs. Herzog.

Fascinated by cast-iron characters with one move? Mesmerized by clunky toys with one trick? Maybe. These were the same kids who rolled hoops and held tea parties for dolls. No PlayStation, iTunes, or even basic cable. And they totally missed *Fortnite.* Poor kids.

"The original idea was to encourage American children to be thrifty and save their pennies," Mrs. Herzog continued. "But these toy banks soon became very popular with adults, too, for the artistic designs and mechanical ingenuity."

Educational toys the parents love. Some things never change.

"They're pretty heavy," said Benny, even as he showed off by hefting the firefighter bank in one hand. "Are they made out of lead?"

"No, but that's a good guess, Benny. This is cast iron—iron melted with other substances and poured into a mold to harden. When all the pieces are put together, each bank weighs several pounds." She nodded to the three of us at the table. "Go ahead and pick them up—with *both* hands this time, Benny."

Ooof. They *were* kind of heavy. Sort of like garden gnomes that ate pennies.

Mrs. Herzog laughed to see us struggling to hoist the banks off the table.

"That's why I needed a few other teachers to help me carry them from my car this morning and then bring them in here from the teachers' lounge."

Kasey picked up a bank that looked like a rooster, winced, and put it right back down. She didn't pick up another one but traced a finger over the elephant. I grabbed a bank that showed the prophet Jonah pitching a penny into the mouth of a whale. A thank-you, maybe, for spitting him out of its belly. I could lift the bank off the table, but not very high, and I sure didn't want to drop it on my toes!

Benny set down a bank that looked like a carousel horse and hefted the firefighter figure, again. I think it was his favorite.

"That bank is one of the heaviest," said Mrs. Herzog. "About seven pounds."

"Oh," groaned Benny, pretending to strain as he put it back on the table. When it touched down, he said, "Crushed it," and flexed his arm muscles—not that he really has any.

"Because they're so sturdy, the figures don't break easily," Mrs. Herzog told us. "But some of the smaller pieces can snap off and get lost, and the mechanisms need special care. Most of the original banks, the true antiques, have missing or replacement pieces. The paint is chipped and worn, or they've been repainted. Still, there are collections of banks in very good or excellent original condition."

"Mrs. Herzog?" I asked. "How many banks do you have?"

"Well, Jill, these six come from the replica collection my father started. Altogether, I guess I have about fifty. That may sound like a lot, but there were hundreds of designs made and each bank was hand-painted, so there was even more variety." She pointed to the clown with the hoop and jumping dog. "For instance, if the clown's suit is painted black, it's worth a lot less to a collector. If the suit is yellow, it will sell at auction for one or two thousand dollars."

"Whoa," I said. I think I whistled, too.

Mrs. Herzog smiled. "Yes, Jill. Yellow clowns like this one are quite rare."

I nodded. "And quite expensive, too." Not to mention ugly. The yellow color made me think of the stuff that comes out of squashed caterpillars. Why not a bright red or purple clown?

Mrs. Herzog rummaged in her big teacher's tote bag and pulled out several slick colored magazines. "You'll see just how serious some collectors are from these auction catalogs." She handed them to Kasey, Benny, and me. "Please pass them around. Next group!"

The next three kids shuffled up to the table to fool around with the banks.

Kasey and I compared photos and prices of some of the coolest banks in the catalogs. We couldn't believe what we were reading!

"Seriously? Who would pay five thousand dollars for a bank that looks like a bank building?" I said. "I'd rather have this lion chasing two monkeys up a tree. And it's only *three* thousand."

"This one's really pretty," said Kasey, pointing to a white trick pony with a colorful saddle and bridle cloth. "Whoa! Only nine *hundred* dollars!"

"Maybe you could pay for it a penny at a time," I joked.

"When I have a lot of money," Benny whispered behind us, "I'm going to buy fun stuff like this fort bank with the cannons and the top-of-the-line VR set and a bunch of sports cars, instead of stupid watches and fancy suits."

"I'm going to buy horses," said Kasey with that dreamy look she always gets for cute animals. "What about you, Jill?"

"I'll ride your horses and race around in Benny's sports cars, but when I have a ton of money I'm going to see the world: Scotland, Egypt, Australia, Japan . . ."

I looked up at the one hundred paper origami cranes dangling from the ceiling grid above our heads. We all made them by folding paper when Lucy Sato brought in a rice paper scroll with two cranes drawn in delicate colored ink. I didn't think cranes did much flying or traveling in flocks, and some of ours were shaped kind of oddly, but they looked a lot better than the bare ceiling panels. And yeah, folding paper into birds and other animal shapes was actually fun.

Every Friday during Social Studies we had the You-Nique Road-show, when we got to bring in stuff to share with the class. Instead of regular show-and-tell, it had to be something special to your family. That's the social studies part. Even Mrs. Herzog got in on it. That's why she brought in her dad's old bank collection. There's fun stuff to do, too, like making the origami cranes.

The wall above our cloakroom was lined with the bright carpet designs we colored when Kasey brought in a small Moroccan rug, like the larger ones that hang on the walls in her home. They put them there, Kasey said, because they're too pretty and too valuable to walk on. When it's my turn, I think I'll bring in the tartan scarf Dad gave Mom when they got married. It's the Macneil of Barra pattern my great-great-great-ancestors wore in Scotland. Dad's got a tartan tie and a cap, but no kilt. That would be *sooo* embarrassing. Mrs. Herzog says we can create our own tartan patterns on a computer and print them for class decorations. I already know Kasey's will be pink and purple. She still likes the girlie colors.

Brrring! Brrring! Brrring! Just as the next group finished playing around with the banks, the school bell sounded in three short bursts, paused, and then rang three more times.

"Fire drill!" announced Mrs. Herzog. "Boys and girls, you know what to do."

I'll say. Mulvihill Middle School had already run three drills for Fire Prevention Month. Don't they think we've got it already?

1. We left everything at our desks and lined up single file by the door.
2. Mrs. Herzog checked the door for heat, then nodded for us to go out to the hall.
3. She closed the door behind us and led us at a brisk walk down the hallway—not too fast, not too slow.
4. We went out the side door and around to the front parking area to our assigned meeting spot.
5. We sat on the ground while Mrs. Herzog took attendance. All present.
6. We waited.

"It figures we'd have a fire drill when we were doing something semifun," I grumbled to Kasey, if it's possible to grumble in a whisper. "By the time we get back to class it will be time for Spanish. After Spanish is lunch and then math."

"I want to look at the banks some more," Benny complained. "I didn't get to feed pennies to the whale. Do you think Mrs. Herzog will let us skip math?"

"We have a test today, Benny," I reminded him. "What do you think?"

"Some kids haven't had any chance to look at the banks at all," Kasey interrupted before Benny could think of a snarky answer. She's our referee. "I bet she'll bring them back in on Monday. That's just fair."

Across the parking lot, Mr. Diallo, our principal, jogged toward the school's circular driveway. The sound of sirens swelled, and two police cars turned into the drive, followed by two fire trucks, a red SUV marked "Fire Chief," and an ambulance. "That's weird." I turned to Kasey. "Isn't the fire department supposed to be here *before* the drill?"

Kasey brushed her wavy black hair behind her ears, something she usually does when she's excited or nervous. "What if it's not a drill? What if there's a real fire?"

Benny pumped his fist in the air. "Maybe we'll get a long weekend! Maybe a whole week off school while they clean up the mess. *Woo-hoo!*"

I wrinkled my nose. "But if the school burns down, we might have to go to class in trailers, *in the winter*, until they build a new one."

Half anxious, half excited, we looked for smoke or any other signs of fire.

Mr. Diallo broke away from the fire chief and crossed the parking lot. He huddled with the school office staff and the teaching specialists who were all grouped together. Then he walked from one class group to another, speaking quietly with each teacher in turn. When Mr. Diallo reached our class, his usually pleasant face was creased in a frown. He turned aside with Mrs. Herzog for a hush-hush conversation.

By this time, the student buzz had reached our line.

"They say somebody pulled the fire alarm!" I whispered to Kasey.

"*Whoa*, somebody's going to be in trouble!" Benny sounded excited, since it wasn't him for a change.

"Boys and girls!" All of our eyes swiveled to Mrs. Herzog. "The fire department has cleared the building, so we will return to the classroom the same way we left, quietly in single file. Please stand!"

Since there was no fire, I don't know why I expected anything to look different. We walked through the same old door and down the same old hallway to our classroom.

"Benny, hold the door," said Mrs. Herzog. "Fifth grade, go in and get settled. I'm going to the office, but I'll be back in two minutes." Her heels made a loud *clack-clack* on the tile floor as she kept walking down the hall.

I figured the teachers were all meeting about the false alarm. In the principal's office. Somebody was *really* in trouble.

Benny opened and held the door, and the first kids entered our classroom. The line suddenly stopped moving.

"They're gone! The banks are all gone!" said a voice from inside the classroom. A bunch of others joined in: "Where did they go?" "Who took them?" "Where are they?" "Look behind the desk . . ."

"On the floor—"

"In the closet!"

Kasey and I pushed our way into the classroom. "Hey, the window's open!" cried Kasey.

"That's how the thief got away, I bet," said Benny.

It looked like the thief pulled our teacher's desk chair over to the long sill that stretched below all three windows. It was positioned directly under the open one in the middle. Books lined up on that part of the sill were knocked over or scattered on the floor.

"Quick!" I shouted. "Can you see anyone out there?"

In two seconds every kid in class crowded around the open window. I locked elbows with Kasey and Benny and we forced our way through to get a good look. This side of the school faced an eight-foot-high wall with only ten feet of scraggly grass in between. The wall was supposed to be a noise barrier to keep sounds from the nearby highway from bothering us. Mostly it was just boring and ugly to look at.

I climbed up on the seat of the chair and crawled onto the window-sill. Kasey grabbed onto my ankles as I poked my head out the window. "They knocked a couple of books out onto the grass, and something else is down there, too. It's . . ." My voice rose in excitement. "It's the fireman bank, the really heavy one! They dropped it!"

Sure enough, I had spotted the firefighter bank lying in the grass below, faceup, as if waiting for more pennies to gobble up. Closer to the building, some of the books from our classroom reading library were jumbled together in a heap. I also spied four or five squashed paper cranes with their strings trailing across the grass. I pulled my head back through the window and looked up at the ceiling. There was an empty spot near the windows where the thief must have become tangled in their strings and pulled them through the window.

"Fifth grade! What is going on?" Startled, I slid from the window-sill, knocking two more books and a couple of cranes to the floor.

"Somebody stole your banks," Benny shouted. "The thief went out the window!"

By then a dozen pointing fingers had directed Mrs. Herzog's attention to the project table. She stood completely still, her hand covering her mouth, her eyes staring at the empty space where there had been six mechanical banks.

"They didn't get them all, Mrs. Herzog," said Kasey in a soft, soothing tone. "They dropped the firefighter bank outside. I'm sure the police can get the others back, too."

I wanted to tell her about everything I'd seen from the window, but Kasey shushed me and whispered, "Wait!"

Mrs. Herzog spun around from the table, and with a slight tremble in her voice, said, "Fifth grade! Take your seats, please." Then she picked up the phone to the school office.

Every kid sat down, but every head was turned to the back of the room, toward the open window.

"I bet Mr. Diallo gets the cops in here," whispered Benny from behind me. "Maybe they'll take all our fingerprints. Maybe they'll bring in the K-9 dogs!"

"They won't be arresting anybody in here," I said. "Nobody in class could have taken the banks. We were all together after the fire alarm. None of the students could have done it, or any of the classroom teachers either. We were all out in the parking lot where we could see each other."

"Then who—?" Kasey broke off at a knock on the door. Mrs. Herzog opened the door to admit the principal.

"Good morning, Mr. Diallo," we all said, the way we were supposed to when any adult came into our class.

"Good morning, boys and girls," he replied in his soft Caribbean accent. "Mrs. Ling will be taking you to the library for the rest of the morning and then down to lunch. After recess, she will supervise your class as you work quietly in the library."

Behind me, Benny whistled between his teeth. "I bet the cops are coming! I wish we could watch!"

"Class," said Mrs. Herzog, "please clear off your desks and take everything that you will need this afternoon and at home tonight." Our teacher's voice lacked its usual cheerful note, and she barely looked at us as she stacked notebooks on her desk and packed pens and a stapler away in her drawer.

"They're clearing the crime scene!" said Benny in his creepy whisper. "Told you!"

We gathered our books and followed Mrs. Ling, the assistant principal, upstairs to the library. We barely had time to drop off our things before it was time for lunch. As soon as we were through the cafeteria door and free to speak, the guessing started. Everyone had ideas about who might have taken Mrs. Herzog's banks and how to catch them.

"I want to know how the thief carried them away," said Benny. "Even without the heaviest, the firefighter bank, he—"

"Or she!" Kasey corrected.

"*They,*" said Benny, sticking out his tongue, "had to carry fifteen to twenty pounds of cast iron."

"They'd clank a lot, too." Kasey wrinkled her nose. "The thief had to be really sneaky."

"Let's try to figure this out over lunch and recess," I suggested. Kasey and I both like mystery books and puzzle games, but we'd never had a chance to work on one in real life.

"I have some ideas—and a notebook to write everything down," said Benny, flipping open the notebook he keeps in his pocket for drawing monsters and aliens (usually when he's supposed to be working in class). "You can't work on the case without me."

Kasey raised her eyebrows at me. I replied with a tiny nod. "Okay, you're in," I said.

"Great! I totally want to nab this perp!"

I plunked my lunch tray down in our usual spot—mine and Kasey's—and unpacked my sandwich of the day, ham and sweet pickle relish on pumpernickel. I automatically traded my apple for Kasey's cherry yogurt. (I like apples, but not how the peel gets stuck in my teeth.) Benny slid in next to Kasey and pulled one of those packs of pepperoni, cheese, and crackers and a cup of chocolate pudding from his lunch bag. Kasey nibbled on a pita pocket stuffed with olives and goat cheese salad.

Benny opened his notebook on the table, took a pen in one hand and a cracker sandwich in the other. "SUSPECTS," he wrote. "Okay, who could have done it? Who wasn't outside after the fire alarm went off?"

"Who could have *set off* the fire alarm in the first place?" I added. "Who could have pulled the fire alarm to get everyone else outside? Especially at a time when the classroom doors were unlocked?"

"Good point, Jill!" Kasey took a crunchy bite of apple that made me shudder. "The classroom is always locked when we go to lunch or any other time there's no one in the room. Except for fire drills!"

"Or false alarms." I pictured the red handles on the wall of each hallway. "They wouldn't want anyone to see them, so they had to have a reason for being in the hall alone. Not a visitor either. They'd have to be buzzed in through the security door and sign in at the office. It's someone who belongs in the school."

"Mr. Diallo! He can go anywhere anytime," suggested Benny. "So could Mrs. Ling or any of the office staff." He wrote all their names in the notebook.

"The custodians," said Kasey. "Not nice Mr. Mott, but that grumpy new guy. And maybe the lunchroom staff."

"And the teachers who don't have regular classrooms," I added. "Señora Biddle"—Benny snorted. It was hilarious that our Spanish teacher had such an un-Spanish name—"that remedial math teacher, Mr. Yancy . . ."

"The cute new PE teacher, Mr. DiNardo," said Kasey. "I hope it's not him."

"But it could be. Put him down, Benny," I said. "Then there's Ms. Ruiz, the music teacher, and the speech therapist—"

"Naw, he doesn't come in on Fridays," said Benny. He continued to add names of other school staff, until we'd thought of nearly twenty adults who could have entered or remained in the school building during the fire alarm.

"We've got to narrow this list," I said. "What else can we look at?"

Benny snapped his fingers. "Who knew the banks would be there?"

"Or who was most likely to know, since we can't tell for sure?" Kasey said. "The lunchroom staff probably wouldn't know about them, would they? Who else?"

After some arguing, we decided to cross off the custodians, who could open classrooms anytime with their master keys, and the office staff who monitored doors during fire alarms.

"And the teachers would notice if Mr. Diallo and Mrs. Ling weren't on duty," said Benny. "It would take longer than a quick minute to carry away those heavy banks, so we can strike them from the list."

"And Ms. Ruiz is so frail," said Kasey. "Besides, I like her."

"Liking doesn't count," I protested. "But she is kind of delicate and wears those skinny high heels, so strike her for now."

We went through the names, discussing each one, through the rest of lunch and recess. When it was time for afternoon classes—or, in our case, library study—we had narrowed the list to our three most likely suspects: Señora Biddle, Mr. Yancy, and Mr. DiNardo.

"They were all in the school building at the time of the fire alarm, but none of them had a class scheduled for that period." I ticked off the points on my fingers. "They could all have seen the banks this morning in the teachers' lounge, and I bet Mrs. Herzog talked about the collection and maybe even showed them the catalogs."

"All three are strong enough to carry fifteen to twenty pounds of weight, and limber enough to climb out a window," Kasey continued. "None of us remember when they appeared in the parking lot after the fire alarm."

As we entered the library, I suggested to the others, "We should ask Mrs. Ling if we can work together as a study group. If you ask, Kasey, I'll bet she says yes. All the teachers like you. Then we can continue our investigation."

Kasey talked to Mrs. Ling and got permission. Actually, we're all pretty solid students—even Benny—so it wouldn't seem too strange we wanted to study together. We picked a corner table and propped open our math books. Benny started a fresh page in his notebook and wrote **"MOTIVE?"**

"That's easy: money," I said. "We heard Mrs. Herzog talking about how collectible those banks are. And her clown was wearing yellow! That's a rare one."

"Wouldn't they be easy to trace?" Benny tapped his pen, not writing anything down.

"Not on eBay or Craigslist or some other online market. You can be anonymous on most of them," I argued. "And Mrs. Herzog did say there are still a lot of these banks in collections, so they're not *that* easy to trace."

"It's the most likely motive, unless someone just wants the banks to keep," Kasey agreed. "Write it down and let's move on. I want to know where the banks are *now*. That's what matters most to Mrs. Herzog—getting them *back*."

"Good luck with that," grumbled Benny. "By now, they could be anywhere."

"I don't think so," I argued. "They couldn't be tossed over the wall without breaking them, and there are no bushes or other hiding places between our windows and the front parking lot." I closed my eyes and tried to picture the groups gathered outside during the fire alarm. "I don't remember anyone carrying a gym bag or anything large enough to hold the banks, do you?"

"No, and they couldn't be carried out the front door after the theft was discovered," said Benny. "Somebody would notice, right?"

"*Clank-clank!* For sure," Kasey agreed.

"What if . . ." I took a deep breath, blew it out. "What if the banks never left the school? What if they're hidden until the thief can collect them without being caught?"

"They wouldn't be in the school, because the thief went out the window, remember?" Kasey said. "They even dropped the heaviest one on the way out."

"Wait a minute! Let's turn that around." My heart raced with rising excitement. "Why would the thief go out the window except to hide the banks? And we just decided there *isn't* any place to hide them outside before the theft was discovered!"

"Sooooo? The window is what? A false clue?" Kasey was getting it, too.

"Misdirection!" I thumped my fist on the table. "Just like magicians make you look over there, so you don't notice what they're doing right here!"

Benny tapped his pencil against the notebook page. "So you're saying that whole scene with the chair and the open window, all the books knocked over and even the firefighter bank dropped outside was a trick?"

"What about the paper cranes?" Kasey objected. "The thief had to climb on the windowsill to pull them down, and for no reason. The knocked-over books and the bank were enough if it was a trick."

"Let me think." I tipped my head back, closed my eyes, and tried to picture all we'd seen earlier, particularly the origami cranes lying on the floor, the windowsill, and the grass outside.

"What are you—" Benny broke off when Kasey poked him in the side. "Shh!"

I opened my eyes to the blank white ceiling tiles and the conviction that we'd been looking at things all wrong. "I'm not sure who the thief is," I said, "but I think I know where the missing banks are and how to catch the thief red-handed." I told the others my plan.

For the solution to this story, please turn to page 354.

THE SCARY PLACE

By Alane Ferguson

nbelievable. Brian texted us *again!*" Min Shi-shi sighed, rolling her dark eyes at her two best friends and fellow members of their club, Geeks 4 Science.

The three "Geekers" met almost every other day to figure out science riddles, just to keep their thinking sharp during the hot summer months. Today they had landed at Min's, a white-and-gray modern home with lots of large, shiny windows and square furniture that looked like boxes. Since it was a hundred degrees with 87 percent humidity outside (Min knew it precisely, because at the moment she was studying meteorology), the Geekers were sprawled out in the family room, which was air-conditioned to a crisp seventy-two degrees.

"Okay, I'll bite. What does Crazy Brian want this time?" Derrick Klar asked, pushing his hair out of his eyes. Tall and lanky, Derrick hunched whenever he read a book, which was all the time. In fact, he read so much Min thought he smelled like paper. "No, wait, let me guess," Derrick said with a crooked grin. "Did he catch the Indiana Bigfoot? Or was it a bug-eyed alien in a cornfield?"

"Nope," Min replied. "Today Crazy Brian swears he's caught a ghost on his cell phone. A real *ooooooooohhhhh* kind of spirit." She waggled her fingers. "He says that he wants us to investigate this case, Ghostbuster style."

"Lame." Jayid Kafir yawned, not even looking up from a map of glowing stars. He was stocky, with ears that stood out from his head like large seashells. Jayid was the one who geeked out over everything in the night sky. He always wore tee shirts with a different planet on the front. Today it was Mars.

"Ghosts are scientifically impossible to prove," Derrick added, his back curled into a question mark. He flipped through a book called *The Ocean Deep*. "I'd rather search for a vampire squid."

"Squids can be vampires?" Jayid gave a loud snort. "Sounds like we should start calling you Crazy Derrick!"

"Don't be stupid, vampire squids are real!" Derrick shot back. "Want to see a picture?" He thrust his book right under Jayid's nose.

Jayid held his hands up. "Okay, okay, as long as you've got proof."

"Brian says he's got proof, too!" Min broke in, trying to get them back on track.

"Come on, it's gotta be fake. Dump it," Derrick jeered.

"I don't know—a vampire squid sounded bizarro, too, but pictures don't lie," said Jayid. "Your call, Min."

Min's thumb hovered over her cell's Delete tab, but something inside her squirmed. Maybe it was the memory of her grandmother, whom she called Nai Nai, preparing an altar for the Chinese Hungry Ghost Festival. Every year Nai Nai lit spicy incense and burned paper money to keep the spirits of her ancestors happy. And her grandmother was one of the smartest people Min knew. What if . . . what *if*? Min bit her lip, thinking. Finally, she said, "Do you suppose, as future scientists, we should watch the clip?" Min pushed her red glasses to the top of her small nose. "Just to be sure."

"Yeah. I kinda love to tell Crazy Brian why he's wrong," Jayid said as he rolled to his feet. Derrick slouched over, too, but he kept a finger crammed into his book to keep his place. All their heads practically touched as they hovered over Min's phone.

The link took them straight to YouTube.

"Science geeks, this one's for you!" Crazy Brian called out from a room glowing with green light. Crazy Brian (adding the *Crazy* to his name was Derrick's idea) had once wanted to be a Geeker, too, but they just couldn't let him join. The problem was that everything he wanted to investigate was, well, *crazy*! In the end, Crazy Brian had formed his own group called Ghosts Were People 2. The Geekers told him to call if he ever turned up *real* evidence of the afterlife. Today, the text had come.

"Do you see it?" Min asked anxiously as a blurry image filled her cell phone screen.

"That isn't proof," Jayid snickered. "Crazy Brian's just got his thumb over the lens."

"I don't know . . ." Min answered, squinting. "It does look like . . . something weird."

Frowning in concentration, the three of them looked closer. Suddenly, the image came into much sharper focus. Brian stood in an old-fashioned basement, one with a high-bricked ceiling and an earthen floor. In an instant Min knew exactly where he was filming, because everybody knew about the most haunted house in Indiana, especially Min, who lived two short blocks away. She'd grown up hearing the stories: ghost children who ran through hallways, throwing pebbles—three at a time—at anyone who dared to come inside. Whispers of a man who haunted its empty windows, his withered skin as white as bone. Tattered curtains moved by the curl of a skeletal finger. Everyone called that house the Scary Place.

Min felt her own grip tighten on her phone.

"Whoa," she gasped. She watched as a thickening swirl of white spun into the room's center. Min could hear the excitement in Brian's voice, could tell that he was breathing hard. "Spirit, ghost— whatever we see you!" he cried. Then another voice shouted, "O-M-G!" Brian's phone zoomed onto some kind of meter. "The temperature just dropped *eleven degrees*! It was sixty-one degrees and now it's only *fifty*! Ghosts make rooms go cold— Geeks," he said breathlessly, "this is as real as it gets!"

Min, her mouth slightly open, kept watching as the mist rose behind Brian's head. It spread out and lapped against the wall like a wave.

Brian flipped his cell phone back onto himself. His white-blond hair was so pale it seemed to glow. "Min, Jayid, Derrick, come tomorrow to the Scary Place at two sharp. And don't worry, I have a way in, 'cause my parents just bought this house." He held up a brass key. "It's the ultimate test—science vs. ghosts. Be there. The spirits are waiting."

And just like that, the clip ended. The screen went completely dark. For a moment no one spoke.

"That was freaky. Which means I can't explain it. So I'm *out*!" Derrick announced, jerking away from the phone as if the ghost would blow right through the screen.

Min shook her head hard. "No way—we're scientists. We can't *not* do this!"

Jayid's eyes were so wide it made his seashell ears stick out even more. He swallowed, then squared his shoulders. "We gotta go, or we'll look like cowards." He blew a puff of air between his teeth. "And no matter what we find, one thing's for sure—we can't call Crazy Brian *Crazy* ever again. Go Geeks hand stack!"

One by one, they put their hands into the center, palm on fist. Even Derrick, whose hands felt like limp fishes.

"Right!" Min cried, trying to sound more confident than she felt. "All of us. Tomorrow. Let's hunt some ghosts!"

"Why are we here again?" Derrick asked, his green eyes narrowing into slits. Beads of sweat gathered along the edge of his hair and his hands were trembling. For someone who studied monstrous creatures from the ocean, Derrick seemed surprisingly nervous about the supernatural. Of course, thought Min, if Derrick didn't want to see a vampire squid all he had to do was stay out of the ocean. A ghost could find you anywhere.

"I already told you—to solve a puzzle," Min told Derrick. "Okay, sure, that whatever-it-was *looked* spooky, but we need facts." She shoved her glasses up the bridge of her nose and tried not to think of Nai Nai, her ancestors, or anything else that might be floating inside that weird basement. Scientists were tough.

The Scary Place was surrounded by tall, leafy trees that seemed to guard the house. Even in their shade, Min felt hot and sticky—another scorching day with enough humidity to make her feel like she was breathing soup. Min, at least, had come prepared. In addition to her cell phone, she had a notebook, a pen, and her own thermometer. Jayid had brought flashlights. Derrick, who had tried to chicken out, had nothing extra at all.

The three "Ghosties," as Min liked to call them, waved eagerly from the weathered porch. Brian Sehen, Amanda Estrella, and Ike Kai all wore matching black tee shirts emblazoned with the words "GHOST HUNTER." Twelve-year-old Ike, who was Hawaiian, had golden eyes and curly, chestnut hair. Ten-year-old Amanda had deep dimples and long, straight black hair tipped in magenta. She was short but had the energy of a firecracker. And of course, there stood Brian, with his white-blond hair and large, gapped teeth that were always visible because he never stopped smiling.

"Come on in!" Brian called to them, scooping his hand through the air. "The stuff lives in the basement."

"Yeah, don't be scared," Amanda giggled. The edges of her hair danced like red flames. "The ghost seems totally cool."

"I heard that the ghost kids throw pebbles at anyone who walks inside the Scary Place," Derrick shouted. "Did that happen to you?"

"*Nah*," answered Brian, while Min (just to be sure) searched every single window for an old man's face, "I think that part's just legend. But this place is *definitely* haunted. That's why my parents bought it, so they could turn it into a spooky bed-and-breakfast. You guys ready?"

There was nothing for it.

"Ready," Min announced, taking the lead.

"Go science." Jayid began to march through the thistle-filled yard.

When the Geekers reached the porch, Brian instructed them to watch their step. "It's rickety out here, but the floor inside is still pretty good."

The six of them walked through the large doorway and made a lopsided circle inside the giant foyer. A dusty smell mixed with rotting wood made Min's nose crinkle. Most of the dingy wallpaper had peeled off; there were large splotches all over the walls, big and dark as thunderclouds. Although the house was completely empty of any furniture, there were plenty of cobwebs hanging from the ceiling like dirty icicles.

"Well," Brian began. He rolled onto his toes and swung his long arms. "This is it."

There was an awkward silence. It occurred to Min that the two groups could not have been more different. They were eyeing each other with no one saying anything. Finally, Min said, "Right, then. Lead the way."

"Down this hall," Brian told them happily. "We already set up our equipment, which we borrowed from Amanda's mom. She's a for-real Ghost Hunter. Amanda's mom told us exactly what to do to get a ghost to come. Like, you have to talk to them like they are people. Which they were."

While Brian chattered, Ike whipped up his hand like he was holding a stop sign. "Wait a sec," Ike said, bending down. He grabbed a large rock and jammed it against the door to keep it wide open.

"What are you doing?" Derrick asked. Min noticed his voice was very, very high.

Ike gave him a look. "Have you ever *watched* a scary show? If ghosts get mad they can lock you inside and you might not *ever* get out. We like to keep our options open."

Falling into the single-file line with Brian in the lead, Min heard the floorboards groan with every step. They made their way down the narrow hallway only to stop at another, smaller door. It squeaked when Brian swung it open. "Twenty stairs to the wine cellar," he told them, pointing down into what looked like a hole.

"Wait—why is there a green glow down there?" Jayid asked, furrowing his brow.

"'Cause we set up my grid lights in the middle of the cellar," Amanda answered proudly. "That way, if something moves, we can see it. Grid lights shoot out a set light pattern. Awesome for tracking ghosts!"

With the cellar door open, a cool, damp draft hit Min's face. Brian's, Jayid's, Amanda's, Derrick's, and then Min's shoes clattered as they began their descent, but not before Ike had placed a second rock to keep the hall door open. "Options," he repeated before taking his place at the back of the line.

When they finally reached the wine cellar, Min could tell they were definitely underground. She was grateful for the grid lights, because without them it would have been pitch black. Bright green polka dots splayed everywhere like a galaxy of stars. Min could make out the uneven bricks in a room shaped like a loaf of bread. Jayid turned on three regular flashlights and handed one to Min and one to Derrick, who muttered, "*I want out.*" Their cells were for filming only.

"Just sit wherever you want," Brian told them softly. "The spirit should be here pretty soon."

They all plopped down around three empty soup cans. Each can held a grid light that pointed upward. There were other gadgets placed in different spots across the floor. "EMF meters," Amanda explained. "Stands for electromagnetic field. They go red when the ghosts are around."

For the first few minutes all Min could think was that her bottom was turning into a block of ice. The Geekers fidgeted with their phones, ready to film at a moment's notice. Brian's ghost hunters, on the other hand, sat like statues. The Geekers shifted around as they waited, waited, *waited* for something to happen.

Ten minutes crawled by: Brian asked, "Is there anyone here with us?" He got up and walked around the entire room, calling out to the air, before settling back down again.

Twenty minutes: Derrick burped.

Twenty-five minutes: Jayid blew his nose so hard Brian accused him of trying to scare off the ghost.

Thirty minutes: Min rubbed her bare arms. It was much colder down here than she expected. Sixty-one degrees again. She knew because Brian held a box with a small wire that read out the temperature on a digital screen. It worked much better than her under-the-tongue thermometer.

At thirty-nine minutes Min had to admit the basement was creeping her out. For one thing, the lights played tricks on her eyes. Every so often something seemed to swim through the dots like a shark, although she could usually trace it to a movement of one of the Geekers stretching an arm or waving a hand. Mostly, but not always. Every crack of a knee made her jump. She noticed Jayid and Derrick had gone quiet, too.

Suddenly, Ike cried, "I sense a presence. It's coming—it's coming *now!*"

At that moment a cloud rolled into the cellar, exactly as it had on Brian's post. Derrick's eyes seemed to pop while Jayid jumped to his feet. Min herself stayed frozen on the ground.

"Geekers, use your cells—film it!" she finally said when she got her mouth working again.

"Who are you?" Ike politely asked the mist. "Why are you here? Are you from the past? Did you *die* in this house?"

The pearly air thickened and coiled. Min could hardly believe what was happening, but she could not deny the evidence right before her eyes. Goose bumps pricked her skin as the cloud revolved like a top. She could sense it, could actually *feel* whatever this thing was.

"The temperature just dropped ten degrees!" Brian yelled, thrusting his temperature gauge into the middle of the cloud. "I told you, Geeks, I *told* you! Paranormal activity!"

"Paranormal *this*!" Derrick yelled as he sprung up like a kangaroo.

There was a *rat-a-tat-tat* like beats on a drum. It was Jayid's and Derrick's shoes as they blasted up the basement stairs, each one shoving the other to get ahead.

That was enough for her. "*Later!*" Min cried. Running as fast as she could (she was the best sprinter) Min was already on her fellow Geekers' heels by the time they reached the hallway. Grateful the cellar door was still open as well as the wide-open one at the front, the three of them dashed like crazy until they all stumbled down the rickety steps right into the yard. Light blinded her eyes; she almost choked in the swamp-like air outside of the Scary Place.

From somewhere far away Min heard the word "Cowards." The sun beat on their heads like a yellow, accusing eye.

"There *has* to be an explanation," Min told Jayid and Derrick when they were safely inside Min's family room. Since they'd run the two blocks back to Min's house, the three of them were still panting. "There just *has* to be."

"I didn't see anything like dry ice or anything fake," Jayid gasped. "I checked it all out with my flashlight before that *thing* came inside."

"We were wrong," Derrick yelled in a cracked voice. "Mind *blown*!"

He, out of the three of them, was the most frightened by the swirling pillar of white, although they were all pretty rattled. Jayid's eyebrows were still high up his forehead, and Min kept taking great big gulps from a water bottle.

"We are the worst," she said, wiping her mouth with the back of her hand. "We acted like little kids on Halloween."

"Did we get anything on our phones?" Derrick squeaked.

They looked at their cells. Every one of them started with white mist, but their shots swiftly changed so that it looked like they were filming on a roller coaster. Mostly they caught their feet running, running, running.

"Okay, that's humiliating. But we've still got our logic," Min told them, trying to gain control. "First step—we need to write everything down. Let's sit." She fell onto her couch and pulled out her notebook, clicking her pen. "According to Brian's text, the first ghost came into the basement yesterday at approximately two thirty," she said, writing as best she could with wobbly fingers. "So that was *Monday.* The people present were *Brian*, *Amanda*, and *Ike.* Now as for today," under the word *Tuesday*, "there was *Brian*, *Amanda*, and *Ike*, and then me," she wrote down *Min*, "plus *Jayid* and *Derrick.* That makes a total of six people." She blew a piece of hair out of her face. "Now, for our constants."

"What does that mean?" Derrick asked. He was so hunched his chin almost touched his knees.

"It means the things that were the same. Like, on both days, the basement was *sixty-one* degrees. But when the 'spirit'"—she made air quotes with her fingers—"showed up, it dropped to fifty-one degrees. It was one hundred degrees outside yesterday and one hundred and one today, which is pretty much the same. Eighty-seven percent humidity both days. Hmmm." She tapped her pen against the paper.

"So what—those are all just numbers!" Derrick almost shouted. "We all *saw* it. We *felt* it! That proves it's *real*!"

"Not . . . yet," Jayid answered slowly. "What about those ghost meters on the ground? Maybe those guys jacked them up. Maybe they used them to prank us."

"Yeah? And how are we going to *prove* that?" Derrick demanded.

That question took a long time to answer. Min chewed the corner of her lip. Derrick rubbed his forehead while Jayid stared at the ceiling. His gaze finally dropped to Min's. As the older two, they'd always been able to signal each other as to what they were thinking. Min shot a look back to Jayid, who nodded back resolutely.

"We can't end our investigation like this. Derrick, we've got to get more evidence," Min told him as gently as she could manage.

"How?" Derrick demanded, brushing Min's comforting hand away.

Jayid said, "We've got to go back there tomorrow. As Geeks 4 Science, we need to find the truth. No lights, no gadgets, or any of their weird EMF meters that can interfere with the facts."

Derrick shook his head. "The ghost hunters will want to use them."

"See, that's just it—they won't be there. Because this time," Min paused, looking from Derrick's whey face to Jayid's dark, resolute eyes, "we go to the Scary Place alone."

It was Friday. Min stared at her logic sheet, completely frustrated. The facts and figures she'd gathered all week were completely useless. She knew the answer was there, if she could only see it, but so far, the only thing that seemed real was that strange, churning, frigid ghost!

She looked at the grid she'd drawn that showed the activity, day by day.

Wednesday: The Geekers had shown up at two o'clock on the dot. Brian had given them the key and the temperature gauge before settling on the porch with his team, leaving the Geekers to hunt on their own. Inside the basement the Geekers had waited well past an hour, but there was nothing. No fog, no cloud, no spirit.

"It's 'cause you guys aren't *believers*," Ike had told them when the Geekers opened the door and stepped outside. The Ghosties had greeted the news of "nothing there" with maddening grins.

"Ghosts can tell," Brian had explained. "Come again tomorrow—but this time it will be all of us. And I'll tell you right now, you'll see the *same ghost*! It comes for us fans!"

Thursday: This time Jayid asked the Ghosties to leave their equipment outside, just in case. "Whatever," Amanda had answered. "It doesn't matter. We can go old school, but our ghost will show up!"

With flashlights and cell phones only, they saw the misty ghost arrive, right on schedule. Six investigators and one very large, swirling entity. Jayid had ground his teeth while Derrick tried to hold Min's hand.

Friday: The Geeks had tried going solo again. Just Min, Jayid, and a very reluctant Derrick.

"Can we borrow your EMFs?" Jayid asked Amanda. He was still suspicious that the meters had somehow generated the ghost in the cellar. To that end he'd tucked a tiny screwdriver into his back pocket.

"Absolutely," Amanda told him. "But remember, a ghost is like Tinker Bell—you've got to have faith!"

That time the Geekers had waited for almost two hours. The meters (which never lit up) had been secretly opened, but there were just wires and batteries inside—no dry ice. "Bummer," Jayid had murmured before screwing them back together. "Guess that's not it."

Legs stiff, rear ends sore, they had tried to be patient, but no ghost, no mist, no *anything* had shown up. Which led to . . .

Saturday: Today. One last, final try before the Geekers would be forced to admit spirits really did exist. Sorry, Nai Nai, Min thought, but real spirits must have something better to do than roll around in a wine cellar. It was only moments away from two o'clock, which meant she had to start walking and meet up with the other Geeks. Still, Min wasn't quite ready to put down her notebook. "The facts," she said aloud, glaring at her figures. "The answer has to be in the facts!"

She scanned the numbers for the hundredth time. Min's information showed the steady temperatures and humidity that had stayed the same all week long, so *that* wasn't the key. And with or without the ghost equipment made no difference in the results. The equipment definitely didn't matter. Truth was, the ghost actually *did* seem to show up *only* when the ghost hunters were there. Maybe the spirit truly preferred the Ghosties over Geekers.

And so, grudgingly and for the last time, at two o'clock Saturday, both the Geekers and Ghosties settled down once more in the dark, dank cellar. Once again and right on time, the thick spirit Amanda had named Pearl showed up.

"Oh, she just *loves* us." Ike laughed. "I'll admit Pearl isn't very talkative, but at least she's consistent. Hi, Pearl! Glad you're here!"

"Okay, this is just stupid. I'm leaving," Min announced. She was so frustrated that she didn't care if Pearl was unhappy with her departure. Stomping on the earthen floor, Min discovered she was just plain mad.

This whole thing made no sense and she hated it when she couldn't figure out a problem. Try as she might, the Geekers had been defeated. Which meant the Ghosties had won.

"Me, too," Jayid grunted as he rose to his feet.

"Don't leave me here," Derrick screeched. "Sorry, Pearl!" He made a peace sign with his fingers. "Later!"

The three of them trudged up the cellar steps. At the top of the stairs, Min's sneaker accidentally kicked the stone Ike had dutifully placed by the door. "Ouch!" she cried, hopping on one foot. "Why do they keep *doing* that? Pearl's supposed to be a friendly ghost, so how come Ike keeps putting those ridiculous rocks at the doors so they can escape? My toe hurts!"

"Yeah," Jayid agreed fiercely. "They think we're the cowards, but *we* never needed an escape plan. We always shut the doors when *we* went into the cellar."

"Actually, I kinda wanted to keep them open, just in case," Derrick admitted guiltily, "but Jayid wouldn't let me."

Suddenly, it felt as though a million bees were buzzing inside of Min's head. "Wait a second! Just—*wait!*" Min looked at her notes. She stared at the rock. She sucked in a breath as the answer hit her with the force of a meteor.

"Hey, Ghosties!" she cried as loudly as she could down the rickety stairs. "Pearl isn't a spirit. I figured it out! I know *exactly* what's down there, and it's *not* paranormal!" Even though her toe hurt, Min did a little dance at the top of the stairs.

"What are you saying?" Brian's voice floated up.

"I figured it out!" Min shouted gleefully. "Come up and see the facts for yourself. *Science wins!*"

THE SCARY PLACE

It was at that precise moment that three small, gray pebbles skittled across the wooden floor like tiny mice. One landed against the side of Min's sneaker, another against Jayid's flip-flop, and the third jumped right inside Derrick's sock. For a moment they stared at each other, slack jawed.

"Are those—are those from the ghost children?" Derrick asked, looking around wildly.

"Never mind!" Min yelled down to the basement. "We'll text you the answer later!"

And then, as fast as their legs could pump, the three of them flew out of the Scary Place for the last time.

For the solution to this story, please turn to page 356.

OTTONETICS

By Peter Lerangis

It is a universal truth that a kid wandering in Central Park after dark is going to die.

Well, so says my mom, Harriet Beers. To her, New York City is a wasteland of crime and devastation, with evil behind every maple tree. So when I walk back from my friend Lizzie's house through the park after sunset, I don't tell her.

Which explains why at 8:07 p.m. on a cold Wednesday last October, I was alone in the park's secluded Ramble section when the shriek came.

It made my knees buckle. It sounded like a tiny child in great pain.

I looked around for help. But the park at night is basically 840 acres of silence in a city of nine million people. All I saw were streetlights, branches, and distant amber windows on Central Park West.

I heard the screech again and realized it was from *above*. My eyes darted up a hill, where the shadow of the Belvedere Castle loomed. Was a baby stuck up there? Or some owl or cat?

"*RrrrrrEEEEEE . . . EEEE . . . kakakakakakaaaaKEEEE!*"

I wasn't going to climb and rescue it. There are people in NYC who do that kind of thing. As I fumbled in my pocket for my phone, my toe banged against the tip of a rock, and I hurtled downward, face-first. I reached out, but my left eyebrow hit the hard-packed dirt. I don't know if I screamed, because I couldn't hear myself.

"KakakakakakaaaaKEEEE!" The screech came again.

Then something was looming over me. A shadow. Its head was lumpy, and it had thick arms. I tried to scramble away, but I felt its gnarled fingers grip my shoulders and pull me to my feet.

This time I know I screamed, because my attacker recoiled. It wasn't a thing. It was a man. As his head jerked away, the lamplight revealed two wide-set eyes, soiled cheeks, and a grimace. I'd seen this guy before in the park, shuffling aimlessly. Right now, he looked like he'd eat me if he weren't completely toothless. "Why you yell like that?" he grumbled.

I pointed toward the sound. "Because of *that*! The noise!"

He gripped my jaw and angled me toward the light. "Raccoons. In tree."

"Wait. That's what *raccoons* sound like?"

"Depends on what they are doing." He examined the side of my face intently. "Looks bad, *hijo*."

He pulled me toward a park bench. On it was an open sleeping bag, several plastic bags, and a jar of peanut butter. A sky-blue wooden box stood nearby, about three feet tall, with four wheels at the bottom and a push handle like a laundry cart. A colorful landscape had been painted in the front, with the words "Otto Geheimnis: Ottonetics for Life" underneath. I figured the box contained this guy's whole life, and the bench was his home.

As he reached into the box, I struggled to get away. But he held tight, yanking me down onto the bench. "Please. Sit. Don't move."

Letting go, he pulled out a plastic bag from the box and dumped onto the bench some Band-Aids, a pack of cotton balls, and some random bottles. The next moment he was daubing my face with alcohol. I flinched, but the touch felt soothing. His eyes were emerald-colored, set deeply under bushy gray eyebrows, and his thick hands moved gently as he bandaged my cut. "Better," he said with a nod.

"Thanks," I said. "Sorry I screamed in your ear."

He let out a hoarse laugh. Then he gave me a long look, like he was deciding whether to tell me something. "I am Hernando," he finally said. "I do something for you. Now you do for me."

He pulled a thick paperback book from his box:

OTTONETICS!

Solving Life's Puzzles

by Otto Geheimnis

"Take this, then go home," he said. "Read it closely."

"Um, thanks." I didn't want this thing, but Hernando looked like he'd cry if I said no. I put it in my pack and then stuck out my hand. "Jake Beers."

But his back was to me, and he was already unrolling his sleeping bag.

"I know," he replied.

Harriet's eyes shot sharp bolts of shame as she yelled, and her big stack of hair moved like a wind-blown rosebush. "WHAT DO YOU MEAN, YOU WALKED ACROSS THE PARK BY YOURSELF?"

"It's all right, the park is empty at that hour!" I protested.

"THAT'S THE POINT! That's what makes it dangerous! That homeless guy wasn't nobody." She reached toward my Band-Aid. "Look at this. He stabbed you?"

"I fell," I said. "He gave me this Band-Aid. He's nice. He paints landscapes."

"SO DID JACK THE RIPPER!" Harriet thundered.

"Really?"

"I don't know! He could have." With a deep sigh, she turned away and pulled open the fridge. "Are you hungry? I made tempeh with Martian seasoning."

Here's what you need to know about Harriet. She once sang and danced in three Broadway shows, but she gave that up when she adopted me. When I ask about my birth parents, she says I was abandoned by a half woman–half selkie, but my baby gills eventually fell off. She wears 1970s clothing, and her hair looks like an alien life form, but she doesn't care about fashion or what people think. She never throws stuff out, including my kindergarten clay sculptures and invisible-ink Valentine's day cards. Most tenants in our building seem confused when they meet her in the hallway, as if they'd just happened upon a wayward yak. All of which makes me love her even more.

Martian seasoning means *whatever spices are left in the cupboard.* "No, thanks," I said.

"What's this?" she asked, pulling the paperback from my backpack.

"A book by Otto Gesundheit," I said. "Hernando gave it to me. The guy in the park."

"Otto *Geheimnis,*" she corrected me. "The founder of the Ottonetics cult. Happiness through puzzles. 'You can't be cross if you do crosswords . . .'"

"That's actually one of his sayings? You've read him?"

"No. But Norman has. Wait till he finds out Ottonetics has reached the homeless community!"

She shuffled over to a landline that hangs on our kitchen wall. Harriet met Norman Kaufmann the same week she adopted me. They talk on the phone about forty times a day. He's slow, serious, and nearly hairless, which makes him the opposite of Harriet. Both of them yell into the phone when they speak.

"NORMAN? . . . YES, IT'S ME, WHO ELSE DO YOU THINK IT COULD BE?"

I went to get some ice cream but noticed a bookmark sticking out of *Solving Life's Puzzles.*

I opened to that page. The bookmark was actually an old photo, facedown. Someone had scribbled on the back in ink that had become faded and splotchy. I held it down, which is hard for me to do, because I was born with camptodactyly, a pinky that can't straighten out.

For H —

A gift for the most gifted man I know, who travels like a zephyr and observes like a falcon. And within this gift, another for our beloved J—when he is ready. You of all people will know when. And eventually, through these words, he will know why.

Yours,

OG

H, I figured, was Hernando, and *OG* had to be Otto Geheimnis.

"Is that a note written by the author, bubi?" Harriet called from the phone. "Avoid fingerprints! It might be worth something!"

As Harriet went back to yelling at Norman, I turned the photo over. And I nearly dropped my spoon.

In the image, a little boy was looking up, offering the photographer a bagel with cream cheese wrapped in wax paper.

I don't know who took the photo.

But the little boy was me.

I ran to my bedroom and texted my friend Lizzie about what had happened. I attached a screenshot of the note on the back of the photo.

Lizzie instantly Facetimed me back. "Dude. You're creeping me out. 'For our beloved J—when he is ready . . . Yours, OG'? You were attacked by a famous author in the Ramble?"

"No, not the author. A homeless guy."

"Was it Hernando?" Lizzie said. "The South American painter dude?"

"Wait. You know his name?"

"Everyone knows him. In the morning all the dog walkers flock around him. He's like Santa Claus. He loves their dogs. It's a big party."

"I've never seen anything like that," I said.

"Duh. Why would you? I have to walk across the park to get to school. You already live on the Upper West Side." Lizzie exhaled dramatically. "OK, so Hernando's been carrying around a photo of you—tucked in a book by a famous author, with a note on the back to Hernando from the author, referencing you."

"He references J," I pointed out.

"But it's a picture of you. Who else could it be?" Lizzie's eyes grew wide. "Jake. Does he look like you?"

"Hernando?"

"The author!" Lizzie said.

"Like, is he my long-lost dad, who gave me up for adoption?" (Lizzie thinks everyone is my lost-lost dad.)

"Well? You're always talking about trying to find your real, non-selkie parents!"

I held the book open to the back flap. Otto Geheimnis had a gray beard, thick glasses, and baggy eyes. As I pointed the phone toward it, Lizzie said, "I'm trying to imagine you at age ninety-five. It's too hard. Any other clues? Messages? Photos?"

I held the phone with one hand and flipped through the book with the other. The pages had yellowed, but they weren't marked up—until the end, where two blank pages had been scribbled on. I showed Lizzie the first.

$$A\ B\ \Gamma\ \Delta\ E\ Z\ H\ \Theta\ I\ K\ \Lambda\ M\ N\ \Xi\ O\ P\ \Sigma\ T\ \Upsilon\ \Phi\ X\ \Psi\ \Omega$$

"Um . . . I'm guessing Otto was studying for the Russian translation?"

"I think it's Greek," I said.

The next page was also blank, except for two lines on top:

Warm milk
2C

"OK, it's something," Lizzie said. "We'll need to do some research on this guy."

Our conversation was interrupted by a knock on the door. "Gotta go, Lizzie."

I quickly clicked off and slipped the photo/note into my shirt pocket. The door opened to reveal a short old guy in a rumpled tweed jacket. A curtain of stringy white hair hung to his shoulder on the left side of his head, in a massive comb-over fail. He smiled at me through smudged glasses. "How's the boy?"

"Hey, Mr. Kaufmann, I think you're supposed to knock and then wait for an answer. But come in. I'm fine." I smiled but glanced back at my phone, where I was already beginning a search on Otto Geheimnis.

Before Norman could answer, Harriet bustled in behind him. "So sorry, honey, I told Norman not to bother you. But you know him. He cares so much . . ."

I was tuning them out, intent on my phone's screen:

Otto Geheimnis (1921–2015), German-born writer, puzzle expert, psychologist. Founder of the Ottonetics Life-style Philosophy (OLP). At its peak in 1974, OLP's chapters were estimated at nearly a million. But they dwindled dramatically in 1991 after a *New York Week* exposé discovered Geheimnis had lived in Argentina as a cabaret singer named El Canario (the Canary), spawning rumors he was among a group of Nazi officers who had escaped to that country after World War II. . . .

"They weren't rumors," Norman said.

His voice startled me. I hadn't realized he was looking over my shoulder. "How do you know?"

"Keep reading," Norman said. "Preferably aloud."

I cleared my throat and recited: "Geheimnis left no known family upon his death in 2015. His effects consisted mostly of notebooks full of crossword puzzles. But hidden among them was a handwritten inventory list, leading to a trove of artworks stolen by the Nazis from Jewish families in Germany and Poland. The note claimed Geheimnis intended to return them to their rightful heirs but chose to stay silent, fearing unjust imprisonment due to what he called 'false rumors' about his Nazi past. Although most items have now been restored, a few are still missing, including the famous Fabergé egg containing the Arkady Diamond, worth approximately thirty million dollars."

At those last three words, Harriet fanned herself with a newspaper and sat at the edge of the desk.

She put her arm around Norman's shoulder. He was wiping his eyes of tears. "Sorry. This is why I came over so quickly. I'm a lawyer. Semi-retired. My firm is involved in finding looted material from the war. I'm not interested in Geheimnis because of crossword puzzles. I entered the legal field because of what happened to my parents in Poland."

Harriet smiled at me. "The Kaufmanns," she explained, "were the owners of the Fabergé egg."

This was freaky.

Otto Geheimnis, the famous writer, was a Nazi disguised as a singer called the Canary, who happened to steal from Norman's parents and many years later wrote me a note, to be delivered to me by a homeless Santa Claus named Hernando.

"For our beloved J—when he is ready. . . . And eventually, through these words, he will know why."

I leafed through the book, hoping to get clues. Geheimnis was all about codes. The age of a tree is encoded in the number of rings. The age of the universe in photons. Even love and friendship could be revealed by solving codes.

At least that's how Norman explained it. But none of that explained the note.

When I got to the doodles at the end of the book, Harriet cried out, "Aha! Look at that—'Warm milk, 2C'! The most sensible thing we've read. I'll heat up some milk. We'll all have a good sleep."

Norman chuckled. "Warm milk to see *what*, darling?"

That was when the solution hit me. "That's it!" I shouted. "2C is a code for *to see*!"

They both stared at me. My mind raced. The blank page reminded me of another blank page I once gave to Harriet. "Remember my Valentine's day card from third grade?"

"Of course, Jakey," she replied. "It's on my dresser. It said 'I love you with all my—'"

"I wrote it in *lemon juice*. Invisible! You had to run a hot iron over it. The heat scorched the juice, so it got brown and you could read it. Like ink."

"You think Geheimnis wrote in lemon juice?" Norman asked.

"Not lemon juice—*milk*. The technique works with different liquids. He's hinting we should warm the milk . . . *to see* something!"

"The boy's a genius . . ." In a minute Harriet was holding a hot iron over the book. She carefully pressed it on the page, then lifted:

Caswell Connor, residing on Tenth Street,
boldly handles my current placements,
assuring the arrival of my most important of hidden, snared eggs.
I rest now.
You act.
Know I am smiling.

Norman fell back, clutching the wall. I thought he was having a heart attack. "Oh . . ."

Harriet touched his arm. "Bubi, your blood pressure."

"I—I know that name," Norman said. "Caswell Connor was Papa's lawyer. Connor owned a brownstone on Tenth Street."

"Wait, *your dad's lawyer* was hiding the Fabergé egg for Otto?" I asked. "That makes no sense. Connor represented *your* family, right? Why would he hide an egg he was supposed to find?"

"The sneak," Norman hissed. "Papa said he didn't trust him. Now I know why." To me, Norman had always seemed like a kind of cartoon character. But he was serious now, shaking as if he were going to explode. "I will track down that treasure if I have to seek out every Connor descendant."

"Maybe if you talk nicely to them," Harriet said, following Norman as he stormed out of the room.

I felt for him. But I also couldn't figure out why this would have happened. And why Otto would want *me* to know it.

The best way I could help was to learn about Caswell Connor. I did a quick search and came up with some historical info, but not much. He had died in 1987 and I found nothing about a diamond or a Fabergé egg.

Not even a hint that the man had committed a crime.

Hernando stared at the note I had decoded. It was a bright, warm Saturday morning, just too early for the dog walkers.

"Cas . . . well . . ." Hernando drawled. "This is not familiar."

Lizzie was with me, wearing a plaid Sherlock Holmes–style hat, with a brim in the front and back. Because Lizzie is Lizzie. "Am I correct, sir," she said, "that you were an acquaintance of one Otto Gehem—Gehamm—"

"Geheimnis," I said.

"Yes," Hernando replied softly. "In Argentina, Otto employed my father on a cattle ranch. Otto paid my parents well. But I was not such a good son. Or husband. I got involved in crime and ran away. I was so ashamed. I could not find work. I was in the snow, in a park, almost frozen to death, when Otto found me. He helped me over the years, but things have not been easy. I live here. I have friends. I'm happy."

"Wow . . ." Lizzie said.

So there was a connection between Otto and Hernando. But that didn't explain the connection between Otto and me.

"So . . . Hernando . . ." I said, "after you gave me the book, I found a photo. Of me. And on the back was a note . . ."

"From Otto, yes." Hernando nodded, his eyes moistening. "I have been keeping watch over you since I got to New York. By the time Otto found out where you were, he was very sick. He wanted me to give this to you . . . when you were no longer a child."

"Aha!" Lizzie shouted. "So Otto *is* Jake's lost-long father! Or . . . grandfather."

"No," Hernando replied. "He is neither."

"The newspapers say he was a Nazi," I said.

"He wore a Nazi uniform," Hernando said. "As long as he could. A spy against Hitler, the most dangerous job in the world. When they stole the paintings, the gold, the jewels, Otto smuggled as much as he could, through the Resistance. Until someone ratted him out. On the morning the Nazis came for him, he escaped."

"To Argentina," I said. "Where he became the Canary."

I sat back. It was all becoming clear. The Fabergé egg had been smuggled away by Geheimnis. Who now wanted to make sure it was returned to . . .

I nearly leaped off the bench. *"Norman!"*

Hernando and Lizzie both gave me a look. "He's here?" Lizzie said.

"No," I said, as the pieces fell into place. "Otto wants to return the diamond to Norman, because he's a Kaufmann. The Fabergé egg—and the Arkady Diamond—belonged to his family!"

Hernando's watery eyes snapped toward me. "What did you say?"

"Wait . . . your father is *Norman*?" Lizzie blurted out. "Oh, is that depressing."

I began pacing. "If Norman is my dad, why didn't he tell me? He met Harriet on the day she adopted me. So he just decided he'd give me up, then hang out with my mom and make bad jokes while she raised me?"

"And why would Otto want to contact *you*," Lizzie said, "when he could contact Norman directly?"

"No . . . no . . ." Hernando was sputtering, trying to get a word in edgewise. "Grobheit . . . you do not know about Putzi Grobheit?"

We both stared at him blankly. "I'll spell it," he said. "You look it up."

I did, and the first hit was a news report headlined "Nazi War Criminal Dies Before Sentencing."

MIAMI (AP)—A trial for convicted Nazi war criminal Karl-Heinz "Putzi" Grobheit ended yesterday, when the 91-year-old suffered a fatal heart attack in court. He had been convicted of stealing $117 million

in artwork, gold, and jewelry from Jewish families during World War II, after which he moved to Miami under an assumed name. In a plea for leniency, Grobheit gave an address of a warehouse in Buenos Aires, where he claimed to have stored his plunder. It was found to be empty. Grobheit had suffered congestive heart failure for many years, according to his sister, Clara Kaufmann of New York City.

The last sentence made me catch my breath. "Kaufmann . . ."

"As in Norman Kaufmann?" Lizzie said. "Clara was Norman's mom?"

Hernando nodded.

It was all clear now. Norman was lying about his family. They never owned the egg. They were the thieves. "But . . . how . . . ?" I sputtered.

"Argentina was full of Nazis," Hernando said. "Real ones, like Grobheit, who wanted me to give him the location of the egg. The diamond. But I could not tell him anything. Otto did not give me the location—he thought he was protecting me."

I began pacing. "We have a problem . . . Norman read Otto's secret invisible-ink note!"

"That sucks," Lizzie said. "He's going after the diamond."

"Through the lawyer, Caswell Connor," I said. "Norman promised to track down all his family."

"Oh Dios mío . . ." Hernando muttered.

I pulled out my phone and called Harriet, trying not to sound frantic. "Hi! Have you heard from Norman?"

"You bet I did," she replied. "We're going to have a big celebration when he returns. I made you pancakes, Jakey!"

"Celebration?" I said.

"Down in the Village he found the granddaughter of that man . . . Connor. Can you believe, she inherited that entire brownstone! You know what that's worth?"

"*What happened?*" I said.

She let out a laugh. "You're breaking my eardrum, hon. He found the . . . the thing. The egg."

"The Fabergé egg with the Arkady Diamond?" I blurted.

"You have such a good memory," Harriet said. "Always have."

Sometimes when I'm upset, I walk until I'm tired.

That didn't happen until Lizzie and I reached the duck pond at the bottom of the park. There I plopped down on a granite outcropping and broke down in tears. "He played me . . ."

"Maybe Norman will marry Harriet," Lizzie said, pacing in front of me, "and you'll be rich."

"That's not the point . . ." I was still clutching the book, and I threw it toward the pond, but it didn't quite make the water. "Look. I can't even do *that* right."

Lizzie scrambled after the book and brought it back, holding it gingerly between thumb and forefinger. "Ew, duck poop."

She put it down on the rock. It had fallen open to the page with the writing on it.

$$A\ B\ \Gamma\ \Delta\ E\ Z\ H\ \Theta\ I\ K\ \Lambda\ M\ N\ \Xi\ O\ P\ \Sigma\ T\ Y\ \Phi\ X\ \Psi\ \Omega$$

Something about that alphabet drew my eye. I stared at it for a minute and began leafing back through the book, starting with the last page. Otto's final sentence was in a huge font:

Remember, every message contains a message, and it's up to YOU to unlock it!

And then I glanced at the alphabet again. "Lizzie?" I said. "What if we missed the message?"

"We didn't," Lizzie replied. "Remember the iron? The milk?"

I nodded. "But everything this guy writes *means* something. That's his philosophy. You look for messages within messages. I mean, he wrote 'Warm milk 2C' and we thought it meant nothing. But we were wrong, right? So why did he write down a Greek alphabet?"

On a nearby park bench, a white-haired saxophone player was setting up. His case was decorated with a light-blue-and-white-striped flag. He waved to us. Behind him, Hernando was approaching, pushing his blue box. "You two are fast," he said.

"Hernando," I said, "do you think Otto was trying to tell us something?"

Lizzie groaned. "Jake, what's the difference? Norman has the loot already. It's a done deal."

As we all sat on the bench, my phone buzzed. It was a text from Harriet:

Jakey, where r u? The pancakes are getting cold.

Is Norman with u? he is not answering my texts!!!

😞😞😞

"I'm not so sure . . ." I said under my breath. "We may never see Norman again."

The sax player was looking at the book over my shoulder now. "Is Greek *alphavito!*" he shouted. "Many Greeks in New York. Good handwriting!"

"You're Greek?" I asked.

The guy nodded proudly. "English alphabet comes from Greek— only Greek has twenty-four letters, English twenty-six. You see—Greek is easier!"

With a big laugh, he stood and started playing.

Twenty-four letters . . .

Carefully I counted out the letters Otto had written down. "There are twenty-three letters here."

"So?" Lizzie said.

"What is missing?" Hernando asked.

I got out my phone again and searched for the Greek alphabet. When I got it, I held up the screen for all to see:

$$A\ B\ \Gamma\ \Delta\ E\ Z\ H\ \Theta\ I\ K\ \Lambda\ M\ N\ \Xi\ O\ \Pi\ P\ \Sigma\ T\ Y\ \Phi\ X\ \Psi\ \Omega$$

The font was a little different, but when I compared letter for letter, it was easy to see what was missing.

"*Pi,*" I said. "Otto's alphabet is missing the letter *pi.*"

"Pi, as in three point one four one five nine?" Lizzie said. "Et cetera?"

The et cetera might be important. I searched for that too:

3.14159265358979323846264338327

"I'm not following," Lizzie said.

Now my eyes were moving from the digits of *pi* to the message in invisible ink.

Caswell Connor, residing on Tenth Street,
boldly handles my current placements,
assuring the arrival of my most important of hidden, snared eggs.
I rest now.
You act.
Know I am smiling.

"Every message contains a message . . ." I murmured. "What if this—all this stuff about Caswell Connor—isn't the real message? What if it's a decoy?"

"But Harriet said Norman already got the egg . . ." Lizzie's voice trailed off.

"Unless," Hernando said softly, "he did not."

"Norman hasn't come home, so Harriet didn't actually see the egg!" I said. "What if Caswell was a spy, too? What if he and Otto had a plan . . . together?"

"Like a prank!" Hernando was clapping his hands.

Thinking the applause was for him, the Greek sax player took a bow.

"OK . . ." Lizzie stared at my phone. Her lips were blue from the cold. "So what if the three in *pi* means the third letter, and then the one means the first letter, and so on?"

Carefully, I matched each *pi* digit to the corresponding letter—3, 1, 4, 1, 5, 9, 2, 6, 5.

After writing S-C-W-C-E-O-A-L-E, I stopped. "Or maybe not."

"Maybe those letters are anagram," Hernando said. "Mixed up."

"But *pi* goes on forever," I said. "How would you know when to stop?"

"I'm freezing," Lizzie said. She was jumping up and down, hugging herself. "Can we go to the food court and continue this over hot chocolate?"

That sounded like a good idea to me. As I stood Hernando was giving her a puzzled look. "Food court?"

"At the Plaza," Lizzie explained. "Right there. Fifty-ninth and Fifth."

I stopped halfway to a standing position.

Fifty-ninth . . .

Fifth . . .

At that moment I was no longer feeling cold.

There were number numbers, like one, two, three, four. But there were also counting numbers like first, second, third, fourth . . .

I flopped back down on the bench. "I have an idea."

Minutes later we were racing around the Delacorte Theater, which was shuttered and quiet. On the other side, behind the park benches, the ground sloped up to a gentle ridge. I knew what it was (because Harriet and I have been on every historical tour of the park)—the buried remains of a stone wall that once contained NYC's drinking-water reservoir. Years ago it was filled in and became baseball diamonds and picnic sites.

At the top of the little slope, a sign pointed out two or three unremarkable stones sticking up out of the ground. They were the only remaining visible signs of the reservoir.

I looked up the pathway. "I just texted Harriet. She should be here soon."

"OK then, let's do this!" Lizzie was shaking again, but not from the cold.

From excitement.

I held up the note, where we had carefully mapped out the code.

3.14159 . . .

Third letter. First letter after that. Fourth letter after that. First letter after that . . .

Caswell Connor, residing on Tenth Street,
31   41   5   9 2   6

boldly handles my current placements,
5 3   5   8   9

assuring the arrival of my most important of hidden, snared eggs.
7   9 3 2 3   8   4   6 2   6   4   3

I rest now.
3

You act.
8   3

Know I am smiling.
2   7

SW CORNER OLD RESERVOIR FIND ROCKS

"What is a grock?" Hernando asked.

I shrugged. Together we crouched by the exposed stones. What were we even looking for? Were we supposed to dig them up? Dig around them? Stare dumbly until a Fabergé egg materialized?

After a while, a little girl skipped up toward us and crouched next to Lizzie. "What are you looking for?"

"Grocks," Lizzie said.

The girl nodded as if that made perfect sense. "That's like rocks, only with a G," she said. "My name is Gelizabeth! Elizabeth with a G!"

"Glizzie," Lizzie said.

I smiled. *Grock* without the *g* was *rock*. Maybe we just needed to think of that. I began digging around the old stones with my hands. Hernando was lumbering over, with a trowel from his box. Together we dug, working our way north, uncovering stone after stone.

A parks department vehicle puttered by. Lizzie was nervous. "This is a historical site," she reminded us in a whisper.

We froze, but the worker didn't seem to notice. We got back to work but all the stones looked the same—jagged and broken, like the teeth of an old, petrified giant.

Until I got to the fifth rock north of the sign.

I dusted it off as best I could. Hernando magically produced a whisk broom and I brushed until the rock was completely visible.

Lizzie's eyes were wide. "Of course . . ."

I nodded. "It's kind of obvious, when it's staring you in the face."

For the solution to this story, please turn to page 358.

GRIDLOCK JONES
CRACKS THE CASE
By Bruce Hale

You wouldn't expect to find the sharpest mind at Vista Grande Elementary in the front office. (No offense to our staff.) But that's where Gabriel "Gridlock" Jones (who's in my grade) volunteered every day—not because he was a kiss-up, but because information is power, and the main office is where it flows strongest.

At least that's what he says.

When I dropped by that Monday before school, Gabe sat in his wheel-chair at a worktable festooned with papers, his neck craned forward so all that showed was the black bird's nest of his hair. It looked like he was redesigning the school's filing system (or something equally exciting).

"Hello, Maya." He gave me a quick up-and-down scan. "Fell asleep studying again last night, eh?"

My hands flew to my hair. Was it still flattened on one side? No, I'd showered that morning. "How did you—?" Even after knowing Gabe for three years, I was still startled by his powers of deduction.

A corner of his wide mouth tugged upward. "Easy. Your socks are mismatched, meaning you dressed in a hurry. Your eyes are puffy. And even though you washed your face, you didn't totally remove that ink stain in the corner of your mouth."

I tugged my jeans legs down over my socks and rubbed at my lip. A girl likes to be noticed, but maybe not that closely.

"You chew on your pen when you study," said Gabe. "Nervous habit."

The outside door opened, admitting a mom, three students, and a gust of chilly November wind. While the kids shuffled up to the secretary, the grim-faced mom cut behind the counter, beelining it for the principal's office.

Glancing up from his papers, Gabe registered everything. "Trouble with the PTA," he said, dividing his mess into four neat stacks.

"Oh, really? How do you know she's not visiting on personal mom business?" I asked, unable to resist taking the bait.

His smirk widened. "Regular parents check with the secretary first, so that makes her either PTA or someone with an appointment. And between that expression on her face and how tightly she's clutching her purse, I suspect bad financial news."

"Wow."

"Plus, I happen to know Mrs. Dunbarton is PTA treasurer."

I whacked his shoulder. "You might have led with that."

"And ruin my fun?" asked Gabe, brown eyes dancing.

Yes, it can be a pain sometimes, having a brilliant friend.

Shortly after Mrs. Dunbarton entered the principal's office, voices rose. Even with all the usual hubbub—kids coming and going, phones ringing—you could almost make out what they were saying behind the closed door.

"Cover for me," said Gabe. With five powerful strokes, he wheeled himself back by the principal's door. Gabe pretended to read the bulletin board on the wall beside it, but I knew eavesdropping when I saw it.

Glancing around, I wondered what *cover for me* meant. Nobody was paying us the slightest bit of attention.

The argument grew louder. I heard our principal, Ms. Braxton, say, "But you don't know for sure. It could've gone missing earlier."

Suddenly the door blew open, and everyone in the office heard Mrs. Dunbarton say, "Well, the PTA holds *you* responsible!"

The treasurer stormed from the office, past Gabe, past the secretaries, and out the door. Behind him, Ms. Braxton appeared in her doorway, jaw clenched and face flushed.

"Problems, Ms. Braxton?" said Gabe innocently.

The principal blew out a breath and sent him a sour smile. "Like you don't already know."

Gabe lifted a shoulder. "Maybe I could help?"

After her sharp brown gaze scanned the office (sending secretaries back to work), Ms. Braxton regarded my friend. Another sigh. "Come in."

Raising an eyebrow at me, Gabe followed her back into her office. I joined them, closing the door behind me.

"It's about Casino Night," our principal said. "Have a seat." She winced when she remembered that Gabe already had a permanent seat.

His face stayed blank. He'd dealt with insensitivity before. So many times.

"It was a profitable fund-raiser?" he said.

"Almost six thousand dollars," said Ms. Braxton, "and now it's gone."

Gabe leaned forward. "Fascinating."

The principal glowered. "It's not 'fascinating,' it's dreadful. The money was stolen from my desk over the weekend."

"Locked office?"

"Of course," said Ms. Braxton. "The desk, too."

Curiosity prodded me. "Who has keys?" I asked.

"Only the janitor, my secretary, and me," said the principal. "And mine never leave my possession."

Leaning back in his wheelchair, Gabe tented his fingers. "Who knew the money was there?"

The principal puffed out her cheeks, considering. "Well . . . the custodians, the PTA president and treasurer . . . and probably Mr. Langley."

"Mr. Langley?" I asked.

Gabe glanced over at me. "Teacher representative on the Casino Night committee."

I shook my head wonderingly. Gabe was right; you could learn a lot by working in the office.

"Any signs of a break-in?" he asked.

Ms. Braxton shrugged. "The door was locked when I arrived today."

Pivoting his chair around, Gabe wheeled over to the door and examined the lock. I peeked over his shoulder.

"No scratches," he muttered, running a hand along the doorjamb. "No signs of crowbar use."

"So they had a key," I said.

"Maybe." He looked to Ms. Braxton. "And the window?"

"Painted shut." The principal clasped her hands. "Look, Grid—uh, Gabriel, I've given you some leeway because you've been . . . helpful in the past."

"'Helpful?'" I bristled. "He's solved three major mysteries here."

She dipped her head in acknowledgment. "But now I'm going to call in the police."

"Wait," said Gabe. "Give me until after school."

Ms. Braxton wavered. "I don't know . . ."

"I'll return at three o'clock to name the thief," said Gabe.

I goggled at him. *Three o'clock?* Was he cocky or just plain crazy?

"One thing more?" Gabe asked.

"Yes?" said Ms. Braxton.

"How were you going to spend that money?"

Her forehead crinkled. "It was earmarked for the general fund."

"Any special projects?" I asked.

"An author visit." Ms. Braxton named a writer that our librarian would have turned backflips over. In fact, he was one of my favorites, too.

"So if we don't find the money, he can't come?" I asked.

"That's right," said Ms. Braxton.

Gabe nodded. "See you at three. Come on, Maya."

And off we went.

Of course, detective work had to wait for classes. School was funny that way. All through our morning lessons, I could tell Gabe's big brain was worrying at the mystery like a terrier with a chew toy. When recess arrived, he wheeled out the classroom door with fire in his eyes.

"Where first?" I asked.

"Custodians, of course," he said.

We soon found the head janitor, Mr. Shamoon, picking up trash on the grass by the walkway's edge. A lean man with glittering black eyes, he looked like a disapproving ferret with a bad haircut. He scowled as we approached. But we didn't take it personally; he scowled at everyone.

"Kids," he growled.

"Mr. Shamoon," said Gabe. "Got a minute?"

Spearing a milk carton and dropping it into his trash bag, the janitor said, "I'm working."

"So are we," said Gabe. His gesture invited me to help Mr. Shamoon.

I rolled my eyes but complied. It wasn't like Gabe could easily pick up trash himself, at least not without his own spear.

"Who has keys to the principal's office?" he asked.

"Me, the principal, and Ms. Bustamante," said Mr. Shamoon.

"The secretary?" I said, picking up a sticky candy wrapper. "Why her?"

He squinted at me. "Backup."

"And where do you keep your key ring?" asked Gabe.

Mr. Shamoon straightened, glaring at my friend. "Is this about that gambling event?"

"Casino Night? Yes." Gabe looked him up and down.

The man spat. "Never should have held it in the first place. Gambling is a sin."

"So is spitting," said Gabe. "Now about your keys . . . ?"

"Locked in my office all weekend." He stabbed at a plastic cup like it had offended him. "And they were right where I left them when I came in this morning."

Even I knew that this didn't mean someone hadn't borrowed and returned them. Gabe didn't bother mentioning this. Instead, he asked, "Who else has keys to your office?"

"Only my assistant. And she's been on vacation since Thursday." Mr. Shamoon slung his garbage bag over a shoulder as if to go. "So I'm doing her work *and* mine."

Gabe raised a finger. "One last thing?"

"Yeah?" The custodian's glare could've boiled concrete.

"Nice boots." Gabe smiled. "Are they new?"

With a harrumph, Mr. Shamoon turned and stalked off.

My friend rolled his wheelchair down the path. "Well, that was productive."

"Really?" I said.

"Absolutely. Those were Filson Highlanders. Three-hundred-dollar boots."

"I can't believe you know that, but I don't see how it helps us."

His gaze swept over the ragged group of kids kicking a soccer ball across the grass. "The world is full of obvious things that nobody notices. Who knows what will prove important?" Gabe loved to say stuff like this.

"So who do we see next?"

Before he could reply, a raspy voice called out behind us, "Hey, Gridlock!"

We turned. Swaggering up the walkway like a gorilla that had just shaved its body and learned to walk upright came Danny Dunbarton, who I now knew was the PTA treasurer's son.

"What do you want?" I asked.

Danny ignored me. "What were you yakking to Shamoon about?"

"The price of fudgsicles in France," said Gabe, craning his neck to look up at our visitor. "Of course."

"Better not have been about Casino Night."

Gabe's eyebrows lifted. "Oh? Why not?"

"People are blaming my mom for losing that money." Danny tried to look tough, but I'd seen fruit chews that were tougher. "It's not her fault, so keep your nosy nose out of it, Gridlock."

Gabe didn't bat an eye at the insulting nickname. In fact, he had embraced it, ever since solving his first case, when Danny had said, "You think you're some kinda Sherlock Holmes, but you're only Gridlock Jones." For a guy of Danny's intelligence, it was actually almost clever.

"But if she's innocent, wouldn't you want me to prove that?" said Gabe.

"Just leave it alone."

"Afraid of what I might find?"

Trying on a sneer, Danny said, "Ha! My mom works her tail off for this stupid school, even though most of the money they raise is for dumb stuff."

"Like books, or an author visit?" I asked.

"That guy's a jerk." Danny glowered. "He wouldn't help my mom publish her story."

Gabe raised an eyebrow at me. "I see. So your mom disapproves of the PTA's choice?"

"Duh," said Danny. He sure had the gift of gab.

"Thanks."

Danny's forehead crinkled. "For what?"

"From what you've told me, that gives your mom a good motive for 'losing' the money," said Gabe.

"Hey!" Danny's fists clenched as he loomed over my friend. "You take that back!"

I put a palm to his chest. "Easy, bucko."

He swatted my hand aside, but he stood down. Danny knew I'd been taking kickboxing and getting beaten by a girl would look bad on his bully resume.

Jabbing a finger at us, he snarled, "Stay away from my mom. Stay away from this whole thing!" And with that, he spun on a heel and stomped off.

"I bet Mrs. Dunbarton did it," I said.

"Maybe." Gabe was maddeningly calm.

"Oh, come on, G," I said. "She hates the author. She could have taken the money before giving the cashbox to Ms. Braxton for safe-keeping."

"Never make deductions until all the facts are in," said Gabe, spinning his wheelchair and heading back in our original direction. "That's sloppy detective work."

"Let's go see Mr. Langley," I said.

"Not yet."

"Why not?"

Holding a palm out, Gabe cocked his head. The bell rang.

"Oh, yeah," I said. "Classes."

Lunch was lunch. What can I say? I've never been a huge fan of cafeteria food. After we finished, Gabe slipped some sugar cookies into a napkin and we headed for the main office.

"What about Mr. Langley?" I asked.

"In a bit," he said. "But first, we consult the gossip hotline."

"You mean . . . ?"

He grinned. "Ermalinda Bustamante."

Ms. Bustamante had a personality as warm as fresh muffins and a nose for gossip that would've put a bloodhound to shame. As the head secretary, she held many of the school's secrets. And Gabe knew the way to her heart.

"Sugar cookies, for me?" she said, her scarlet-painted lips splitting in a smile. "Aw, Gridlock honey, you're the sweetest." Ms. Bustamante snagged one of the treats in her long, violet fingernails and took a dainty bite. "Mmm, nummers."

Pulling up his wheelchair beside her desk, Gabe said, "We haven't had a chance to catch up lately."

"Ooh, let's," she said. "Did you kids hear that they had to get a special aide for the youngest Bumblecombe boy? Turns out, he's a biter."

"No fooling," said Gabe. After some more small talk, he asked, "Say, do you know if any of the staff has money problems?"

She giggled like a lovesick dolphin. "Honey, we work in a school and get paid peanuts. Who *doesn't* have money problems?"

"How about Principal Braxton?"

"Or Mr. Langley?" I added.

"Old Iron Toes Langley?" she said. "Not that I've heard. He's got family money. And he's an awesome poker player—never loses. He was top scorer at Casino Night."

I raised a hand. "Back up a second. *Iron Toes?*"

Her eyes twinkled. "A tragic dance class accident. His partner was limping for a week."

"And how about our principal?" asked Gabe.

"She can walk just fine," said the secretary.

Gabe rolled his eyes. "Her money issues?"

Glancing at Ms. Braxton's closed door, Ms. Bustamante leaned forward, her voice softening. "Poor Aisha. She got upside down with her mortgage. Now she owes more than her house is worth." The secretary clucked her tongue, a sympathetic mother hen.

"Will she be all right?" I asked. For a principal, Ms. Braxton was pretty decent. I hated the thought of something bad happening to her.

Gabe waved a hand impatiently. "Our principal always lands on her feet. She'll be fine."

Then it struck me: Could the *principal* have taken the missing money? I shook my head, not wanting to think that about such a nice lady.

I was sure Gabe shared my thoughts, but you'd never have known it to look at him. He traded some gossip with Ms. Bustamante before wrapping things up with, "Thanks for your help. I'll be sure to remember you next time my dad bakes his famous Kahlúa brownies."

"Num-num-nummers!" said the secretary.

"Oh, one more thing," said Gabe.

"Yes?"

"Where do you keep the key to Ms. Braxton's office?"

She patted the purse on her desktop. "Right here. And before you ask, it never left my possession." The phone rang and she excused herself to answer it.

As soon as her attention was engaged, Gabe wheeled over to an open computer, shoved aside the office chair, and opened a program.

"Heck of a time to play video games," I said. "An author visit is at stake."

"Research," he muttered, scrolling down the page.

I glanced at the wall clock. "You know we've only got lunch period to solve this thing, right? We don't get a hall pass to play detective."

"I know." Scrolling down further, he clicked on a link. "A-ha!"

"Found something?" I asked.

"No, I just like saying *a-ha*. Check this out."

I leaned in closer. "Danny Dunbarton's record? Wondering how many D grades it's humanly possible to achieve?"

He pointed to a line. "Danny's on the free-and-reduced-lunch program. The Dunbartons must have gotten into financial trouble, too."

"So?"

"So Principal Braxton isn't the only one who needs money."

We were silent for a beat, absorbing this.

Finally, I straightened, raking a hand through my hair. "Augh, too many suspects!"

"Nonsense," said Gabe. "We still don't have all the facts."

"So . . . *now* we visit Mr. Langley?"

"Precisely."

Gabe's my buddy and all, but honestly, what kind of sixth grader says *precisely*?

Just outside the teachers' lounge, we bumped into Mr. Langley—literally. Or at least I did. His satchel fell, spilling its contents onto the floor. I squatted down to help him gather his things.

"Oh! I'm so sorry!" I collected some student tests, an airline itinerary, a paperback book, and a protein bar, and handed them over.

"No permanent damage," said Mr. Langley with a stiff chuckle. I hadn't seen him around in a while and was surprised to notice that he looked tired and unshaven.

"Just the man we wanted to see," said Gabe. He leaned over, snagged a red pencil with his fingertips, and handed it to the teacher. "You've heard about the missing money from Casino Night?"

Mr. Langley winced. "Such a shame. And after all that hard work."

"You were the teacher representative for the event?" I asked.

"That's right." He frowned, returning the last items into his satchel. "What's your interest?"

"Just trying to help Ms. Braxton," said Gabe. "Did you have an eye on the money the whole time?"

"Not *all* the time," said Mr. Langley. "I did play some poker."

"But someone was always watching it?" Gabe asked.

"Of course," said the teacher. "Mrs. Dunbarton counted the money at the end of the night, then passed it to me for a recount. After I finished, I gave it back, and that's the last I saw of it."

I scratched my head. "So why didn't she just deposit the money at the bank? Why leave it at school?"

He made a rueful face. "Amanda doesn't trust ATMs, and she was going to be tied up all day Saturday during bank hours." Mr. Langley shrugged. "We thought it'd be safe at school."

Gabe cocked his head. "In your opinion, who could have stolen it?"

Mr. Langley's eyes narrowed. "Shamoon. He hated the idea of gambling at school, and he's got keys to everything."

"But he—" I began.

"Thanks for all your help," said Gabe. "This whole thing must be so upsetting."

Mr. Langley blew out some air. "You have no idea. And the worst part is, the money we raised wasn't nearly enough. We need three times that much, just to keep up." The corners of his mouth pulled downwards.

"Well," said Gabe, "we've spent enough of your time."

And speaking of time, ours was up. Lunch period ended, the bell rang, and we headed back to class.

It's hard to focus on lessons when your eyes are glued to the clock. I tried not to, but couldn't help worrying. Sure, Gabe was brilliant, but how could we possibly solve this mystery before three o'clock while we were stuck here in class?

My friend maintained his poker face, but I caught him chewing his pencil eraser a couple times, a sure sign that his mental wheels were spinning. Still, aside from a longish bathroom break during our last period, he stayed at his desk, apparently doing schoolwork.

At last, the final bell rang. Gathering up our notes and textbooks, we joined the kids streaming up the hallway.

"So who did it, G?" I asked, pushing his wheelchair along. (He let me help sometimes when he was tired.)

"Patience," he said. "All will be revealed."

Easy for him to say.

When we reached the principal's office, we found we weren't alone. Mr. Langley and Mr. Shamoon were standing before her desk, arguing. And right after we arrived, Ms. Bustamante ushered Mrs. Dunbarton into the office.

There was officially no more room for another body.

"What is the meaning of all this?" huffed the PTA treasurer.

"Yeah," said Mr. Shamoon. "Why'd you call us in?"

"That's what I'd like to know." Principal Braxton cleared her throat. "Gabriel, what's going on?"

"I invited them in your name," he said. My friend let his gaze roam over the adults' faces, one by one. "We're here to solve the mystery of who stole the Casino Night money. And the thief, ladies and gentlemen, is right here in this room."

For the solution to this story, please turn to page 360.

THE CASE OF THE MYSTERIOUS MYSTERY WRITER

By Tyler Whitesides

hat's next?" I asked my little sister as I switched off the mixer and watched the cookie dough tumble to a halt.

She quickly checked the recipe and answered, "Chocolate chips."

Dusting flour from my hands, I stepped over to the pantry and pulled out the half-empty bag of chocolate chips. "Aha!" I suddenly shouted. "You've been snitching chocolate!"

"What are you talking about?" Jules defended. "Dad used half of the chips when he made cookies last week."

"Exactly," I said. "*Dad* made cookies. *You* didn't help that time."

"So?"

"So the twist tie closing this bag is wrapped left over right." I held it out for her inspection. "A right-handed person wraps a twist tie the opposite way, which means that this bag of chocolate chips was last opened by a left-handed person. That's not Dad or Mom. And that's not me . . ."

I saw her squirm under the proof. I had her now!

"Well," she said, "at least I wasn't the one who ate the last doughnut from the box Mom bought on our way home from my ceramics lesson."

"That was Dad," I said.

"Are you sure?" she taunted me.

"All I know is that the doughnut was there when I went to bed at ten, and gone when I woke up in the morning," I answered.

"There is a difference between going to *bed* and going to *sleep*," said Jules. "You snuck back into the kitchen at approximately 10:20 p.m. and ate the doughnut." She narrowed her eyes in challenge.

"Proof?" I asked.

"Your bedroom light was on until 10:30."

"I was reading."

"Your book was in the bathroom," she said. "And I checked your toothbrush. It was dry."

"I must have forgotten to brush."

"I checked it again at 10:45," said Jules. "It was damp."

I squirmed under the proof. She had *me* now.

"I don't see why I need to mention the chocolate chips to Dad," I said quietly.

"And the doughnut will remain our little secret." She stretched out her hand, a bit of dried cookie dough stuck to one finger. We shook in a truce.

Jules was getting good at this. Too good. Together we were becoming unstoppable. We hadn't had a single case go cold in the last year.

In a few more months, Jules would have her tenth birthday. Once she reached the double digits, we'd probably start charging for our investigative services.

The doorbell rang.

I set down the open bag of chocolate chips and headed for the front door, but Jules beat me to it. Sofia Diaz was standing in the doorway, an anxious look on her face as she wrung her hands together.

"Um . . . hi?" I said. Sofia and I were in the same sixth grade class, but it wasn't like we were friends. She was talkative and popular. And I was, well . . . *me*. Sofia and I had been partners during a social studies lesson, but we didn't hang out at recess. And she'd certainly never been to my house before.

"Hi, Theodore," she said. "This is kind of awkward, but . . . I've heard things about you."

I tilted my head curiously. "Like what?"

"That you're smart," Sofia said. "Good at figuring things out."

Jules and I glanced at one another. "Where did you hear such things?" I asked.

"Weren't you the one who found Erica Powell's birthday present when it went missing?" Sofia asked.

"Technically, *I* found the birthday present," Jules cut in. "Theo didn't think to follow the footprints in the dirt by the porch."

I spun on her. "They were *hoof* prints. I wasn't expecting our thief to be a goat!"

"Goats will eat anything," Jules said. "Even birthday presents."

"And you discovered that Cooper Mahoney was the one who'd been sneaking into the teachers' lounge and drinking their sodas," continued Sofia.

So she'd been following my career.

"That was me," I admitted. "But my sister and I usually work together."

"Julia and Bro. Detective Agency," Jules declared.

"We're still working on the name." I cleared my throat. "But the Smetler siblings are here to help. What do you need?"

Sofia Diaz swallowed hard. "It's my dad's job."

I knew Mr. Diaz was the director of the Felding Public Library. "What's wrong?"

"Did you hear about the Young Writers Contest the library was sponsoring?"

I shook my head. "No."

"My dad was in charge of it," Sofia said. "Kids from all over town could submit short stories. The grand prize was a hundred dollars."

"Let me guess," I cut in. "Someone stole the prize money?"

"I'm afraid it's much more complicated than that," said Sofia. "My dad has all the details. That is . . . if you think you can help."

I glanced at Jules, but she was absently picking at the dried dough on her hand.

"We'll take the case," I answered.

Sofia's face cracked into a relieved smile. "Thanks," she said. "We should head over to the library. You can talk to my dad."

I pulled off my apron. "Let's do it."

"What about our cookies?" Jules whined, looking up sharply. Sometimes I had to remember she was only nine.

"We can put the dough in the fridge and bake them later."

Jules folded her thin arms stubbornly. "I'm staying with the cookies. Besides, *someone* has to clean up this kitchen before Mom gets home from yoga or we'll never be allowed to bake again."

"Thanks," I said. Since when was Jules the responsible one?

My sister shrugged. "You can fill me in on the details of the case when you get back."

I turned to Sofia. "Let's go."

I knew the Felding Library almost as well as my own house, but I had never been behind the checkout desk before. Sofia led me back to her dad's office, where Mr. Diaz was rubbing his tired-looking eyes. His desk was strewn with papers and his shoulders were slumped in discouragement. He pasted on a smile when we stepped in, and Sofia quickly introduced us.

"Have a seat." Mr. Diaz gestured to a little sofa against the wall. I plopped down on one cushion, Sofia beside me.

"Thanks for reaching out to me," I said. It was always a little awkward doing business with adults. They often didn't take Jules and me seriously.

"That was Sofia's idea," Mr. Diaz said. "I'm doing plenty of investigating on my own."

"What exactly are you investigating?" I asked, getting down to business.

"Last night was the award ceremony for the library's third annual Young Writers Contest," Mr. Diaz began. "The evening was going well until I finished reading aloud the winning story. At that point, I asked the author of the story to come forward and claim the prize money. At first, no one moved. And then *three* kids came forward at the same time."

"They wrote the story together?" I wondered.

Mr. Diaz sighed. "Actually, that's the issue. Each of these kids claims to be the true author."

"Whose name matches the one on the story?" This seemed simple enough.

"None of them."

"Then they are all lying?"

Mr. Diaz shrugged. "All three claim to have used the same pen name—the name that was used on the story."

"What's the name?" I asked.

"Tucker Murphy."

"The name sounds familiar," I said. But I couldn't remember exactly who or why. "What else can you tell me about this contest?"

"Anyone age ten to twelve is allowed to submit a story," said Mr. Diaz.

"How many entries did you have this year?"

"Eleven," he answered.

"Hmm. Not very many," I muttered.

"We didn't do a lot of advertising," replied Mr. Diaz.

"Did the three kids who claimed to be Tucker Murphy also submit stories under their real names?"

"They did," he said. "But contestants aren't allowed to submit more than one story."

"Then that explains why they might have tried to use a pen name," I said. "Double their chances of winning." I scratched my chin in thought. "What was the story about?"

"It was a mystery story," he answered. "The Case of the Stolen Painting."

"Would you mind if I inspect the pages?"

"Be my guest." Mr. Diaz slid a few papers across the table toward me.

I stood slowly. Careful examination was a crucial part of my job. I was usually pretty good at noticing details other people missed.

The pages in front of me were lined papers, the left edges tattered from being torn out of a notebook. There was a staple in the top left corner and two horizontal folds, dividing the pages into thirds.

The story was written in thick strokes from a dull pencil, and the text looked smudged off to the right. That could have been from folding the pages, the pencil graphite smearing as the papers rubbed together. But why would it only smear in one direction?

"That's some strange handwriting," Sofia commented, inspecting the pages over my shoulder.

It certainly was. Whoever had written the story had used a strange combination of uppercase and lowercase letters throughout the sentences.

"Why would they write it like that?" asked Sofia.

"Obviously, they don't want to be identified by their handwriting," I said. "It makes sense if they were trying to illegally submit a second story." I looked up at Mr. Diaz. "How were these stories submitted?"

"We provided specific envelopes," he answered. "The kids were supposed to come to the library, grab one from the stack on the help desk, and drop their stories in a submissions box."

"No stamps, addresses, or names, then?"

He shook his head. "It was all done right here."

"Do you have the envelopes?"

It only took him a second to find one amid the clutter on his desk. "I believe this is the very one our mysterious story was delivered in." He handed it to me.

It was a large orange manila envelope with a label printed across the front that read, "Young Writers Contest." Other than that, there were no markings or clues. But one thing seemed strange to me. The envelope was definitely large enough to fit a full sheet of paper. So why was the story folded?

"Do you mind if I take the story home?" I asked, picking it up and thumbing through it. Just seven pages long.

"I don't think that's a good idea," answered Mr. Diaz. "Those papers are the only clues we have. Better to keep it safe here at the library."

I nodded. "Understood. I'll just need a moment alone to read it."

"Of course." Mr. Diaz and Sofia stood to leave.

"Before you go," I said. "I'll need the names of the three kids claiming to be the author. My sister and I will question the suspects and see if it turns up anything new."

"Sure." Mr. Diaz took a moment to write three names on a piece of paper.

Cassandra Coleman

Nathan Hansen

Randall Jones

"Everybody wants that hundred-dollar prize," Mr. Diaz said. "These three kids got pretty upset at the awards ceremony. Lots of yelling— each one calling the other a liar. Be careful if you go sniffing around."

I took the paper. "Sniffing around . . ." I repeated, as something clicked inside my brain. "I know who the real Tucker Murphy is!"

Mr. Diaz didn't look too convinced. He shook his head and sighed. "I checked through the whole list of library patrons last night. There's nobody in this town named Tucker Murphy."

"That's because he's not a person," I said. "He's a dog."

"You're saying that a *dog* wrote the winning story?" Sofia cried. I could tell by the look on her face that she was having second thoughts about hiring me.

"Of course not," I answered. "But I *do* know a dog named Tucker. And he's owned by a Mr. and Mrs. Murphy that live on Foothill Street. My sister and I will begin our investigation there. After all, there might be a connection between the pen name and the dog."

"It's actually a really good story," I told Jules as we rode our bikes toward Foothill Street. "I can see why it won first place."

"What's it about?" she asked.

It hadn't been easy to convince her to join me. Jules had finished baking the cookies, but I'd found her curled up on the couch with her latest book—*Goldilocks: A Retelling.* I'd practically had to drag her outside.

"The story is about this fancy vase worth thousands of dollars because the clay was flecked with gold," I explained. "The owner was a rich lady that told the detective exactly how her day had gone. She woke up, had a cappuccino, and took her dog for a walk. When she got home, she exercised while the maid started cleaning the house. Her personal chef made lunch and went home because the lady was going out to shop and have dinner at a restaurant. When the woman came home at nine o'clock, the vase was on the floor, broken into a hundred pieces."

"Easy," Jules said. "Sounds like the maid was the only one home. She bumped the vase while she was dusting."

"That's what the detective thought at first, but the maid had proof that the vase was still intact when she locked the house to leave."

"So no one was home when the vase broke?" Jules said, pedaling hard. "No, wait! The dog was home! I bet the lady's poodle bumped the vase and it shattered."

I shook my head. "Actually, it was the chef. He had propped the kitchen door open so he could slip back into the house after the maid locked up. He knocked over the vase on purpose."

"Why?" she asked as we coasted up to the Murphys' house.

"The detective reassembled the vase and discovered that one of the broken pieces didn't match the rest of the pottery," I explained, hopping off my bike. "The chef had stolen one of the gold-flecked pieces and replaced it with a fragment that he had sculpted and baked in the kitchen oven. But the detective realized that the piece was fake because it hadn't been fired in a kiln. There were a bunch of clues, but ultimately, our genius detective recognized the lingering smell of baking clay in the kitchen oven and figured out it was the chef."

"Wow," Jules said. "That *is* a clever story."

"And whoever wrote it did a good job disguising their handwriting," I said, heading up to the front porch. "They used uppercase and lowercase letters to throw us off."

Jules rang the doorbell.

"Wait!" I whispered. "What are we going to say?" I could hear the dog barking inside.

She shrugged. "I thought you knew these people."

"Not any better than you do," I said.

Mom had worked with Mr. Murphy before he took an early retirement because of some health problems. Last fall, we'd spent an afternoon raking the Murphys' leaves. Mostly, that meant I had raked, and Jules had jumped in the piles with the dog. We didn't *really* know the Murphys. They probably wouldn't even remember us.

The door opened and Mrs. Murphy appeared. She sort of reminded me of my grandmother—short and plump, with hair dyed jet black.

"Down, Tucker!" she called, pushing back the small white pug that was jumping excitedly.

"Umm," I stammered. "We have some questions . . . about your dog . . ."

"Smetler Detective Agency," Jules took over. She was young enough to get away with that kind of talk. Most grown-ups probably thought she was cute. This was confirmed by the broad smile that spread across Mrs. Murphy's face.

"What can I help you with?"

"I'm wondering if you recognize any of the names on this list," I said, handing her the note that Mr. Diaz had written for me.

She squinted down at the square paper, glancing at it from three different angles before answering. "Why, yes! Randall Jones lives just down the street. He takes care of our dog when we go out of town."

I shared a victorious glance with Jules. "Anyone else?" I asked.

"Cassandra Coleman," Mrs. Murphy muttered. "Isn't that Jeremiah Coleman's daughter? His lawn company takes care of our yard." She handed back the note.

Two leads. Two connections to Tucker Murphy.

This was good.

"Can I ask what this is all about?" said Mrs. Murphy.

"Nothing serious," I said. "Just a case of stolen identity."

"One last question," Jules added. "Has your dog been writing stories lately?"

✦ ✦ ✦

"Randall Jones?" I said when the boy opened the door. I had to be sure I was talking to the right person even though I recognized him from school—he was a year younger than me.

"Yes?" he said suspiciously, twirling a blue mechanical pencil between his fingers.

"We're here to talk to you about the Young Writers Contest," I continued.

He grinned. "You're here to bring me the prize money?"

"Not yet," I said. "Does the name Tucker Murphy mean anything to you?"

"Of course. It's my pen name. I used it when I wrote 'The Case of the Broken Vase.'"

"How long did it take you to write that story?" Jules asked.

"About two weeks," he answered.

"You wrote it here?" I asked. "At your house?"

"Here and there," he said. "I take my notebook with me everywhere I go."

"Would you mind if we take a look at it?" I asked.

"So you can steal my ideas?" Randall cried. "No way!"

"At the very least, we'll need a sample of your handwriting to compare to the original story."

"Are you serious?" Randall disappeared into the house for a moment. When he returned, he had a lined page torn from a notebook, the left edge tattered. On it he had scribbled:

I wrote the story, so the money should be mine.

I studied the sample. The pencil strokes were thin, and the letters stayed neatly between the lines on the paper.

"Of course, I didn't use this same handwriting on the story,"

Randall explained. "I was trying to be secretive."

I frowned. "How did you write this?"

"Uh . . . With my hand," he said slowly.

I rolled my eyes. Obviously.

"I was guessing you used your feet," Jules snapped.

"I mean, what kind of paper and pencil did you use?" I tried again.

"Same as all my stories," answered Randall. "From my notebook with my lucky pencil." He lifted his mechanical pencil and clicked the eraser twice.

"Well . . ." I sighed. "Thanks for your time." Jules and I turned away.

"Come back when you have the prize money!" Randall called after us.

We found Cassandra Coleman sitting under a tree in her front yard, her backpack open in the grass in front of her.

"Writing a story?" I asked as we drew closer.

She glanced up from her three-ring binder. "Yes, actually."

"Will you be using your own name this time?" I asked. "Or the dog's?"

Cassandra narrowed her eyes at me. "You know Tucker Murphy?"

Jules and I nodded. "He's quite the poetic pug."

Cassandra shrugged. "It wasn't against the rules to use a pen name. The Murphys' dog was the first one I thought of."

"But it *is* against the rules to submit more than one story to the contest," said Jules. "So, even if you did write 'The Case of the Broken Vase,' you can't claim it without getting disqualified."

"Who says I submitted two?" she asked.

"Mr. Diaz told us you submitted another," I replied.

Cassandra shook her head. "That could have been anyone."

"Your name was on it."

She shrugged. "Maybe somebody used Cassandra Coleman as a pen name."

Ooh. That was devious and clever. I didn't believe her for a moment, but she'd clearly thought this through.

"Can you tell me exactly how it went the day you submitted your story?" I asked.

"Sure," answered Cassandra. "I went to the library, took my story out of my binder and stuffed it into one of those big orange envelopes. Then I dropped it in the box and walked out."

"Would you be willing to give us a handwriting sample?" I asked.

Cassandra thought about it for a second before writing something down on a piece of paper. Then she popped open her binder rings and handed me the page. It was a simple sentence:

I aM tHe ReaL AuTHor of ThE STOry.

Just like the mystery story, some letters were big and some were small.

"This is very helpful," I said to Cassandra as I passed the note to Jules. "Thank you for your time."

"Why did she write it like that?" Jules asked once we were out of earshot.

"Two possible reasons," I said. "Maybe Cassandra doesn't know what the writing is like on the real story, so she was trying to disguise her handwriting for us."

"And she ended up matching the real story by coincidence?" Jules said. "That doesn't seem likely. What's your other idea?"

"Or Cassandra Coleman is the real author and she wrote this

sentence to match the handwriting on purpose."

"If that's true," said Jules, "then she still cheated by submitting two stories. She just thought up a way to lie about it."

I shrugged. "Well, I guess that's it for today."

"What about our last suspect?" Jules asked. "Nathan Hansen?"

I waved my hand. "He had no connection to Tucker Murphy."

"No *known* connection," she corrected. "Besides, we might as well pay him a visit. Unless, of course, you already know who the real author is."

I didn't. And I felt like Jules was just rubbing it in.

Mrs. Hansen led us into her dining room, where we found Nathan seated at the table. Before him was a large mound of clay that he was shaping into a bowl.

"We're here with the Felding Library," I explained as his mom stepped out of the room. "Did you submit a story to the Young Writers Contest?"

"Yep," he said, opening another package of air-dry clay and adding it to his bowl. "And I won, too. Except they won't give me the prize money for some reason."

"They're just having trouble proving who actually wrote the story," I said. "Why did you decide to use a pen name?"

"Some of my friends don't think writing stories is cool," he answered. "But it would have been worth it if I won a hundred bucks."

"How did you choose the name Tucker Murphy?" I asked.

He shrugged. "It sounded like the name of a tough guy."

"Or a dog," Jules added.

Nathan laughed. "That's ridiculous. Why would I want people to think that a dog wrote my story?"

Okay. So Nathan Hansen clearly didn't know about the Murphy dog. But there was another clue right before our eyes. Whoever wrote 'The Case of the Broken Vase' clearly knew a lot about clay and pottery.

"That's a nice bowl you're making," I said.

"Thanks," he muttered. "Almost finished. Then I just need to glaze it and fire it."

"When did you submit your story?" Jules asked.

"About three weeks ago," Nathan answered. "But I wasn't the only one to turn mine in early."

"What makes you say that?" I asked.

"After I dropped my envelope in the box, I hung around so I could see who my competition would be. A few minutes before the library closed, somebody ran up to the help desk and grabbed one of the big envelopes. I tried to follow them, but they lost me in the bookshelves."

Now *that* was interesting! I gave my sister an excited glance before asking Nathan my next question. "What did this person look like?"

He shook his head. "I was too far away to tell. They were wearing a big jacket with the hood up. But it was definitely a kid."

"Did they have their story with them?" I followed up. "Any papers that you could see?"

"Nope," said Nathan. "Now that I think about it, that's kind of weird. The only thing they had was a book."

"What book?"

"I couldn't see the title," he said. "But I thought I saw a couple of grizzly bears on the cover."

As soon as Nathan Hansen said those words, everything started falling into place.

"Come on," I said to Jules. "We've got to get back to the library!"

I had solved the case. I knew exactly which kids *hadn't* written the story. But more importantly, I knew exactly which kid *had*.

For the solution to this story, please turn to page 363.

TRICKED!

A Framed Story

By James Ponti

Can you keep a secret?

I hope so, because I've got one that's totally hush-hush.

My name's Florian Bates and I'm a seventh grader at Alice Deal Middle School in Washington, DC. Okay, so that's not secret. All you have to do is open up a yearbook to find that out. No, the secret part is that when I'm not in school, riding my bike, or doing other typical twelve-year-old stuff, I'm a consultant with the FBI.

Yes, *that* FBI.

My best friend Margaret and I are part of the Bureau's top-secret Special Projects Team. We've recovered priceless masterpieces stolen from the National Gallery, rescued a classmate who'd been kidnapped by foreign agents, and even exposed a deep-cover Russian spy. But for our most recent case we weren't on assignment for the bureau. We were just trying to tape a segment for the afternoon announcements.

"Hello, I'm Margaret Campbell, reporting from backstage at the Alice Deal Auditorium," she said holding a microphone and doing her best impression of a news reporter. "Dating back to 1893, the Stanley Cup is the oldest professional sports trophy in the world."

"Cut!" I called out from behind the camera.

"Why?" she asked. "What's wrong?"

"You need to speak up," I said. "It's really loud in here."

She cleared her throat, double-checked her script, and nodded when she was ready. I pressed the record button and signaled her to start.

"Hello, I'm Margaret Campbell, reporting from backstage at—"

"Cut! Still too quiet."

She gave me a look. That Margaret are-you-just-messing-with-me-or-are-you-being-serious look. "Any louder and I'll be yelling," she said. "That'll look ridiculous."

"How do you think it'll look if it seems like your lips are moving and nothing's coming out?"

Our problem was on the other side of the curtain. The entire student body had filled the auditorium and was now stomping to the beat coming from a band made up of sousaphones, trumpets, and drums.

They also chanted, "Rock the red! Rock the red!"

We weren't the only ones battling the noise. A woman nearby had to practically yell into her phone just to be heard, and a reporter from the local news huddled with her producer and cameraman to figure out how to set up a shot.

I spied on them to see how they solved the problem.

"Try standing closer," I said motioning Margaret to step toward me. "And lean forward when you speak. Look how she's doing it."

Margaret moved closer and I had to adjust the focus. Once I was ready, I signaled her to start. But she just stood motionless.

I figured she'd missed my signal, so I exaggerated it.

Still no response.

Finally, I whisper-shouted, "Go!"

Frozen like a statue.

That's when I realized Darius King, all-star center forward of the Washington Capitals, was walking right toward us. His nickname was Deke, and Margaret was one of the hard-core super fans who called themselves "Deke's Geeks."

She could tell you all of his stats and accomplishments. She knew the name of his dog (Puck) and his birthday (November 20). She even knew that he ate grilled chicken, brown rice, and steamed broccoli before every game. There wasn't anything about Darius King that Margaret didn't know.

Except how to talk to him.

She was totally fangirling as he walked up wearing his red number 42 jersey with a blue *C* on the upper left signifying his role as team captain. He flashed a huge smile and said, "Hi, I'm Darius."

"Nice to meet you," I replied shaking his hand. "Florian."

We turned to Margaret, but all she did was nod. Repeatedly. Like a bobblehead. After an awkward silence, I nudged her with my elbow. "And you are . . ."

"Oh . . . yeah," she stumbled. "I'm . . . Margaret Campbell reporting from backstage at the Alice Deal Auditorium . . ." She froze again, totally mortified. "I mean, I'm Margaret and I'm a geek, Deke . . . no, wait . . . A *Deke Geek*."

Darius totally ignored the stumbles and said, "So nice to meet you."

She went to shake his hand, which might've gone better if she hadn't forgotten she was holding a microphone. By the time he walked over to the woman on the cell phone, Margaret was trying to disappear into the folds of the curtain.

"Tell me the camera wasn't running," she said desperately.

"Oh, no. It was running. The whole time."

She shook her head. "I can't believe I told him I was a geek."

I laughed. "I can't believe you think that was the worst part."

Margaret had been a fan ever since Darius joined the Caps. Part of that may have been because, like her, he was African American, not too common in professional hockey. He also led the team in scoring, just like Margaret was the top scorer on our school soccer team. Mostly, though, she admired all the work he did in the community.

Darius ran street hockey clinics all around the district. He sponsored a citywide book club with the DC Public Library. And he did whatever he could to connect with local schools, which is why he was at Deal. Just five days after winning the Stanley Cup, he'd brought it to our campus so we could see it up close.

The Stanley Cup was the oldest professional sports trophy in the world. It was silver with a bowl at the top, stood just under three feet tall, and was awarded every year to the champions of the National Hockey League. According to tradition, each player on the winning team was given temporary possession of the cup to celebrate as they wished.

As a result, it'd been drunk from and eaten out of, dropped and dented, misplaced and mishandled. One time it was even left in a snowbank on the side of the road when some players changed a flat tire on their car and forgot to put it back in the trunk.

It had also been stolen.

Multiple times.

In 1970, someone nabbed it from the Hockey Hall of Fame in Toronto. And, not long after Margaret got all tongue-tied and called herself a geek, someone snatched it from Deal Middle. Although we didn't learn that until later in the day.

First, there was an assembly. Darius gave an inspirational talk. He showed hockey highlights on the screen. And he opened a large black case to reveal the Stanley Cup. The crowd roared. The Capitals' pep band, which had come along for the fun, started playing, and Darius carried the trophy up and down the aisles so that everyone could take pictures. It was beyond cool!

Next, we went out in groups to the parking lot, where Darius led street hockey clinics. Margaret redeemed herself during one of these by putting three straight slap shots into the goal. Each time Darius yelled, "AND SHE PUT THE BISCUIT IN THE BASKET!"

Finally, he got a break while preparations were made for an after-school parade. It was scheduled to start in our parking lot and go down Nebraska Avenue to Wilson High. This was during sixth period, which is when we heard our names over the loudspeaker.

"Will Florian Bates and Margaret Campbell please come to the office? *Immediately*." It was our principal, Mr. Albright, and it sounded urgent enough that Coach Latham told us to forget about our algebra quiz and go.

"Any idea what this is about?" Margaret asked as we walked down the hall.

"Maybe Mr. Albright saw the video of you with Darius and wants to know if you'd like to transfer to a different school."

She gave me a look. "I'll remember this the next time you do something foolish. Which probably won't be too long from now."

"I know," I said, still laughing. "That's why I'm making the most of this while I can."

We were surprised to find Mr. Albright waiting for us in the hall outside of the office. He appeared more frazzled than usual. "I'm sorry to put you two on the spot like this," he said, looking around to make sure no one could hear us. "But we have something of an emergency."

"Okay," said Margaret. "Why call us?"

He took a deep breath and dived right in. "I don't know what you do for the government," he replied. "I just know that from time to time the FBI comes for you. And when they do, I don't ask questions."

"We're not allowed to talk about it," I said.

"I understand and I'm not asking you to. It's just that we have a *puzzling* situation and I thought with your experience and skillset . . ."

"You need us to solve a mystery?" asked Margaret.

"Exactly," he said. "And preferably without involving the authorities."

"That shouldn't be a problem," I replied, intrigued.

He sighed and said, "I was hoping you'd say that."

We bypassed the front desk and went straight to his office, where there were already two people waiting: Darius King and the woman we'd seen backstage talking on her phone. They looked extremely troubled.

Mr. Albright introduced us. "Florian, Margaret, this is Darius King, as I'm sure you know, and Juliette Tremblay. She's with the community relations department for the Capitals."

"Who are they?" demanded Juliette.

"They're here to help," said Mr. Albright as we took our seats.

Juliette frowned. "But they're kids. You said you had experts."

"They're the experts," he said. "Trust me."

"This just keeps getting worse," she said, resigned.

"What keeps getting worse?" I asked. "What's the problem?"

"This," said Darius. Between them was a large black case. He opened it to reveal foam padding with a cutout where the Stanley Cup was supposed to be.

"Where's the cup?" asked Margaret.

"We don't know," answered Darius.

I quickly shifted into detective mode. "Then tell us everything you do know."

"Why?" asked Juliette. "How can two kids help?"

"By using TOAST," I answered.

"TOAST?" she said.

"TOAST stands for the Theory of All Small Things," said Margaret. "It's how we solve problems like this."

"The idea is that big things can be misleading," I explained. "So we focus on the little details. The ones that get overlooked. If you add them up, they lead to big answers. Like where the trophy is."

"I'm sorry but this isn't going to work," she said. "I need to call the team and let them know what happened. Even if it means losing my job."

I needed to convince her, which meant I needed to show her how TOAST worked. I studied her as quickly as possible. She looked to be in her late twenties and was dressed in a red business suit with a blue blouse. She had a Capitals lapel pin and the wallpaper on her phone was a picture of her holding the Stanley Cup. Everything about her was neat and tidy, except for the pencil she nervously wiggled between her fingers. It was covered in bite marks.

That's when I knew how to get her.

"Look," I said. "I know you're stressed. You're worried about your job and the cup. And that's on top of everything to do with your wedding. But give us a chance before you give up."

She gave me a perplexed look. "My wedding?"

"Aren't you getting married this weekend?"

"Yes," she said incredulous. "But how did you know that?"

"Watch this," Margaret whispered to Darius.

"First of all, you're wearing an engagement ring," I said.

"That doesn't tell you I'm getting married on Saturday."

"No. But your fingernails do."

She gave me a confused look.

"Everything about you screams Washington Capitals team spirit," I said. "Your clothes are team colors. You're wearing a Caps lapel pin. And in this picture your nails are red and blue as you hold the Stanley Cup."

I pointed to the photo on her phone.

"That couldn't have been taken more than a few days ago," I continued. "But in the middle of all the madness that's followed the team winning the championship, you've already had your nails redone a subdued shade of ivory."

She reflexively checked her fingers as I talked.

"You've also stopped biting them," I continued. "Probably so they'll look good in the pictures. Now you bite your pencil instead. You know, the pencil with the logo of the bridal shop in Georgetown."

She went to interrupt, but I just kept going.

"Earlier, when we were backstage, you made two phone calls."

"You were eavesdropping?" she said.

"Not on purpose. But you were talking pretty loudly. The first call was to check on the weather forecast for this weekend. My guess is that the wedding is outside. The second call was about seating arrangements."

"That call was to my mother," she said. "We were speaking French."

"I speak French, too," I answered. "I lived in Paris for three years. Although, judging by your accent, I'd guess you're French Canadian. Montreal, maybe?"

There was stunned silence around the room until Margaret turned to Darius and said, "See what I mean? TOAST is freaking awesome."

"I don't know about you," said Darius. "But I think we should give them a chance."

"Definitely," answered Juliette. "What's our first step?"

"Let's go back to the auditorium," I said. "That's where this all started."

Moments later, we stood on the stage and looked at a sea of brown wooden seats. "We have to establish a timeline of events," I said. "First the curtains were closed, the band was playing, and everyone was chanting 'Rock the red.' We were backstage when Darius walked in and Margaret made a fool of herself."

"Hey!" Margaret said as she gave me a sharp jab in the side.

"Just re-creating the scene," I said. "Facts are facts."

Darius leaned over to her and said, "You didn't make a fool of yourself at all."

"Darius talks," I continued. "We see highlights from the season, and he unveils the Stanley Cup. Did I miss anything?"

"No," said Darius. "So far, so good."

"What did you do with the cup after that?" asked Margaret.

"Put it back in the case," said Juliette.

"And who took the case?" I asked.

"I did," said Juliette. "It's my responsibility."

"It's really big," I said. "Is it hard to carry around?"

"No, it's got wheels and a handle like a suitcase," she explained. "It's easy."

"So then you wheeled it outside for the hockey clinic?" asked Margaret.

"No," said Darius. "First we did an interview with . . ." he turned to Juliette. "What's her name?"

"Kinzly Vance," sneered Juliette.

"You don't like her?" I asked.

"I don't like it when TV crews show up unannounced," she replied. "If she wanted to interview Darius, she should have put in a request to the team."

"Sorry about that," the principal said sheepishly. "Her daughter's a student here, and I told her she could come."

"Yes, but she knows better," said Juliette. "And it wouldn't have mattered, except Kinzly's famous for throwing out surprise questions. Always looking to trip someone up and get a scoop. That's why I stood next to her for the whole interview. I wanted to hear everything."

"Where was the cup during the interview?" I asked. "In the shot?"

"They wanted that, but I told them no," said Juliette. "It's big and silver and reflects a lot of light. It would've taken them at least fifteen minutes to set up the lights and we had to be at the clinic in five. So I told them if they wanted the interview, they'd have to do it without the cup."

"If you were watching the interview," said Margaret. "That means you weren't watching the trophy."

Juliette realized she was right. "Yes, but only for a few minutes. And there was just the four of us: Kinzly, the cameraman, Darius, and me."

"What about the producer?" I asked. "Earlier there was a producer with them."

"I didn't see any producer," said Juliette.

Margaret and I shared a look, thinking this might be significant. Before we left, I pulled Mr. Albright aside and said, "I know you don't want the authorities involved. But if we can't find it, this may become a crime scene."

He understood what I meant and used his walkie-talkie to call the chief custodian. He had him lock all the doors to the auditorium and told him not to let anyone in without his permission.

We went out to the parking lot where preparations were underway for the parade. There were cars and floats and some fans already lining the street. They cheered when they saw Darius and he waved back and smiled, giving no hint that anything was wrong.

"The parade starts in thirty-nine minutes," Mr. Albright said checking his watch. "If we haven't found the cup by then, it's going to be pretty obvious."

He motioned to the convertible at the rear of the parade lineup. A sign on the car read, "Darius King and the Stanley Cup."

"That's not our only problem," I said surveying the parking lot. "Everything's been taken down from the hockey clinic. The crime scene's already changed."

"Actually, no," corrected Juliette. "I was worried about all the people running around, so I locked the cup up with the band's equipment."

In the corner of the parking lot was a truck with a cargo trailer. "Washington Capitals Pep Band" was painted on the side along with pictures of the team's logo and the Stanley Cup.

I couldn't believe it. "You've had the cup for less than a week and they've already put it on the trailer."

"They're hard-core fans," said Darius.

"Sometimes a little too much," added Juliette.

"What do you mean?" asked Margaret.

"They're not officially part of the organization," she explained. "Sometimes they forget that. They expect to be treated like employees instead of fans."

"I always thought they worked for the team," said Margaret. "Does that mean when they play at the games they have to get their own tickets?"

"Yes," she said. "Which they often complain about. We reserve them a special spot and let them use an employee entrance to bring in their instruments. But they're ticket-buying fans just like you."

"Deke!" called out one of the band members. "Come take a picture!"

The man was Robert Besserer, sousaphone player and leader of the band. He excitedly took some selfies with Darius next to the trailer.

"I can't believe you've already got it painted," said Darius.

"That's just the tip of the iceberg," he said excitedly. "Check these out."

He opened the trailer to reveal an extremely well-organized instrument storage area. There were sousaphone and trumpet cases held in place with bungee cords. Three bass drums were stacked on top of each other like a column and (catching my particular attention) there was a large wooden storage case that looked to be the perfect size to hold the Stanley Cup.

Besserer, though, wanted to show us drumheads. "Look at these!" There were five and each featured a bright silver Stanley Cup. "I had them specially made."

"They're great!" said Darius. Then he changed the subject. "Listen, we need to ask you some questions."

"Sure," he said. "Anything."

"But it's got to stay between us," added Juliette. "We have to keep it in the Caps family."

He shot her a look. "Oh, so *now* I'm part of the family?"

There was tension, but Darius quickly defused it. "Of course you are." Then he added, "And maybe I can sign some things for your shop."

It turned out Besserer owned a sports memorabilia and card shop in Bethesda.

"Of course," said Besserer. "Anything for you, Deke."

Darius looked at me. "Go ahead, ask him your questions."

"Where was the Stanley Cup while Darius taught his clinics?" I asked.

"Right in here." Besserer motioned to the trailer.

"Did you keep an eye on it?" asked Margaret.

"Didn't have to," he replied. "I closed the trailer and locked it." He motioned to a padlock on the door. "Me and the other sousaphones had to practice. We've got a new number we're premiering at the parade today." He turned to Darius. "You're going to love it. It's called 'Deke to Deke.'"

"I can't wait," Darius said.

I was just about to ask another question when something caught Juliette's eye. "What's she doing here?"

We saw Kinzly Vance and her cameraman watching us from across the parking lot.

"She already got her interview," Juliette said. "I can't believe she'd wait around all day just to get some video of the parade."

"She didn't wait around," I said. "She must've left and come back because she's wearing different clothes."

"You're right," Juliette said. "Now that really makes no sense."

"What do you mean?" I asked.

"She can't edit the video together with what she shot earlier," she explained. "It'll look wrong if her clothes change in the middle of the story. It's called a continuity error."

"So that means she's here for a new story," Margaret said.

No one said it out loud, but we knew what that story might be. The disappearance of the Stanley Cup would make for a huge scoop. She noticed us watching her and smiled.

Before we left, I had one more question for Besserer.

"What goes in there?" I asked pointing at the wooden storage case.

"A glockenspiel," he said. "It's like a xylophone with a harness, so you can play it in a marching band."

"I don't remember one earlier," I said.

"That's because Tony plays the glock and he couldn't make it," he explained. "He's a dentist and had to work."

"Can I see it?" I asked.

"The glockenspiel?" said Besserer. "It's not in there. Tony keeps it at his house to practice."

"No," I said. "Can I see inside the box?"

The moment turned suddenly tense. In effect, I was calling him a liar and he didn't like the implication. But I was also with Darius, so he went along with it.

"Sure." He stepped up into the trailer and opened the case. "See. Empty."

"Thanks," I said.

I turned to Mr. Albright and gave him a little look.

"Right," he said. "I'm going to get a resource officer out here to secure the scene and make sure nothing gets disrupted."

"Wow," Besserer said shaking his head. "Now it's a *scene*." He pulled the trailer door shut and padlocked it. "Don't bother," he said handing Darius the key. "This is the only key. You keep it." Then he shot a look at Juliette. "You know. In the family."

"Thanks," Darius replied.

As we went back into the school I felt guilty. Robert Besserer was a huge fan, so excited about the Stanley Cup that he'd already repainted his trailer and ordered special drumheads. And we'd just made him feel like a criminal. But that's part of working a case and there was nothing I could do about that.

"Where to next?" asked Margaret.

"Cafeteria," said Darius.

Margaret and I both gave him a look. "Why?"

"I wanted to thank the staff," he answered. "You know my favorite saying, right?"

"Put the biscuit in the basket," said Margaret.

"So as a present they made me a basket of biscuits," he explained. "Absolutely delicious."

We got to the kitchen and Ms. Wilkes, the cafeteria manager, lit up when she saw Darius.

"Looking for more biscuits?" she asked.

"Not now," said Darius. "But don't be surprised if I show up for breakfast tomorrow."

"Ms. Wilkes, we're wondering if you can help us," Mr. Albright said. "We're trying to re-create the activities from the day."

"Is something wrong?" she asked.

"It's . . . *complicated*," he replied.

She could tell he didn't want to go into specifics. "How can I help?"

"Do you remember when Mr. King came in here?"

"Sure," she said. "Right after the last lunch. In between fifth and sixth periods."

"So the students were all gone?" he asked.

"It was just the kitchen staff and the two of them," she responded. "And that big black case they were wheeling around."

"What happened while you were here?" I asked Darius.

"I thanked everyone for the biscuits and we all posed for pictures."

"Well, not *all* of us," said Ms. Wilkes. "Doug Thiel's from Chicago. He's a die-hard Blackhawks fan and since the Caps beat them in the finals, he's been a bit of a sore loser."

"Where was he during this?" I asked.

"Unloading a delivery," she replied.

"Here are the pictures," Juliette said showing us her phone.

"And where was the case while you took them?" I asked.

"Right there by the pantry," she said.

"And where was Mr. Thiel taking care of the delivery?" asked Margaret.

"In the pantry," said Ms. Wilkes.

I looked at the angle of the photos and realized that, while she was taking them, Juliette's back was turned to the case.

"And it was just a few seconds?" I asked.

"I took the pictures," she answered. "And then I got everyone's email addresses, so I could send them copies."

"Hmmm," said Margaret. "So your back was turned for at least a minute or two. That might be enough time."

Juliette slumped. "I've just made one mistake after another."

Darius put his arm around her shoulder. "Don't be so hard on yourself. We're in this together."

Inside the pantry we were surprised to see a row of fifty-five-gallon storage drums. They were the perfect size for hiding the cup.

"What are these?" I asked.

"We cook over a thousand meals a day," said Ms. Wilkes. "So we order lots of ingredients in bulk."

We spent the next ten minutes opening each drum, but they all checked out clean. Still, Ms. Wilkes admitted that some drums may have been put on a truck and taken away after the delivery. She also said that Mr. Thiel had already left for the day, explaining, "He gets here a few hours before school to start cooking, so he gets off early."

Mr. Albright thanked her for helping us and we returned to his office. It was obvious Juliette had given up hope but Margaret and I still worked the case.

"Let's talk it through," said Margaret. "The first question is 'do you really think Mr. Thiel would steal the cup just because the Caps beat his favorite team?'"

"I don't think so," I said. "But it's possible. Just like it's possible Kinzly Vance's producer stole it, so she could get a big story. And it's possible Robert Besserer stole it because he's angry at how the team treats the pep band."

"Which means we're right back where we started," said Juliette.

I went to protest, but she held up a hand to stop me. "I'm not blaming you. You did great. You two are super smart. The problem is that I'm dumb. Or at least I was dumb today. The cup is my responsibility and it was taken because I didn't watch it properly."

The parade was scheduled to start in five minutes. We could hear the pep band warming up outside.

"If Darius doesn't have the Stanley Cup when he's riding in that convertible, it will be all over social media before the parade makes it halfway down the street," said Juliette. "I can't let the team find out that way. I have to tell them I lost it."

"Say it was my fault," Darius offered. "I scored fifty-three goals and was the MVP of the Stanley Cup Finals. They're not going to fire me."

She laughed. "I appreciate it. But I'm telling them it's my fault because it is."

The bass drums began to pound, and people started chanting, "Rock the red! Rock the red!" Time was up and we didn't have the cup.

And then it hit me.

Something was wrong, I wasn't sure what, but something was out of place. Suddenly, images started flying through my mind. The Stanley Cup. Biscuits in a basket. Sousaphones. Storage drums. Bass drums. Kinzly Vance's clothes. The cafeteria. Street hockey. Blackhawks. It was all a blur.

And then I saw it as clear as day. Suddenly everything made sense and all I heard was, "Rock the red! Rock the red!"

TRICKED!

Juliette looked distraught as she waited for her boss to answer the phone. Just as she was about to talk, I snatched it from her.

"Sorry, wrong number," I said using a fake deep voice. Then I ended the call.

"Why'd you do that?" asked Juliette.

"Because I know where the Stanley Cup is," I said with a Cheshire grin.

"How?" exclaimed Darius.

"It's complicated," I answered. "But the first thing you need to know is that 'Rock the red' changes everything."

For the solution to this story, please turn to page 366.

SOLUTIONS

Solution for Snow Devils

"It wasn't Hubert Montgomery," Riley told Mr. Ball.

He and Mongo were sitting in the vice principal's cinder-block office. Mongo looked nervous. Riley did not.

"Go on, Mr. Mack," said the school's disciplinarian. "I'm listening. But only until two twenty-five. Then I'm calling the police."

Riley glanced up at the square clock on the wall. It clicked from two nineteen to two twenty.

He had five minutes.

"There was a pair of snow devils involved in this prank, which, actually, wasn't a prank."

"Excuse me?"

"That FART out back?" Riley gestured toward the window. The big word was still there. "It wasn't a joke. It was a giant cheat sheet created by an eighth grader named Brandon Kilmeade."

Mr. Ball nodded. "I know Mr. Kilmeade. We've had a few . . . discussions. Go on."

"Kilmeade charged Steve Duffy, who, by the way, has to be the laziest student on the planet, twenty bucks to steal the answers for his makeup history quiz in Mrs. Henkin's class."

Mr. Ball bristled. "How could you possibly know such a thing, Mr. Mack?"

"Easy. Steve told me. But even after Kilmeade gave him the answers, Steve Duffy was still freaking out."

"He must have severe test anxiety," said Mongo.

"I'm guessing having the answers to the quiz wasn't enough for Duffy," said Riley. "So Kilmeade gave him a giant cheat sheet."

"I'm not following your logic," said Mr. Ball.

"The history quiz was only four questions long," Riley explained. "And it was about American presidents. The answers? Franklin Delano Roosevelt, Abraham Lincoln, Richard Nixon, and Thomas Jefferson."

"I still don't . . ."

"Take the first letters of their first names."

"F-A-R-T," mumbled Mr. Ball.

Riley nodded.

"What about the boots?" asked Mr. Ball.

"Well, sir, I confess I don't have any proof to back me up, but I believe Mr. Kilmeade 'borrowed' them from Mongo last night. My friend here keeps them on his porch overnight when they're wet."

"Those are my mom's rules," said Mongo. "You want me to ask her to check our security cameras?"

"You have security cameras?" said Mr. Ball.

Mongo nodded. "We had a dognapping incident at our house not too long ago. We installed them after that."

Mr. Ball stood up behind his desk.

"Mr. Mack?"

Riley stood up, too.

"Yes, sir?"

"Job well done." Mr. Ball extended his hand. Riley shook it. "Now, if you two gentlemen will excuse me, I need to locate a certain pair of eighth graders."

Mongo raised his hand.

"Yes, Hubert?" said Mr. Ball.

"May I have my boots back? The sidewalks are still kind of slushy."

"Of course. Here you go."

Mr. Ball handed Mongo his boots, exited the office, and scurried down the hall, barking into his walkie-talkie. "This is Ball. I need a 10-20 on Brandon Kilmeade and Steven Duffy. ASAP!"

Mongo and Riley followed him out of the office and sat down on the bench so Mongo could pull on his boots.

"Hey, Riley?"

"Yeah, Mongo?"

"Why'd Kilmeade march all the way over to my house in the snow to steal my boots? He could've put on anybody's boots. His mom's. His dad's."

"He was going for a twofer," Riley explained.

"Huh?"

"He wanted to earn his fee from Steve Duffy, sure. But he also wants to take over our territory. So he tried to take a shot at breaking up the gnat pack. He probably thought I'd kick you off the crew for doing something dumb like writing FART in the snow."

"Would you?"

"No way," said Riley. "Come on, you're the biggest gnat in the whole pack. We're nothing without you."

"Thanks, Riley."

Riley grinned and remembered something his dad, who was in the Army, always told him: "Protect your country, protect your family, protect your friends, and defend those who cannot defend themselves."

Yep.

That's just how Riley Mack rolled.

Solution for Possum-Man and Janet

Janet pushed the big button that had been hidden under the Danger sign.

Instantly, the paint stopped rising and the door out of the tank popped open. Thousands of gallons of paint went pouring out onto the factory floor—carrying Uncle Jim and Janet with it.

"It said 'Manual override'!" Janet shouted as she rode the big blue wave through the door. "'Push in case of emergency'!"

"Ohhhhhhhhhh!" said Uncle Jim.

The paint swept them another twenty yards from the tank as it spread out in every direction. The second he came gliding to a stop, Uncle Jim popped to his feet, blue from the bottom of his boots to his thick neck.

"Now to catch Limerick King!" he declared, slamming a fist into an open palm. Speckles of paint sprayed onto his face, but he didn't notice. He was too busy bolting away. He almost slipped and fell on the slick floor, yet managed to make it to the hallway leading outside.

Janet got up more slowly, took a deep breath, and followed.

She found her uncle outside looking disappointed. There were police cars everywhere, and Limerick King and his minions were already in handcuffs.

"Darn it," Uncle Jim said. "I didn't get to punch anybody."

"Oh, there you are," said a familiar voice.

Janet turned to find Lieutenant Celeste Wroblewski of the Cleveland Police walking their way with Uncle Jim's Possum Belt in her hands.

"They wouldn't tell us where you were," the lieutenant said, jerking her chin at Limerick King and his gang.

Punk—or maybe it was Skunk—gave Limerick King a kick as they were being shoved into a squad car.

"You and your dumb limericks," she grumbled.

"How'd you know to come here?" Janet asked Wroblewski.

The cop handed Uncle Jim his belt, then pointed at the Night Glider. All its lights were flashing, the windshield wipers were on, and a flamethrower was spitting a stream of fire from the front.

A dark shape sat in the pilot's seat—a shape that was wagging its tail.

"We got a call about a dog in a flying saucer trying to burn down the Spreadz-Easy factory. I had a feeling you two were involved." Wroblewski looked Uncle Jim and Janet up and down. "What did they do to you, anyway?"

"No time for chitchat," said Uncle Jim, buckling on his belt. "There's still important work to be done."

Wroblewski looked surprised. "Some of Limerick King's gang is still on the loose?"

Uncle Jim shook his head.

"It's worse than that." He nodded at Janet. "She's up past her bedtime, and there's a math test tomorrow."

"To the Night Glider!" Janet cried.

She and Uncle Jim took off running.

Solution for Monkey Business

"It wasn't any of the suspects," I explained. "It was Padgett. I don't think she's really a keeper at all!"

I then explained my reasoning:

Padgett had said that the giraffes probably reminded Zipper of home. But giraffes are African animals and spider monkeys are from the forests of the Americas, ranging from Mexico down to the Amazon. In fact, no monkey with a prehensile tail lives in Africa; those monkeys only live in the New World. Any keeper working with primates should have known that.

Once I had told them this, Hoenekker quickly dispatched his team after Padgett, who realized the jig was up and bolted for the exit. Marge O'Malley tackled her, and both tumbled to the ground, taking down the poor person playing Kazoo the Koala that day, resulting in another traumatic mascot beheading.

It turned out that Padgett wasn't named Padgett at all. Her name was Matilda Bleeker. She had slipped into the employee area of the park and stolen keeper Padgett's uniform with the intention of making off with a monkey—because she had always wanted a monkey. However, Matilda ended up learning the hard way that monkeys make bad pets. While being carried away from the scene of the crime, Zipper escaped the net and, recognizing Matilda as the person who had tried to steal her, promptly bit her on the nose, resulting in her needing fourteen stitches.

As for the fluffy object Zipper had dropped, it turned out to be part of one of the eyebrows of the Uncle O-Rang costume. It was returned and reattached without incident.

The three suspects were each given free passes to FunJungle and coupons good for a complimentary $11.99 soda as an apology for being wrongly accusing of monkey theft.

For my help in solving the mystery, I was treated to a free corn dog.

Solution for The Fifty-Seventh Cat

Everyone started talking at once. Anya ran around the cat homes in excitement, and then Mom showed up, frantic. "Where did you girls go?" she thundered, relieved and angry at the same time. All the while, Div stared down the pebbled walkway, her mouth dry. Should she say what she thought? What would happen if she did?

Then Judy came down the walkway. Their eyes met and she gave a sad smile.

"It was you, wasn't it?" Div asked softly.

Anya stopped running. "It was *her*?"

Everyone stopped talking.

"It's not right," Judy cried. "He works so hard. Harder than all of us. It's not easy looking after fifty-six cats! And in a few weeks when Marilyn Monroe has her litter, it will be sixty-four!"

"Kittens!" Anya said, delighted.

"Shush," Div told her. She turned to Judy. "You hid the statue in the cat house. Why?"

"When I saw the statue break," Judy said, tears streaming down her face, "I knew Shel would get in trouble. It happened when Elvis jumped off the bed. His tail knocked over the statue."

Shel's mouth fell open.

Judy nodded at him through her tears. "Luckily it happened between tour groups. There was no one in the room for about two minutes. Still, there were cat biscuits on the ground. So I had just enough time to hide the statue under my shirt, grab the biscuits, and run to the cat house. And um, dispose of the biscuits along the way."

"By eating them!" Anya said admiringly. "That was smart."

"Judy," Shel said, finding his voice at last. "You took a big risk to protect Elvis and me. I don't get it; why would you do all of that?"

Anya snorted. "Duh!"

Mr. Frost spoke up. "This is quite a story," he said gently. "I'll see that the museum doesn't press charges. After all, the cats are part of the museum, aren't they? And . . . let me see, maybe that Wally knows something about art restoration?"

"Wally?" Anya asked.

"You know, the man wearing the red suit," Div said.

It turns out Wally didn't, but his partner, Lizzie B., did. Restoring old art was her specialty. For a fee, of course. In no time, the police officers were sent away, the gate was reopened, and plans were made to repair the broken statue and have it back on display soon.

"Maybe we haven't made it easy for you," Mr. Frost said to Shel after the police were gone. "You understood all along, we have to keep this place the way Hemingway wanted. It would be wrong to sell the Picasso cat."

"Yes," Shel said. "And it would be wrong to relandscape. I see that now."

"Maybe we can still replace the magnolia bush with something else," Mr. Frost said. "We don't want poor Fred getting sick." Then he added gently, "But also, Shel, fifty-six is a *lot* of cats for one person to take care of. No one realized that until now. No one except Judy."

It was decided that Judy would sign on as Shel's assistant. She had two cats of her own at home.

"Only until I train her," Shel said quickly. "After that we're equals on the job."

When Div and Anya and their mother were heading out, they could see Shel and Judy holding hands in the garden, a family of cats surrounding them.

"Aw, I told you she likes him," Anya said.

"Yeah, well, he likes her, too," Div said.

"Bye, girls," Mr. Frost said at the gate. "The Hemingway cats are forever grateful to you!"

Just behind him stood Elvis the tuxedo cat. "*Meow,*" it said. "*Meow, meow!*"

"Come on, girls," Mom said. "It's time for Dolphin Paradise."

Div and Anya followed their mother to the street, where the afternoon sun shone bright.

"I wonder," Div said to Anya, "if there will be fifty-seven dolphins, too!"

Author's Note:

This mystery was inspired by a recent trip to Key West where I got to visit the Hemingway House and see all those cats! I also saw a replica of the Picasso cat that was given as a gift from Pablo Picasso to Ernest Hemingway. The original statue was stolen and broken in real life before it was found. This story is my imagined version of what happened!   —SC

Solution for The Perfect Alibi

Frankie figured Mr. Cumberland was the mastermind, because he was wearing a fancy watch just a month after the burglary. Later, when pressed, his grandmother remembered her husband had worn the exact same pocket watch.

Secondly, Frankie knew Shana Cooper's alibi was fake because of the church clock. The burglary happened on Sunday, March tenth, when daylight saving time takes effect. She was actually seen running up the church steps at *one o'clock*. The church's maintenance man, as Frankie learned on her field trip, always set the clock on Mondays. On Sunday, the church clock was still set to standard time. Shana Cooper helped her boyfriend Petey steal the jewelry, then went to church. She lucked into her fake alibi until Frankie figured it out.

For Shana and Petey to have cleaned out the house so quickly, they had to know where the most valuable jewels and items were stored. They needed inside information, which the grandson was only too eager to provide.

Frankie and George solved the mystery. Were you able to figure it out?

Solution for Three Brothers, Two Sisters, and One Cup of Poison

Hannah smiled. She walked over to the silver goblet filled to the brim with poison. "When you think about it, only two of your sons had motive to poison you all these months. And those are the two sons getting something from your will."

"Blake and Jake!" Aunt Bea said. "So they're working together?"

"No," Hannah said. "They both have motive. But only one of them has the means."

At this, Bubbie looked confused. "What do you mean, Hannah? Both Blake and Jake have been taking care of Bea in this house. Any one of them could have slipped the ethylene glycol into Aunt Bea's food or drink at any time."

"True," Hannah said. "But only *one* of them had easy access to antifreeze in the first place."

She looked at the triplets, who all looked very nervous.

"Aunt Bea told us that Jake works part time at a soup restaurant and that Blake works part time at an auto shop. So which place would have a very poisonous chemical like antifreeze?"

"You put antifreeze into cars," Aunt Bea whispered.

All eyes turned to Blake.

"I—I'm being framed!" he said. "It's Jake—I swear!"

Hannah shook her head. "Oh, Blake," she said in mock pity. "We know it isn't Jake . . . because Jake was the only one eating the food tonight. He dug right into the feast without hesitation or fear. He had no idea the food or drinks had trace amounts of poison in them. But you knew—that's why you said you weren't hungry."

Beads of sweat formed on Blake's forehead. His smile had completely fallen from his face. His eyes darted to the door. But Drake stepped back and blocked the doorway.

"I can't believe this," Aunt Bea said. "You were making me sick on purpose?! Why?!"

"This smile of mine? It was all *fake*," Blake said sourly. "I wanted my fortune! I wanted it now! I'm tired of living in this house, waiting on you hand and foot. I wanted to be like Drake—to move away and follow my dreams, but you felt so betrayed when he left that you decided to cut him out of your inheritance. I put in too much hard work and too many years of my life for you to write *me* out."

"And . . . how did that work out for you?" Isaac asked.

Blake snarled.

"Thank you, Hannah. Thank you!" Aunt Bea said. "I will write Blake out of my will. Jake will get my necklace, now. And Drake will get the house. Jake and Drake are the only ones I can trust—"

"Not so fast," Hannah said, holding up the goblet. "The person who poured poison in this cup . . . was *not* Blake."

The triplets looked at each other. Then Jake pointed at Drake, while Drake pointed at Jake. And Blake pointed at both of them.

"Isaac and I were sitting on the couch, waiting for your lawyer, when we heard some pots and pans clanging in the kitchen. Bubbie was sleeping, but Isaac and I got up to investigate. We opened the door just in time to see a triplet pour the rat poison into the goblet. But there was something very fishy about the whole scenario."

"Fishy? I think you mean *ratty*," Isaac said.

"Why would someone make loud noises in the kitchen before quietly tipping the poison into a cup? How is it that we would crack open the door just in time to see the crime?" Hannah threw her hands up in the air. "You see? Someone wanted to make sure we saw him poisoning the cup. He wanted to get caught!"

Bubbie scrunched her nose. "But why?"

Hannah grinned. "*This* goes back to motive. Who had the most to gain from tonight?"

All eyes turned to Drake.

"You're crazy!" Drake said, adjusting his glasses. "You—you have no proof! You even said you weren't sure which of us you saw!"

"Here's the clincher," Hannah said. "The poison Blake was using was ethylene glycol. The poison used tonight was rat poison. Only the people who saw the note Bubbie gave Aunt Bea would think that rat poison was correct."

"I never saw the note," Drake said.

"I didn't either!" shouted Jake.

"True. Bubbie wrote the note, then Aunt Bea got the note at the dinner table. When she left to call her lawyer, Isaac stole the note immediately. Isaac and I read the note out loud in the pantry closet, and Isaac ate the note right after."

"Yum!"

"But," Hannah said, "Drake was the one who came to fetch us from the pantry to bring us back to dinner. He heard us talking about rat poison through the door."

Drake shook his head. "If I had the most to gain from tonight, then why would I poison my mother? After all, if I got caught, I would never see any money!"

"This was because of something Aunt Bea said," Hannah explained. "She gave Blake and Jake until midnight to prove that they were trustworthy—and that their brother was the liar. If either of them had any proof at all, you could kiss your new fortune goodbye. So you decided to act like *both* your brothers while pouring the poison, knowing that we wouldn't know for sure if you were Blake or Jake."

Isaac's face lit up. "Oh yeah! You had a huge smile, like Blake. But you were burping and talking about how full you are, like Jake would."

"Exactly!" She nodded at her brother. "Drake was *never* going to poison you, Aunt Bea. He purposely got caught with the poison, pretending to be his brothers, so that you wouldn't know who to trust, and so you'd stick to the plan of giving him the whole inheritance at midnight."

Drake glared at her with molten-hot hatred.

Aunt Bea's jaw was slack. She stared between her three sons, and a little panicked hiccup escaped her throat. "I . . . Jake! Protect me!"

Jake shielded his mother from the other two.

"You've poisoned my mother against me!" Blake cried.

"What an odd choice of words," Bubbie said, as Blake turned on his heels and ran. But he flew right into the arms of the police, struggling and howling as they dragged him into their car.

Bubbie pulled the cell phone out of her pocket. "I dialed them ten minutes ago, when you first revealed Blake."

Drake gave himself up to the police without a fight.

By the time Aunt Bea's lawyer arrived, Hannah and Isaac were nearly falling asleep. Jake received Aunt Bea's total inheritance, having neither poisoned his mother nor tried to frame his brothers for poisoning. At least there was *one* good brother.

On the way out, Hannah and Isaac linked arms with Bubbie. Even after Bubbie saved Aunt Bea's life, Bubbie didn't get their mother's necklace or the cottage. She didn't even get her pop-pop's silver goblet. But, in the end, Bubbie didn't need it. She had a relationship with her sister again, and she had sweet, nonmurderous grandchildren.

Family is better than fortune, and her cup runneth over.

Solution for The Haunted Typewriter

"Are you mad that we figured out it was you?" said Kevin, turning toward the person responsible.

All eyes turned toward the person Kevin was looking at.

Tara wasn't sure why the other two people in the room were surprised. They all had the same information she and Kevin had. They had all the information they needed to solve three mysteries:

First, *decoding* the cipher.

Second, *how* the person responsible had gotten into and out of the locked room.

And third, *who* was the person responsible, along with their *motive* for impersonating a ghost.

Kevin's brother, Braden, shoved his hands into his jeans pockets and looked at the floor.

"Braden?" said Mrs. Byrne. "It was you?"

When Braden didn't say anything, Kevin spoke.

"I think he did it for me," he whispered. "If you solve this latest cipher, you can see *why*."

```
/ \ / \
\ / \ /

N....H....E....U....L....N....D
.E...I.C..Y.R...I.O...I.E...O.G...O.
..R.L..R.O...O.G..Y.K..M.R..I.N..
...D....U...N....E....E....T...

SINCERELY,
THE GHOST OF SOMA
```

Braden looked up and nodded at his brother, but neither spoke. Tara took Kevin's hand and pulled him into the living room to talk in private. They only needed a minute to confirm they both had the same idea.

"You start," Kevin said when they got back to the others.

"Braden, who we call Salmon as a code name from its Irish Gaelic meaning, knows how to do the same type of magic as Sanjay," Tara said. "*Misdirection.* That's when you get people's attention so they'll look one place while you do something in another place without them seeing it."

"If we assume there isn't really a ghost," Kevin said, "there had to be a trick."

"A trick made us think of the magician," Tara said, "and how Braden loves magic. Remember the first coded message appeared before the door was locked? Anyone could have gone inside the room and put the paper in the typewriter."

"But we heard the typing," Mr. Byrne said.

"Misdirection," Tara said.

"It was probably his cell phone," Kevin said, looking at his brother, who nodded. "He turned on a recording of the sound of typing keys on his cell phone, which he didn't have with him at the table where we were eating either meal. Because of our family rule about no electronic devices at the table, we didn't notice Braden's missing phone as strange. His phone must have been near Dad's office, hidden somewhere."

"In the entryway cabinet," Braden mumbled, speaking for the first time.

"But we locked the door of the room," Mrs. Byrne said. "Misdirection from the sound of the typing keys is one thing, but getting a message into the typewriter through a locked door?"

"The second message *wasn't* in the typewriter," Tara said. "Braden had the note with him when we opened the door."

"Impossible," Mr. Byrne said. "We all saw the note in the typewriter."

"Did you?" said Braden. A hesitant smile was on his face. "One of the main principles of misdirection is to make people see what you want them to see. I called out 'look!' and pointed. But then I blocked your view with my body as I ran forward. You *believed* there was a note because of my words and actions, but I was the first person to reach the typewriter. I had the note in my hand. I'd printed it out earlier, after writing it using an app on my phone with a typewriter font. When I held up the paper, you all *assumed* I'd pulled it from the typewriter, because that's what made sense based on your expectations. You believed what made sense, not what you really saw."

"Why?" Mrs. Byrne asked.

"Read the latest note," Braden said.

"It's the same rail fence cipher," Kevin said. "There's an extra line, but the same idea. However, the hash markings on the top are the *opposite direction* of the first cipher. You can decode it in the same way—and then read the letters *backward*."

```
/ \ / \
\ / \ /

N.....H.....E.....U.....L.....N.....D
.E...I.C...Y.R...I.O...I.E...O.G...O.
..R.L...R.O...O.G...Y.K...M.R...I.N..
...D.....U.....N.....E.....E.....T...

SINCERELY,
THE GHOST OF SOMA
```

"Decoded," Kevin said, "here's the first string of letters:

"N-E-R-D-L-I-H-C-R-U-O-Y-E-R-O-N-G-I-U-O-Y-E-K-I-L-E-M-E-R-O-N-G-I-T-N-O-D.

"Backward, that's DONTIGNOREMELIKEYOUIGNORE-YOURCHILDREN.

"With spaces between words, DON'T IGNORE ME LIKE YOU IGNORE YOUR CHILDREN."

Braden shrugged. "Kevin got it right. I did it for him. You missed his sixth grade graduation, Mom. You missed most of the things that were important to him. Ever since you and Dad went to work at that start-up, you've been away *all the time*. Most of the time it's cool, but the important stuff?" He shrugged. "When I took your jewelry, I thought you'd be worried that a thief had gotten inside the apartment with Kevin inside all alone, and you'd realize that it wasn't cool to leave him on his own so much. But all you did was get upset at building security. I felt bad for Ms. Weber when I heard you yelling at her."

"Stealing your mom's jewelry wasn't the answer," Mr. Byrne said, shaking his head.

"The earrings are only hidden," said Braden. "I didn't do anything with them. But that first idea didn't work. After the Hindi Houdini moved into the building and he learned I was into magic, he talked to me about the principles behind successful illusions: misdirection and a good story that fits the audience. That gave me the idea to try something else. Since Kevin loves codes, I knew he'd solve a mysterious coded message. And Mom and Dad love to watch scary movies, so I thought a ghost might scare them into making changes."

"Were we really away that much?" Mrs. Byrne said to her husband.

"Temporarily," Mr. Byrne mumbled.

"Nearly a whole year," Kevin said.

Kevin's parents hadn't realized just how much they'd been away. They worked in a place where a lot of people didn't have kids. Long hours were expected, so the Byrnes meant well, but they'd lost sight of their priorities.

The Byrnes apologized to the building manager, planned a week of vacation to spend with their sons, and found a balance that allowed them to work long hours but also be there for the important events they'd been missing. Braden was still grounded for half the summer, but he was allowed to go out as long as it was to spend time with his brother or parents.

Tara, who had never especially liked magic before, now appreciated what it could do. Her parents took her and Kevin to one of the Hindi Houdini's magic shows, and she didn't guess how he performed a single trick. Part of her wanted to figure out the tricks like she did codes and ciphers, but, in the end, she decided she liked the mystery better.

Solution for Surprise. Party.

Only the low hum of air through the floor vents could be heard as Sherman paced before the torn paper and empty box.

"Well?" Erica said.

"Scratch the paper."

"What?"

"With your fingernails." He pointed to a swath of untarnished paper.

Erica huffed, but did as told. A scraggly line along the paper's surface remained.

"The finish on this paper is so delicate," Sherman said, "the slightest abrasion scrapes it away. I can't think of any shipping company that could transport a box like this without scuffing the sides, or corners. As you all can see, there's little damage to the paper besides where it was initially opened, and the scratch Erica just inflicted."

Murmurs in the crowd. The Sorcerer Farnsworth loudly proclaimed, "Well, ain't that something."

"This box wasn't shipped from anywhere. It was wrapped here. Isn't that right, Mister Erica's Dad?"

Mister Erica's Dad turned about as red as the wrapping paper. "Now wait just a minute!"

"Certainly," Sherman said. Everyone in the room looked to Erica's father.

Erica said, "What's he talking about, Daddy?"

There was an extended, awkward silence that Sherman interrupted after checking his watch. "A minute has passed. I will continue. There's a tiny shard of broken glass by the staircase, from a mirror. There are no broken mirrors downstairs, and Mister Erica's Dad never told any of us to watch where we step, even though he required we remove our shoes at the home's entrance. Isn't that right, James?"

James, with the bandaged foot, stepped forward. "I guess it is. My foot still hurts. Though I appreciate the bandage, Mister Erica's Dad!"

Mister Erica's Dad did not respond.

"It's the least you could do," Sherman said to him, "since you didn't know your mistake had made it all the way downstairs."

"Okay, I'm calling everyone's parents now."

Sherman stared at his own fingernails. They needed clipping. "Will you also call Erica's mother and tell her you broke her gift? A mirror of some sort."

"You broke my Sea Breeze Blue fashion mirror?" Erica's face was frozen in a snarl. "Why?"

"Sweetie, it was an accident!"

The party crowd gasped.

The Sorcerer Farnsworth said, "Why give the kid an empty box? That's cruel."

"You're fired!" Mister Erica's Daddy said. "Pack up your rabbit and go."

This started a shouting match between the two adults in the room. Sherman slipped to the gift table, lifted a slim box in metallic blue paper. He unwrapped it, and only Erica noticed. "Hey, that's mine."

Sherman did not stop, lifting the top from the box, revealing the necklace inside. He held the slim chain so the charm dangled from his fingers. It said "Daddy's Little Girl."

Sherman said, "I take it you don't live with your father. But you could if you wanted. He really wants that. So he does silly things sometimes. Like try not to get shown up by your mom. I don't think he's such a great planner. Though I think he does love you."

Outside, a horn honked.

Perky, Sherman said, "That's my mom. Gotta go."

The party crowd seemed stunned and shaken as Sherman grabbed his blazer, and on his way to the door, a slice of sausage-mushroom pizza. "Thanks for the party. It was fun."

Sherman trotted outside, and on his way to the street, footsteps pattered behind him. The boy Otis, and Erica's (former) BEARY Best Friend, Paisley.

"Hey," said Paisley, "you think your mom could give us a ride home?"

Sherman nodded stiffly. "I don't see why not."

Otis said, "I wasn't having much fun in there. Erica and her dad are a hot mess."

"Agreed." Sherman opened the minivan door. "It doesn't escape me that many at our school consider me a hot mess, too. It's why Erica's father had to insist on my attendance at this gathering, though I'm sure he regrets that now."

Otis said, "Okay."

Sherman felt it fair to be clear here. "There are other classmates staring through the blinds at this very moment. If they see us ride off together, they will likely associate you to my particular brand of hot messiness. It isn't always pleasant."

Otis and Paisley exchanged looks.

Otis shrugged.

Paisley leaped into the vehicle. "I get the back row all to myself."

Sherman's new friends accompanied him without reservation.

It was the best surprise that day.

Solution for The Dapperlings

Milo took a deep breath. "The specimen jars are in the flashlight."

"The *flashlight*?" Meddy started to laugh. The others stared from Milo to Kip to Kip's bed, where the cabin's big spare flashlight was now lying suspiciously close to the Senior Dapperling's rucksack. Kip kept his mouth shut, but it looked a bit like he might want to smile.

"You took out the batteries and replaced them with our little test tubes," Milo continued, "which is why you looked like you were going to pass out when I threw the light to Josh and when he shook it when it wouldn't turn on. All you had to do is sneak the flashlight into your bag and carry it to the mess hall that way."

Kip sighed. "Well played, Pine." He picked up the flashlight, unscrewed it, and upended it over his palm. Two small, cylindrical glass specimen tubes just about the size of a kid's thumb slid out. "And not so much as a crack in the glass. I thought for sure they were going to get destroyed, the way you two were throwing the flashlight around."

As Kip passed the tubes to Milo, Josh groaned. "I should've guessed the minute it wouldn't turn on."

"He's right," Meddy said, looking down at the tubes. "You guys have never used that flashlight, and of course the counselors would've checked the batteries at the beginning of the week." She frowned. "I'm equal parts impressed and creeped out that this whole thing has been about getting some weird old fungus back."

"And now we're going to go capture some more weird old fungus." Milo checked his watch. "Five minutes to breakfast. Should we get moving?"

"Absolutely," Kip said, somehow able to shift effortlessly back into Senior Dapperling mode despite his recent humiliations. "Thanks for the second chance, Dapperlings. Let's go win this thing!"

Milo and the others cheered, but the effect of both apology and pep talk was somewhat dampened as Kip, taking a step toward his personal effects to get dressed, went flying, sprawling headlong and landing flat on his face with no apparent provocation at all.

Milo bent and examined the knot that connected Kip's left shoe to his right.

"Couldn't resist," Meddy said, dusting off her hands. "But seriously, it's out of my system now. Probably. I think. Go Dapperlings!"

Solution for Codename: Mom

I grabbed the phone from Dad and punched in the numbers 3-1-4-1-5-9. The phone opened. Dad took it without a word and went back outside to call his friend.

It was a long wait. Finally, Dad came back. He was smiling.

"Your mom is fine," he said. "She had photos on her phone of that guy along with his name and address, everything they needed to find him. It seems like your mom has been worried about this fellow for a while."

Mom got home a couple of hours later. For once, Dad had a lot of questions, and not just for her.

"How did you figure out the password?" he asked me.

"Mom left us a clue," I said. "That picture of us at the pie-eating contest. Pie sounds like pi, the math constant. The picture on her phone isn't just us having fun, it's a math pun. Her password was six numbers, so I put in the first six digits of pi: 3.14159."

"A math pun," he said. "That is so like your mom." He squeezed her hand. Mom looked tired but happy to be with us.

"So who was that guy?" I asked. "Rival intelligence agent? International smuggler?"

"Disgruntled grad student," Mom answered. "He was going to hold my phone hostage until I had set him up with a fellowship." She shook her head. "That kind of shoddy logic is why he failed my class in the first place."

I crossed my arms and stared at her. I couldn't believe she thought I'd swallow such a flimsy story.

"After all I did?" I asked. "After I kept your phone safe and figured out the password and helped to catch this guy? You're still not going to admit that you're a spy?"

"Certainly not," she said. "Because I'm not a spy."

"Right. Because all families have code words like *Euclid* to signal that everything's A-OK."

Mom raised her eyebrows and gave Dad a look. He cleared his throat and quickly stood up. "I'm off to bed," he said. "Don't stay up too late, you two."

He left. It was just me and Mom.

I stared at her. She stared back at me. The seconds ticked by.

"I'm not a spy," she said finally. "Here, I'll put it in writing so you can remember it."

She picked up one of Rosa's crayons and a pad of construction paper. She wrote in big, block letters NOT A SPY!!!

I got really angry. I thought about all the things that had happened that day and how here she was, treating me like a five-year-old, writing a sign in crayon. She held the sign out to me and, at first, I wouldn't even look at it.

"Take it," she said. "Read and remember, because I won't have this discussion again."

Reluctantly, I took it. It was written in blue crayon on green paper, and she'd put three exclamation points at the end for emphasis. And then I saw it.

In front of the words was a small horizontal line.

When read in front of a number, that would be a minus sign. But in front of a variable—a letter—Mom said that you read it as "the opposite of." Which meant that "- NOT A SPY!!!" should be read as "the opposite of NOT A SPY!!!"

I looked up at her. "That's okay," I said, keeping my voice even. "I don't need a reminder."

"Good," she said, taking the paper back from me and crumpling it up. And then she winked.

My mom is a lot of things: pie-eater, math teacher, and the coolest spy I know.

Solution for The Red Envelope

Catherine stands up. "Our question was 'This man's name is synonymous with the order of things.' The answer is ROY G. BIV, the mnemonic for the colors red, orange, yellow, green, blue, indigo, and violet. It's a memory aid for the order of the colors in the rainbow.

"Mr. Michael gave us three big clues that ROY G. BIV was the *right* answer:

"First: the *colors*. We started with a red envelope and ended with a puzzle picture of a purple envelope. In between, Mr. Michael led us to find green books, messages on yellow paper, and blue bags containing jigsaw-puzzle pieces. The puzzle had a picture of oranges and indigo—deep blue—flowers.

"Second: the *letters*. Mr. Michael left us clues with backward letters, dashes, dots, raised dots, numbers, and musical notes that stood for letters. We solved a crossword-puzzle message by combining the first letters of each word.

"Third: the number *seven*. We found seven green books, seven yellow messages, and seven blue bags. The note in the puzzle picture mentioned 'a round seven.'

"ROY G. BIV: A man's name synonymous with the order of the colors in the rainbow: seven colors, seven letters." Catherine stops talking.

"When did you know the answer?" Mr. Michael asks.

"I thought I knew when we talked about the northern lights. Tony mentioned 'almost all the colors of the rainbow,' and it clicked.

"I was sure once we found the math book by Sir Isaac Newton. He developed the seven-color spectrum that ROY G. BIV represents. Before Newton, people said the rainbow had five colors. Newton thought that seven was a more elegant number because there are seven notes in the musical scale. He added the colors orange and indigo and used a color wheel to explain. That's what 'for a round seven' means in the puzzle."

"Why didn't you submit sooner?" Tony asks.

"I was having too much fun." Catherine glances over at Kevin. "Plus, I was the one who said we needed to work together . . ."

"—Instead of bolting like I did?" Kevin walks to the front of the room. "Catherine, you should never play poker. When we found the Newton book, you lit up like a Christmas tree. I looked Newton up in the encyclopedia while you all worked on the crossword. Thirty seconds flat and I figured out he was the rainbow-colors guy. I grabbed an answer envelope, but I didn't know what to write down. The name Newton is only synonymous with fig cookies.

"ROY G. BIV came to me in a flash when I jumped off that chair. I think best when I'm moving. I ran out here and submitted."

Catherine looks confused. "If you turned in the right answer first, how did I win?"

"I put your name on the envelope," Kevin admits. "I wouldn't have found the answer without you telling us what to do. You deserved the Golden Answer Award. Time was running out, and I was afraid you weren't going to submit."

Catherine opens her mouth to disagree, but Kevin cuts her off. "I didn't show it before, but I am a team player." He pantomimes shooting a basketball. "Maybe even a team captain if I remember to give credit to my teammates who deserve it."

"Well done," says Mr. Michael. "Please bring that team spirit to my honors class next week."

Solution for Whiz Tanner and the Pilfered Cashbox

Whiz looked around at the crowd that had gathered. He didn't like crowds, but he could talk in front of a hundred people as easily as he could two. And while he wasn't purposely trying to generate tension—he generated it.

"Everyone who was near the cashbox in the moments before or after it disappeared is present. Chuck, Thorny, Megan, and Jennifer. I believe Tyrone's alibi will hold up, so let us forget about him for now and see what plays out."

"I wasn't anywhere near the table," cried Jennifer. "You can't believe I had anything to do with it."

"Then how did you see Chuck putting a box in the kitchen?" Bonnie asked.

Officer Van Dyke was about to say something also, but Whiz raised his hand to stop him. It's not every sixth grade kid who could stop an adult cold like that—but Whiz does it all the time.

"Let us start with that, Jennifer. Please tell us where you were?"

She looked at the policeman and he just nodded. That took the boldness out of her.

"I had just come from fishing down by the Little Marsh River. I put my fishing pole in the kitchen to keep it out of the way. I didn't want anybody playing with it."

"I didn't see you in the kitchen," Chuck said.

"Well, I saw you."

"That is precisely what I thought after finding the dried river mud on the table," said Whiz. "But that raises the question as to why Chuck did not see you in the kitchen."

"I don't know, but I was never near the table."

"I believe you were not near the table, Jennifer. But you were not exactly in the kitchen, either," countered Whiz.

What happened next was quite unusual—especially since it was Whiz who did it. Whiz looked directly into Jennifer's eyes and stared without blinking. I could tell she was trying not to blink or look away. Her boldness was coming back. She was several years older than us, and tried to look intimidating.

Whiz then turned his eyes to the ceiling. Jennifer did likewise and then looked away. She turned around looking at the crowd that had gathered. She seemed to be looking for an opening to run through. But, while Whiz was doing his thing, Bonnie had moved behind Jennifer. Bonnie just shook her head and Jennifer seemed to lose her boldness again. Talk about squirming!

Officer Van Dyke placed his hand on her shoulder. "Jennifer. Do you have anything you want to tell us?"

Her menacing look seemed to change to a hint of fear and then quickly to determination. "No!"

"Whiz." Officer Van Dyke turned back to Whiz. "You haven't told us anything new yet. Do you have more to say?"

"Let us turn our attention to Megan. Will you tell us how you hurt your hand?"

Megan instinctively pulled her hand to her chest and covered the bandage with the other hand.

"After Thorny couldn't find a purple shirt, I left to find Jennifer. We went to get her fishing pole from the kitchen, but I jabbed the hook into my hand as I lifted it. I'm not much of a fisherman."

"That's right," added Jennifer. "She was in the kitchen with me when it happened."

Whiz then rubbed his fingers over the red dots on the table. Megan seemed to do the same looking-for-an-escape move that Jennifer had done earlier. But Bonnie was right there, and I wasn't too far away. That makes two squirmers.

After seeing how Whiz rattled Megan and Jennifer so easily, I began to rethink my original suspect. Thorny wasn't smart enough to pull off this heist in the middle of a crowded room—even with Chuck's help. Now how was Whiz going to make Tyrone squirm?

"Well, Whiz," said Officer Van Dyke, "you seem to have upset Megan and Jennifer. But what's the story?"

"The story is quite simple. Megan and Jennifer are rattled because they are guilty, and they know I know it."

"How?" I asked. "You haven't said anything yet. Jennifer was fishing before she came to the fund-raiser and Megan caught her hand on the hook back in the kitchen. And what about Tyrone?"

"Tyrone's alibi is too easy to check out. He could not have been involved in the actual theft."

"They all have alibis," said Bonnie. "So where does that leave us?"

"And none of this points to the stolen cashbox," I added, wondering if Whiz had finally gone over the deep end.

"But it does, Joey," answered Whiz.

"Please tell us," Officer Van Dyke said. He flipped his little notebook to a clean page.

Patrolman Bailey just stood there looking between Officer Van Dyke and Whiz. Officer Van Dyke outranked him, so he wasn't going to interfere. Whiz continued.

"Jennifer did go fishing this morning. She got mud on the bottoms of her sneakers as she fished off the bank of the Little Marsh River. Some of that mud found its way onto the top of the table."

"But how?" asked Thorny. "She's right, she wasn't near the table."

"Look beyond the obvious, Thorny," said Whiz. "Why did Jennifer have a fishing pole with her in the first place?"

"She was fishing," I replied. "And then came here."

"Yes," Bonnie agreed.

Thorny just looked confused—and a little teary-eyed.

"Granted," replied Whiz. "But her house is nearby. Why not drop the fishing pole at home before coming here? That would be much more convenient than finding a place in the community center to keep it safe. Unless you needed it in the community center."

"Sounds interesting, Whiz," Officer Van Dyke said. "Go on."

"When she arrived, she did go into the kitchen, but not to store her fishing pole. She climbed, with her fishing pole, up the ladder that leads to the catwalks above us. While she was above the table, some of the mud that was embedded in her shoe fell off."

Everybody looked up.

"It was from there that she saw Chuck carry a box into the kitchen—which explains why Chuck did not see her. She waited until there was significant distraction down at the stage end of the room. The raffle drawing was a perfect chance. Everybody would have been looking toward the stage or down at their tickets. That was when Megan, her accomplice, made her move. Megan had two jobs. The first was to distract Thorny and Chuck. I think Chuck going to the restroom made her job a little easier. All she had to do was ask for a purple shirt."

Both Megan and Jennifer squirmed a little more, but they didn't run—Bonnie and I were still close behind them.

"When Thorny had his head bent over the shirt cartons and everybody else was concentrating on the stage, Jennifer lowered the fishing line with a hook on the end. Megan's second job was to place the hook on the handle of the cashbox. However, being nervous about Thorny seeing her and the fishing line, she was probably not paying as much attention to the fishing hook as she should have. When she grabbed it, she jabbed herself with the hook. Some blood from her wound dripped onto the table and has since dried—or nearly so."

Everybody looked at the table. Whiz rubbed his fingers over the red dots as he continued.

"When the handle of the box was hooked, Jennifer reeled it in. Megan held her hand to stop the flow of blood as best as she could and walked away . . . most likely, she headed to the restroom for some paper towels. We only have her word that she went to find Jennifer at that time."

"I saw her leaving the girls' restroom," said Tyrone. "We'd all started looking for the missing cashbox and she came out with a bunch of paper towels wrapped around her hand. Jennifer was looking for her, too. She looked concerned about Megan's hand, but now that I think about it, she looked more mad than concerned. She tried to help with the bleeding and so did I."

"Shortly after that is when we came in," Whiz continued. "We saw neither Jennifer nor Megan—nor Tyrone—walk out with the cashbox, so I think we can safely assume it remains inside the community center. Possibly hidden among the boxes on the catwalks where they store the unused lights."

Whiz was looking up at the catwalk as he spoke, but since he often looks around as he speaks, I didn't follow his eyes, until he resumed talking.

"I have not seen the cashbox in question, but I do see a corner of what could be a small metal box of the proper size wedged among the other boxes up there."

We all looked up. Thorny jumped up and ran to the back of the kitchen. He climbed up the ladder and, in a moment, shouted, "It's here!"

"I knew your stupid plan wouldn't work!" Megan shouted at Jennifer.

"If you didn't grab the hook like an idiot, it would have!"

"But you wore your muddy shoes! That gave us away."

"No! You did by not paying attention and jabbing your hand."

Then, they both looked at Whiz. Boy, did they have an icy stare!

Even though I'm a full-fledged partner of the Tanner-Dent Detective Agency, I moved a little farther to the side so I wasn't in their line of sight. I didn't need a couple of high schoolers mad at me and was willing to let Whiz take all the blame—uh, credit—for this one.

Solution for The Magic Day Mystery

After the assembly, Madison Reilly led Principal Greeley, Jose, and me to her locker.

"I'm really sorry," she said. "I don't know what happened. I was just so frustrated that I couldn't practice this morning. I didn't mean to cause all this trouble."

She opened her locker, revealing the bounty of stolen items. Principal Greeley checked the items off Jose's list. She pulled the blue cups out of the locker and handed them to Jose.

"Thank goodness," Jose said. "Dad would kill me if I lost these."

Principal Greeley put her hand on Madison's shoulder.

"Let's go to my office," she said. "You and I need to have a little chat before we call your parents."

Madison swallowed hard and nodded. She followed Principal Greeley down the hall. After a few steps, she stopped and turned around.

"Marlon," she asked. "How did you know it was me?"

I gave her my usual answer.

"Magic."

She shrugged and continued down the hall.

"You'll tell me how you figured it out, right?" Jose asked.

"When we talked to Madison earlier," I explained. "She said she hoped you found your cups."

"Yeah, was that to throw us off?"

"Maybe, but you had already told me that you hadn't told anyone what you brought, and we hadn't told her you were missing your grandfather's cups. The only way she could have known was if she was the one who took them."

Jose pumped his fist. "You're a genius!" he said. "Wait till I tell everyone."

I put up a hand.

"Let's just keep this to ourselves," I said.

"But what do I say if someone asks me how you found all that other stolen stuff?"

"Do what I do," I said. "Tell them it's magic."

Solution for Puzzling It Out

Jeremy stared at the numbers, panic rising inside him. He'd done the one with the five in the middle. How different could this be? Nineteen was the middle. They knew that.

What was next? He shut his eyes, trying to remember what they'd done that day in Puzzle Club. Find the magic constant.

Chloe already had her phone out and the calculator app pulled up. She added the numbers from fifteen to twenty-three. "The magic constant is one hundred seventy-one," she said.

Jeremy pulled out his phone and divided one hundred seventy-one by the number of rows and got fifty-seven.

"This will go faster if we work together, Jeremy," Chloe said. "I'll do the math and you write the numbers down."

Jeremy felt frustration rising up in his chest. It was like a ball of tightness that made it hard to breathe.

Chloe glared at him. "There's no time for you to go all solo cowboy on this."

Jeremy opened his mouth to protest and then shut it again. She was right. There was no time, and Chloe was better at these puzzles than he was anyway. "What do we need to add to nineteen to get to fifty-seven?"

"Fifty-seven minus nineteen equals thirty-eight. So now we need all the pairs that add up to that." Chloe fired off numbers and he wrote them down as fast as he could. "Fifteen and twenty-three. Twenty and eighteen. Twenty-two and sixteen. Twenty-one and seventeen."

He hesitated. "Should I put the 15 on the top row or the bottom?" he asked Chloe.

"It won't matter. The middle row will be the same no matter what."

He wrote fifteen in the middle square of the top line. That meant the middle of the bottom row would have to be twenty-three.

"Twenty-three is the biggest number. We're probably going to need smaller numbers around it," Chloe said. "Put the eighteen and sixteen on either side of it."

What she said made sense. He could see how she made her decisions. He put the numbers where she directed. "So that would mean the other numbers that go with them in the other direction should be larger, right?"

"Exactly!" Chloe said. "Put the twenty in the top left corner and the twenty-two in the top right."

There were only two numbers left. Seventeen and twenty-one. Jeremy scribbled them in. He looked up at Chloe. "But the 17 and 21 could switch places."

"We've only got two options, though."

She grabbed the combination lock, spun it to the right until she got to seventeen, then to the left past the seventeen and ending on the nineteen, then back to the right to twenty-two. She yanked down and the lock came open.

A flash drive sat by itself on the shelf. Jeremy grabbed it. "How much time do we have left?"

Chloe looked at her phone. "Fifteen minutes."

The courthouse was two miles away. If they managed a five-minute mile, they'd be there in ten minutes and still have a few minutes to spare to get the flash drive to Ms. Sullivan. "Let's go!" They ran to their bikes. Chloe jammed her bike helmet on, curls sticking out in all directions. "Ride, Jeremy! Ride!"

It was five minutes to nine when they skidded off the bike path into the street in front of the courthouse. They threw their bikes down, not stopping to lock them, and ran up the stairs to the entrance, dashing in, only to be stopped by a line heading to two big metal detectors.

"Empty your pockets and put everything in the bin and walk through, please," the security guard said in a tone that made it clear he said the same thing a hundred times a day. Then he yawned. Jeremy looked at the flash drive in his hand. He didn't want to let go of it for even a second. Plus, it was taking forever for people to go through the security line. Jeremy had never seen people empty their pockets of keys and change more slowly.

He looked around and saw Ms. Sullivan. She was on the other side of the metal detectors behind a plant. He yelled her name and she stepped out.

"Chloe!" Jeremy yelled and tossed the flash drive toward her.

Without even thinking, she crouched down and did a perfect volleyball bump, sending the flash drive flying over the top of the metal detectors directly to Ms. Sullivan, who snatched it out of the air.

The bored security guard looked at the other security guard and pointed toward the ceiling. "Did you see something up there?"

"You're seeing things, Frank. You need a vacation," she said.

Jeremy slumped against the wall, Chloe beside him.

Two hours later, Ms. Sullivan was done with her testimony. Chloe and Jeremy had managed to get through security and into the courtroom to listen. She laid out exactly when Dynamic Recreational first learned that one of the chemicals in Origanisms was harmful to children and how they'd hidden that information. Her testimony was backed up by the documents from the flash drive Jeremy and Chloe had retrieved from the school basement.

When Ms. Sullivan stepped down out of the witness box, she walked straight out of the courtroom, giving Jeremy and Chloe a little nod to follow her. When they got out into the hall, she grabbed them both into a big hug. "I knew you'd be able to figure out the square, Chloe."

Chloe wiggled out of the hug. "I didn't. We did it together."

"You were right," Jeremy said. "Doing it with Chloe helped it make more sense to me."

"So working together wasn't so bad?" she asked.

He smiled at Chloe. "Not bad at all."

Solution for The Mechanical Bank Job

"I don't know how to thank you!" said Mrs. Herzog, gazing teary-eyed at the five recovered banks, plus the firefighter, back on display on the project table. "My father loved his collection, and it reminds me of the fun we had playing with the banks together."

Mr. Diallo beamed at us. "Such clever children to figure out where the banks might be hidden and how to catch the thief!"

"Did you know it was Mr. Yancy?" asked Mrs. Herzog.

"Well, he was one of our top suspects—" Benny began.

"But we didn't know it was him," I interrupted. We'd agreed it was better not to name our other suspects and risk flunking gym and Spanish. "We didn't know for sure until he came to get the banks from his hiding place."

"We couldn't figure out how anyone could have taken the banks out of the school building during the fire alarm. They're too heavy to carry easily," added Benny. Once again, he flexed his biceps. "Even if you're really strong."

"So then we thought they might be hidden in the school," said Kasey. "It was really Jill who figured out the rest."

"We *all* worked on the problem and all those thoughts together just . . . gave me an idea," I said. "If the banks were hidden in the school, then the window wasn't open for someone to escape. Then why?"

"Misdirection!" Benny flung out his hands. "*Alakazam!*"

I ignored him. "And I thought of the messed-up books on the windowsill, like they were pushed aside to make room for someone to go through the window *or get up on the windowsill!*"

"But that didn't explain how all the paper cranes got knocked down," said Kasey. "The thief might have gotten tangled in a few, but why so many? Tell them, Jill!"

I picked up one of the slightly squashed cranes from the table. "What if they weren't knocked down by someone going through the window, but fell down when someone *lifted up the ceiling tiles*? I thought there might be enough room above the drop ceiling to conceal the banks! They seem heavy to us when we hold them, but they're not too heavy for the ceiling tiles to support their weight—especially the way Mr. Yancy spread them out on the crosspieces of the grid."

"And she was right!" Kasey was so excited she almost levitated. "After school, we waited outside the window, and we saw Mr. Yancy sneak into the classroom behind the custodian and hide in the cloak-room."

"By the time Kasey and Benny got Mr. Diallo from the office, he was up on the windowsill, in the dark classroom, trying to recover the banks," I added.

"Serves him right to get conked on the forehead by Jonah and the Whale," said Benny. He turned to Mrs. Herzog. "That knocked him off the windowsill, too, so Mr. Diallo and the custodian could hold him till the police came."

"I've known Mr. Yancy for years. I just can't imagine why he would steal these banks from me!" Mrs. Herzog stroked a finger over the Trick Dog bank with the clown.

"For the money, of course!" said Benny. "We figure he meant to sell them online to a wealthy collector."

"Oh," said Mrs. Herzog. "I thought he knew. I thought everyone knew. My father didn't collect the originals. These are replicas, copies made much later! All six together are worth less than two hundred dollars."

I laughed. "Someone should have told Mr. Yancy to just save his pennies, because crime doesn't pay."

Solution for The Scary Place

Min and the Geeks 4 Science had all the information needed to explain the "ghost" right at their fingertips, especially Min, who had been studying meteorology! (Meteorology: the branch of science that deals with weather.) Min noted the temperature outside plus the temperature inside the wine cellar. She even wrote down the humidity, which—clue!—was very high. The only thing Min had *not* written down was the fact that two rocks had been wedged, one each against the front door and the other against the cellar door (in case members of the Ghosts Were People 2 needed a fast exit). The opened doors allowed the one hundred–degree hot, moist air to creep inside. It swept into the basement of the Scary Place and hit a cold, damp area. Once cooled, the humid air reached its dew point. When this occurs, something called *advection fog* forms, especially when there is dust present.

It's easy to solve this using a super simple logic puzzle! Put an *O* for *Yes* (when the ghost was seen) and an *X* for *No* (when the ghost wasn't there). Same thing for the rock. Now check for the only times the "ghost" didn't show up—the days when the Geeks 4 Science shut the doors! And there you have it—logic wins!

As for the pebbles hitting the Geeks' shoes, well, that's another story . . . 😊

	Min	Derrick	Jayid	Brian	Amanda	Ike	Ghost	Rock
Monday								
Tuesday								
Wednesday								
Thursday								
Friday								
Saturday								

Easter Egg Bonus:
GEEKS 4 SCIENCE Names and Their Meanings

Min Shishi: (Chinese) Intelligent Fact

Derrick Klar: (German) Direct Clear

Jayid Kafir: (Arabic) Good Unbeliever

Easter Egg Bonus:
GHOSTS WERE PEOPLE 2 Names and Their Meanings

Brian Sehen: (Dutch) Honorable Belief

Amanda Estrella: (Spanish) Love Star

Ike Kai: (Hawaiian) Ghost Seer

Solution for Ottonetics

Hernando began laughing. "It is not a *grock*. It is a *G rock*!"

A couple more minutes revealed another one—two old granite stones with the letter G chiseled onto them.

"G for Geheimnis . . ." Lizzie said.

Together we edged our fingers around the rocks and pulled upward. I kept a wary eye on the road. It took about twenty minutes, but the rocks came out of the ground like stuck Legos. Under them, wrapped in old, decayed burlap, was a small box.

None of us breathed until Lizzie said, "You do it, Jake. I think I might throw up from the tension."

Carefully I lifted the object out. The burlap fell away, disintegrating into dust. The box was shut tight, with a combination lock.

"Oh, great," Lizzie said.

"Otto always gives you everything you need . . ." Hernando reminded us.

I took a deep breath. I needed a combination, and so I dialed the only thing I could think of.

Pi.

3 . . . 1 . . . 4 . . . 1 . . . 5 . . . 9.

I heard a click. The lid moved. I pulled it open.

Inside was an oval-shaped object wrapped in moldy velour that may have once been red. But what was inside *that* looked like it hadn't ever been touched.

The egg was cool and heavy, about the size of my palm. As I held it toward the sun, it glinted red, gold, and blue—rubies the size of fingernails, clusters of tiny sapphires, gold leafing like snakes. At one end of it was a tiny gold clasp.

Lizzie's mouth was hanging open. Hernando's eyes, which were always watery, now sent thick tears down his cheeks.

I flipped the clasp. Inside, a clear diamond seemed to pulse with its own light. Its edges were razor-sharp, and it sat in a bed of soft, thick crimson padding.

"That thing could make engagement rings for all of Queens," Lizzie said.

I shut the egg, gently putting it back into the box, which I slipped into my backpack. Looking up at Hernando, I smiled. "Dude, where would you like to live? East Side or West? I'm buying you an apartment."

Hernando threw his head back with a laugh. "Teeth first, then apartment!"

"Teeth first," I said.

"You always were a good boy."

He held up his hand as if to wave goodbye. This time I noticed his left pinky, bent at a forty-five-degree angle. "Camptodactyly," I said.

He smiled. "It is genetic."

Now I started to cry. I should have known it from the start. Hernando had been looking out for me—not only because of Otto. He knew he couldn't give me the life he wanted me to have. He knew he had to get through his own problems. But he had stayed near. He had made sure I was in good hands.

My dad was the Santa Claus of the Ramble.

"Helll-oooooo!" came Harriet's voice from up the path.

Lizzie ran toward her, jabbering away with the news.

I smiled. I sat on a discarded grock. Hernando sat with me.

There would be so much to tell.

Solution for Gridlock Jones Cracks the Case

Mrs. Dunbarton gasped. Mr. Langley's eyes narrowed.

Clenching a fist, Mr. Shamoon said, "Are you really going to listen to this little twerp?"

Gabe kept his cool. "We invited you here because all four of you—even you, Principal Braxton—had motive and opportunity to commit this crime."

All the adults began talking at once. Gabe just held up a palm and waited. When they paused for breath, he said, "You, Ms. Braxton, have mortgage troubles and a key to this office."

The principal drew herself up, brown eyes fierce. "True, but you can't possibly—"

"That's ridiculous," said Mr. Shamoon.

"And you," I said, turning to him, "also have keys. Plus, you believe gambling is wrong."

He glowered. "It *is!*"

Mrs. Dunbarton put her hands on her hips. "Surely you can't believe *I* did it. That money was my responsibility. And besides, I don't have a key to the office."

"You didn't need one." Gabe spun his chair to face her. "You had the money all to yourself before you gave it to Ms. Braxton." Glancing at the principal, he asked her, "Did you actually *see* the cash?"

She frowned. "No, just the box."

"So it could have been stuffed with cut-up comic books, as far as you knew."

After a long look at the treasurer, Ms. Braxton said, "That's right."

Over Mrs. Dunbarton's protests, Gabe said, "Plus, she had her own financial troubles and a grudge against the author whose visit that money was going to fund."

"That jerk!" snapped Mrs. Dunbarton.

"But what about Mr. Langley?" I asked Gabe. "He didn't have an opportunity or a motive."

"Didn't he?"

"Oh, come on," said the teacher.

Gabe asked Mrs. Dunbarton, "When you gave him the money to recount it, was Mr. Langley ever out of your sight?"

A vertical line creased her forehead. "Uh, yes, he took it backstage to count. He said he didn't feel safe, flashing all that money in front of people."

"That's opportunity," said Gabe.

Mr. Langley spluttered, "But what earthly reason would I have to steal it? I love this school, and I inherited enough to make me comfortable."

Gabe spread his hands. "You said it yourself—that money wasn't nearly enough for our needs. I think you took a little trip with it and tried to turn it into big money."

The teacher's jaw dropped.

I flashed back to the contents of Mr. Langley's satchel. "The airline itinerary!"

"Precisely," said Gabe. "LAS is the airline code for McCarran Airport in Las Vegas. You flew there this weekend, hoping to use your poker skills to win big. But you lost, didn't you?"

Mr. Langley looked stricken. His hand scrubbed at his face, and his eyes grew moist. "I-I've never lost before. All that money . . ."

"Jason." Ms. Braxton's eyes reflected hurt, anger, and sympathy, all at once. "Oh, Jason."

"I think the police will want to know about this," said Mrs. Dunbarton, pulling out her cell phone.

"No! Please!" said the teacher. "I can break into my retirement savings. I'll . . . pay it all back."

Crossing her arms, the principal said, "Why don't you and I and Mrs. Dunbarton sit down and discuss this."

Mr. Langley sagged into one of the visitors' chairs like a deflated balloon. With a triumphant glare at all of us, Mr. Shamoon said, "Gambling. I told you!" and marched out of the office, head held high.

Ms. Braxton turned to Gabe. "Thank you, Grid—uh, Gabriel. You've done this school a great service."

"It's okay, you can call me that." My friend grinned. "Solving mysteries is all in a day's work for Gridlock Jones."

Solution for The Case of the Mysterious Mystery Writer

"I hope you were more successful than me," said Mr. Diaz. Sofia and I were in his office again, this time with Jules. "I talked to all the other contestants," he continued. "None of them wrote our mystery story. So I'm hoping it was one of your three suspects."

"Let me tell you what we learned." I stood up to present my facts. "It wasn't Nathan Hansen. He had no idea that Tucker Murphy was a dog, while both of our other suspects had connections to the pug."

"What about the clay Nathan was using?" Jules asked.

"Air-dry clay," I answered. "He said he was going to glaze it and fire it, but that's not the right kind of clay. He clearly doesn't know as much about pottery as he wanted us to think."

"Go on," said Sofia.

"Randall Jones didn't write the mystery story, either." I clasped my hands behind my back. "He claims to have written it with a mechanical pencil, but 'The Case of the Broken Vase' was written with a regular wooden pencil."

"How do you know?" Sofia repeated skeptically.

"A mechanical pencil always stays sharp, making very thin lines," I said. "But our story was written with a dull pencil."

"Then it was Cassandra Coleman?" said Mr. Diaz.

I shook my head. "It couldn't have been her. Cassandra told us that she'd written the story in her three-ring binder. But our mystery pages were clearly torn out of a notebook."

"Who was it, then?" cried Sofia. "Who wrote 'The Case of the Broken Vase?'

I sighed heavily. "I'm afraid we'll never know. I have disproven the imposters, but it seems this case has finally bested me. It is my recommendation that the library keep the prize money and run the Young Writers Contest again next year."

Mr. Diaz's shoulders slumped in defeat. "Thanks anyway," he said, as Jules stood up. We exited the library and rode our bikes home in silence.

"How about we try some of those cookies to celebrate the case," I said to Jules once we were back in our kitchen.

"Celebrate?" she cried, putting a few cookies on a plate. "We failed!"

"Did we?" I pulled the jug of milk from the fridge and poured us both a glass.

The cookies were delicious, and I took a big swig of milk. "Your story *was* really good," I finally said. "And you almost got away with it, sister."

Jules stopped chewing and looked up. "How did you figure it out?" she finally asked through a mouthful.

"Too many clues," I said. "Starting with the handwriting."

"But I disguised it."

"The pencil graphite was smudged," I explained. "All of the letters were smeared to the right. That's what happens to left-handed people. Their hand drags over the letters and smudges the text."

"That wasn't enough to go on," she said.

"You also had a connection to Tucker Murphy from the time we raked leaves," I said. "But the biggest clue came from Nathan Hansen. He saw you at the library three weeks ago, turning in your story. You wore Dad's jacket as a disguise, but you were carrying a familiar book with three bears on the cover."

"Ah," said Jules. "What does *Goldilocks* have to do with this?"

"You used the book to smuggle the papers into the library so no one would see you. That's why the papers are creased, even though the envelope was big enough for a full page. You had to fold the story to hide it inside your book."

She chewed her cookie in silence, so I decided to go on.

"Last, but not least, was the topic of the story. The author had to know a lot about pottery and you have a ceramics class every Thursday night. And when I was telling you about the story, you accused the poodle of knocking over the vase."

"So?" she asked.

"So I never mentioned that the lady's dog was a poodle. The only way you could have known that detail was if you'd read the story . . . Or *written* it."

She took a long swig of milk. "You're probably wondering why I did it."

"Nope," I replied. "I know exactly why. The Young Writers Contest was only open to kids age ten to twelve. You weren't old enough to submit a story, but you wanted to see if you could win anyway."

"I didn't care about the money," she admitted. "I knew I could win and not get caught."

"Except, you *did* get caught." I took another bite of cookie. "By me."

"Why didn't you turn me in?" she asked.

"Because next year, you're going to write a story even better than 'The Case of the Broken Vase,'" I said. "And then you'll win *two* hundred dollars. Fair and square."

My sister smiled.

Solution for TRICKED! A Framed Story

The parade was about to start as I led the others out to the parking lot. I still hadn't told them the solution to the mystery. I wanted to run it through my head one more time to make certain I had it right.

I scanned the cars and floats waiting in line. I heard the band warming up. And I saw Kinzly Vance and her cameraman getting ready. I headed right for her.

"Are you sure about this?" Darius asked.

I looked over my shoulder and nodded.

Margaret saw my face and smiled. "He's sure. I call that his Sherlock look."

Kinzly saw us coming and told her cameraman to start rolling. She hurried into position to interview Darius while he was walking.

"Darius, can we get a few questions?" she asked.

"Sorry," Juliette said, stepping between them to block the interview. "We're busy at the moment."

"I just want to know if there's any truth to the rumors that the Stanley Cup is missing," Kinzly said with a devilish smile. This was her gotcha moment.

Darius stammered and Juliette jumped in to rescue him. "Where'd you hear a rumor like that?" she asked.

"A reporter never reveals her sources," Kinzly answered smugly.

"You don't have to," I said taking over the conversation. "We know you got an anonymous phone call and rushed back to cover the story. And we know who made that call."

"We do?" asked Margaret surprised.

I shot her a wink. "Yes. We do. It was Robert Besserer."

The others had been so focused on Kinzly that they hadn't noticed we'd stopped at the band's trailer, which is where I was headed the whole time.

"Go ahead," I said to Darius. "Unlock it."

Robert Besserer, meanwhile, had seen this going on and rushed over from the band's position. He ran as fast as he could while carrying a sousaphone.

"What are you doing?" Besserer demanded.

"Getting the Stanley Cup," I said. "Darius is supposed to carry it in the parade."

The anticipation was palpable as Darius unlocked the trailer and pulled up the back to reveal . . . nothing except for some empty instrument cases. This is when it dawned on me that the cameraman was rolling. If I was wrong, this was going to make for some very bad television.

"Florian?" Margaret said with concern. "Do you know what you're doing?"

"Absolutely," I said. "It's in the glockenspiel case."

"Unbelievable," said Besserer. "You've already looked in there. Face it. I didn't steal the cup."

I smiled broadly. "Then how'd you know it was stolen?"

"What do you mean?" he asked perplexed. "You guys gave me the third degree earlier. You know, when you checked in the box and saw that it was empty."

"You see, that's your first problem," I said. "None of us ever said that it was stolen. It didn't dawn on me until after we'd left. You never asked us why we were looking around. That's because you already knew it was missing."

"Well, maybe you never spelled it out," he said, backtracking. "But it was obvious what was going on. I'm not a stupid guy."

"You're not a stupid guy," I said. "But you did make one stupid mistake."

Everyone was quiet for a moment as he scrambled through his memory to figure out what he'd done wrong.

"What was that?" he finally asked.

"You gave us the key to the trailer while the instruments were still inside. Yet, now the band is playing them. That means you have a second key. You lied when you told us there was only one."

"He's right," said Darius. "The drums were in here. All the instruments were."

Besserer slumped. He knew he was beaten.

"I realized it when I heard everyone chanting, 'Rock the red,'" I said. "That could only happen if you'd gotten the instruments. The part I didn't understand was why hadn't you just taken them out before you gave us the key."

"The bass drums!" said Margaret solving it.

"Yes," I said. "It was because of the bass drums."

"The heads had been taken off because you showed them to us," said Margaret. "And the drums were stacked on top of each other like a big column."

"And without the heads," I said. "It was hollow and a perfect place to hide the cup. But you couldn't take the instruments out without revealing that. So you had to wait until we left and then use the other key to unlock the trailer and move it to the glockenspiel case."

Margaret climbed up into the trailer and opened the case to reveal the trophy hidden inside.

"I don't believe it!" gasped Juliette.

"The biscuit is in the basket!" exclaimed Darius.

Besserer confessed to everything. His plan was to alert the media so the story became public. After keeping the trophy for a few days, he was going to use his memorabilia connections to make it look like he'd recovered it, so that he could return it to the team. He thought it would make him a hero. Instead, it got him arrested.

The parade went off as planned, with one slight alteration. Two of Deke's Geeks joined Darius and the Stanley Cup in the convertible. I'm sure the people lining the street wondered what Margaret and I were doing with him. But we didn't care. We were having the time of our lives.

About the Authors

Chris Grabenstein is a #1 *New York Times* bestselling author. His books for kids include *Escape from Mr. Lemoncello's Library*, *Mr. Lemoncello's Library Olympics*, *The Island of Dr. Libris*, and *Welcome to Wonderland #1: Home Sweet Motel*. He is also the coauthor of numerous fun and funny page-turners with James Patterson, including *I Funny*, *House of Robots*, *Treasure Hunters*, *Jacky Ha-Ha*, and *Word of Mouse*.

Steve Hockensmith says he's extremely bad at puzzles and riddles, but fortunately for him he's not too shabby when it comes to writing. He's the author of more than a dozen novels, including the science-themed mystery *Nick and Tesla's High-Voltage Danger Lab* and its five sequels. (One of those sequels, *Nick and Tesla's Secret Agent Gadget Battle*, was a finalist for the Mystery Writers of America's Edgar Award.) You can learn more about him and his books at www.stevehockensmith.com.

Stuart Gibbs is the *New York Times* bestselling author of the Spy School, FunJungle, and Moon Base Alpha series, and he has been nominated for an Edgar Award twice. His newest book is *Charlie Thorne* *and the Last Equation*, and he is currently writing the screenplay for the *Spy School* movie for Disney.

Sheela Chari is the author of *Finding Mighty*, a Junior Library Guild Selection and Children's Choice Award Finalist; and *Vanished*, an APALA Children's Literature Honor Book, Edgar finalist for best juvenile mystery, and Al's Book Club Pick on the *Today* show. She is currently working on a novelized series called *The Unexplainable Disappearance of Mars Patel*, based on the Peabody Award–winning mystery podcast by the same name created by Gen-Z Media. Sheela has degrees from Stanford University, Boston University, and New York University, where she received an MFA in fiction. She teaches fiction writing at Mercy College, and lives with her family in New York.

Fleur Bradley has loved puzzles and mysteries ever since she first discovered Agatha Christie novels. Fleur is the author of many short mysteries and mysteries for kids, including *Midnight at the Barclay Hotel* and the *Double Vision* trilogy. Originally from the Netherlands, she now lives in Colorado with her husband, two daughters, and entirely too many cats.

Lauren Magaziner grew up in New Hope, Pennsylvania, and is a proud graduate of Hamilton College. She currently lives in Philadelphia. She is the author of humorous middle grade books: the Case Closed series (*Mystery in the Mansion* and *Stolen from the Studio*), *Wizardmatch*, the Pilfer Academy series, and *The Only Thing Worse Than Witches*. She has also written Haunting at the Hotel for the puzzle-packed and interactive "pick your path" Case Closed series.

ABOUT THE AUTHORS

USA Today–bestselling and Agatha Award–winning author **Gigi Pandian** is the child of cultural anthropologists from New Mexico and the southern tip of India. She spent her childhood being dragged around the world on their research trips, and now lives in the San Francisco Bay Area. Gigi writes the Jaya Jones Treasure Hunt Mystery series, the Accidental Alchemist mysteries, and locked-room mystery short stories. Gigi's debut novel, *Artifact*, was awarded a Malice Domestic Grant and named a Best Debut Novel by *Suspense Magazine*, and her later fiction has received the Agatha, Lefty, Rose, and Derringer Awards.

Lamar Giles is a published author and a founding member of We Need Diverse Books. His recent books include his debut middle grade fantasy, *The Last Last-Day-of-Summer*, and his fourth YA thriller, *Spin*. He is a two-time Edgar Award finalist for his young adult thrillers *Fake ID* and *Endangered*. His third YA thriller, *Overturned*, received a glowing *New York Times* review, and was named a *Kirkus Reviews* Best Book. He contributed to the YA anthology *Three Sides of a Heart*, is the editor of the forthcoming We Need Diverse Books YA short story anthology *Fresh Ink* and is a contributor to the forthcoming YA anthology *Black Enough: Stories of Being Young & Black in America*, and to a forthcoming We Need Diverse Books middle grade anthology.

Kate Milford is the *New York Times*–bestselling author of *Greenglass House* (winner of the Edgar Award for juvenile literature, long-listed for the National Book Award for Young People's Literature, and a nominee for the Andre Norton Award and the Agatha Award for Children's/YA) as well as its sequel, *Ghosts of Greenglass House*, and five other books set in the same world: *The Boneshaker, The Broken Lands,*

The Left-Handed Fate, the crowdfunded companion book *The Kairos Mechanism*, and her newest release, *Bluecrowne*. Kate grew up in Riva, Maryland, and now lives in Brooklyn, New York, with her husband, two children, and their dog.

Laura Brennan's eclectic writing career includes television, film, theater, web series, fiction, and news. She has taught pitching workshops at several MFA programs and universities, including UCLA, USC, Boston University, National University, and Stephens College. A graduate of Yale University, she has won awards for journalism, television writing, and fiction. Her short stories have appeared in multiple anthologies, including the upcoming Malice Domestic anthology *Murder Most Edible*. Her podcast, Destination Mystery (DestinationMystery.com), features interviews with mystery writers and combines her love of books with her background in journalism. Her children's book, *Nana Speaks Nanese*, tackles the confusing changes brought on by dementia in a reassuring and straightforward way. She has also written a second children's book, *Papillon*. Contact her at Laura@LauraBrennanWrites.com.

Lara Cassidy is a high-stakes litigation attorney and author of "The Red Envelope," a middle grade mystery story. Her lifelong love of mysteries took root when she met Nancy Drew with a flashlight past her childhood bedtime. Lara juggles practicing law for big businesses and writing mysteries for children and adults. Her stories feature bright women unraveling perplexing riddles, finding missing people, and quashing corporate greed. She lives in northern Virginia with her husband and middle grade daughter, who edits over her mom's shoulder. Follow Lara on Twitter @ladcassidy.

ABOUT THE AUTHORS

Fred Rexroad's life has been an eclectic array of locations and interests. He's lived in the Northeast, Mid-Atlantic, West Coast, Midwest, South, Europe, and on a boat. He's printed cigar boxes, owned a magic store, flown airplanes, built an ultralight, did financial and statistical analysis, photographed oil spills and shifting sandbars from a helicopter, taught at Wright State University, solved logistics problems for the US Air Force, trained NATO personnel, wandered unarmed in war zones, did top secret analysis for the Joint Chiefs of Staff, and found time to write stories. He lives with his wife, Susan, in Vienna, Virginia.

Bryan Patrick Avery discovered his love of books at an early age, when he received his first Bobbsey Twins' Mystery. His short mysteries, poems, and essays have been published in the *Buffalo Soldier Newspaper*, *The Case Online*, *The National Examiner*, and other publications. He relishes the opportunity to create stories for children. In addition to writing, he also enjoys the art of magic, and is a life member of the Society of American Magicians and a charter member of the International Association of Black Magical Artists. Bryan lives in Northern California with his family.

Eileen Rendahl is the national bestselling and award-winning author of the Messenger series and four Chick Lit novels. Her alter ego, Eileen Carr, writes romantic suspense. She writes cozy mysteries as Kristi Abbott and Lillian Bell. Born in Dayton, Ohio, she moved when she was four and only remembers that she was born across the street from a Baskin-Robbins. Eileen remembers anything that has to do with ice cream. Or chocolate. Or champagne. She started writing for the worst reason (she thought it would be easy!) and has since spent years working on her craft, earning an MFA in creative writing at Antioch University in Los Angeles. She now teaches creative writing at Southern New Hampshire University. She has had many jobs and lived in many cities and feels unbelievably lucky to be where she is now and to be doing what she's doing.

Mo Walsh wrote her first mystery story, "The Clue in the Picture Frame," for a fourth grade spelling assignment. After years working for newspapers and advertising agencies, she returned to writing mysteries for magazines and short story anthologies. She also writes silly poems called doggerel verse, and two of her favorite words are *prestidigitation* and *serendipity*. She grew up in St. Louis and now lives in Boston with her husband, near their three grown-up sons. Visit her online at www.mowalshwriter.com.

Alane Ferguson has written more than thirty books and is currently completing her most intense and autobiographical book yet, *Dragonfly Eyes*, the first in her latest paranormal trilogy. A recipient of the Edgar Award as well as the Belgium's Children's Choice Award for her young adult novel *Show Me the Evidence*, she also received a Edgar nomination for her young adult novel *The Christopher Killer*, the first in the Forensic Mystery series. Alane won the Children's Crown Classic Award for *Cricket and the Crackerbox Kid*, the American Booksellers Association's "Pick of the List" for her picture book entitled *That New Pet!*, and has been on numerous ALA Recommended Books for Reluctant Young Readers and Young Adults' Choice lists.

ABOUT THE AUTHORS

Peter Lerangis is the author of far too many books. Nine of them have been *New York Times* bestsellers, to his parents' relief. After writing the Seven Wonders series and several 39 Clues books, he promises his next work will not contain a number in the title. His friendship with R. L. Stine was forged over a dinner with Vladimir Putin, who kept his shirt on. Ever since, he has been very careful about emails. Peter is now locked away working on a new series called Throwback, and he would deeply appreciate if you sent chocolate.

Edgar-nominated author-illustrator **Bruce Hale** is passionate about inspiring reluctant readers to open books (and read them). He has written over forty seriously funny books for children, including the award-winning Chet Gecko Mysteries, *Snoring Beauty* (one of Oprah's Kids' Reading List picks), and the Clark the Shark books, one of which ended up in a McDonald's Happy Meal (not the way you think). An actor and Fulbright Scholar in Storytelling, Bruce is in demand as a speaker, having presented internationally at conferences, universities, and schools.

Tyler Whitesides was born in Washington state. He developed a love of books from a very young age, and with that came a desire to write his own stories. Tyler attended Utah State University, where he received a bachelors in music. While there, he got a part-time job at a middle school as a night custodian, and wandering the halls sparked the ideas that eventually led to the Janitors series, published by Shadow Mountain Publishing. During the course of the series, Tyler had the opportunity to visit many states, presenting at more than 600 schools across the country. He lives in Northern Utah with his wife, Connie, and their son.

James Ponti is the Edgar Award–winning author of the City Spies, Framed!, and Dead City book series. He's written and produced television shows for Disney Channel, Nickelodeon, PBS, and NBC Sports. He lives in Maitland, Florida, with his family, and his favorite guilty pleasure is going to the movies on a weekday afternoon. His Twitter handle is @JamesPonti and you can visit him online at www.JamesPonti.com.